Cold Blooded

by Bernard Lee DeLeo
Paperback Edition
Copyright 2013 Bernard Lee DeLeo
Published by RJ Parker Publishing

ISBN-13: 978-1494378431
ISBN-10: 1494378434

This book is a work of fiction.

The unauthorized reproduction or distribution of a copyrighted work is illegal. Criminal copyright infringement, including infringement without monetary gain, is investigated by the FBI and is punishable by fines and federal imprisonment.

Chapter One
Nick and Rachel

"Hello, Mr. Robinson." A seated man's shadowed face appeared on the screen.

"You have an urgent matter?"

"We found someone -"

"You're running my location. The price just doubled." The man referred to as Mr. Robinson closed his notebook computer with satellite uplink and packed it away. He left the empty Pacific Grove beach after taking a last look at the surging waves. The overcast dawn gave the ocean surface a grayish hue.

It took him only minutes to travel the road which ran along the coastline. With his gear safely stowed in the trunk, the man mentioned as Mr. Robinson drove his nondescript gray Chevrolet Malibu away from the beach to Lighthouse Avenue, where he parked near Monte Café. With a different laptop, the man walked into the nearly empty restaurant and sat down. He smiled and nodded at the middle-aged couple having breakfast a few tables over.

"You're up early, Nick."

Nick grinned over at the balding man with deeply lined, tanned face. "It's not that early, Dan."

"Working on a new novel?" Dan's wife asked.

"Always, Carol," Nick answered. "What are you and Dan doing up? I thought you retirees hated getting up before noon."

"Yeah, right. We haven't been in a bed past seven in fifty years, you slacker. Carol and I actually accomplish things in reality. We can't all make a fortune writing about killers."

"Dan!" Carol admonished, slapping her husband's shoulder.

"I asked for it." Nick chuckled as a harried man in his forties, wearing white cook's garb rushed toward Nick's table. "Uh oh, you short again, Joe?"

"Nancy's still out with the flu. What can I get you, Nick, the usual?"

"Yep, and I'll get my own coffee. Don't hurry my order. I'll fool around on the computer for a while," Nick replied, standing up.

"Thanks," Joe said, on his way to the back again. "I'll bring you your rye toast in a few minutes, big spender."

Dan and Carol laughed at Nick's stricken look as he trudged to the coffee pot. Nick brought the coffee over to the couple. He refilled their cups before retrieving a cup and saucer from the coffee station for himself. Nick returned to his table, ignoring Dan's remarks about slow help. He opened his notebook computer and accessed the internet. An anonymous bulletin board carried the message with the identifying code he was looking for. The post contained only one word: agreed. Nick typed in a new time for one hour later and closed his notebook.

"Wow! That was a quick entry." Dan helped Carol get stiffly to her feet.

"I'm outlining today, nothing serious."

"That killer of yours is scary, Nick," Carol said. "How do you come up with those awful plots?"

"I do the job and then I write it out like a diary."

Dan chuckled appreciatively. Carol clucked her disapproval at Nick's ad lib.

"Why don't you write a nice romance for your next one," Carol urged, as the couple walked toward the door. "I'll bet –"

4

"Oh, yawn," Dan cut in, glancing at Nick. "Don't you dare, Nick. I want to read all about a new Diego assassination gig. Have him blow up congress like Tom Clancy did in his book."

Nick laughed. "I'll think about it. Hey, Carol, Diego had a romantic interlude in the last one. Didn't you –?"

"Nick, that was so nice." Carol turned around excitedly, leaving Dan holding the door open for her. "You should give him a steady girlfriend."

"Might as well give him gardening and quilting hobbies, too, while you're making him into a sissy." Dan scowled at Carol as she took another shot at his shoulder, and the two shuffled out the door, still arguing.

"You set off Dan and Carol again. I can't believe those two both read your pulp. Here's your rye toast, Hemingway." Joe set the plate down in front of Nick with an exaggerated flourish. "Thanks for getting your own coffee. Give yourself a big tip."

"How about I find a new restaurant to get insulted in?"

"Oh no, Nick." Joe played along, wringing his hands on the way to the kitchen. "There goes my vacation in the Bahamas."

"You'll be sorry when you don't have Nick McCarty to kick around, Joe," Nick called out after him, before digging into his rye toast breakfast.

Within the allotted time, Nick again sat out on the Pacific Grove beach. Although a few joggers and walkers passed by along the stone divider separating the road from the sand, no one had descended to the chilly beach.

"We were taking precautions," the man on Nick's screen explained.

Nick rearranged his ear piece. He projected only a blank screen, his words in text form, with a computer generated voice. When Nick was satisfied his contact had no tracking gear on him, he spoke.

"Send the package, and I'll be in touch." After the transmission was completed, Nick acknowledged reception.

"This is a small window of opportunity."

"I'll let you know," Nick ended the conversation and packed up his portable satellite uplink once again.

Nick drove to Lighthouse Avenue again; but turned right on 12th Street, stopping two blocks down in front of a two story home with a white picket fence, porch, and balcony. It was one of his few excesses. He loved the sprawling four-bedroom place more than anything else in his life.

Inside, tan walls highlighted the dark oak woodwork throughout. Oil paintings of seascapes dominated the wall space. With the satellite gear stored in his downstairs safe room, Nick took a cup of coffee with him to the balcony. He opened his notebook computer at the table. After scanning and opening the burst transmission, the attached picture gripped him as nothing had in decades.

A young woman with sandy hair and shining blue eyes peered out at him, her smile accenting the sprinkle of freckles across the bridge of her nose. She looked so much like a woman he had known in high school that Nick's sense of reality slipped momentarily. He swallowed and searched the data in her file. At thirty-three, she was five years younger and in no way the girl he had known. The file revealed her name to be Rachel Hunter. Nick's prospective employer wanted her dead by week's end. Rachel was under federal witness protection in Pleasanton, California, just north of Nick's Pacific Grove place.

Nick locked up his house. It took him under two hours to reach the Applebee's restaurant where Rachel worked. He followed the greeter in and was seated at a window table with a menu. Rachel's tables were in an area further down on Nick's right, where he could see her movements without obstruction. She had to pass by his table to reach the kitchen. Nick ordered the soup and salad special with iced tea. He noticed Rachel glance his way as she walked by. Nick smiled at her, and Rachel blushed as if embarrassed he had noticed her looking at him.

* * *

Six days later, an immaculately dressed man entered his plush office on the Upper East Side of Manhattan. He walked to the huge window behind the desk, where it seemed the world lay at his feet. Gazing out at what he thought of as his world, he wondered if the detestably arrogant Mr. Robinson had brought the little blue-eyed canary to room temperature yet.

The fifty caliber slug went in dead center between his eyes, opening after impact to leave little of his head intact. The man was never to be disturbed during these morning hours. His secretary would not discover the body until nearly noontime. By then, Nick was off the island and on his way west.

* * *

"Hey look there Carol, it's Mister Pulp Fiction."

"Shush, Dan, quit repeating Joe's insults! Hi Nick."

Nick sat on a camping chair in the sand of Otter's Point Beach. The ocean vista fronting the small beach calmed considerably as it flowed into the narrow cove. A steep rocky cliff poked out to blunt the ocean's force on the left, while waves crashed rhythmically against the craggy rock barriers jutting out of the water on the right. Although the nearness to the path and road made satellite uplinks a bad idea, Nick loved to visit Otter's Point in the early morning hours. He liked the cold and salty-tasting air.

Nick looked behind him to the stone wall separating the beach from the road above. It snaked along unevenly to a roughly hewn beach access stairway. He waved at the old couple picking their way carefully down the rock steps to the sand and stood up to greet them.

"Joe told us you stopped in for coffee and insults again this morning," Dan said, shaking hands with Nick. "He mentioned you were headed here. Where'd you take off to these past couple weeks?"

"Don't be so nosy, you old goat." Carol rebuked her husband, but looked at Nick expectantly anyway.

"Field work for Diego's new adventure," Nick answered with a smile. "I journeyed to the Moonlight Bunny Ranch in Las Vegas for research on romance."

"Oh…you…bugger." Carol gasped, shaking her finger at Nick as Dan laughed.

"You suggested I needed more romance in my creepy novels, Carol," Nick replied, while innocent confusion beamed expertly from his features. "I aim to please."

"I never…oh, I see…it's 'poke fun at the old lady' day." Carol tried to look at Nick with stern reserve but started giggling as if she were eighteen instead. "You never give Diego a sense of humor either, by the way. You're funny, Nick. Diego could be funny."

"A funny assassin?" Dan snorted. "Oh please…"

"Between you and me, Carol, I can't give Diego too much of my personality." Nick looked both ways for witnesses before leaning toward Carol conspiratorially. "It would give away my secret identity."

This drew laughter from both Dan and Carol. Dan held out the thermal cup he had in his hand to Nick.

"Here, Hemingway, we bought you a cup of coffee for the beach."

"God bless you, sir." Nick took the cup in both hands, imitating a street urchin in a Dickens' novel. "You do the Lord's work this gray morning."

"Notice how we've been talking for ten minutes, and he still hasn't told us anything," Dan said. "The least we could get is a straight answer to one simple question in payment for hauling that heavy coffee all this way for you."

"I went east for research. I took pictures and notes all along the route for stops I'm using in my work-in-progress. Then, I came back. Simple as that."

"You take pictures, of course." Carol thought about it for a moment. "Then you'd have something to jog your memory for a particular piece in your writing."

"Damn, you've dragged the secrets of bestsellers from me. Now, what will I do? You know, of course, that the Writer's Guild will send people after me for this, don't you?"

"We thought maybe you had a girlfriend somewhere," Carol persisted, ignoring Nick's humorous sidestep.

"Actually, up north, I did see a woman I'd like to know better. It was –"

"Is this another joke?" Carol cut him off.

"Give him a chance to finish a sentence, oh Grand Inquisitor." Dan needled Carol with practiced ease.

"I'm sorry, Nick, go on." Carol reached out a hand to touch Nick's windbreaker while glaring at Dan.

"I'm making Pleasanton one of the main points in the story I'm doing," Nick went on, grinning at the couples' continuous repartee. "I stopped in for lunch at an Applebee's up there and saw a waitress I took a real liking to. I have to do more field work in Pleasanton and I figured to haunt the Applebee's restaurant while I'm working."

9

"I don't know that I approve of you dating a waitress," Carol replied, stunning Dan, who gaped at her as if she had grown a third eye.

"You were waitressing when we met." Dan recovered quickly, smiling with satisfaction as his factual addition to the conversation made Carol blush.

"See." Nick put his arm around Carol's shoulders. "It worked out for you."

"On second thought…" Dan said, cupping his chin as if in deep thought, "Carol may have a point."

"I need more caffeine before taking both you weasels on at once this early in the morning." Carol sighed, shrugging off Nick's arm. "Sorry, Nick, that came out wrong. When are you going to Pleasanton again?"

"Later in the day, when the rush hour traffic's over."

"You're really taken with this waitress," Dan speculated.

"And with my research, so I can remain in this lap of luxury," Nick added.

"We'd better get going." Carol tugged on Dan's jacket. "My knees are starting to ache. It's cold down here in this wind, and I've had enough morning exercise."

"I can go get the car, honey," Dan offered quickly. "You can sit here with Hemingway while I get it."

"No… I'm not that sore." Carol grasped Dan's hand. "Let's move. Bye Nick."

Nick waved. "Bye, Carol. I'll see you two at the café."

Nick watched the couple trudge up the rock steps to street level, still gripping each other's hands. Something sharp and annoying stabbed into the dark recess of his mind, bubbling unease to the surface, bringing a bitter taste to his mouth. Nick sat down again on the camp chair. He pulled the windbreaker hood over his short cropped brown hair, squinting out at the waves again as the cold sea breeze blew across the beach.

* * *

Timing his entry after carefully watching the ebb and flow of patrons into the Applebee's restaurant, Nick entered as a table opened in Rachel's area. The greeter, a young teenage girl, grabbed up a menu and led him to the table he had hoped to get.

"I'll have this cleaned up right away," she told Nick, handing him the menu.

"No hurry," Nick said. A busboy came over to clean the table only moments after the girl returned to the front.

Rachel hurried over to the table, having seen Nick sit down. Nick noticed her nametag had 'Kim' on it as she smiled at him in greeting.

"Hi, I'm Kim. I'll be your server today. Can I get you anything to drink?"

"Iced tea, please, and I'll have the soup and salad." Nick pointed out the entry in the menu. "Blue cheese dressing on the salad."

"Coming right up, I'll get your iced tea. Be right back."

Rachel returned a few minutes later with Nick's iced tea. As she set the table for him and put the ice tea down, a fortyish woman slipped into the chair across from Nick.

"I'm sorry." The woman apologized excitedly. "Are...are you Nick McCarty?"

"Yes," Nick answered. The best-selling author had forgotten for a split second that his picture was on millions of book covers.

"I knew it! I'm Denise." The woman held out her hand and Nick shook it. "I've read all your books - mostly because my husband made me - at least in the beginning."

Denise laughed at her own admission as Rachel looked from Denise to Nick curiously, knowing she should get moving, but unable to command her body away from the table.

"My husband will freak." Denise put a piece of notebook paper in front of Nick with a pen. "Can I get your autograph? Ron will go ballistic when I show him."

Nick wrote 'to Ron and Denise, thanks for your support,' signed it, and passed the pen and paper back. "Nice meeting you, Denise. Tell Ron I said hi."

"Oh… I sure will," Denise stood up and walked quickly away, waving the paper in front of two bored looking pre-teen girls which Nick figured were hers.

"You're a writer?" Rachel glanced around at her area tables. "Oh crap…I mean…I'll be back with your food."

Nick watched Rachel go into hyper-drive as she caught up with her orders and drink refills. She brought his food ten minutes later.

"Here you are."

"Thank you."

Rachel started to walk away, but turned again.

"Are you a writer?"

"Yes. I write creepy killer novels," Nick smiled up at Rachel. "I don't normally get asked for an autograph except when I do book signings."

* * *

"I saw you in here a couple weeks ago." Rachel remembered the lean-faced man with the butch cut dark hair, smiling up from a table she passed almost as if he knew her. She had watched Nick, meeting his gaze several times before he left. *There was something about him -maybe the dark eyes.* "Do you live in the area?"

"No, I live down in Pacific Grove, near Monterrey."

"Wow, it's beautiful there. I..." Rachel glanced around, seeing the lunchtime crowd had thinned considerably and the tables in her area were not being filled. She hesitated for a moment before making a decision. "Listen. Mr. McCarty, I have a break coming, and...well...ah..."

"Would you like to join me?"

"Can I?"

"Sure, but it's Nick when you sit down, okay?"

"Of course."

She walked up front and spoke to her assistant manager. The man nodded in agreement. Rachel returned to Nick's table and sat down where Denise had sat earlier.

"I don't normally do this, but..."

"I'm honored," Nick cut in gently, eating a forkful of salad.

Rachel laughed. "You're kind of a smartass, aren't you?"

"Guilty."

"What are you doing visiting this furnace, instead of enjoying the ocean coolness, Nick?"

"I'm on a field trip, researching the area for a part in my next book."

"You're not going to put Applebee's in it, are you?"

"Yeah, I am, and you in some form, along with a host of other details."

"Me? In your book? I…"

"Not you in person, but possibly a waitress who takes breaks with her customers."

Rachel giggled. She looked away from Nick. Rachel remembered how happy she'd been upon hearing the news which her contact with the US Marshalls had delivered a week ago: Hayden Tanus was dead. The possibility of returning to her old life in New York had been breathtaking. Now, sitting opposite Nick, it didn't feel as exciting. Rachel shook her head. *He's a stranger. What the hell's wrong with you, girl?*

"You look like something stung you."

"It's…it's just that I…received some good news last week about maybe returning home."

"Where's home?" Seeing Rachel hesitate, Nick quickly added, "No need to say. I was making small talk."

"No, it's all right," Rachel smiled, meeting Nick's eyes again. "I don't want to talk about it until I have an actual chance to do it."

"It sounds like you've already decided." Nick kept his voice carefully neutral, but his voice was the only thing in neutral. "Well, I better get moving."

Suddenly, seeing Nick walk out was the last thing on Earth Rachel wanted. She reached over to take his hand as he started to stand.

"Wait, Nick, do you have to go back tonight?"

"I have a room at the Marriott in Pleasanton. I had planned to stay over."

"Great, I live close to there. Why don't we have dinner so we could talk some more?"

"I'd like that. I have to warn you though. I'm not as funny when you've been around me more than fifteen minutes."

14

"I'll take the chance. We'll meet at the Marriott and have a drink together. If you're still funny after the first drink, we can have dinner. Deal?"

"Deal."

Chapter Two
US Marshalls

As Rachel walked out to the parking lot she spotted the familiar black Lincoln next to her Honda. Anxiety made her breath come in short gasps, amplified by the discomforting sweat from leaving Applebee's air conditioned building into the Livermore, California heat. Rachel opened the Lincoln's passenger side door and slipped quickly inside, thankful they had the air conditioning going. She took a deep breath and gave the couple in front a tired wave.

"Is it still good news, or not?"

"We're in gathering mode back east but it looks good," the brunette in the driver's seat said. "Tanus was the only one you could help us with. We suspect Tanus had the whole operation on his shoulders. We're hoping his import/export network will be falling apart, instead of someone jumping right into his shoes. Our overseas contacts are already moving on his holdings there. You may be home free, but I'm not sure going home to New York right away would be a good idea."

"Tim said –"

"Yeah, I know what Tim said." The woman interrupted Rachel as she skewered the man with dark hair on her right with a grim look. "Want to take it from here, Tim?"

"Sorry, I made a slight jump in logic" Tim acknowledged. He looked back at Rachel. "Grace pointed out the probability of trouble if you popped up in New York all of a sudden. Who was the boyfriend?"

"What boy... oh... you mean the guy I sat with on break. His name's Nick McCarty. He's some kind of writer doing –"

"Shit! Are you kidding me?" Grace exclaimed. She looked over at her partner. "Do you remember the book I gave you to read titled *Diego's Way*?"

"Yeah, the assassin for hire," Tim replied. "McCarty must be loaded. How many bestsellers did you tell me he had?"

"Eleven so far, all about the same badass killer," Grace explained excitedly to Rachel. "He lives down near Monterrey. What's McCarty doing up here?"

"Nick told me he's researching the area for his next book, using Pleasanton as one of the locales. He's staying at the Marriott there."

"Oh it's Nick already. Gee, that's cozy," Tim said. "So is the fact that you only live a couple blocks from there, Kim."

"By the way, is there any chance of losing the Kim Hunnicutt moniker?"

Grace nodded. "That may be doable. We should know more in two weeks. So, do you have something going on with Nick, Kimmy?"

Rachel growled, evoking laughter in the front. Grace's continual banter from their first meeting had put Rachel at ease in a horrid situation. Although professional in all aspects relating to her client, Grace used her jokingly blunt persona to make a connection with people she handled in the program, and to extract bits of information vital to doing her job. Having witnessed the many verbal sparring matches between Grace and Tim, Rachel could tell Grace's manner was no affectation.

"You know I hate that name."

"Yeah… What's your point?" Grace needled her a little more. "You've been in the program nearly a year and this is the first social meeting we've seen you have."

"Being afraid for my life has that effect on me," Rachel retorted. "For the first six months I thought any guy who looked at

17

me was a potential killer. When Nick looked at me…I…it seemed like he knew me."

"Writers are like that," Grace stated as if she were an expert. "Did you initiate the interest?"

"A woman came up and asked for his autograph when I brought him an iced tea. I guess I did come on kind of strong after that."

"I don't blame you," Grace said. "Spill it. Are you going on a date or what?"

"I'm meeting him at the Marriott bar at seven and then we're going to dinner if things work out."

"We'll have to check him out, right Tim? I think a double date is in order. Besides, Tim here's been trying to get into my pants for the last two years."

Tim started choking comically.

"No way!" Rachel gasped, pushing Grace in the back of her head. "I'm not going on a first date with you two."

"I'm afraid I'll have to insist," Grace began; but one look at Rachel's face, and she turned to pleading. "Please…please… please…"

Rachel tried to keep from laughing but failed. Grace added hands clasped in prayer over the seat back to her mantra.

"Okay…okay…" Rachel relented. "One look at you two and my romance with Nick will be over before it begins. But what the hell? I came on to him like a cheap hooker. Maybe he'll think I'm more reserved if you two show up."

"No, he'll tell you to take a hike," Tim warned. "Don't listen to the Black Widow here. She wants to meet the famous author at any cost and throw our low profile presence to the wind. Take my advice, and tell Grace to get a life. The moment Grace walks into the bar she'll throw herself all over this McCarty guy

18

like the attack of the Gorgon. She'll turn him to stone before you get to first base."

"I have a gun, pencil-neck," Grace threatened, while Rachel laughed at Tim's send up of his partner. "One more word out of you and you'll be on life support."

"You two can come for a drink," Rachel relented. "After that I want you both gone."

"Good enough. Now get out of the car," Grace ordered. "I have to find a book store and buy Nick's latest novel. I'm getting his autograph tonight."

Rachel opened the car door, gritting her teeth at the blast of heat. "You two better be on your best behavior."

"See ya at seven, Kimmy." Grace waved while Tim mouthed, 'I told you so,' through the passenger side window.

Rachel let Grace back the Lincoln out and leave before opening the driver's side door of her white Honda Civic. She pulled the reflectors from the front and rear windows and threw them on the backseat. They were the only reason she could enter the car after it had baked all day in the sun. Rachel smiled as she started the car and put the air conditioning on full blast, wondering what Nick would say when he met Grace and Tim.

* * *

Nick, parked a block up from where the meeting between Rachel and the US Marshalls had taken place, put away his earpiece. He had picked the two agents out earlier and bugged their car while they went inside the restaurant. *They were pretty funny for US Marshalls,* Nick thought, driving his Malibu toward the Marriott Hotel.

* * *

19

"Grace, could you come here for a second?" Tim called out from the kitchen of Grace's apartment in Dublin, California.

Tim had his notebook computer open on the kitchen table searching databases while waiting for Grace to get ready.

"What?" Grace walked into the kitchen still brushing her hair.

"Check out Mr. McCarty's file, Princess," Tim urged, getting up and gesturing at the screen.

"He's a New York Times best-selling author, for God's sake, what...shit...!" Grace had started out scanning the screen, but ended up throwing her brush aside and sitting down in Tim's seat. "Special Forces...Delta...and then...Jesus...file transferred to DOJ in 1998. What the hell does all this mean?"

"It shows him still in the reserves and the rest of his file after 1998 is blocked. That's when his writing career took off and he bought the house in Pacific Grove. I pulled up his passport activity. He's a traveler."

"His novels are about an assassin who kills people all over the world. He'd say it was research," Grace muttered, standing up. "I don't like this. I'll finish getting ready, and you call it in. Maybe Richards has more pull and can find out about McCarty."

* * *

"I figured they'd hit the databases next," Nick mumbled to himself after deciphering the scrambled message he received by logging on to the anonymous bulletin board on-line. He took out the satellite phone from his bag, fingered a number in, waited five seconds, and hung up. It beeped thirty seconds later.

"Hello, Romeo." The gruff voice on the other end of the line greeted Nick. "What the hell do you think you're doin'? I told

20

you your damned involvement ended with that rogue sanction on Tanus."

"They put out another hit on her this morning. Apparently, the leak at DOJ is still bleeding information. There's no way Tanus would have shared his knowledge of Rachel's location or my involvement. Even with my cover, I can't…"

"No contact, Nick! You're the deepest we've ever been into this network. You've been a ghost, thanks to that goofy writing career you managed to pull off. In one day you pissed it all away. We have US Marshalls hacking into the DOJ databases trying to access your record, and now you're romancing the mark?"

"You wanted the leak found out. When Tanus bought the hit on Rachel, you ordered me to stall the deal. I stalled it. What happened to 'we don't work domestic'? As long as I keep Rachel alive, you have time to nail the leak at DOJ. Who was it that told me the entire Witness Protection Program is for sale to the highest bidder, Frank?"

"Who the hell gave you permission to write your own ticket, genius?"

"Some folks just need killin'."

"You son of a…okay, listen up cowboy, drop off the radar immediately. Let's salvage what we still have. Get the hell out of Pleasanton."

"That's a negative, good buddy. It was all okay when Tanus ordered hits on scumbags overseas. What were you thinking – sacrifice a witness to keep Tanus in business and find the leak at DOJ as a bonus? You keep hunting for the leak, and I'll do whatever the hell I want to do."

"You've watched 'Bourne Identity' too many times, Nick. Get your head out of your ass. You have too much to lose. We can take it all away."

"Don't threaten me, Frank. I don't like it. Tanus threatened me once."

"Why you arrogant... Did you just –"

"I didn't just anything. I've played this game by your rules for ten years. I'll play this one a little different. Take some time to think it over. Call me tomorrow morning. I have a date tonight."

Nick disconnected. *That went well.*

* * *

Nick stood up from his table in the Marriott hotel bar. Rachel spotted him and walked over. She self-consciously smoothed her black scoop-neck dress with gathered bodice. The hem ended inches above her knees. Her blonde hair, no longer tied back, lay loosely past her shoulders. At six feet tall, Nick was only a couple inches taller than Rachel in her black high-heels.

"Hi," Nick greeted her with a smile. "You look nervous."

"Good, because I am," Rachel conceded, sitting down in the chair Nick pulled out for her. "On the other hand, you look like you do this all the time...I mean, date nearly complete strangers."

"Hardly," Nick replied, sitting opposite Rachel as a waitress came over. "Would you like something to drink? I held off on ordering."

"Long Island Iced Tea, please," Rachel told the waitress.

"Dos Equis dark," Nick ordered.

"I'll be right back with your drinks."

Nick grinned. "A Long Island, huh? You must be nervous."

"I already copped to that, smartass." Rachel giggled. "Look, I know this is weird, but two of my friends who are really big fans of yours are stopping by for a drink with us. Will that be okay? If not, I can –"

"I don't mind," Nick cut in gently.

"I...I think my friend Grace is bringing along one of your novels for you to sign."

"Okay. One book signing coming right up."

"You're upset, aren't you?"

"Nope, if I was I'd already be on my way out the door. I'm not much on hiding my feelings. You look stunning."

"Thank you." Rachel glanced away, her face reddening under Nick's gaze. The waitress arrived and set the drinks down on the table with their tab.

"I thought we'd have dinner here, too, if I don't scare you away during our 'have a drink together' tryout." Nick liked Rachel more with each passing moment. "I didn't bring anything with me other than slacks, jeans, and a few pullover shirts, so I'm reluctant to go anywhere fancier."

"I'm overdressed is what you're saying?"

"No." Nick laughed at Rachel's dig. He saw Tim and Grace entering the restaurant bar. "I was trying to explain why I only wore slacks and a shirt."

Grace appeared to be a couple inches shorter than Rachel in Nick's peripheral vision, while he thought Tim looked a little taller than he was. Noticing the grim look he was getting from the agents Nick wondered if they found out more than they should have. Grace carried a hardbound book in her hand. She wore a blue sleeveless dress, so Nick figured it couldn't be too bad. Tim wore black slacks and a brown pullover shirt. Their appearance startled Rachel, who had been in the middle of telling Nick there weren't really any dress codes anywhere in the area.

"Hi." Rachel greeted Grace and Tim, moving over into the chair next to Nick. "Grace, Tim, this is Nick McCarty. Nick, this is Grace Stanwick and Tim Reinhold."

"Happy to meet you." Nick stood and shook hands with each of them before gesturing at the empty chairs. "Please join us. I see you have *Cold Terror* with you, Grace. Would you like me to sign it for you?"

"Uh…sure, if you don't mind." Grace glanced down at the book in her hand as if having forgotten she'd brought it along and then handed it to Nick. "I was wondering if we might borrow Kim for a moment."

"Huh?" Rachel looked up in surprise at Grace.

"Just take a moment," Grace urged.

"I'm sorry, Nick. We'll be right back."

"I'll be here." Nick unclipped the pen from the book jacket. While watching the three walk away he signed it *to my friend Grace* with his signature.

* * *

"Hey, thanks a lot," Rachel hissed at Grace as they entered the lobby area side by side with Tim bringing up the rear. "As if this date isn't strange enough."

"We found out a few disturbing items of interest about Nick." Grace handed Rachel a folded sheet of paper she took from her purse.

Rachel unfolded the paper with ill-disguised irritation which quickly turned to shock.

"You can see why we're a little concerned about Nick," Tim added as Rachel continued reading.

"Okay." Rachel handed the paper back to Grace. "Nick's a little more than a writer. He's a war hero, travels a lot and I saw your note about his file being blocked from 1998 on. Apparently, when he writes about violent people, Nick probably has some real life experience. I'm surprised, but I don't see anything on the paper to make me think he's a danger to me. According to your info, he's owned a house in Pacific Grove since hitting it big as a novelist in 1998. Maybe that has something to do with his file being vague since then."

"Restricted access doesn't mean vague," Tim pointed out.

"Look, Kimmy, we don't think Nick's here to kill you. Hell, he wouldn't invite you out on a date so he could pop you…at least in the bullet type sense," Grace explained. "We wanted you to know there's more unexplained stuff about the guy than there are facts."

"Well, this puts a new kink in the first date deal." Rachel sighed. "There's nothing like having my own personal investigation staff running info on potential suitors."

"See, Tim, it's not registering." Grace told her partner with a knowing look. "Kimmy's panties are wet already thinking about danger boy in there."

"Grace!" Rachel shoved the now laughing agent against Tim, who steadied her while shaking his head in commiseration with Rachel.

"Sorry…did…did I say that out loud?"

"I need to finish my drink." Rachel walked toward the bar. "Thanks for the report. Feel free to leave the moment you get your book back, bitch."

"I'm having a Margarita no matter how offended your sensibilities are." Grace yanked Tim along with her.

* * *

Nick watched the trio's return with some concern. Rachel was at least a few paces in front of the agents as if she were trying to outdistance them. He stood up and pulled the chair out next to him. Rachel smiled at him crookedly and sat down, taking a gulp of her drink. Nick handed the book to Grace. The waitress came over right after the Marshalls sat down.

"I'll have a Margarita."

"Make it two," Tim added.

"So, Nick, where do you get your material for the novels? They're so realistic. Diego always knows exactly what should be done at every instant and he's so matter of fact about it. Doesn't your agent or editor complain about him not having any real conflict?"

"Not bad, Grace." Nick smiled, as their waitress returned with the Margaritas. "You must know a little about the publishing business. That was one of the hurdles I had to overcome. They liked the writing but complained how one dimensional it was. I explained one of the traits a world class assassin would have is the skill to foresee every possible scenario on a job. It would be idiotic to have him stumbling from one situation to another as if he were Peter Sellers in a 'Pink Panther' movie."

"The details do sell the character," Tim piped in. "When Grace loaned me *Diego's Way*, I figured it would be one of those thrillers with James Bond type action. Instead, it read as if an assassin kept a diary with every gruesome detail. A third of the way through the book I'm rooting for Diego to pull off the hit, collect the money, and return to his place in Venice."

"Yeah, and the way you describe his life in Venice…that whole other life he leads in complete obscurity," Grace added. "I like how you handle his sex life too. It's realistic and pretty sad. If Diego ever got too involved with anyone, his life would be in jeopardy."

"I appreciate the feedback," Nick said with some surprise. "Other than my agent urging me to throw contrived obstacles in Diego's path, romance is the second most complained about aspect. I have it in there but romantic ties have to be handled with the utmost care."

"This assassin of yours." Rachel looked into Nick's eyes. "Does he kill people indiscriminately? I mean…is he a real bad guy?"

"He kills people for a living," Nick answered without turning away, noting Rachel had finished off her drink already.

"Because of what he does, I think he would have to be classified as a bad guy."

"Diego kills bad guys though," Grace argued as if she were defending the character, having downed her Margarita already. "He takes hits where a bad guy orders a hit on another bad guy. It's not like he's out mowing down regular folk."

"Whatever made you start writing a book series about an assassin?" Rachel asked.

"You –"

"Can I get you folks anything else?" The waitress had returned, having spotted empty glasses on the table during her rounds.

"I'll have another," Grace held up her glass.

"Same here." Rachel handed her empty glass to the waitress.

"Maybe we should get some appetizers too," Nick suggested, hearing a slight slur in Rachel's words.

"No, we'll be eating dinner soon anyway," Rachel replied.

"I'll have one more." Tim drank the last of his Margarita and put his glass on the waitress's tray.

"Since we are having dinner together after all, would you and Tim like to join us, Grace?"

"Sure, that sounds –"

"Don't you and Tim have a party to go to?" Rachel asked innocently, while staring laser beams at Grace, who grinned and shook her head.

"No, Kimmy, Tim and I canceled out already. We'd love to have dinner with you two."

"Oh, wonderful," Rachel said without enthusiasm. "Nick, why did you decide on writing a series with an assassin as the main character?"

"I was always into action/adventure books and movies, even as a kid. I really liked the James Coburn movie series where he played a super suave secret agent named Flint. Have any of you seen the series? Flint was always two or three steps ahead and super slick. Using the same template, Diego formed in my head."

"I'll put those Coburn movies on my list of ones to see," Grace said. "It's neat hearing where a writer's ideas come from first hand. We thought maybe you were basing the books on real life experience."

"Funny you should say that." Nick chuckled appropriately, pretending he thought Grace was making a joke instead of going on a fishing expedition. "I tell everyone who asks me that very thing. Usually I get laughs."

The waitress arrived with their fresh drinks.

"I'm getting hungry," Nick announced as he sensed Grace was going to continue with her questioning. "Why don't we take our drinks into the dining area?"

No one objected, and the four were soon seated in the restaurant area. After ordering their dinners, Nick quickly warded off more questions with a stream of his own.

"How long have you all been friends?"

"About a year," Grace answered. "Kim waitressed for us a couple times and we hit it off."

"Are you and Ted married?"

"No, we work together," Ted cut in before Grace could answer.

"Oh, where do you two work?" Nick launched ahead.

"We work together out of the Federal Courthouse in Sacramento," Grace filled in quickly. "Luckily, our work doesn't involve a commute thanks to the computer age."

"Nice," Nick said. "I don't envy any of you three. I hate the heat."

"How long are you planning to hang around Pleasanton?"

"Probably another day. I'll make the trip up here again whenever a plot line requires it."

"Then your assassin will be killing someone in the US this time?"

"Not that I don't trust you implicitly, but I can't divulge the plot of a work in progress," Nick answered, patting Rachel's hand.

"Of course," Rachel nodded her head in understanding. "I don't know much about –"

The waitress arrived with their orders. Dinner proceeded with little conversation other than small talk. Nick insisted on picking up the tab for meals and drinks.

"You had some very strong drinks," Nick mentioned to Rachel as they left the restaurant area. "Did the food and coffee help, or would you like me to drive you home?"

"I'll be fine." Rachel smiled at Nick. "Thanks for the offer though. You can walk me to my car if you want."

"I want. It was nice meeting both of you," Nick told Grace and Tim as the four walked toward the Marriott's front exit together. "When I get back up here, maybe we can do this again."

"I'd like that," Grace chirped in immediately. "Knowing a famous author is so cool."

"You are such a groupie," Tim needled his partner with over-enthusiastic zeal.

"Don't let those two Margaritas you downed make your mouth write a check your ass can't cash, Sparky," Grace fired back, eliciting laughter as they cleared the entranceway.

Chapter Three
Hit Still On

Nick saw a glint in the darkness and jerked Rachel to the left by her arm as the glass behind them shattered. He snatched the befuddled Rachel off her feet, carrying her along until they were behind a car parked near the Marriott's entrance. Knowing the shooter would not stop with one shot after missing Rachel, Nick pressed her to the ground. He then ran straight at Tim and Grace, who had dropped into shooting crouches with weapons drawn. He hit into Grace hard from the left and slightly behind, launching her against Tim as more shots passed where the two Marshalls had been.

"Get down by those cars to your right!" Nick ordered. "I'll go back to Rachel. Watch for muzzle flashes straight out and to the left."

"We almost shot you," Grace gasped, but Nick was already streaking in a zigzag pattern back to Rachel.

* * *

Tim saw the muzzle flashes from what he guessed could have been hundreds of yards away. He pulled the struggling Grace toward cars parked on the right side of the entrance. Grace had her Glock 9mm trained on Nick as she allowed Tim to guide her. When she saw Nick shield Rachel, holding her pressed up against the parked car, Grace quickly snatched the cell-phone from her purse and pressed a number on speed dial.

"Code Red...I repeat...Code Red," Grace stated calmly into the phone, knowing her ID would be flashed automatically. "I want everything you can launch in an outgoing radius from the

Marriott Hotel at 5zero5niner, Hopyard Road, in Pleasanton. We are taking sniper fire. I repeat, we are taking sniper fire."

"If that guy's just a writer, I'm Bill Clinton," Tim stated after Grace ended the call. They stayed behind the cover of parked cars on their side.

"Yeah, well at least he's on our side." Grace motioned with badge in hand for the people approaching the shattered entranceway to get back. "He was in Delta. It's not like you forget all that. He did just save our lives."

"Duly noted."

* * *

"Are you okay?" Nick asked Rachel, turning so he could look into her eyes.

"I...I'm okay...I guess," Rachel answered. She took stock of her physical condition, while trying to calm her heart rate down before the organ burst from its chest cavity position. "Did somebody try to shoot me?"

"Does anyone want you dead? A few of my readers have e-mailed me about pooling their money together for my demise, but —"

"How did you know?" Rachel broke in, ignoring Nick's attempt at levity. "I'd have been dead if —"

"Hey...you two alright?" Grace called out, as the sound of sirens drew closer. "I think it's over."

"We're okay. You're probably right, but maybe we should stay where we are until some help arrives," Nick suggested. "Hey, Grace, you civil servants are pretty well armed."

Nick heard a stifled laugh from across the way.

"Tim and I are trying to figure out whether you paid for this just to impress Kimmy," Grace shouted back, drawing laughter from Nick as the first approaching squad car screamed up in front of the Marriott entrance, joined by three others in short order.

31

Nick turned to see Rachel staring at him questioningly. He stopped laughing. "I hope you don't think –"

"How did you know, Nick?"

"I saw a glint in the distance and decided looking like a fool would be preferable to one of us getting shot," Nick answered truthfully, lowering his voice as the police sirens cut off. "So, I yanked you to the side. I figured if I was wrong, I could tell you I tripped."

"That was fun." Grace leaned down to give Rachel a hand up. "Nice moves for a writer, Nick."

"I wasn't always a writer." Nick stood up away from the car, allowing Grace to handle Rachel.

Tim walked over to join them. "Maybe we should go back inside."

"Another Long Island sounds pretty good to me," Rachel said.

"I have no objections," Nick added. "I'm staying here."

"Margaritaville, here I come." Grace guided Rachel back inside the Marriott's entrance, walking carefully over to the side away from the glass. Tim walked slightly behind Nick and to his right.

"May I make a suggestion?" Nick stopped, when they were all inside the lobby area. "I think every person walking through any entrance here should be on camera: a good camera, not those grainy, piece of crap, security cams. Also, if it's not being ordered yet, every person through the doors should be monitored. Anybody expressing interest in my name or room at the front desk should be investigated."

"You don't think the sniper's out of the area by now?" Tim asked.

"Professional assassins have complete disregard for law enforcement and they won't panic. A silencer was used, so pinpointing the source, even if your investigators narrow down the trajectory, is remote. It might be possible to catch one unawares. They'll want to know if you're going to move Kim or not, and any new acquaintances she has in or out of the area."

"You're beginning to worry me, Nick." Tim exchanged concerned looks with his partner.

"I could pretend I'm stupid. I wrote a book titled –"

"*No Protection*," Grace broke in excitedly. "I loved that one. Diego takes a –"

"Can I get that drink now?" Rachel interrupted.

"You go ahead, Grace. I'll run these suggestions by the locals and see what I can come up with. I don't want to steal your thunder, Nick, but can I speak as if these suggestions are mine?"

"If you want any chance of them getting followed, you'd better."

Tim nodded with a smile and left. Grace, Rachel, and Nick took seats again at the same table Nick had reserved earlier. Grace and Rachel ordered their drinks but Nick ordered Iced Tea.

"Not drinking with us, huh partner?"

"Nothing personal, Grace, but I'm not your partner, and I have a sneaking hunch I might end up answering questions all night long in front of a spotlight."

Grace laughed. "Fair enough."

The waitress brought over their drinks, including the extra Margarita Grace ordered for Tim.

"You don't really think he had anything to do with this, do you?" Rachel asked Grace, after gulping a quarter of her drink.

"I'll have to get back to you on that one, right Nick?"

"She'll have to get back to you on that, Kim." Nick relayed the answer as if he were an interpreter.

"I'm sorry I mixed you up in this –"

"Kimmy!" Grace cut her off. "Slow down on the booze, girl."

Tim arrived at their table a moment later. He took a grateful sip of his Margarita. "They like the suggestions, mostly because they don't have William Petersen and the CSI Las Vegas cast here to do all those magic tricks like on TV. Did I miss anything? You were saying something about one of Nick's books?"

"Diego takes a job involving this murderous scumbag who had decided to turn on the mob in exchange for witness protection and a new life. He buys his way in at twenty-five grand a pop, picking people he can get info from in the justice department until he locates the scumbag."

"Did he shoot him from long range?" Rachel leaned forward uneasily.

"Nope." Grace shook her head. "Diego blew the crap out of him with a car bomb. The interesting part of the book is how every one of the people who tipped Diego off ended up behind bars but they couldn't finger Diego. Nick here knows a lot about the Witness Protection Program, don't you, Nick?"

"Six months of intense research went into that one," Nick admitted, remembering the hit on Paulo Cortesa. He had scared Cortesa into fleeing the program to Mexico, by planting notes where only Cortesa could find them. "I wrote the whole book first and filled in the details concerning the US Marshalls' service afterward."

"You're just dying to ask us, aren't you, Nick?" Grace kidded him.

"I'm a writer. I have an imagination and I can add two plus two. No, I don't care to know anything more than I do right now. If I could put Pandora back in the box, I would have eaten my meals at Denny's instead of Applebee's. That's all you're gettin' out of me, Coppers."

Even Rachel laughed this time.

34

* * *

"Hello, Nick." Grace waved animatedly as she walked into the interrogation room with Tim behind her. "Sorry about all this."

"I'm okay with it. I didn't figure you'd let me toddle along as if I weren't there. The Detectives have been very nice. The good cop was good and the bad cop was good. Is it time for you two to take a shift? How's Kim doing?"

"Kim's getting some sleep at a safe house until we figure this out. You're a little too calm in interrogation, Nick." Grace raised her hand in warning as Nick started to speak. "Don't give me that 'I wrote a book on it' nonsense either. I know you did."

"They've been going over my military record since you left me off here last night. You know I was in Delta. We do train for anything, including interrogation."

"We told them, Nick." Tim sat down opposite Nick. He placed a cup of coffee in front of him. "We told them you saved Kim and us."

"We told them we know right where to get you." Grace sat next to Nick, a big smile on her face. "Want to hear what finally got through to them?"

"Will it get me out of here?"

"They caught him. It was like you wrote the scene. He waited until five in the morning, when everything was quiet, and approached the desk dressed like a business executive. When he asked if you were still checked in, our guy at the desk hit the switch and sniper Sam was surrounded – false ID, false documents, false passport, the whole smear. The bad news is he picked you as his accomplice."

Nick burst into laughter, nearly choking on his coffee, with Tim and Grace joining in.

"I told them we were acting on your suggestions," Tim informed him after many moments. "They believe you had nothing to do with the hit – and it was a hit."

35

"Interpol lit up like a Christmas tree when we put out the guy's picture and fingerprints," Grace added. "We can't tell you anymore about him, but you're off the hook."

"Well, in that case." Nick stood up "Can I go home now? I'm thinking maybe I have enough Pleasanton material after all."

"Kim would like to see you," Grace said.

"That's very funny." Nick smiled, running both hands through his hair as he stretched. "I believe the stars are not right for Kim and me. Tell her I said no hard feelings."

"Sit down, Nick," Tim urged. "We have a proposition for you."

"No offense," Nick proceeded carefully, hoping they were going in the direction he'd been steering them. "But if this proposition has anything to do with me and Kim, forget it."

"We have a leak in the program." Grace patted the chair until Nick reluctantly sat down. "No way anyone finds out where Kim is without a leak. First, the guy she was to testify against grew a third eye in Manhattan and now there's an attempted hit on Kim."

"Maybe it was the same guy."

"He was in France when the Manhattan guy went down."

"Tanus? I read the papers."

"You know too much. Nobody likes a smartass."

"So I've been told. That's why I live alone. What's the proposition?"

"Your house in Pacific Grove has two safe rooms," Tim stated.

Uh oh, Nick thought, trying to keep his face in neutral.

Grace put an arm around Nick's shoulders. "Now what would a cute writer-type like you need with not one, but two safe rooms? Bet you're wondering how we found out you have them, aren't you?"

Nick shrugged. "It's public knowledge. Any two-bit hack could get into city planning."

"You're one of those damned computer nerds too?" Grace pulled her arm back and pretended to pout.

"Want to tell us why you have two?" Tim asked quietly.

"One's downstairs, one's upstairs. I'm a little paranoid."

"What would you have to be paranoid about?" Grace eased up over the table until she was smiling in Nick's face, resting on her arm in front of him.

"No reason. I'm just naturally careful." Nick smiled back.

Grace sighed and slid into her seat again. "I told you he'd say that."

"We'd like you to take Kim with you, Nick, until we get this leak business straightened out," Tim explained. "Grace and I will go down with you, while some people we trust implicitly find the leak."

Yeah, that'll work.

"You two are out of your ever lovin' minds." Nick registered the right amount of shock and awe. "Kim and I just met. I don't even know her."

"Ah…but would you like to?" Grace laughed at her own play on words. "C'mon Nick. It'll be fun. You have a huge house. Tim and I will stay in Monterrey so we're near if you need us. US Marshalls put people in places where other bad people can't find them. We aren't exactly bodyguards. It'll only be for a couple weeks."

"Does Kim know about this?"

"She's very excited about it, Nick. Kimmy loves the idea."

* * *

37

"You want me to what?" Rachel cried out in astonishment, with Grace trying to shush her, while Nick tried not to laugh.

"For the record, I knew you lied about Kim knowing all about this idea."

"Shut up, you," Grace ordered, pointing a warning finger at Nick. She turned to face the enraged Rachel. "It's the best we can do until we clear this up, Kimmy. No one knows about Nick. He has those safe rooms you can run into and lock behind you like a people vault."

"You agreed to this?" Rachel stared at Nick in amazement.

"He's very excited, Kimmy. I —"

"I want you to be safe," Nick cut in. "Like Grace says, I have a huge house you can get lost in. Tim and Grace figure it'll only be for a couple weeks. It would be very easy for you to avoid me at my house. The living room and kitchen are really the only communal areas. There are three bathrooms. If Grace and Tim manage to keep your whereabouts secret, you could move around outside without a problem. I'm not much of a bodyguard either. The way to keep you safe depends on my address remaining secret."

"You haven't told him, have you?" Rachel stared accusingly at Tim and Grace.

"Just like you, we were waiting for the proper time." Grace smiled confidently over at her increasingly distressed partner.

"I have a seven year old daughter named Jean, alias, Sarah," Rachel blurted out, still staring at Grace.

Oh shit! I'm well informed.

"The more, the merrier," Nick stated without hesitation. "I'll put you two up on the other side of the house."

"And...and an Australian Sheppard dog named Deke."

"I love dogs." *Great God in heaven, I am so screwed.*

38

"Do you mean that?" Rachel, tears running freely down her cheeks, met Nick's unwavering gaze.

"Absolutely," Nick answered. *I'm a dead man if Frank finds out about this.*

* * *

Nick's Chevy Malibu, loaded with bags in the trunk, also had a pile behind the driver's seat. Jean and Deke sat on one side of the rear passenger seat, with Deke's head out the window and body spread over Jean. Rachel sat on the front passenger side looking around the dark parking lot worriedly.

"You have yourself a low rider, Nick." Grace stepped back, assessing how low the Chevrolet was to the ground.

"Don't come to my house with the rest. Leave a message at the number I gave you when you come down with the other stuff. I'll meet you," Nick replied, standing with his hand on the driver's side door handle.

"Will you know if you're being followed?"

"Yeah, for all the good it would do me. If they have my license number how long would it take to find out where I'm headed? Our advantage is if no one knows about me. When will you and Tim be following? Did you put the block on my DMV records."

"Yes, yes, yes, and we're coming tomorrow night. We won't approach unless you call the code," Grace promised, trying to hug Nick. "You're my hero...my widdle bunny...my..."

Nick grabbed Grace's hand and in seconds Grace was standing on her tip toes dancing around. "Ow...ow...ow...ow... ow..."

"Don't touch me." Nick released her and opened his door to laughter from both Rachel and Jean. "I'm writing you into my

39

next novel and it won't be flattering. I'll make it so bad – yet exactly like you – your whole family will sue me even though they won't be able to win."

"No need to get nasty." Grace held the hurt look until Nick was behind the wheel and then she waved happily at Jean. "You be good and do what Nick says."

"Okay, but what's in it for me?" The seven year old asked, staring out at Grace over Nick's shoulder with a serious face. Deke barked on cue, sending Grace into peals of laughter.

"This is like you've entered the Twilight Zone, isn't it?" Rachel asked, when Nick drove away from Grace and out of the underground parking garage.

Shit, she reads minds.

"No, I'm not like the writer Jack Nicholson portrays in *As Good As It Gets*. Very little bothers me when I write – except for women, kids, and dogs."

Rachel laughed so long, Deke began to bark, with Jean giggling. She slapped Nick's shoulder in a way that reminded him of Carol's affectionate scolding of Dan. Rachel calmed down and leaned back in her seat with a sigh.

"It wasn't that funny." Nick smiled over at her.

"Why didn't you quote the line from that movie you really like? Go ahead and say it. I'll give you the lead in…'How do you write women so well?'"

"Okay…'I think of a man, and I take away reason and accountability.'"

"Feel better now?"

"Surprisingly, yes. How about you?"

"I'll be okay."

"I'm hungry," Jean spoke up from the back.

"Sarah!" Rachel whipped around. "I asked you if you were hungry before we left."

"I wasn't hungry then."

"Give me about forty-five minutes, Sarah, and we'll stop, okay?" Nick checked his rear view mirror every few seconds. He had swept the Malibu for bugs before they left when he had been alone.

"Okay," Jean agreed.

"It won't be safe to stop, will it?"

"If it's not safe in forty-five minutes, it won't be safe at all," Nick stated matter-of-factly.

"I'll have to start reading your novels. Your main character, Diego, must be like a superhero."

"He's a cold-blooded psychopath with only a thread of humanity left."

"Oh…"

"You'd be surprised how many people read the novels and start rooting for Diego as Tim admitted to doing. We have a mean streak in us and sometimes a character like Diego touches the black part of our souls. There are other readers who would like to have a book burning with my novels as the guests of honor."

"Grace really likes them."

"Yeah…well…Grace is a psycho."

"She is?" Jean popped up past Deke to get closer while the dog jammed in behind her with his head out the window. "What's a psycho?"

"If you want to stop in forty-five minutes you'll have to ignore anything you hear me say." Nick grinned back at Jean for a moment. "I live alone. Sometimes I say things better left unsaid because I think I'm talking to myself."

"How about after the forty-five minutes?"

"Sarah!" Rachel reached around attempting to tickle Jean who started squealing before the hand reached her. Deke interceded, grabbing Rachel's wrist lightly in his jaws. "Deke!"

Nick started laughing, while glancing over at the interchange. Hearing the tone in Rachel's voice, Deke released her and plopped down with head in Jean's lap, ready for another attack.

"You didn't tell me Deke was an attack dog."

"He attacks me without any problem. I'm not sure about anyone else. He's been doing it since he was a puppy. If I reach quickly for Jean in any way, Deke grabs me. If I escalate, he escalates."

"Neat."

"Figures you'd think so." An enigmatic smile formed as Rachel looked over at Nick.

"What's that supposed to mean?" Nick asked rhetorically, recognizing a setup when he heard one.

"Men and dogs recognize abhorrent behavior, think *oh well, that's nature*, and move on."

"You know us so well it's scary, right Deke," Nick prompted the dog and earned a 'grrruuffff' in response. "Hey, let's play the women and cats game now."

Rachel giggled. "I don't think so."

Twenty minutes later Rachel noticed Nick watching the rear view mirror even more than at the start of their trip.

"You're looking worried."

"Did Grace or Tim mention anything about putting a tail on us to you?"

"No, I thought they wanted only the two of them to know we were headed to your place."

"That's what I thought. We're almost to Gilroy. There's a McDonalds near the exit where we can get something to eat. In the dark, I'll know if the car I'm suspicious of follows us off."

"Yaaaaaaaaayyyyy, McDonalds!" Jean cheered.

"You will have a salad and glass of milk, young lady," Rachel told her.

"Yeah, right, Mom." Jean gave Rachel the wave off. "I'm having a Happy Meal and a milkshake."

"Do you have kids, Nick?"

"No."

"Want one?"

Chapter Four
Getting To Know You

Nick drove off the exit he knew led to the McDonalds and noticed the pair of headlights he had been watching leave the freeway too. In the McDonalds parking lot Nick, watched the car go past. It was a tan colored late model Buick Lacerne. The Buick kept going without slowing down and Nick could not get an angle to see the plate. He ordered and paid for the food after only a slight debate between his charges. They took the order over to a table Nick had picked out away from the front windows. Nick let Rachel divvy up the drinks and food, staying on his feet while sipping from the iced tea he'd ordered.

"Let me have Deke's leash and one of his waste bags. I'll take him for a walk."

"They came off the freeway with us, didn't they?"

"I'm going to see if they're parked where they can see who gets into or out of my car. Relax, I'll be right back."

Rachel nodded hesitantly and handed Nick the dog's leash and a baggie she had brought with her, planning to walk Deke after having something to drink. Nick took his iced tea with him. He leashed the overjoyed Deke and walked him out of the parking lot. Nick stopped every time Deke sniffed anything, allowing the dog to stay engaged with whatever aroma appealed to him. Nick drank his iced tea, looking around as Deke proceeded slowly up the street. The Buick was parked in the darkness nearly fifty yards away, facing Nick from across the street. After continuing another thirty feet, Nick took a look up at the sky casually and tugged Deke toward the parking lot.

Rachel smiled at Nick in relief as he walked toward their table after returning Deke to the car. "How we doing?"

"Not so good." Nick sat down. "I'm going to take them for a little ride. I'll call Grace while I'm doing it. If I'm not back in half an hour, call a cab and have the cabbie take you to a hotel. I'll have to take Deke with me."

"Why not call Grace right now?"

"You're not going to hurt Deke!" Jean chimed in.

"Calm down you two," Nick urged. "Deke and I will lead these clucks away, ID them, and be back in no time. I'm covering all our bases. If they're dangerous people, Deke and I will lead them on a wild goose chase until Grace and Tim get here."

"Okay...okay, we'll wait," Rachel agreed, picking up her cell-phone. "You'll call me, right?"

"I'll have Grace call you. Sorry this trip's taking longer than we figured but we need to be careful."

Nick walked out to the Malibu and opened the trunk. He moved luggage out of the way until he could reach the rear trunk area. Lifting up a section of fiber board, Nick took out a small leather case. He reloaded the car and took the case up front with him. Deke looked at Nick from the front seat expectantly. Nick laughed and opened the rear passenger door. Spreading the bags out on the floor and seat, Nick evened the surface before motioning Deke into the rear passenger compartment.

"Deke, buckle up, you're in for a bumpy ride. Sorry, but no hanging out the window this trip, buddy."

Great, now I'm talking to the dog.

Nick sat in the driver's seat, closed the door, and opened the leather case. He took out his satellite phone and a MAC 10 machine pistol with a forty round clip. Nick popped the clip into place and set the weapon on the passenger seat. With the phone in its Velcro cradle installed on top of the center storage compartment, Nick drove away from McDonalds within sight of the Buick. Instead of entering the freeway, Nick drove onto Gillman Road, heading East.

45

The Buick followed, nearly a hundred yards back. Nick called Grace's number, putting it on speaker. He turned off his lights, wheeled hard left, feathered the brake pedal, and slid smoothly in the reverse direction. Nick passed the Buick and repeated the maneuver, bringing the Malibu up behind the Buick.

"Grace Stanwick."

"Grace, I have a bogey here and I'm wondering if it's one of yours." Nick flashed his lights on and hurriedly read off the license plate number as the Buick's brake lights lit up.

"How'd you get through without your ID flashing on my screen, Nick?"

"Quit talking and get looking, Grace," Nick ordered, swerving around and ahead of the Buick once again, glancing back to make sure Deke was still okay. The dog had spread his paws to stabilize motion.

"Wait one, damn it, I'm checking!"

Nick accelerated far ahead of the Buick, turned out his lights, and reversed his direction once again. This time, he opened the driver's side window, picked up the MAC 10, and cradled it over the window frame.

"Hurry, Grace, time's running out." Nick calmly slowed the Chevy. The Buick decreased speed but kept coming. Nick anchored the MAC 10, the top pad of his right index finger gently beginning to squeeze the trigger.

"They're ours, Nick! Where are you and what do you mean time's running out?"

Nick turned on his lights, set the MAC 10 down, and accelerated back toward McDonalds. "I'll be with Kim and Sarah in a few minutes at a McDonalds on Arroyo Circle in Gilroy. I'll let you find out what this is all about. Call in to Kim's cell-phone, okay?"

"Count on that," Grace retorted angrily, ending the call.

Slowing his Malibu down, Nick picked up the MAC 10, cradling it next to his chest as the Buick Lacerne shot by him. A block away from the McDonalds parking lot, Nick packed away his phone and weapon. He let Deke jump to the front while Nick reformed the baggage in the rear passenger compartment. Nick shook his head in disbelief as he entered the McDonalds parking lot and saw both Rachel and Jean standing outside the door. Nick parked the Chevy. He eased out of the seat looking over at Rachel with undisguised disappointment.

"Do you have any survival instincts at all?"

"Grace called me. She said we no longer have a tail and to call her when I saw you."

"Can we at least go back inside please?" Nick motioned them to the restaurant door. "I'll get another iced tea and then give Grace a call. Please don't come out in the open again when we're still determining our situation."

"Sorry...I'm glad to see you," Rachel added.

"I'm growing on you, huh?"

"No, I left my purse in your car with all our money and credit cards."

Nick laughed, pointing at Rachel. "Good one. Want anything else to drink."

"No...and neither do you," Rachel said to Jean, just as the little girl was about to order.

A few minutes later, Nick had his iced tea, and Rachel's cell-phone with Grace on the other end of the line.

"It will amuse you to know my co-workers in the Buick never saw anything like what you pulled off out there on the road in the dark."

"I –"

"Already read it, Nick," Grace cut him off. "Our Diego learned racing skills for *Racing Terror*, and of course you again

47

have a cover for your antics. Do you have any idea how annoying you're getting to be?"

"Shouldn't we be talking about how I grew a tail in spite of complete secrecy?"

"I'd rather not."

"I'll bet," Nick chuckled. "Someone's watching you and Tim. Do you know either of the people in the Buick?"

"Both of them, and yes, Tim and I will be talking to them tomorrow morning in Sacramento. I wish I could tell you how confident I am about your trip home and continued anonymity. We shouldn't have brought you into this but we're in over our heads now. Think of this as a writing research bonanza, Nick."

"I'm going to give you a huge black mole right on your nose in the book, Grace, and you'll be a bed wetter, and you'll scratch inappropriate places, and even the pet gerbil you'll have as your only companion will hate your guts... and –"

Nick paused as Grace had already lost it and was howling in laughter while trying to repeat his threats to Tim. She didn't come back on for a minute.

"Okay, Nick, head home, watch your back."

"And you'll have an 'I Love Dad' tattoo on your ass, and..." Nick heard Grace losing it again and then the disconnect. He handed the phone back to Rachel, who had been playing Hangman with Jean on a sheet of notebook paper.

"That sounded like a very strange conversation," Rachel noted.

"Can we go now?" Jean asked.

With Mother and Daughter both looking at him almost with the same expression, the resemblance was startling to Nick. The blonde hair tied back coupled with light blue eyes made him smile. "This is like traveling with the Double-mint Twins."

48

Rachel laughed but Jean looked at him as if he had just landed from outer space.

"C'mon, we can go now. The good part is we're not all that far from my place."

An hour later, Nick pulled into his driveway, stopping where he could carry their bags into the house easily. Rachel gasped as motion detector security lights came on and she saw the huge Victorian house with a white picket fence.

"I've never seen anything like this." Rachel stepped out of the Malibu and stared up at the house front. Is there a place for Deke in the back?"

"If he's housebroken and doesn't chew on furniture, he can stay inside. I do have a fenced-in backyard he'll like. I'll check my security system and then we'll go inside. I'll haul in the luggage after I let you three in."

Nick led them up the stairs in front to his porch where he checked and then deactivated his security system. He left the door open so Deke could rove around his small front lawn while he unloaded the car.

"Oh my God." Rachel stared around her. "This is gorgeous."

"Thanks." Nick pointed straight ahead. "The kitchen is in there and there's a bathroom on the way. I'll go check my upstairs security cams before I unload the car."

Nick jogged upstairs and did a room by room search. He never left the house without locking away all his gear in a small vault within the safe room downstairs. After making sure the safe room upstairs could be shown and all else was in order, Nick went downstairs to begin unloading the Chevy with Deke dogging his every step. When the luggage was inside, Nick went into the kitchen, where Rachel and Jean sat in a comfortable but awed silence.

"We can take whatever necessary bags you need upstairs now and you two can unpack the rest tomorrow," Nick offered. "Help yourself to anything in the cupboards and refrigerator."

"Nick...this is too much."

"Too much what?"

"We've never stayed in a place like this before," Jean said. "Not even in New York."

Deke 'grumpfed' and laid down on the kitchen floor, head on paws.

"Deke doesn't look that impressed so follow his lead. Pick out the bags you can't sleep without and I'll take you to your rooms."

Other than having Carol and Dan over, Nick had never had anyone inside his house. He did his own housecleaning and gardening. Rachel and Jean picked out a couple of bags to take with them upstairs, and followed Nick to their adjoining rooms to the right of the staircase.

"You two can fight it out as to who sleeps in which room," Nick joked. "I'm down at the other end of the hall if you need me."

"Where do you usually write?" Rachel asked, after Jean called first and ran into the room on her right.

"I have a balcony you probably noticed from below. Normally, I do most of my writing out there. I take my notebook computer along everywhere I go when I'm on my home turf, so if I get some inspiration, I have the tools along with me to work. Lighthouse Avenue is my favorite walkway and the beach is usually my destination."

"I don't know what to say. I envy you."

Nick gestured with his hands. "I love this place. Would you like to see the balcony?"

"Do you have to ask?"

"Nick!" Jean ran out of the room she had picked and grabbed Nick's hand. "Can we go to the ocean?"

"Sure, I'll take you with me on my morning walk down to the beach. Deke will probably need a bath before he can come back in the house afterward though. How is Deke with strangers he meets on a walk?"

"Real good," Rachel answered. "He only gets upset if someone grabs at either Jean or I. Will it be safe for us to go out?"

"Your guess is as good as mine," Nick admitted. "Grace and Tim wouldn't like it, but I'll leave it up to you. Why don't I get us some wine, and a juice for Jean. We can drink them out on the balcony and talk it over."

"Thank you." Rachel leaned in and kissed Nick, her lips softly brushing against his, sending a chill through him all the way to his feet.

"You're welcome. I'll be right back."

* * *

"Mom, why don't you marry Nick?" Jean suggested, her face alight with the possibilities. "Then we could –"

"We're here for a couple weeks, kid," Rachel interrupted, stroking her daughter's face. "Let's enjoy the stay here without scaring Nick any more than he already is."

"I don't think Nick gets scared, Mom," Jean replied, looking over the rail.

* * *

On the balcony with Deke at their feet, Nick poured wine for Rachel and himself. Jean sat as close to the railing with her

51

juice as she could get, looking out at the incredible view of Pacific Grove and the ocean beyond. The fog had begun moving in ever so slowly, beginning to obscure the housetops below them.

"I'm no wine connoisseur. I hope this Berringer White Zin is okay."

"Wow, something you're not an expert at," Rachel said in mock surprise. "White Zin is my favorite. I don't know how you ever leave this place. It's incredible."

"It's not easy to leave here, but it makes me appreciate what I have more when I finally return. I'm going to like seeing it through your eyes. I take a lot for granted."

"It gets pretty cold down here, huh?" Rachel pulled up the collar on her jacket more as a chilly breeze blew in off the ocean.

"I hate hot weather. I can adapt to about anything, but I sure wouldn't choose to live in a furnace like Pleasanton. Then again, you didn't either. What –"

Jean nodded off where she sat, nearly pitching off the chair. Nick righted her in the chair before she ever knew what happened, stunning Rachel with how fast he moved.

"I think someone needs some sleep if they want to hit the beach tomorrow." Nick leaned down to look into Jean's half-lidded eyes.

To Nick's surprise, Jean wrapped her arms around his neck. With a smiling nod from Rachel, he picked Jean up gently and carried her to bed. Pulling the covers down, Nick tucked the little girl in. It was the first time he had ever tucked anyone in. He turned on the miniature lighthouse nightlight, and turned off the room light. Nick returned to the balcony.

"Jean and I are kind of pushy, huh?"

"I'll get over it. Did you think any more about how you want to handle your stay here?"

"If Grace or Tim don't come unglued, I'd rather live like a normal person."

"Tanus is dead, Kim. Why —"

"My name is Rachel Hunter," Rachel interrupted. "I don't like the name Kim and I detest the name Kimmy."

"Which is why Grace calls you Kimmy." Nick laughed. "I like the name Rachel; but unless we're alone like this, I think you'd better stick with Kim. Why do you think they're still taking shots at you, since Tanus is dead?"

"My husband worked as a computer security consultant for Tanus's firm." Rachel took a gulp of wine and looked at the eerie fog-covered vista below. "We lived in a tiny apartment on the East side. Rick was always complaining about money. He tried blackmailing Tanus, threatening to turn the flash drives he'd made up over to the FBI. I had no idea what he was doing."

Nick watched Rachel pause as she glanced over at him speculatively. She maintained eye contact with him in the low light of Nick's balcony.

"I had taken Jean to school, hanging around as a teacher's aid in the mornings to cut down on our tuition costs. Returning to the apartment, I fumbled with the keys at the door, and heard Rick's muffled screams…and…and I ran."

"Lucky you did," Nick replied gently. "If you hadn't, you would have joined Rick. You didn't actually see Tanus then?"

"I ran to the end of the hall. We were only a few doors down from the stairwell. I hid in the stairwell and phoned 911. Only a minute after I called, our apartment door opened, and Tanus came out with two other men. Thank God they took the elevator. I stayed in the stairwell with the 911 operator on the phone until the police arrived. They didn't get what they wanted from Rick. That's why they're still trying to kill me."

"Meaning the flash drives are in a safety deposit box somewhere and there's someone a rung up the ladder from where Tanus was." *Well, maybe I'll get off Frank's shit list after all.*

"I know where the box is located and I have the key." Rachel leaned over and took Nick's right hand in both hers. "I didn't know if the Marshalls could actually protect us. I didn't turn over the key because I figured if they found us, I could buy Jean's life with it."

I have fallen into the shit pile and emerged smelling like the proverbial rose.

"Nick, aren't you going to say something?"

"Putting aside your seemingly legitimate distrust for the US Marshalls' service, I think you acted very well under pressure. You did consider Tanus's boss is implicated on one of those flash drives, right?"

"Yes…but listen…those guys have more money than God. They buy and sell politicians, police, and judges. I'd hand over the key. The cops get the files. The files get lost, and I'm a dead mom with a dead little girl. Fingering Tanus was my ticket out of New York to a new life and possible safety. Even after a year, Tanus was only now coming up for trial to be indicted. The chance of anyone arresting the guy above him is a joke."

"I'm having trouble faulting your logic," Nick admitted. "Since you have to be signed in on their list to get into the safety deposit box, having the –"

"I am signed in on the box," Rachel cut in.

"Where's the box located?"

"Sarasota, Florida. Rick opened an account with five hundred dollars and obtained a safety deposit box attached to the account. Any fees would be debited from the five hundred dollar balance. He did it while we were on vacation with Jean and the account is under my maiden name. Jean is my daughter's real name."

"Jesus...." *She's good.* "I can really understand your reticence in giving over the key. I'm sure the same questions popping into my head would have been popping into the cops' heads."

"I didn't know what he was doing, Nick." Rachel squeezed his wrist with attitude as if she could physically press the point into Nick. "Rick put gold and silver coins in the box he had showed me. He said they were our little nest egg the government wouldn't know about and if something happened to him I would have a little safety line. I saw him put a small plastic baggy with the flash drives in there. Rick told me they were backups to our financial records."

"Easy, Rachel... I believe you." *No, I don't. You picked the wrong guy to tell this story to. I don't believe anyone. Shit list, here I come.* "Your explanation is plausible. I only meant I can understand how you would think the FBI might look at what you've told me."

"No one will believe me now. I am so screwed."

Birds of a feather. Nick smiled at his own weird commiseration with Rachel.

* * *

Rachel let go of Nick's wrist. "You think this is funny?"

"I write fiction for a living. That means I'm a paid liar. Let me tell you a story. Once upon a time, there was a computer security guy, married to a beautiful blonde haired, blue-eyed woman and they had a beautiful little blonde haired, blue-eyed daughter. The computer security guy tells his wife all about some of the very strange dealings the company he's working for is into. Wifey suggests digitizing the strange dealings for a rainy day, just in case they run across something they need. The computer guy's a

55

little uncomfortable with this idea but it sounds like a nice insurance policy.

"Computer guy copies the company's strange dealings. He and wifey then take the daughter down to Florida on a nice vacation, where they set up their emergency nest egg. Low and behold the day arrives when wifey thinks they're not living quite the way she thinks they should and talks computer guy into cashing in on their insurance policy."

Nick paused, watching Rachel's shoulders slump as she turned in the chair, picked up her glass and drained the wine. She poured another glass out of the bottle on the table with a shaking hand.

"How'd I do?"

"On a scale of one to ten on my annoyance meter, you've blown the top cap on the tube," Rachel stated tiredly, keeping her eyes on the fog.

"That good, huh?"

"I killed Rick as sure as if I had put a gun to his head and pulled the trigger. He...he was a good man. Jean idolized him. He created computer games for her, and...and taught her how to play softball."

Rachel's lower lip trembled as she took another gulp of wine. "He didn't want to do it."

"And he died without revealing your part in the nest egg," Nick added quietly.

Rachel nodded, unable to speak without bursting into tears.

"Rick stepped up," Nick continued. "What are you willing to do?"

Rachel turned to him, setting her wine glass aside. "What do you mean?"

"I mean it appears you've figured out what matters in life now, and dangerous games can and will get you killed. You want to make sure nothing happens to Jean. What would you do to keep her safe?"

"Who do I have to kill?" Rachel asked, without a hint of tremor in her voice.

"That's the spirit." Nick poured himself another glass of wine.

"Who the hell are you, Nick?"

"I'm what they call a 'Jack of all Trades'. I think I can help you and Jean."

"You're already helping us."

"You're going to need more help than a place to hide out in for a couple weeks."

"How would you be able to help with that?"

"I have contacts but I don't plan to get on the wrong side of the US Marshalls Service. I will make a few calls tonight and do some bargaining. Something I've been working on in a peripheral way is the leak in the Witness Protection Program. Our friends Grace and Tim may be on their way to closing it. Whoever jumped the gun and sent US Marshalls to follow us tonight either is the leak or knows exactly who the leak is. I'm thinking one of my contacts has already closed the leak. What took place tonight did not go unnoticed."

"That would mean we're safe here." Rachel wondered where the conversation was headed. *Who is this guy? Is he delusional?*

"Not a hundred percent but probably around ninety-five percent. If I manage to help you work things out, I might have a proposition for you."

"Damn it, Nick! Who the hell are you?" Rachel demanded again in frustration.

"I'm a cold-blooded psychopath with just a tiny thread of humanity left," Nick answered, patting her hand.

57

"Oh, c'mon, Nick, I've seen you with Jean and Deke."

"I killed a woman once while I petted her dog. I blew Tanus's head off with a fifty caliber sniper rifle and had brunch in Pennsylvania later in the day. Tanus hired me to kill you."

"Oh my God!" Rachel pulled her hand away. She stared into Nick's unblinking eyes and knew the truth. "You're Diego?"

"Diego's a campfire girl compared to what I am," Nick replied bluntly. "Now that we know a little about each other, what say we work out a way to keep you and Jean in one piece?"

"How…I mean…I don't know any more than I already told you."

"I figure it this way, if the leak is plugged, my boss will get the hell off my back. It will make him more amenable to my taking on a team. We're going to visit your safety deposit box and I'll get a name or possibly a couple names. I'm going to trade the flash drives to my boss for an okay to sanction the top of the Tanus ladder."

"What do you mean take on a team?" Rachel whispered, with sudden dawning realization of what team Nick meant.

"As you said, I have a nice place here. After ten years in this business, I'm getting a bit frayed around the edges and in a position to pick and choose what I want to do. Business takes me all over the world and –"

"…and you need a cover," Rachel continued for him with growing horror. "You think your novelist persona is wearing thin. With a family, no one would suspect what you are."

"I knew you were smart." Nick smiled. "The only way this works is if I make it safe for you and Jean to get famous and photographed. Being a best-selling novelist's wife will mean a lot of exposure, so naturally, all the people who want you dead are going to have to die first."

"And if I refuse?"

"I return you to Grace and Tim. You and Jean hit the outlaw trail again with Deke. Maybe everything will be okay once the leak in the program is patched."

"What if I go with Grace and Tim and trade your ass for something nice?" Rachel continued to stare directly into Nick's eyes.

Rachel shivered slightly as a cold smile wavered and spread outwards on Nick's mouth. The smile did not stretch to his eyes.

"Why don't you sleep on it, and let me know what you decide when we walk to the beach tomorrow morning?"

"Does this proposition involve partnering up with you in the biblical sense?"

"You can sleep on that too."

"When I saw you the first time at the restaurant, were you staking me out?"

"No, I was deciding whether to take Tanus out or not. The picture I had of you reminded me of someone from long ago. You still reminded me of her when I saw you in person."

"And if I hadn't?"

"Then I wouldn't have been there to pull you out of the way last night."

"Is this what they mean by being caught between a rock and a hard place?" Rachel nodded with a smile at Nick's admission.

"No, this is between a rock and a cold, hard place," Nick replied, smiling back.

"Nick." Rachel looked up as Nick stood and gathered the glasses and wine bottle. "The woman you killed, she was bad... right?"

"She was to someone."

Chapter Five
Deal Goes Sour

"Well, well, well, I can sure understand why you missed checking in after your date," Frank's voice greeted him as Nick answered the satellite phone following his initial call in. "If you were ready to start a family why didn't you say so, Nick? How is the family? How did you know the sniper wasn't shooting at you, Pappy?"

"Maybe we should skip the sarcasm for now."

"Very well." Frank paused for a moment. "We plugged the leak. I can't say I'm pleased with your methods, but you damn sure lured the dummy out into the open. What the hell made you think taking Hunter and her daughter to your place would work?"

"We have differing views, Frank. You keep looking for criminal masterminds, and I look for impatient dolts who like the money but not the precautions. Let's tackle the next order of business."

"Don't you want to know anything about the leak?"

"Why should I? The mark won't know anything anyway. The FBI can trace the money trail to the dead end I'm sure is waiting for them."

"You don't do detective work but it seems you're pretty good at it. Did you enhance your rep as Sherlock Holmes by consulting with the Marshalls and local PD? I know those idiots didn't get the shooter by themselves. I thought maybe you were figuring on opening a detective agency or something."

"You've developed quite a sense of humor, Frank," Nick replied, without a trace of humor. "I have a kink in this case I think you'll like if you're all through with the comic act."

"Give it to me but it better be damn good. The thought of you playing house and risking the asset we've built for ten years will eventually lead to an adjustment. Know this, Nick: it won't be me who clips off all the loose ends you're creating. If it comes, I'll be the first one tied on the tracks with the train coming."

"Acknowledged." *Oh boy, I wonder if I should get my hanky out.* "Let's see if I can get you in the good graces of whatever monstrous entity is pulling your strings. The Hunter woman talked her husband into blackmailing our buddy Tanus, which left her a widow with a safety deposit box. Some very interesting flash drives are stored in it."

Nick smiled as the silence stretched on for a very long moment.

"I could have the US Marshalls pick her back up."

"And she would, of course, not know squat about any safety deposit box."

"What do you want, Nick?"

"I get a sweet family cover for the heinous deeds I do, and a little company. You get the flash drives with the whole Tanus network documented...after I take a look at them. We agree on the upper echelon of the network meeting with inexplicable accidents and everyone's happy."

"Have you been watching reruns of 'Father Knows Best' on Nickelodeon or something?" Frank asked with obvious disdain. "You have a psych profile making you the original Lone Wolf. You don't play well with others."

"I need a change."

"Go to Barcelona."

"Did I say something to make you think this was a debate?"

"Okay...listen pal, there's no use in me pretending I don't care about those flash drives, but what happens after you get tired of playing house? I wager Hunter knows too much already and her kid will...shit...why am I talking about this? You're insane."

"If things don't work out, I'll set them up real nice somewhere. Rachel Hunter is a bit more complex than you think, Frank. In the meantime, I acquire an added family dossier to waylay suspicion overseas. It's not like they can find out about you or your puppet masters. Hell, I don't even know about them, but if you think I need to, I could find out."

"Now wait a minute…you're playing a dangerous game, Nick."

"Oh, I'm so scared."

"The trouble with you, Nick, is you're getting delusions of grandeur…and invincibility."

"Not at all," Nick reasoned. "I know my value. In addition, while we're on the subject, you do realize that taking me out will have some unintended consequences, do you not?"

"Overseas?"

"I sure wouldn't hide implicating evidence in Podunk, USA. It would be embarrassing for you if I'm ever unable to touch base with my contact."

"I'm going to miss Tanus's taste in hits." Frank sighed audibly as Nick heard him take a deep breath. "It will be extremely interesting to finally find out from those flash drives why his choice of bad people intersected our own so often. What do you need from me?"

"Nothing," Nick answered. "If you take a hand in this to get the US Marshalls off my back, it'll be way too suspicious. You plugged the leak, but they know someone still wants Rachel dead. You'll have to be patient. I'll take Rachel to get the flash drives as soon as possible."

"Tanus was your biggest employer with needs closely tied to ours. What are you going to do about work?"

"It may be time for you to stop waiting for bad guys to pay me to kill other bad guys. You're the one making sure all the info and equipment materializes when I need it."

"That's funny, Nick. You want us to admit we double-oh-seven your ass around the world to sanction people dangerous to the USA. Yeah, that'll happen. Don't forget who pockets the money from the hits."

"I didn't say put it out in the New York Times, Einstein," Nick retorted. "Fine, we keep the status quo. I'll be in touch."

"Make it sooner rather than later, Pappy."

* * *

Nick woke up. He slid silently out of bed in an instant, listening intently. The click of a door downstairs triggered the subconscious alarm Nick had spent decades honing. A glance at the bedroom wall told him his security system had been disabled. *Frank, you stupid son of a bitch.* He already held his Heckler & Koch USP-Tactical .45 caliber handgun with fitted silencer which had been on his nightstand. Even knowing the house plans intimately, Nick calculated it would take the intruder at least five minutes to move upstairs. The assassin would have been told to take no chances.

Moving out his open bedroom door while staying low to the floor, he came face to face with Deke. Nick smiled and gave the dog a quick stroke before moving quickly down the hallway to Rachel's room with Deke following. In seconds, he maneuvered to her side. Nick clamped his left hand over her mouth while keeping the bedroom door covered. Rachel's eyes flew open in shock. She saw Nick shake his head in the dark, and the hand moved away from her mouth. When Nick knew she was awake, he walked quickly over to the bedroom's walk-in closet. Opening a door at the closet's rear wall revealed a recessed armored doorway with digital security keypad. Nick opened the reinforced door. The interior safe room lights came on. He then returned to Rachel's bedside.

"In two minutes time, run into Jean's room, pick her up, and get her and Deke into the safe room. Make noise doing it," Nick whispered close to Rachel's ear. "Count the minutes now."

Nick pointed at Deke purposefully and the dog sat down. Nick hurried silently toward the stairwell and down the stairs, his weapon trained in the direction of the house entranceway. He moved next to the ornate, open sliding oak door, separating the front entrance from the interior of his house. Nick heard the intruder threading his way slowly through the adjoining rooms. When Rachel made noise upstairs, Nick waited with weapon at the ready. The intruder quickened his assault, thinking Nick was moving upstairs. Nick fired two silenced rounds into the back of the assassin's skull as the man went past. Nick's .45 caliber rounds propelled the man face first onto the hardwood floor. Nick fired one more round into the man's head, and retrieved the weapons he found on the body.

Knowing he had time now, Nick ran into the kitchen, pulled out a black plastic kitchen bag and duct tape from under the sink. He quickly returned to the body, slipped the bag over the dead man's head, shoulders and chest. Nick duct taped the bag opening tightly around the body as he rolled the corpse over. He ran upstairs. After retrieving his satellite phone, Nick called the communication activation code and hung up while moving downstairs again. When the phone vibrated, Nick answered it.

"Hi honey."

"Shit! Nick...don't do anything hasty. It was out of my hands. We can –"

"Shut up, Frank," Nick told him. "You should have nuked me from orbit asshole."

"Let me talk to Jenson. I'll..." Frank paused as he heard Nick chuckling.

"I'm too old for unarmed combat, Frank. It's hard on the furniture, and it might have been Jenson talking to you now rather than your favorite novelist. Now, let's get the mess cleaned up first so we can talk. Did you send that dickhead Morris with him?"

Silence.

"Good, he can handle Jenson. Have him come in noisy, pick up Jenson, and leave."

"Christ, Nick, you and Jenson –"

"Yeah, Jenson and me chewed the same dirt once upon a time," Nick cut him off. "On the other hand, I can't stand the sight of Morris. If he even sneezes in my house, I'll take my time and send him to you in pieces. Hurry up – I'll hold."

Fifteen minutes later, a hulking figure in black stamped through the rooms. He stooped next to Jenson's body and shouldered the burden carefully. Backing out, Morris spoke as he scanned the darkened room, his night vision headset casting an eerie light.

"You're lucky Jenson came in for you instead of me, Nick," Morris's gruff voice broke the silence.

"The only difference is Jenson would have had to drag your fat ass out, leaving marks on my hardwood floor." Nick trained his USP-Tactical on Morris's head from the adjoining room.

When Morris was out of the house, Nick moved to the front entrance, where he could see Morris loading the body into his car trunk. Nick brought the phone up.

"Obviously, you didn't believe me about the overseas package I have stashed away."

"I told them, Nick. They thought they could absorb it."

"Tell you what, just to keep this in the family, I'll send you a hint of what will come out. Check the bulletin board for a coded file in fifteen minutes. Call me when you get a look at it."

Nick disconnected, went to his safe room downstairs, opened the safe there and brought out his notebook computer with satellite uplink. Minutes later, Nick uploaded a file. Twenty minutes after that, his satellite phone vibrated.

"Are you out of your God damned mind?" Frank shouted in a smiling Nick's ear. "Where the hell —"

"Now you know how serious this is, Frank," Nick interrupted. "Let's keep our eye on the prize. Your friends don't think they can absorb my enlightenment anymore, do they, buddy?"

"Small doubt about that, you prick. You better pray we don't find out where your package is overseas."

"Did I say I had only one? Sorry."

"Shit!"

"I've had a lot of years 'absorbing' the way things work, Frank."

"Call me when you have the flash drives. You have a blank check for now."

"That's the spirit. See ya'." Nick ended the call and went to clean up the small mess he had made taking out Jenson.

The safe room door opened and a smiling Nick entered. Rachel, Jean, and Deke huddled together on the bed in Nick's upstairs safe room. Deke's body lay sprawled over his companions' laps.

"Sorry about that. You three can come out now and go back to bed."

"What happened, Nick?"

"Negotiations."

* * *

66

Rachel smelled bacon and coffee. She walked down the stairs, breathing in the enticing aromas with relish. Sleep had come in fits of dozing nod-offs in between jerking upright at every sound. Rachel arrived at the stair landing and noticed the newly cleaned and freshly polished section of hard wood floor to her left. She skirted it carefully and continued into the kitchen. Nick, in black pajama bottoms, gray strapped t-shirt and slippers, stood at the stove watching a griddle. He smiled at her as she walked up next to him. Deke was already prone next to Nick's feet.

"I bet you make killer pancakes."

"Hardy har har." Nick chuckled, looking surprised and impressed with her ad lib. "I have to watch these, so you can get your own coffee. With your vast expertise though, I'm sure you'll have no trouble at all."

"I'll manage." Rachel giggled, filling the cup already set out for her. "You didn't say how well the negotiations went last night."

"Very well, with only a few rough spots I'm sure are now worked out. After our walk to the beach, I'll introduce you to the owner of my favorite café on the avenue. He's always shorthanded, and the hours would be flexible."

"I thought if I decided to stay it would be as the wife of a rich novelist," Rachel replied, sitting down at the table.

"I've found over the years it's best to make yourself appear handy and a hard worker. Projecting an image of wealth will usually draw attention we could do without. You don't want your skills getting rusty, do you?"

"Surprisingly, I like waitressing. The majority of people I've met are real nice. I'll talk to your friend about the job. If I get any difficult customers, I'll have you kill them."

Rachel felt relieved when Nick laughed in appreciation of her needling.

67

"Good one. Jean won't be a problem either. We'll get her into a school and I can help with dropping off and picking up. To make it all work we have to go real soon and pick up those flash drives. I've done business using Florida as a base of operations in the past. We'll stay at a condo down in Sarasota I know about."

"Will there be any more negotiations?"

"I don't think so, but let's not kid ourselves, there will always be tradeoffs, Rachel."

"Does Jean have to be involved?"

"She's a very big part of my anticipated cover. It's not an ideal life for a kid, but it's a hell of a lot better than the alternative on your horizon with the US Marshalls. Give it six months. If it's too much for either of us, I'll set you up somewhere nice."

"Sounds fair, but what in hell made you decide to do this? I mean, you could quit the Diego part of your life and keep making money writing."

"Not to put a frown on your logical musings, but I believe you're leaving out the psychopath part of my makeup. We don't do well in retirement."

"Oh...yeah, I...I did forget." Rachel felt the hairs at the nape of her neck stand up. She watched the pajama clad Nick smiling as he made pancakes. "Do you think it possible you could care for me eventually?"

"I care for you already. Otherwise, I'd have dumped you at the first sign of complications," Nick answered, meeting Rachel's gaze. "It's all new to me, which is sometimes a good thing. We psychos don't like a lot of changes. We're neat to a fault, precise in our language, good with kids and dogs, and we like our patterns. When I find something out of the ordinary I want, even with the changes in my patterns it brings, the positives usually outweigh the negatives.

"Like being an assassin?"

"I am an assassin. What I was referring to is my writing. It made an incredible diametrical enhancement in every aspect of my life. I had a persona and work I could talk about. I even do book signings."

"We're an experiment then?"

"Life is an experiment, full of choices. You have a choice now," Nick stated plainly. He brought the covered dish full of pancakes to the table, along with a spouted serving cup with heated syrup. After taking the bacon out of the oven warmer, Nick called up to Jean, but didn't get an answer.

"Well then for now I choose life."

"I'll try to keep your regrets at sixty/forty."

"Huh?"

"You'll be relatively satisfied with your choice over half the time." Nick grinned, pointing at Deke. "Deke, go get Jean."

The dog streaked off upstairs, much to Rachel's amazement. "I can't get that damned dog to sit, let alone fetch."

"Deke's already made his choice."

* * *

Rachel huddled into her coat, hunching her shoulders against the cold salty-tasting breeze blowing in from the ocean. Blue sky peeked out amidst the multi-grey colored clouds roiling across the sky. Nick had ordered his two charges to dress in practically winter clothing. Walking down 12th Street and across Lighthouse Avenue toward the ocean, Rachel and Jean quickly understood why. Nick and Rachel sat on the two fold up beach chairs Nick had brought along, watching Jean and Deke explore the rock formations on Otter's Point Beach. The ocean surface, unlike the strong breeze, was dead calm. The waves lapped gently at the rocks. Large kelp formations covered sections of the water offshore. Nick pointed out two otters zipping around amongst the thick, green leafy vines.

"Is it always this empty down here in the morning, Nick?"

"Yes, except on the weekends. I usually walk down around five-thirty in the morning on weekends. Weekdays, I seldom see anyone until nine out here, except a couple joggers."

"Are you going to write me into your next book?" Rachel watched Jean poke into a tide pool while Deke romped around her, expecting something to be dislodged from the water.

Nick shook his head, snorting derisively.

"Why don't I just surrender myself to the law while I'm at it? This writing gig is supposed to be a cover for us not an autobiography."

"Don't you write Diego's adventures using your own hits as a template of sorts?"

Nick stared at Rachel as if she had sprouted a horn out of her forehead until Rachel started laughing.

"Okay, I'm stupid. Tell me why."

"Think about it, Rachel. How many plots using real life hits would it take before someone saw a pattern? I thought you were an up and coming psycho. Now, I'm afraid you'll have to be satisfied with simply being the decorous wife cover."

"That's so cute. You were going to train me to be a psycho like you." It was Rachel's turn to stare grimly at Nick. "Don't law enforcement people figure out a connection when you arrive somewhere supposedly doing research and someone ends up dead? Forget I asked. This is where you say *I could tell you, but then I'd have to kill you.*"

"Let's just say I'm a bit more devious. When the mark arrives where needed, I'm staying on the same continent. You can cross many borders in a short space of time in Europe, especially when some very strong strings get pulled. Intel is the key, coupled with area familiarity. It helps if the mark won't be missed by anyone important, and doesn't get discovered until I'm far away. Having you and possibly Jean along, staying where I'm researching, will allay virtually all local suspicion."

"Do you ever kill anyone in the US?"

"Tanus was my first here, and he wasn't sanctioned. I've had business offshore though."

"I could get used to the in-betweens around here." Rachel clasped Nick's hand. "Maybe I do have some psycho in me."

* * *

They sat together in silence for a moment, watching Jean and Deke. Nick patted her hand.

"Nah, you're a survivor," Nick looked up toward Ocean View Blvd. He saw Carol and Dan walking toward Otter's Point. "Here come a couple old friends of mine you and Jean will like. I was hoping we made it down here early enough to see them. They know nothing about me other than I'm a novelist."

"You have friends?" Rachel's face dropped comically into open mouthed wonder, drawing laughter from Nick. "You're a more personable psycho than you've led me to believe."

"Repartee is a dual-edged sword, Kimmy," Nick retorted, standing and helping a now growling Rachel to her feet.

"I...hate...that...name!" Rachel whispered through clenched teeth as Dan and Carol descended to the beach area waving animatedly.

"Well, damn. What the hell have you gone and done, boy?" Dan asked gruffly, shaking Nick's hand while smiling brightly at Rachel.

"Dan!" Carol cringed before holding her hand out to Rachel. "Hi, I'm Carol Lewis and big mouth here is my husband Dan."

"Dan, Carol...I'd like you to meet Rachel Hunter." Nick caught up on the introductions. "The little girl over there is Jean and the mutt is named Deke."

"Very happy to meet you," Rachel shook Carol's hand, happy to hear her real name after so long.

"Did Nick order a family from an on-line catalogue without telling us?" Dan smiled at Rachel, taking her hand in both his weathered ones. "You do realize you've taken up with a serial killer, right?"

Nick grinned, noting as Rachel nodded gamely, covering up for the split second of utter confusion that rolled over her.

"Why yes, I believe he did mention something about being a cold blooded murderer. That's why I brought the family down to visit."

Oh, that was good, Nick thought approvingly, laughing along with Dan and Carol.

"You're okay, Rachel." Dan pronounced between laughing and warding off Carol. "So, you're down from Pleasanton to stay at the big house, huh?"

"I told them I'd met someone while researching up in Pleasanton," Nick filled in when Rachel looked at him questioningly. "Carol thinks I need more romance in my novels. I figured I'd better get some experience if I'm planning on giving my assassin, Diego, a love life."

"I'm a research project?" Rachel entertained Nick with enough credible outrage to worry Dan and Carol until she started laughing. "Just kidding. I've never read his books, so I wouldn't know if he were researching a project or not."

"You and Nick make quite a match." Dan nodded speculatively.

"Are you two stopping at the Café on the way back, or going there now?"

"Neither this morning, Nick," Carol answered. "Dan has his annual check-up in an hour. They have to keep checking each year to make sure all his blood hasn't turned to vinegar."

Nick saw Jean and Deke approach the laughing adults together before waiting with impatience for the hilarity to subside. After introductions, during which Nick made Deke sit and shake hands with Dan and Carol, irritating Rachel to no end, the older couple continued home. Deke, sensing something different in Rachel's attitude began hopping around snapping at Rachel's heels, grabbing her pant leg and pulling.

"Why you...no good...ungrateful cur...call your damned dog off, Nick!" Rachel ordered.

"C'mon, let's go get coffee and hot chocolate at the Café. We'll get them to go, so you can grab an application, and Deke won't get into trouble tied up outside." Nick whistled a short two-tone *come on* to Deke, who immediately ran over, sat down, and waited for his leash to be attached.

"You're lucky you're already fixed, traitor." Rachel shook an angry finger at Deke's perpetually smiling face. "Maybe we can get the vet to do a follow up just to be sure."

"Mom!" Jean ran over to hug the docile Deke. "Don't you dare!"

Nick, who had been viewing the interaction with intense amusement, leashed Deke. "We'd better move along, Dawg, before Rachel goes postal on your hairy butt. Did you like the beach, Jean?"

Jean nodded in the affirmative, but immediately qualified her answer. "Are there ever any kids around here my age?"

"We'll find some," Nick promised, taking Rachel's arm.

Chapter Six
Road Trip

"Bring him in, Nick." Joe beckoned from the counter as Nick poked his head in after holding the door to the Monte Café open for Rachel and Jean. He held Deke within sight on his leash. "It's a slow morning, and a good thing, too, since Nancy's still out. Where'd you pick up the strays, Hemingway?"

Nick chuckled. "Up North, along the side of the road. This is Rachel Hunter, her daughter Jean, and Deke the dog. I don't want you to get into trouble for having Deke in here, Joe."

"Glad to meet you, Rachel, Jean, and of course, Deke." Joe gestured at the first table by the window. "I'm the owner of this establishment, Joe Montenegro. Now, if you see anybody come in, act like Deke's your seeing-eye dog, Hemingway."

"I have my sunglasses right here," Nick agreed instantly, holding them up. "Two coffees and a hot chocolate, please Sir."

"Coming right up." Joe left to get their order.

"Another friend?" Rachel needled Nick.

"Any more out of you, Kimmy, and I'll have Deke herd you up to the house."

Deke gave out a short 'grumphf' in agreement and on cue.

"Okay, for you, Hemingway," Rachel retorted as Jean giggled.

After collecting an application from an eager Joe, who offered to hire Rachel on the spot, the four walked up 12th Street to Nick's house as sunlight streamed through the dissipating clouds. Nick saw that Rachel kept glancing over her shoulder at the ocean's colorful transformation under the sun's rays.

"It's gorgeous when the sun comes out," Rachel noted, as they stood on Nick's porch.

"Yep, it's nice. We can go up on the balcony. I'm working on my outline for Diego's next adventure." Nick disabled the alarm system, propping the screen open, and kneeling down to check over Deke. "You didn't collect much sand, Deke. I guess we don't have to give you a bath this time."

Nick opened the front door. Jean skipped over the stoop and a huge hand grabbed the little girl up. Nanoseconds later Deke clamped onto the wrist with snarling ferocity. Morris cursed, dropping Jean, while pivoting to the right, swinging the attached Deke with him. Rachel scooped up Jean and Nick stomped his booted right foot into Morris's left Achilles tendon. Morris collapsed, gritting his teeth against the blinding pain while trying to swing his silenced automatic toward Nick. With Deke out of the way, Nick swung his left boot up in a roundhouse kick which smashed into Morris's face like a jackhammer. Morris's weapon clattered to the hardwood floor. Morris pitched over on his back, blood gushing from his shattered nose. Nick had the automatic pointed at Morris in the next split second. He kicked the front door closed.

"Take Jean and Deke upstairs, Rachel." Nick directed, watching Morris roll around in misery.

Rachel carried the stunned Jean upstairs, pausing only to call Deke.

"Go on, Deke. Thanks for the save, mutt."

Deke gave out a sharp bark and ran after Rachel and Jean.

Nick waited, keeping his distance from Morris. Morris coughed up blood after rolling to his hands and knees. He tested his left leg, falling on his right side with a grunt of pain. Getting back to his hands and knees Morris looked up at Nick sullenly.

"You'll hav' to call. The tendon's busted," Morris said nasally.

"What the hell are you doing here? Frank and I have a deal."

"You ain't got a deal with me. If not for that Goddamn dog, I'd –"

Nick fired two shots into Morris's right temple and one more into his forehead after tipping the shuddering man onto his back. Nick went into the kitchen and pulled out two black plastic garbage bags and his duct tape. After pulling Morris into a sitting position, Nick covered the head and upper torso with doubled black plastic bags, duct taping them tightly into place. It took Nick twenty minutes longer to clean up the blood spatter. He retrieved the satellite phone and made initial contact. Fifteen minutes later the phone vibrated.

"Clean up on aisle seven."

"What the hell did you do now?"

"Morris went rogue on you, Frank."

"Did you have to kill him?"

"That was rhetorical, right?"

"You'll have to find a way to speed up the flash drive retrieval, Nick. I'm going to have some trouble fixing this without them."

"I talk to the Marshalls tonight. I'll try and get them on board with a family trip within the week."

"The best I can do is two hours for clean up."

"Call me before they get here. Morris is next to the front door. It's strange, Frank. If Morris wanted me dead, why didn't he send a long range postcard? He knew we had a deal; but he tried to get leverage against me like he wanted to barter. You wouldn't know what he would've been bartering for, would you, Frank?"

"You could have asked him." Frank's nonchalant tone was not fooling Nick at all.

"He was bleeding all over my hardwood floor. It would've been a noisy question and answer session. As you know, I have company."

"I'll ask around." Frank disconnected.

Sure, you'll ask around. Nick put the phone and weapon up on the hutch inside his dining room. He walked upstairs and knocked on Rachel's door.

"Come in."

"We have a problem," Nick stated, seeing Rachel, Jean, and Deke huddled up on the bed together. *There's an understatement.* "I don't think my insurance is enough. I may have overestimated my value. The man downstairs was trying to get you and Jean. If not for Deke, he would have. I played dumb with my boss, but we need a new plan."

"What do you have in mind?"

"Road trip."

"All of us in your Chevy? How soon?"

"We have an hour. Any longer and we'll be cutting it close. I have something a bit more comfortable for us to travel in. Sorry we didn't get much time to rest up. We'll call Grace and Tim after we're on our way. I'll tell them we had to leave because we spotted trouble. I think we may have to use your nest egg to deal with them, Rachel."

"You're screwed, aren't you?" Rachel wrapped her arms around Jean.

Nick shrugged. "Hey, new choices mean new gambles." *You sell this, you should get into the movies next, killer.* "Grace and Tim will not be happy with this decision, especially since they'll have to stay in the dark until we finish our scavenger hunt."

"Are...are you going to stay with us, Nick?" Jean asked.

"I'm stuck, Jean. Deke saved my bacon. A life for a life, little one. If your Mom and me manage to find the right owner for your nest egg we might even make it back here soon." *Right after I kill a few people.* "Get packing if you want aboard Nick's Adventure Express. Otherwise, we call Grace and I deliver you three to them right now."

"I want to stay with Nick."

"This won't go away," Rachel said. "They have the Marshalls under surveillance. They know where we are and apparently the identities of the ones hunting us down may be on those flash drives. Did I miss anything?"

Yeah, how the hell I managed to get myself into this.

"You forgot about my boss getting in the game and deciding a high value asset with very high blackmail potential takes second place to what's on the flash drives. This goes beyond the network you compromised. Someone has managed to get into a position of power who knows what's on the drives. Some players in this want you dead before anything surfaces, and others want the drives as leverage. My cavalier remarks about making people-adjustments according to what I found on the drives triggered somebody's survival instinct – either my boss, or someone in on briefings he gives."

"Gee, you have it all figured out." Rachel grinned up at Nick to take the edge off her sarcastic tone.

"Not everything." Nick smiled back, admiring the way she took the news. "I'd still like to know what made my boss think the guy downstairs could pull this off by himself."

"You said except for Deke he would have got you," Jean put in, reminding Nick they were debating this in front of a seven year old.

"Very true, smarty, but my boss assumed without divine intervention in the form of Deke the dog, I would have been handled. I surmise from that fact either I've dropped a few notches in the eyes of my superiors or they have less assets to send after us. I'm hoping for less assets, because two of them have already been retired."

"Couldn't they recruit others?"

"From where, 'Psychos Are Us'? There are very few 'no questions asked' people working at my level. This conference is over, my dears. If you want aboard the Express, get packing."

Nick left the room. He used the remaining time to gather weapons and gear he did not already have stashed in his hidden away Cadillac Escalade. After forty-five minutes Nick stored his own Heckler & Koch USP-Tactical with extra clips in the recessed compartment he'd built under the driver's seat of his Malibu. He next set up his satellite phone and went in to help Rachel and Jean. Nick retrieved Morris's Glock automatic with silencer from the top of his hutch. He took off his shirt and put on a black pullover sleeveless shirt with a sewn in weapon pocket. The Glock fit into the pocket. Nick put on a windbreaker jacket over it, then threw a blanket over Morris's body.

"The Express leaves in five minutes," Nick called out, jogging up the stairs.

Nick went into Rachel's bedroom, where Rachel was hurriedly zipping up the two bags on her bed. Nick picked them up the moment she finished and headed to the car.

"Bring Jean and Deke. We have to go."

Minutes later, Nick started the Chevy and drove around the block. He parked it.

"What's going on?" Rachel asked with a bewildered look.

"I have to meet my guests, who will be arriving unannounced very quickly," Nick told her, leaving the spare Chevy key in the ignition. "I'll call your cell-phone when I want you to drive the Chevy around to the house again. From there, you'll follow me in a vehicle yet to be determined."

"What's this about, Nick? Why don't we just leave?"

"Mainly, this is about asset reduction. It's also because I don't want to be set up by having the other unmoving asset discovered inside my house. Plus…I don't like being played."

79

"You…you mean…the guys being sent over –"

"Yeah, sucks to be them." Nick shut the driver's side door with satellite phone in hand.

Nick jogged to his house, went inside and dragged Morris's body into the entryway closet. He quickly retrieved his duct tape and another black plastic garbage bag. With a box cutter from his kitchen, Nick made a slit on each side of the bag, and put the bag over his head, carefully cutting two slits for his eyes. Nick put the bag and duct tape aside and then made sure Morris's silenced weapon was operational with a full clip.

Nick's satellite phone vibrated. "Find out anything useful?"

"No. Cleanup arrives in ten minutes. They don't want any trouble, Nick, so wait upstairs. If they see anything move, they'll spray everything in sight."

"I'll be upstairs in the back bedroom with the woman and her daughter. All they have to do is remove Morris's body, wrapped in a black plastic bag, leaning against the wall to the right of the front door. They won't even have to step inside the house."

"Good, I'll tell them. We'll talk after they remove the body."

"Fine."

Nick pulled the bag over his head, aligning the eyeholes with his arms through the slits. He wrapped the duct tape around the bag at his waist, and positioned himself sitting next to the doorway, with his right arm free behind him. His left side leaned against the entryway door frame with legs splayed out sideways. After making last minute adjustments to his eyeholes, Nick waited, his right hand holding Morris's weapon slightly under his right leg.

Minutes later, the front door opened. Without more than a glance at Nick's bagged figure, the two men entered the house, pausing when they reached the stairwell. Nick raised his right arm and fired with deadly accuracy from only fifteen feet away. The silenced shots from Morris's 9mm Glock struck the two men's heads. Nick fired four times, two striking the man in the rear over his right ear. The third shot struck the second man through the jaw as he turned and the fourth through his forehead. Rolling to his left, Nick propelled himself up after one spin with his left hand. He shot twice more into each man's head as they lay twitching on the floor.

Nearly forty minutes later, Rachel's cell-phone rang. She jumped as if touched with a cattle prod. Rachel had been taking turns with Jean on her daughter's Nintendo DS. Opening the cell-phone with a shaking hand, Rachel said hello.

"Drive around to my house. You'll see a black Ford van parked out in front. I'll wave and you follow me down to the Monterrey Marina."

Rachel drove around the block and followed Nick as he drove the Ford van. When they reached the Monterrey Marina, Nick waved Rachel around, pointing toward the curb. He parked the van and took a last look around the van's rear cargo compartment. Morris sat propped against the rear doors, his Glock with silencer in hand, and his legs splayed out in front of him. Morris's weapon pointed in the general direction of the two men Nick had shot after they entered his house over an hour ago. The corpses stared sightlessly at Morris from where they were slumped against the front seat backs. Nick straightened the body behind him slightly with gloved hands and then locked up the van. He set the vehicle alarm. Nick ran up to his Malibu's driver's side and opened the door for Rachel.

"Where to now?"

"Las Vegas, baby," Nick answered. "I have an emergency place out in the desert there. We can hole up for a few days until we're off the radar. Get in."

"Nick..." Rachel grabbed Nick's arm before he could get into the driver's side seat. "Were those guys in the van assets like you thought?"

"Absolutely." *Probably.*

* * *

"Thanks for stopping, Nick." Jean settled into the seat with Deke's head on her lap. "I was starving."

"I noticed. I think I saw the McDonald's assistant manager send out for more food after you ordered."

"Did not." Jean made a face at Nick as he watched her in the rearview mirror. "Where'd all the cars come from?"

They were on their way to California Route 46 East, near Bakersfield. The McDonald's stop had been the first rest break since leaving the Monterey area. While heading toward the freeway on-ramp, they encountered a traffic jam up. A State Highway Patrol car with lights flashing was visible along the roadside a hundred yards ahead. Nick could see the route lay open past the patrol car, with vehicles speeding up from there on.

"There must be a fender bender up where the patrol car's parked," Nick speculated, as the traffic inched ahead. "Naturally, the looky-loos have to jam us all up."

Rachel opened her window, getting a blast of hot air from the Bakersfield desert area, while craning her head out the window to see around the vehicle ahead.

"Nick!" Rachel gasped, jerking back inside. "Some guy's kicking the crap out of a state cop! They're wrestling around on the ground and no one's stopping except to look."

"People know they can end up getting killed sticking their noses into something like that," Nick explained calmly. "Hopefully, he called for backup, and they'll be here soon. Sometimes you...what?"

Rachel stared at Nick in open-mouthed surprise, all the while knowing it was ridiculous to think Nick would react any differently. "What if the cop didn't get a chance to call in? Couldn't you help?"

"You do realize we're on the run, right?" Nick was unable to disguise the irritation her question provoked in him. "I could get killed. I could help and end up on the six o'clock news. I could be a star on a You-Tube vid thirty seconds after I get involved, with all the cell-phone freaks out there."

"Stop the car. I'm going to help him," Rachel ordered.

"Are you out of your –"

"Stop the damn car now!" Rachel turned on Nick, her mouth a thin line of angry determination.

Oh great, Dudley Doright to the rescue. Nick glanced at Jean in the rearview mirror. It looked as if both the little girl and Deke were looking at him accusingly.

"Jean, hand me my windbreaker, quick." Nick sighed. "Hold the wheel, Wonder Woman."

Jean handed Nick his windbreaker while Rachel held the steering wheel. Nick slipped into the jacket and pulled the hood up over his head, cinching it tightly. He reached across Rachel and popped open the glove compartment. Nick extracted the pepper spray and stun gun he had stored there.

"I'll stop, jump out, and you get your Good Samaritan ass over into the driver's seat. Keep going no matter what you see and wait for me at least twenty yards past the incident. If it doesn't turn out well for me, get turned around and head back to Grace and Tim."

* * *

Rachel tensed as Nick stomped on the brake, shifted into park, and leaped out of the car. Rachel exited her side and moved quickly to take his place. It took Rachel only a few seconds to get into the Malibu driver's seat and shift the car into drive. She watched Nick jog toward the flashing lights. Rachel only caught brief flashes of his windbreaker hood as Nick moved along, staying close to the slow moving line of cars.

* * *

Nick saw the faces of mildly interested people gawking ahead, anticipating their soon to be front row seats to a possible tragedy. As he suspected, Nick saw cell-phones held out windows nearer to the fight. He shifted the stun gun to his left hand while positioning the pepper spray nozzle with his right. As he drew nearer, Nick saw the State Highway Patrol officer slip and go down on his back hard. His attacker straddled him with arms cascading closed-fisted blows on the downed officer. Nick noted the guy on top wore only a white t-shirt and jeans. His unkempt dark brown beard and long hair lent a wild aspect to the hulking figure.

Nick heard the mixed grunts and cries of rage, fear, and pending exhaustion, as the life and death struggle played out toward disaster for the patrolman. The bearded attacker stopped his assault and grabbed for the officer's gun. The patrolman, spitting blood and gasping for breath, tried to cover the man's access to his holster with both hands. This drew his attacker's ire in the form of a one-fisted pummeling the officer had no defense for. Nick kept close to the cars, breaking into a run, knocking into arms and cell-phones, as he covered the remaining distance.

The patrolman gave up defense of his weapon, unable to withstand the pounding he was taking to his already shattered face. With a yelp of triumph, the bearded man seized the 9mm automatic, wresting it out of the patrolman's holster with his left hand as he continued to smash the officer with his right fist. The side of Nick's booted foot struck with the full power of his running leap into the man's right ribcage. Rib bones cracked and the attacker shrieked in pain, pitching sideways off the patrolman, the weapon falling from his hand.

84

Nick followed through his kick, landing over the fallen officer, spraying the still screaming attacker full in the face with pepper spray. With calm, calculated movements, Nick then stunned the convulsing man, blue crackling arcs highlighting his relentless assault, until the man made no sound. Only the man's heaving chest and jerking limbs gave any indication the attacker still lived. Nick heard cries of shock from the vehicles' open windows as they passed by. He made sure he kept his face turned away from the people's cameras. Nick pocketed his pepper spray and picked up the patrolman's handgun with the sleeve of his windbreaker pulled over his right hand. He leaned over the officer, who had groggily rolled to his left, wheezing and gasping for air. Nick stuck his handgun into the empty holster and helped the patrolman up into a sitting position against his squad car's rear door. The officer blinked tears and sweat away, his arms hanging at his sides limply.

"I doubt this clown will be moving, but if you'll allow me, I'll cuff the prick for you." Nick looked closely at the officer's eyes, trying to determine the patrolman's state of consciousness.

Not in a condition to question his savior, the officer nodded slightly, and turned to allow Nick access to his handcuffs. Nick took them out of the pouch at the patrolman's belt and went over to flip the bearded man over on his face, dragging the man's hands behind his back and expertly cuffing him. Nick leaned down and wiped the cuffs with his windbreaker before returning to the patrolman.

"I have to leave. Will you be okay?"

"Tha...thank you...they...they just watched. He had my... gun...I –"

"Easy now," Nick soothed, holding his hand up in front of the officer's eyes. "Keep your focus. Did you get this called in?"

"No...I didn't have time, he –"

"I'll get it." Nick noted the officer's name was Tomlinson. He opened the driver's side door, reached in with his windbreaker-covered right hand and called in an 'officer down' call, naming Tomlinson.

Nick left the driver's door open and leaned over to Tomlinson again. He saw some clarity returning to the patrolman's eyes. "Help's on the way. Want me to kick the sucker on my way by for you?"

In spite of his painful condition, Tomlinson grinned a little, but shook his head slightly.

Nick ran off, ignoring the mixture of cheers and accusations, while he ran for the Malibu parked ahead. He ripped open the passenger door and dived in.

"Go, go, go," Nick ordered Rachel.

Rachel spun the wheels slightly, kicking up dirt and loose gravel getting onto the road again. In minutes she had the Malibu on the freeway heading East, with Nick watching for possible looky-loos following them from the scene. Nick stripped off the windbreaker. He was drenched in sweat, and leaned back in the seat taking slow, deep breaths while enjoying the blast of cold air from the vents.

"I...I was wrong, Nick." Rachel gripped the steering wheel stiffly. "That guy was a monster. He'd have killed me...and...I saw all the cameras. If –"

"You were right," Nick interrupted, thinking of Tomlinson's smashed face. "You made me do what was right and I don't often know what's right anymore. He would've killed the cop."

Suddenly remembering Jean, Nick whipped around in his seat, peering back at the little girl appraisingly. "I don't suppose you looked away as your Mom drove by, did you?"

"Nope," Jean replied with a mixture of fear and awe. "Did you kill that guy?"

"No, but he ain't happy."

86

Jean giggled.

"Great." Nick sighed, turning to the front again. "Another psycho in training."

Chapter Seven
Las Vegas

"Holy crap, Nick, this is yours too?"

Nick chuckled at Rachel's tone as he drove the Chevy up into the driveway of a two story brownstone with an arched, extended stone patio entranceway. He left the car, ran over to the keypad at the entranceway and then reentered the Malibu. It was nearly three in the morning. They had stopped as infrequently as possible after the incident in Bakersfield and interacted with no one. Nick triggered the garage door with a remote he took out of his glove compartment. A late model black Cadillac Escalade could be seen shining in the lights which came on as the garage door opened. Nick parked the Malibu next to the Cadillac and used his remote to close the garage door. He shut off the engine and leaned back rubbing his eyes.

"Sorry we had to drive straight through like that."

Rachel glanced back at Jean, whose head rested against a pillow, mouth hanging open in sleep, with Deke across her lap. "It was fine. Those two have been dozing on and off for the last few hours. Do you have this house furnished?"

"Yep. It may be dusty though. I only get out this way a couple times a year. It gets hotter here than in Pleasanton, so other than stopping in to check everything over, I really don't visit very often. I pay the bills through an on-line PayPal account, so everything's on and working. Want me to carry Jean in?"

"No, she needs to get ready for bed anyhow," Rachel replied as they both exited the Chevy. "Do you have a backyard for Deke?"

"Yes, but it's a stone yard, a lot like the front. Water is in short supply out here, and other than cactus plants, you can't trust much to grow without everyday care. I'll get the bags and let Deke out. You go ahead and get Jean up and moving."

Deke was ready and leaped out over the suitcases on the backseat the moment Nick opened the car's rear passenger area. Nick led the dog through a door he unbolted, opening into a stone patterned area, graced with only resilient desert plants as landscaping. A six foot security fence ringed the large rear of the property. Nick left the door open and went over to unlock the garage entrance to the house interior for Rachel and a yawning Jean. He switched on lights as he led them inside. Nick paused in the huge living room and pointed to the stairs.

"The bedrooms and big bath are upstairs. Take any room that suits you. I'll get the bags."

"Nick... thank you."

"Don't thank me yet, Wonder Woman, the adventure continues." Nick waved her off on the way back to the garage.

* * *

Rachel woke with a start, sitting straight up in bed, her heart thumping. She looked around the bedroom, furnished in western fashion with a dark oak dressing table, nightstands, dresser and headboard. The matching blinds only let in a small amount of light. The alarm clock on the nightstand read 10:45 AM. Remembering their journey out of California, Rachel hurriedly went to check on Jean and found her still fast asleep. After stopping in the bathroom and putting on a light robe, Rachel went downstairs. Nick was sitting at the kitchen table typing on his notebook computer. He wore only a sleeveless gray t-shirt and jeans. Not for the first time did Rachel feel a familiar warmth flow over her, looking at this man who killed people for a living. *I must be nuts.*

"Good morning." Nick smiled up at her.

89

Deke grunted at Rachel from where he lay near Nick.

"You look like you've been up a while," Rachel noted, walking over to the coffee pot and pouring a cup for herself. "I see traitor-dog came down with you."

"All this adventure inspired me." Nick chuckled at her reference to Deke. "I decided to get a few thousand words down on my new novel. If I run out of steam later I'll take a nap."

"Psychos take naps?"

"You have to be careful taunting psychos in the morning," Nick told her, getting up and moving as close to Rachel as the cup she held allowed.

"Is that a threat?" Rachel met Nick's eyes questioningly as she set aside her cup. "When did you go to bed this morning?"

"About four," Nick answered, undoing her robe and spreading it out. Rachel wore only a bra and panties underneath. Rachel shivered as Nick put his hands on her sides. "I had to take a shower after the workout I got in Bakersfield."

"Are you writing another Diego novel?" Rachel asked, her heart speeding up into the danger zone. Nick gently stroked his hands up and down her sides slowly. She could tell he liked the shortness of breath his ministrations caused.

"No, I'm trying my hand at an erotic novel."

"I'll bet. So...this is research?"

"Absolutely," Nick whispered, leaning in to brush his lips over hers, gently touching and then sealing Rachel's mouth with his own.

Rachel moaned, and wound her arms around Nick's neck, her body moving sensuously against him.

"Eeeeewwwww!" Jean exclaimed from the doorway, her face contorted into a grimace. "Young child here."

Rachel blushed, pulling away from Nick, and laughing at Jean's reaction. Nick turned and pointed a finger at Jean while Rachel closed up her robe.

"Don't make me have to put a bell around your neck."

Jean giggled. "I'm hungry."

"I'm shocked," Nick muttered, going to the cupboard, "shocked, I tell you. All I have is canned goods for now. How about Spaghettios?"

"For breakfast?" Jean questioned doubtfully in return, and then nodded enthusiastically. "That sounds good."

"How about you, Wonder Woman?"

"Do you have crackers to go with them?"

"I have a box of unopened Ritz crackers only a year old."

Rachel grinned. "Yum. Count me in."

Fifteen minutes later they sat around the table eating Spaghettios and Ritz crackers, with glasses of orange juice Nick had made up from frozen concentrate. Nick had served himself only a small amount and pushed it aside after a few bites. Jean finished hers and asked for seconds which Rachel dished up for her.

"Tasteless muck. I don't know why the hell I ever bought it."

"It's good," Jean said, her mouth half full of Spaghettios.

"Glad you liked it." Nick made a face at her. "What's the verdict, Wonder Woman? Is Spaghettios the breakfast of champions?"

"Absolutely," Rachel mocked Nick's one word answer for nearly everything, holding up a Ritz cracker covered with Spaghettios before popping it into her mouth.

"Speaking of the breakfast of champions."

91

"Don't even tread down that trail, Psycho," Rachel warned, covering her mouth as she lost a few crumbs in her haste to rebuke a now laughing Nick. Rachel felt her face flush hotly.

"What's so funny, Nick?" Jean looked intently from one adult to the other.

"He only thinks he's funny," Rachel told her, trying to stare warningly at Nick, but only succeeding in heightening the sudden desire she had for him.

"Our time together has been pretty scary, huh Jean?" Nick changed the subject. "I guess you'll have to be in therapy until you're forty."

"Huh?" Jean asked, and then smiled back at Nick. "Oh, you're kidding me. I'm not scared. I saw Terminator II. It was my favorite. You're like the good Terminator in the movie, and I'm like the little John Connor."

This caused Nick to nearly unload the swallow of coffee through his nose. He coughed and cleared his throat while Rachel and Jean laughed at him.

"I didn't see that one coming," Nick muttered, clearing his throat while pondering Jean's take on the insanity since leaving Pleasanton. "What makes you think I'm a good Terminator?"

"Come with me if you want to live." Jean's brows knitted in an attempt to gain a threatening aspect. She lowered her voice into a cracking mimicry of Arnold Schwarzenegger, at which Nick and Rachel convulsed in fits of laughter.

"Okay..." Nick held up his hands finally in a gesture of acquiescence. "I see why you might make the comparison."

"Will you show me how to make pipe bombs and stuff?"

"Jean!"

Nick laughed again, shaking his head. "Ah...no. While we're all here, I better check in with Grace again. It will have to be

92

a short call. If they're under surveillance, a long conversation will put us in danger."

"You didn't give Grace a chance to speak last night."

"I gave her the highlights. This time you and Jean talk to her. I'll get the phone and connect for you. Don't say anything revealing," Nick directed on his way out of the kitchen.

Rachel wondered as she watched Nick leave the room if *pipe bombs and stuff* were in their immediate future.

* * *

Nick rigged his satellite phone to a small attachment with a blinking green light. He had decided to take no more chances with forces outside his control. He brought the altered phone with him into the room where Rachel and Jean waited.

"Everything's fine until this light turns red." Nick showed both Rachel and Jean the phone. "Hit this button if or when it turns red."

When they nodded their understanding, Nick made the connection. Tim answered the phone.

"Tim, we've reached the destination and I'm —"

"Nick, what the hell's going on!?"

"Like I told Grace last night, we were in danger, and I knew a safe place to go."

"Let me talk to Kim."

"Here she is." Nick handed the phone to Rachel, noting the less-than-friendly tone of Tim's voice. *Into each life a little rain must fall, Marshall Dillon.*

Nick pointed at the light again before handing the phone to Rachel, and going into the living room. He switched on the television set, listening with one ear to the conversation in the

93

kitchen. Nick had been reluctant to check the news, more worried than he let on about the Bakersfield incident. As he suspected, grainy videos and camera shots of him in action were highlighting every major news broadcast. He breathed a sigh of relief when it became apparent no one had any clue as to who he was. Rachel came in and handed the phone to Nick with the green light still blinking.

"Wherever you are, stay there, Nick," Grace's voice told him. "We're still compromised. You were right to leave. Did you use any credit cards getting where you were going?"

"No, cash only, everywhere," Nick replied, glad someone was taking this seriously.

"Do you have enough to stay out of sight for a while?"

"Yes."

"Good. Can you update us and stay in touch? We're working all the angles right now, but there've been some complications. I'm sorry we dragged your ass into this, Nick; but it seems you're a lot more than you appear, old buddy. Any thoughts?"

"Like do I have a red cape tucked away somewhere? The answer is no."

Grace laughed. "No, but I must admit, Tim has come up with some interesting coincidences involving you and your overseas travels."

Uh oh.

"If I keep partnering up with you and Tim, I may not even be alive much longer. Maybe you and Timmy should concentrate more on who's trying to kill us, and less about bestselling authors, namely me."

"Fair enough," Grace allowed. "Maybe you could give us a little more direction, Mr. Big Time."

"Let me get back to you on that, Grace. Rachel and I are working on a course of action you and Tim would have to be a part of to make it work. How long do you think we need to lay low?"

"Oh, it's Rachel now, is it? Can you keep your heads down for at least two weeks? We're close to sealing up our agency and looking for branches into it."

Nick considered the two-week time frame, glancing over at Rachel and Jean, who were avidly watching news coverage of the Bakersfield stunt. "Two weeks might be doable. Did you make any headway with the shooter from our night on the town?"

"Yeah, about him…ah…he had a little accident, Nick. We —"

"I'll bet he did." Nick cut her off. "I hope to hell you're putting everyone who even sneezed his way under a microscope."

"Tim and I are out in the wind a bit right now."

"Well, either start flying kites or get into the cellar kiddies. There's a storm on its way."

"What's that supposed to mean?"

"It means you and Timmy better figure out what line can't be crossed. We all know there are some bad people involved in this. If the two of you want to stay safe let me know now."

"Am I ever going to know who the hell you really are?" Grace asked with only a slight trace of resentment.

"Absolutely." *If I'm dead.*

* * *

"Is this your morning surprise? I thought you hated the desert." Rachel looked around at the forbidding landscape as she walked with Nick, Jean, and Deke away from the Cadillac Escalade, parked well off the main route.

95

"Did we have to get up before dawn?" Jean added.

Even Deke voiced a quick 'gruff'.

The dim light barely gave the group enough illumination to walk safely along the mostly level hard-packed surface. They walked together over the desert moonscape with Deke wandering far and wide around them, examining every hole, crevice or shrub. Silence was palpable. The motley group created the only audible sounds while walking along. Nick carried a pack weighing over eighty pounds, with Rachel shouldering a much smaller one.

Nick grinned at his soon-to-be sniper team. "Unfortunately, we need to do this at least every other day until we leave for Florida. I have an area set up already, where we can be relatively certain not to be disturbed, and we won't start deep frying until later in the morning. I told you it was a surprise because of the way you two are reacting now. Every day we do this, and no one complains, we go to the waterslides in Sin City after we get back. Any complaints, and we sit in the house and mope all day."

"Waterslides!" Jean yelped, dancing around with Deke joining her, while nipping at Jean's cuffs.

"That's a pretty neat bribe. What do I get? Can I go to the casinos?"

"Oh sure." Nick gestured at the sky in supplication. "I'll send you over to the most intensively videoed area in all of creation, where security cameras are so high tech, they reproduce themselves every five seconds."

"Ah...point taken, waterslides it is," Rachel replied. "Couldn't Jean and I have waited for you at the house? Devil dog could keep you company."

"I'm going to train you in spotting and shooting, Wonder Woman," Nick explained. "Can you get your head around that?"

Nick noticed how Rachel clamped her lips together by force of will, as he imagined every anti-gun, peace at any risk, Kum-Ba-Ya cliché she'd ever heard threatening to pour out of her mouth. Nick saw the inner battle being waged and pulled out the card he had been saving.

"Think of watching Tanus through a spotter scope, knowing he would never order another death ever again. It's no different than ordering me out in Bakersfield to help the cop."

"Going on offense has done wonders curing my tendency toward insomnia." Rachel nodded in agreement. "I'll do what I can but I hate having Jean with us."

"Hey!" Jean chirped, yanking on Rachel's arm. "I'm part of this Terminator team too."

"I'm going straight to hell," Rachel whispered, covering her face.

Twenty minutes later as they walked around a small rock formation, Nick stopped. He took off his pack in a spot shaded by the small hill. He pointed across the small sloping valley of sand and rocks to another craggy upheaval of boulders. Nick knew it looked only a few hundred yards away, but in actuality was nearer to a mile distant.

"You'll be able to see the targets I have set up across the way better once I give you the spotting scope. I have two scopes, Missy Connor, so you'll be able to watch and spot too."

"Cool!" Jean exclaimed. "What's a spotting scope?"

Nick helped Rachel out of her pack, and unloaded the three small cases he had put into it. He opened the larger of the cases and removed the spotting scope.

"This is a Leupold Mark 4 spotting scope." Nick spent the next few minutes explaining the basics of using it, refraining from burying his audience in details.

Nick gave Jean the smaller, but very powerful, digital range-finding binoculars he had brought along, schooling her on how to use them and estimate distances. Next, Nick unpacked his M107 Barrett .50-caliber long range rifle with special silencer for noise suppression, setting it up firmly in the packed ground at their feet. He then steadied the spotting scope on its tripod near him and handed Rachel yet another digital tool.

"This is a Kestrel 4500 wind and weather meter. If the wind whips up a little in about an hour, you'll see the differences it makes in a 1500 meter shot without correction. It also reads wind direction, temperature, relative humidity, altitude, and a bunch more items you'll get used to checking," Nick explained. Both Rachel and Jean were listening raptly to him while glancing at the sniper rifle with a mixture of excitement and fear. "I have six four-inch-thick cast iron plates anchored at various spots against the rock wall over there. See if you two can find them through your scope and binoculars."

Once Nick showed Rachel and Jean how to make minuscule movements, in scanning for targets within invisible quadrants, they were able to pinpoint each of the plates within minutes. Nick took three earmuff type protectors out of his pack and helped Rachel and Jean put theirs on. He also handed out safety glasses.

"My silencer here will reduce the noise so it won't bother Deke at all. The ear covers are for safety. I'll hit the plate all the way on the left first. The spot in the middle, gouged out the most by prior shots, is my target. I'll hit the target first and then the dirt near it. Try and gauge how far off my miss is. Tell me when you have the target in sight. Don't look away from the target. You will hear the discharge and a moment later see the hit."

Nick donned his vest with shoulder pad and made ready to fire. Rachel and Jean told him they had the target in sight. Nick fired. The plate jolted from the concussion. Nick had hit the plate inside the already gouged middle. He shot a second time and dust kicked up near the plate.

"You hit two feet to the right, and three inches below center," Rachel said.

"Very good." Nick was impressed with Rachel's concentration in spotting the missed hit amidst the dirt explosion. "How'd it look to you Jean?"

"I saw a lot of dirt fly. I think I blinked."

Nick laughed. "It happens." He noted that Deke had taken up a position next to him in spite of the sudden sound. "The barrel heats with every shot and accuracy diminishes slightly. You two take turns spotting and calling out the target you want hit. I'll fire at your choice. Keep glancing down at the wind and weather meter Rachel so we can track gradual changes over the next half hour."

After completing all he had planned for the day, Nick packed up his gear, and passed out cold water and trail mix. Deke received a small plastic bowl of water and some food Nick had packed in a baggy. When they were ready to begin hiking back to the Escalade, Nick showed them the digital compass built into the Kestrel 4500. He also pulled out his plain plastic Sunto compass, going over the differences.

"We'll map our way out here day after tomorrow using a terrain map," Nick added, fending off Deke, as the dog snapped at the loose pack straps waving around as Nick moved. "I think we made a good start today."

"I hope we have some kids in the neighborhood," Jean said. "I'm getting tired of hanging out with you two. This Terminator stuff's pretty cool, but it's hard work."

"Maybe you'll meet some locals at the waterslides. I never paid much attention to the neighbors around my place so I'm not sure if they have kids or not. As the good Terminator, I'm hurt you no longer wish to hang out with me."

"Don't worry, Mom'll help you over the rough spots."

"Jean!"

Chapter Eight
Choices

"This is wonderful." Rachel gestured at the inside of the cabana, featuring plasma television, refrigerator, and ceiling fan. "Thanks for the wardrobe, you pervert."

Nick glanced over at Rachel from his lounger next to her, admiring the black bikini with very little material. *Oh yeah.* "You're welcome. Man, am I lucky the Excalibur had this cabana available for rent."

"Jean can be a bit difficult when she has her mind set on one thing and it doesn't work out." Rachel laughed. She looked out at the giant pool with splashing children and adults with what Nick thought was satisfaction. "At least you found a place with lots of kids."

"Tell me about it. How was I to know they closed the 'Wet & Wild' back in '04?"

"Are we taking a big chance coming here?"

Nick shrugged. "I have the beard going a little. With this ball cap, I doubt any book fans will recognize me. It's not like I'm a movie star."

"I don't know." Rachel turned on her side, lowered her sunglasses and peered speculatively at Nick. "You look pretty good in swim trunks, Psycho, six pack and all. Navy blue is your color. Growing the beard does make a difference, especially since you razor trimmed it. I was surprised you had a whole other identity here."

"It wouldn't do much good to hide out in a place under my real name."

"Ouch! I was just making conversation. What in the world made you pick Roscoe Weatherby?"

"Roscoe Nikolas Weatherby to you. It took me a while to establish the residence and driver's license under the Roscoe name, so show some respect. Don't forget, you'll have to pick out a different name if you're asked around here. I was thinking you can get away with Rachel Weatherby."

"I like it." Rachel reached over and stroked Nick's thigh. "Jean's excited. She ran into a little girl and her brother who live around the block from you on Ketchikan Street. They knew Fort Bowie Street right away when Jean mentioned it. The brother's her age and the sister is only a year and a half older."

"Oh good." Nick shook his head, looking up at the sky, his thigh feeling as if it were on fire. "This is what happens when I assume facts not in evidence, like the need to not volunteer information to strangers. My bad."

"I was playing around with them in the pool and I happened to mention your house was on Ft. Bowie. I'm sorry, Nick."

"Forget it. Stop stroking my thigh." Nick turned toward her, breaking contact. "Any more of that and I won't fit in my trunks. We'll get better at this. I have to think like I'm not alone. It takes some getting used to. You didn't meet the parents and invite them over for dinner or anything, did you?"

"No!" Rachel reached for Nick, but had her hand enveloped in his instead. "I said hello to their Mom. They pay for access to the Excalibur pool. She wasn't real friendly after hearing we had rented a cabana. How are you paying for all this, Nick?"

"I have credit cards to go with Roscoe, but only as a reference when they demand it. I pay cash. Trust us psychos to be flush with cash. We're also paranoid to a fault about leaving financial trails. I keep a fund here at the local Citicorp bank, too, under my Roscoe ID."

"I want you," Rachel whispered.

"I'm not that easy," Nick responded casually while trying to keep from jumping Rachel right there in the cabana. *Lord have mercy, did that ever sound good.* "Okay... maybe I am. I'm disappointed in you though."

"Huh?"

"You never questioned me at all so far about my taking you and Jean out in the desert."

"I've accepted my need-to-know position." Rachel pulled Nick's hand over to her bare side. "Being two steps behind in this from the beginning gave me an inferiority complex."

"I like your instincts." Nick ran his hand lightly over Rachel's hip. "There's nothing inferior about you. This will hurt a bit, but Rick gave up the Sarasota safety deposit box location and your maiden name on it."

Rachel swung her legs over the lounger and sat up, grasping Nick's hand in both hers. "What do you know?"

"I know Tanus wouldn't have killed Rick until he gave up the location. It's only in the movies that people endure torture without breaking. If you hadn't gathered Jean up and gone to the cops immediately, Tanus would have had you down in Sarasota with the key. He'd have had someone with a knife at Jean's throat until you opened the box for him."

"My...my keeping the keys kept us in it?"

"I can't say. Tanus may have considered you and Jean as loose ends to be dealt with. It was lucky you had the keys and saw Tanus at your apartment. The rest is water under the bridge." Nick pulled his hand free while swinging his legs over and around Rachel's. He took both her hands in his, their faces only inches apart. "I doubt they want you dead, Rachel. I think the shooter's mission was to put you on the run, out of the program where they could take you down to Sarasota. They figured to get Grace and Tim running around with you and Jean. I've done something similar in the past. When they chased you to the right spot, it would have been goodbye Grace and Tim, hello safety deposit box, and the end of all loose ends. Then I got involved. The people who run me probably had a hand in this all along."

102

"But Tanus sent you to kill me."

"I believe Tanus was going to cut his losses. When he fingered you, I'm thinking he cleared it with someone over me. He wouldn't have needed you, with an outfit capable of obtaining a federal warrant to get into your safety deposit box. Now, any number of folks are watching the bank in Sarasota expecting us to waltz in there with the keys to the kingdom."

"Why bother telling me all this now?"

"Need-to-know, and you need to know. We're going down to Sarasota and stir things around. If I can find out who their people are watching the bank —"

"We take them out, get the flash drives, and vanish."

"I love it when you talk psycho," Nick whispered, covering Rachel's mouth with his own.

"Hello!" Jean called out, peeking into the cabana, with her two friends giggling behind her.

Nick pulled away reluctantly as Rachel had not moved from him at all. He waved at the kids in the cabana entrance. "Look who's here, Rachel, our long lost daughter, Jean. Her timing is remarkable as usual."

"Your...oh..." Jean caught on quickly. "Yeah, Dad, my friends and I want to watch the plasma for a while and eat."

"Fine," Nick agreed, reaching behind him and grabbing two towels. He pulled Rachel to her feet. "We'll go for a swim. Don't wreck the joint. It's only rented."

"Okay...Dad," Jean agreed happily, gesturing her friends inside.

Rachel poked Jean's shoulder. "Of course you know, my daughter – this means war."

"Oh bring it, Mommy. Bye Mom, bye Dad. Don't drown."

Nick and Rachel swam together for a time, before Rachel pulled Nick over to the side of the pool. She moved into his arms, giving him a quick kiss.

"It just occurred to me how weird your involvement in all this really is, Nick." Rachel encircled her feet around Nick's ankles and pulled close to him. "One glimpse of me and you turn the world upside down. I think that's kind of hot."

"Considering the body count so far, Wonder Woman," Nick whispered, the center of his being turning to molten lava, "we better keep the coals white hot."

* * *

"I had a great time, Nick!" Jean cried out from the backseat. "I'm going to see Kelly and Garth tomorrow. They asked if I could come over to their house and hang out. We don't have Terminator duty tomorrow so it should be okay, right Mom?"

Rachel looked over at Nick, who shrugged noncommittally.

"I guess it's okay. They seem like nice kids. You have to be careful what you say, just like in Pleasanton."

"I'm Jean Weatherby. My Dad is Roscoe Weatherby, and my Mom's name is Rachel. We're staying here for a little while because my Dad's a killer and we have to hide out until the coast is clear."

"Not funny!" Rachel whipped around with her hand up threateningly, causing Jean to squeal and cringe defensively in her seat. She looked over at Nick, expecting some form of reaction but he was watching the road and smiling. "Aren't you going to say something, Dad?"

"We all handle this mess in a different way," Nick answered. "Any way a seven year old wants to handle what Jean's dealing with is okay by me."

104

Nick glanced at Jean in the rear view mirror. "As long as the seven year old doesn't get us all killed by forgetting to play her part in front of strangers."

"I'll be eight next month, August thirtieth," Jean announced. "I won't forget, Nick."

"Good enough. It's going to be hot in the house. I left the sliding glass door open for Deke and set the thermostat at eighty-five. We can take him for a walk when it gets dark."

"Aren't you afraid we might have a break in?"

"I have a vault in the house it would take more than your average goon to even find, let alone break into. Besides, we can't put Deke out in the back all day."

"I think you like our dog more than you do Jean and me."

"That obvious, huh?" Nick asked, getting a punch in the shoulder for his trouble.

Nick brought up the rear as Rachel and Jean walked from the garage through the connecting doorway. Hearing Rachel gasp, and Jean start laughing, Nick caught up with them at the entrance into the living room. Every loose cushion in the home's lower floor had been dragged through the sliding door into the back yard. Rachel turned to Nick as he glanced between the bare furniture and the cushion mound in his backyard with tight-lipped surprise.

"Please don't kill him, Nick," Rachel pleaded.

"Hey Nick, it looks like Deke found his own way of dealing with our mess." Jean gestured at Deke, who lay on his back at the very top of his pillow mountain, paws curled against his chest as he stared sideways at his human companions.

Nick glared at Deke and then grinned. "Well at least he didn't rip them apart first."

* * *

Nick vacuumed the last of the cushions. He handed it to Rachel. "I needed to do a cleaning. Nice of Deke to remind me."

Deke 'gruffed' from where he lay, next to the couch where Rachel placed the cushion.

"See, he's really sorry." Rachel threw the cushion into place and stroked Deke's head.

"Yeah, he looks real repentant." Nick laughed. "We should have taken a picture of him up on his cushions. What's Jean doing?"

"Playing video games in her room. I bet you like us better than the dog now."

"Even with dragging them out into the shade, it was hot work." Nick ignored Rachel's dig. "Deke needs a challenge. Did he ever rearrange your furniture while you were at work?"

"No, but he used to take all Jean's stuffed animals out of her room and throw them around the house. He's still a puppy. Deke turned three only a couple months ago."

"That's twenty-one in dog years." Nick pointed at the attentive Deke. "He's old enough for the death penalty."

Deke immediately sat up and extended a paw.

"Very shrewd." Nick shook the dog's paw. When he released it, Deke gave him his other paw to shake. "I'm going to the grocery store and get this clown a few soup bones. Want to make out a list for me? I have a barbeque stored in the garage. Does Jean eat steak?"

"Sure." Rachel nodded. "I'll make a list. Do you want us to go with you?"

"I'd rather not leave your four legged furniture mover alone for the time being." Nick pushed Deke's head playfully before standing. "You make the list, and I'll check in with our US Marshal connection."

106

Nick retrieved his satellite phone and called Grace. The indicator he'd attached to register a trace went from green to red almost instantly when he heard Grace's voice.

"I see you're tracing us." Nick watched for the red light to start blinking.

"It's not us, Nick, I...hey...how do you know we're tracing the call?"

"I'm checking in. So far, we're okay on this end. We only have seconds left on this call. Anything you need to tell us?"

"Keep your heads down. If you hear some other voice besides Tim or me when you call, run."

"Noted. Any luck getting the one who accidentally killed our shooter?"

"We hit the cover-up wall on this, hence the phone tap. There are also rumors starting to fly around about what a bad guy you are. Anonymous tips from official sources are telling us you may be more dangerous than the people we're trying to bring down."

"I told you, writers are very dangerous people. I can make you into a complete idiot in one sentence."

"Oh really?" Grace snorted derisively.

"The frumpy US Marshall named Grace leaned against the alleyway wall, picking her nose, glancing up periodically while looking for witnesses to the loathsome act."

"Frumpy? What do you mean, frumpy? I-"

"Times up," Nick said as the red light began blinking. He disconnected.

Nick found Rachel at the kitchen table writing out a grocery list. He sat down next to her, liking her choice to stay in the black bikini. Nick ran his hand lightly over Rachel's nearly bare back. She shivered under his touch, but kept working on the list.

"You're disturbing my grocery list concentration."

"I assumed you stayed in the bikini so I would disturb you."

"I need you to install a tracking device on my daughter. Her appearances seem connected to the first moment I feel your hand on me."

"I'll get right on it," Nick promised, kissing the back of Rachel's neck. "Jean had quite a workout today. Maybe she'll go to bed early."

"Maybe...oh, Nick...don't stop..."

Nick had stood up behind Rachel, massaging her shoulders and neck, trailing his hands down her back, thumbs kneading the spine, while his fingers splayed out along her sides with feathery touches. When he reached the base of Rachel's spine, his hands worked slowly back up to her neck again. Rachel dropped the pen, head leaning forward to the table surface, a groan escaping her lips as she shuddered under Nick's hands. Her breathing quickened as Nick's fingers moved down past the hip area and his thumbs manipulated deeply into her spinal column all the way to the base. Sweat beaded on Rachel's lip, and the goose flesh from a moment ago felt on fire now. Rachel almost cried out for Nick to keep his hands where they were, as his fingers and thumbs crept up her back once again. By the time Nick completed the cycle to Rachel's neck and shoulders, her fists were clenched on the table, and her breathing sounded closer to a pant. When Nick again reached the base of Rachel's spine, his fingers gripped her hips. Rachel's head shot up and her back arched.

"Oh...oh God..." Rachel moaned, her arms clasped around herself as if a sudden chill of arctic air had swept through the kitchen. She collapsed against the chair back, ankles crossed under the chair, and her thighs pressed together tightly.

Nick leaned around in front of Rachel, his lips caressing hers briefly.

"Like that?"

"What…what did you do to me…? Jesus…" Rachel opened her eyes. She reached for Nick's face with her own trembling hands.

The doorbell rang. A forbidding look swept over Nick's face. He could see his violent change of mood infected Rachel in an instant as she straightened quickly in her chair, looking up at him expectantly.

"I'm going to have to kill something pretty soon." Nick gave Rachel a quick and final kiss. "I'll get it. I'm coming…strike that…I'm walking."

Deke lay in front of the door, a low growl emanating from the base of his throat. Nick motioned Rachel back into the kitchen. Looking out the door's security eyehole, Nick saw a heavily built man in tan slacks and a dark blue short-sleeved shirt, with the shirttail pulled out over his pants. The man's dark hair was fashionably long, his face lined, clean shaven, and menacing. Nick made some mental calculations and then opened the door.

"Hi," Nick smiled up at the man, holding onto Deke. "Can I help you?"

"No, but I think I can help you. May I come in?"

"Well, actually, I was on my way out to the grocery store."

"In your swim trunks and t-shirt?"

"I hate the heat." Nick shrugged.

"Let's talk." The man pulled up his shirt to reveal a holstered automatic. "It'll only take a moment and you'll be happy you took the time."

"Okay… honey, come get Deke," Nick called to Rachel, who hurried into the room. "Take him upstairs with Jean."

Rachel nodded, exchanging smiles with the man at the door. After Rachel went upstairs with a reluctant Deke, Nick unlocked the heavy screen door and stepped aside for the man.

"Come on into the kitchen. Are you a cop?" *If he's a cop, I'm the Easter Bunny.*

Nick gestured for the man to sit down and then Nick sat down at the head of the table to the man's right.

"Security. My name's Brewster. I look in on a family who lives near you, over on Ketchikan."

"The kids we met over at the Excalibur... Kelly and Garth?" Nick realized the conversation was going in a completely different direction than he expected.

"Yeah, their Mom's name is Suzan. I work for her husband. I watch out for the family when he's away. I was doing my job this afternoon and saw your little family. Suzan said your wife's name is Rachel and the daughter's name is Jean. That right?"

"Yes it is," Nick answered, resigned to the fact he had blundered once again. *I'm better at this alone.* Then Rachel in the black bikini and Jean making faces at him from the backseat with Deke draped over her lap popped into his head. Nick took a deep breath and let it out slowly. "What's this all about? Why come over here with a gun?"

"I have –"

Rachel walked into the kitchen. She had put on her shorts and a blouse over the bikini. "Is something wrong?"

"I have a photo I'd like to show you." Brewster pulled a picture from his right breast pocket and set it down on the table in front of Nick.

Rachel leaned over Nick's shoulder, saw the picture, and then stumbled back away from the table. It was a picture of Rachel, Rick, and Jean. "Who...who are you?"

"I figured I could make a call and maybe get a pat on the head, or I could come to you with this. I figure it's worth ten grand easy." Brewster leaned back in his chair.

"How do we know you haven't already made the call?" Nick stopped smiling.

"You don't for sure." Brewster waved his hand in an expansive gesture. "Anybody holding back info like this can get whacked. I figure to make a little money and no one's the wiser. That is, if you two play it smart."

"Sorry about all these questions. How do we know you won't take our ten grand and still make the call?"

"You don't." Brewster chuckled and patted his holstered weapon. "I could make a whole lot more by –"

Nick's strike was a blur. Brewster's head jolted backwards with a sickening crack. Brewster's body flexed in an eerie series of motions as if all the parts were acting on their own without direction. Blood trickled from his nose. Brewster's nose appeared flat, as if the bone and cartilage inside it were somewhere else. Nick could see that Brewster's eyes froze Rachel's blood. Brewster gazed at her in surprise, small gurgling noises issuing from his throat. Seconds later, the eyes looked on into eternity. Nick hurriedly unbuttoned Brewster's shirt.

"Get a towel quick, Rachel," Nick ordered.

"What...what did you do?" Rachel turned toward the sink as if she were a marionette, her limbs moving jerkily to the task.

"C'mon, Rach, get the towel and hold it over his nose! He's dead, so it won't be fresh blood. Keep it from dripping while I strip him down."

Nick paused, seeing Rachel's face lose all color. The towel she had retrieved dropped from nerveless fingers, her mouth worked but no sound came out. Nick tilted Brewster's head onto the top of the chair back. Taking Rachel in his arms, he half carried her out to the living room, guiding her onto the couch.

"Look at me, Rachel!" Nick shook her a little.

Rachel's eyes regained focus slowly. She blinked a few times, recognition overtaking her features once again.

111

"Hey, are you with me?"

"I…I think so."

"I have to get Brewster's clothes off him. Stay here and take deep breaths. Don't let Jean and Deke down until I tell you it's okay."

Rachel nodded without speaking. Nick ran into the kitchen and carefully stripped Brewster out of his clothes, leaving the man in his underwear on the kitchen floor. Nick put the holstered weapon from Brewster's belt up in the cupboard over the refrigerator. He then emptied Brewster's pockets onto the kitchen table, reclaiming only the Toyota keys. Putting on Brewster's clothing and a ball-cap, Nick went into the garage and activated the door opener. Thankful the sun had gone down, he backed the Escalade out to the street. A Toyota Camry was parked in front of the house. Nick used the remote to unlock it before driving the Toyota into the garage.

With the garage door shut again, Nick donned plastic gloves. He wrapped Brewster in black plastic garbage bags: one over his upper torso, one with cut out leg holes over the middle part of the body, and another over Brewster's legs. He duct-taped the body tightly, and half dragged, half carried it out past the Malibu to the Toyota. Nick had some difficulty crushing the body into the Toyota trunk, but managed with some sickening adjustments. Nick put bleach, rags, and a shovel on the floor behind the front seats along with two other garbage bags.

He went inside the house to check on Rachel. She wasn't in the living room, so Nick called to her from the stairwell. Rachel walked down the hall towards the stairs hesitantly, gritting her teeth upon seeing Nick dressed in the dead man's clothes. Holding on to the railing tightly, Rachel trudged down the stairs.

"It's getting dark." Nick kept eye contact with Rachel. "I have to get rid of Brewster and then drive the Toyota somewhere it won't be noticed in town for a while. When I find a good spot for it, I'll call the house phone. It works. Can you come pick me up?"

"I think so. Jesus, Nick. Did you have to kill him?"

Nick watched Rachel's lip trembling in her attempt to keep from crying.

"You're reacting and not thinking. We will always have very few choices. When we choose, it will be quick, and there will be no time for regrets. Can you pick me up?"

"Yes."

Nick started toward the garage, and then turned back. "This is all still a trial time until we get those flash drives to Tim and Grace. Afterward, you'll be free to choose again."

"I know."

Chapter Nine
Complications

By the time Nick drove back to the Las Vegas city limits, it was nearly ten o'clock at night. He had decided to leave the Toyota in a low-income housing project on the outskirts of the city. He parked the Toyota and carefully went over the inside of the car again with his rags, cleaning the vehicle meticulously, wiping every square inch of the trunk and passenger compartment. Nick wrapped the shovel, rags, and bleach bottle in a black plastic bag, took the bag with him and abandoned the vehicle. When he reached the corner of East Sunset and Pabco, Nick called Rachel, giving her specific directions to his location. Twenty minutes later, she drove up next to him in the Escalade with Jean and Deke in the back. Nick threw the black bag into the rear storage compartment and got into the front seat.

"Is everything okay?" Rachel asked.

He could tell she was relieved he no longer wore Brewster's clothing. "We'll know soon. Did you bunch eat without me?"

"It's almost midnight." Jean replied, yawning. "We ate a long time ago. Where were you?"

"Running errands," he answered, and left it at that.

* * *

Nick took his beer out to the back patio with Deke trailing him. He felt much better after a shower, but knew from experience it would be a while before he could sleep. The sliding glass door opened behind him, startling Nick. Rachel pulled another chair

114

over near his, holding out a fresh beer to him. Rachel wore the same shorts and blouse she had worn earlier.

"I thought you went to bed," he said.

"I couldn't sleep. I keep seeing Brewster staring at me with the 'I'm dead' look."

"It was all nice and cozy there for a few moments, wasn't it?"

"Yeah, Nick," she said with a sigh, "It really was."

* * *

Nick glanced down at Deke where he lay near his chair. He nudged Deke's flank with his foot, smiling when Deke replied with a short growl without looking up. Nick had been typing away on his new manuscript since getting up at six. As usual, writing smoothed the rough edges of reality. A mobster put out a hit on his character Diego, endangering the assassin's way of life. Nick had enjoyed turning Diego loose to cut a swath through the mobster's ranks, killing indiscriminately until the mobster rescinded the order and paid Diego a million dollars. He heard footsteps and looked up as Jean walked into the kitchen. The little girl waved at him before fending off Deke, who was now leaping around in front of her. Nick gave out a short whistle, and Deke returned to his place beside Nick's chair.

"You're up early." He noticed it was only twenty minutes past eight. "I figured you'd wake around noon after being up so late."

"I'm excited about hanging out with Kelly and Garth today." Jean slipped into the chair next to his. Nick had cleaned and moved the chair Brewster had died in, and Jean sat in the same spot. He dropped the image of Brewster's last moments at the same kitchen table from his mind and patted her hand.

115

"What can I get you for breakfast? Your mom did the grocery shopping for me while I was doing my errands. We have lots of food."

"Could I have toast and tea?"

"I remember having toast and tea when I was a kid. The tea has to be strong, mixed with lots of sugar and milk, while the toast has to be crispy with butter, right?"

Jean nodded. "You know a lot of stuff, Nick."

"Do you dunk the toast like I did?" He hung a teabag in one of his larger mugs, filled it with water, and heated it in the microwave. "It used to drive my mom nuts. The tea would end up filled with crumbs and I'd slurp it up. She'd look at me like I was from outer space."

"That's what my mom does!" Jean laughed, nodding her head excitedly. "She always says, 'that is so gross'. Is your mom still alive?"

"No, honey, she passed away many years ago." He put the bread in his four-slotted toaster and took the margarine from the refrigerator.

"Nick, is Mom mad at you?"

"She was a little upset because I had to go out on those errands last night and leave you two alone. I'm sure she'll be fine this morning. You're a pretty neat little girl, Jean. You don't complain, and none of the awful things happening around you for the last year has messed with your mind too badly. What's your secret?"

"I was messed up real bad when my dad was killed." She clasped her hands in front of her in serious fashion. "That's why I like you, Nick. See...ever since Dad died, everyone's been running us around looking all scared and worried, even Grace and Tim. They're US Marshalls, but they can't really do anything. Bad guys killed Dad. Bad guys are tryin' to kill us. Bad guys are why we had to leave New York. I kept wondering how come we can't just kill the bad guys before they hurt us."

Nick laughed, pointing at Jean appreciatively. "You're all right, kid. I'm sorry things aren't as easy in real life, or as straightforward."

He spread margarine on the toast and doctored the tea up as he remembered from his own childhood. After cutting the toast diagonally, he placed the tea and toast in front of Jean on saucers.

"Better sip the tea, Jean. Make sure it's perfect or the whole tea and toast thing will be ruined."

She sipped the tea and made an audible 'ah' sound in satisfaction. "Yep, just right."

Nick made more toast and filled his cup, joining Jean for breakfast with toast and coffee. She made a face as he dunked his toast in the coffee and gobbled it up.

"That's gross! You're supposed to dunk the toast in tea." She giggled.

"Why you little elitist." He reached over toward Jean as if to swat her, only to earn a no nonsense warning growl from Deke, who had appeared instantly at Jean's side. "One of these days you won't be with your bodyguard. You'll be sorry then."

"I still like you, Nick," Jean petted Deke. The dog started lapping at the crumbs and bits of margarine on Jean's hand. "Can I give Deke a piece of toast?"

"Sure, if he'll eat it. He already scarfed a whole can of dog food this morning."

Deke gulped the toast down as if he hadn't eaten in a month.

"Wash those yucky hands after you finish giving Deke his treat, young lady."

"Nick," Jean said suddenly, sipping her crumb-filled tea. "How come you're allowed to kill bad guys?"

117

Nick grinned. "Uh...actually, I'm not allowed to kill bad guys. You should know by now that no one is allowed to kill bad guys. They had tough childhoods. Their mommies and daddies beat them. Their self-esteem was lowered from the time they were in diapers. No one wants them to be bank presidents. People flash devil's horns on their heads when they get their pictures taken. Animals growl at them. Pigeons decorate their cars. Even their –"

"What's going on in here?" Rachel asked from the doorway, seeing Jean laughing raucously as Nick barked out his bad guy excuse list, counting them off on his fingers.

"Nick was..." Jean suppressed her laughter. "Nick was explaining why no one's allowed to kill bad guys even though they keep trying to kill us."

"Oh wonderful." Rachel gave him a malevolent look, geared to make his toes and testicles curl up simultaneously. "Perhaps it would be better if you left off on teaching Jean from the psycho training manual for now."

"At least Nick does something about bad guys!" Jean turned on Rachel. "Maybe if Nick kills enough of 'em, we won't have to run anymore, Mom. I'm tired of being scared all the time. I want the bad guys to be scared!"

Deke barked, lending his support. A few toast crumbs exited his mouth. Rachel's shoulders sagged. Jean climbed off her chair and walked over to hug her around the waist.

"Don't be mad at Nick. We weren't really talking about killing. Mostly, we were talking about toast and tea."

"I know." Rachel held Jean's head to her gently. "I'm cranky from sleep deprivation. Sorry, Nick, I'm just jealous from hearing you two yucking it up in here. What's this about toast and tea?"

"Nick ate toast and tea when he was a kid, just like me. He even slurps up the tea and crumbs same as I do."

"Eeeewwww!" Rachel exclaimed, making a face. "There's an image I could do without."

Jean laughed and ran back to her seat. She held up her crumb-filled tea for Rachel's disgusted reaction, and then sipped it noisily. Nick followed with his crumb-filled coffee.

"I think I'll just have coffee," Rachel announced, walking to the coffee maker with her left hand held up to the side of her face like a horse's blinder, preventing the sight of crumb tea and coffee slurping on the way by.

"Jean reminded me of her scheduled get-together today," Nick said, when Rachel was seated at the table across from Jean. "I think we should introduce ourselves to the mom, and have a chat."

"No, Nick...don't even –" Rachel began, a horrified look on her face.

"Calm down." He cut her off with some disappointment, but understanding her leap in logic. "I meant a simple chat to be sociable."

"Oh... Sorry."

"God, Mom, what'd you think he meant, kill her?" Jean clucked, while shaking her head at Rachel. "I'm done. Thanks for breakfast, Nick. I'm going to take a shower and get ready."

"You're most welcome, my dear." He watched Jean run off. He could feel Rachel looking at him appraisingly. "I think your daughter likes me better too."

"Yeah, right! That's because she doesn't know you like I do. It's all fun and games until someone gets their nose bone driven into their brain."

"Ouch."

* * *

"I hope Suzan isn't a Diego fan," Rachel whispered sideways at Nick, as Jean ran ahead to her new friends' door. "Your beard is coming in nicely, but Brewster freaked me out."

"I'm more worried about whether it was Brewster's idea to come visit, or Suzan sending him to check us out. You said she acted strange at the pool when you told her we were renting one of the cabanas," Nick replied in an equally hushed voice, glancing up at the noon day Las Vegas sun. "Damn, it's hot out here."

"Deke should be happy grinding his soup bone into dust rather than rearranging furniture today."

"We won't be long." Nick grinned, thinking of Deke working over the soup bone on his kitchen floor.

Kelly and Garth opened the door before Jean reached it. Nick heard their mother admonishing them for answering the door without her. The kids' laughter receded as they ran together away into the house. A mid-thirties brunette in blue shorts and a white blouse smiled at them from the doorway, opening it for Nick and Rachel. Nick watched the woman for any sign of recognition.

"Come in. I'm Suzan Benoit, and I believe you've already met my two children," she greeted them, gesturing Nick and Rachel inside. "I'm sorry we didn't get to talk more at the pool, Rachel. The guy my husband hired as security for us gets really obnoxious when we meet anyone new while my husband's out of town."

"No problem – this is my husband Roscoe."

"Just call me Ross." Nick shook Suzan's hand.

"Would you like something to drink?" Suzan led them through the western ranch style house into her kitchen. "I have soda, iced tea, juice…"

"I'll have a soda," Rachel said.

"Iced tea sounds good," Nick added. "We were wondering about Mr. Brewster. He came over to see us yesterday afternoon, mentioning he worked in security for your family. He asked us some questions about our stay in Las Vegas, and then left."

"He actually stopped by to see you?" Suzan looked genuinely surprised, as she served the drinks, taking iced tea for herself. "Carl usually asks my husband if he should check someone out. I hope he didn't upset you. Carl can be rather abrupt and a little scary."

"Not at all," Rachel put in immediately. "Mr. Brewster was very nice to us."

"Good." Suzan sounded relieved. "I'll ask him about it Monday when he comes over. He has the weekends off, because we locals stay away from the crowds. Carl knows we don't go anywhere on the weekends, other than the smaller restaurants and grocery stores away from downtown. My husband, Jim, has been getting more and more uneasy about the new gang conglomerate formed in the city called 'Squad Up'. He says they don't need a reason to shoot at someone. Gang members even fired into a gated community just for the hell of it."

"Thanks for the warning. We'll watch ourselves."

"Rachel said you own a house over on Fort Bowie. It's funny we haven't run into each other before."

"Actually, I've owned the house for quite a while, but only spend a couple weeks a year there," Nick explained. "Do you have much gang activity around here?"

"No, not really, and the school near here is real nice. What do you do for a living, Ross?"

"I'm a troubleshooter for a large firm," he answered, hurrying into the question he wanted answered. "What does your husband do?"

"He's in the import/export business on both coasts, which is why he's away a lot."

"Maybe it's a good thing we met. My parent firm deals off shore. Do you have one of your husband's business cards around?

121

You never know when a need for someone with your husband's expertise and contacts will come in handy."

"Sure, I'll get you one." Suzan left the table and the kitchen for a few minutes before returning with a couple of cards. She handed them to Nick.

"Thank you." Nick pulled out a business card he had made up that morning with his name and the Fort Bowie phone number on it. He handed one to Suzan. We're going to have a barbeque later after Jean gets home. Would you and your kids like to join us?"

"Sure," Suzan accepted gratefully. "It's a treat being with adults. Should I bring anything?"

"Nope," Nick answered, standing. "We'd better move along, hon. It was nice meeting you, Suzan. We'll see you later then. How about around five?"

"Great, I'll bring Jean with me." Suzan walked Nick and Rachel to the door.

"That'll work. If Jean starts acting up, call me, and I'll come drag her home."

Suzan laughed. "I don't think that'll be necessary. Goodbye."

"It's a Tanus subsidiary," Nick said, handing Rachel one of Jim Benoit's business cards in the car. "I'll check on Benoit when we get home. It does explain how a mook like Brewster came to have a picture of you, Jean, and Rick."

"And you invited her over for a barbeque…why?" Rachel asked caustically.

"Suzan will do one of two things, call her husband immediately, or take us at face value and forget the whole thing. I want to see which one she does."

"You'll actually know without her telling you?"

"I'll work it into the conversation. Tanus Import/Export is a huge conglomerate on both coasts, which means they've been able to hide some very big undertakings. I'm certain their employees were given your picture long ago. I doubt more than a few people even knew Tanus was under indictment. I'd wager Mr. Benoit gave the picture to Brewster because he couldn't be bothered with it."

"Having Suzan and her kids over a day after you whacked their security guy would be unthinkable for anyone human...no offense meant." She smiled at him, leaning a little so she could see his reaction.

"None taken." Nick pulled the Escalade into the open garage and shut the door. "It's all the more reason to have them over. I don't suppose you'd like to model your black bikini for me until Suzan arrives with the kids for the barbeque."

"You write some more Diego and research Jim Benoit. I'll prepare everything for our get together."

"Throw the potatoes into the microwave, brush barbeque sauce on the steaks, cut up the French bread, and boil the corn on the cob. That's about five minutes work. You'd have a long time left to model," Nick pointed out as he exited the Escalade.

"Ever hear the old Jim Croce song 'You Don't Mess Around With Jim'?" Rachel began singing as she danced into the house. "You don't tug on Superman's cape. You don't spit into the wind. You don't pull the mask off that old Lone Ranger, and you don't mess around with...Nick."

Nick laughed. *Damn, she can carry a tune too.* "Ah...when I was asking you to model the black bikini, I wasn't considering it as a prelude to unarmed combat, Rach."

* * *

Rachel spun around, only to find Nick had covered the intervening space more quickly than she had anticipated. "Weren't

123

you? Why don't we take a step back for the time being? I haven't been assimilated completely into my new Terminator mentality yet."

"Sure," he agreed, taking her left hand in his right at the doorway. "I wasn't trying to give you a hard time."

"Yes you were." She smirked at his double entendre, putting her right palm against his chest as he moved closer. Nick's nearness, coupled with Jean's absence, forced the more unpleasant aspects of the day before from her mind. "Hey, you're invading my airspace."

He pulled her right hand away from his chest and down to her side. They had dressed casually, he in t-shirt and jeans, Rachel in a burgundy cotton dress. As he forced her hands back around her hips, very little material separated them. She looked away from his face, feeling the heated flush enveloping her from where their bodies touched. Nick drew her tightly against him, making sure she had no question what the 'hard time' he had in mind really was. Deke stuck his nose up under Rachel's dress, touching cold wet nose to bare back of thigh. Rachel jumped away from Nick with a cry of surprise. She laughed, seeing Deke sitting between her and Nick, looking questioningly from one to the other.

"Thanks Deke. Good of you to stick your nose into my business, Butthead."

Rachel, her hand still suppressing her laughter, watched Nick frown and then grin at the attentive Deke. He shrugged and walked around her. "I'll be up in my room on the computer if you need me. Maybe I can get Diego laid."

Rachel bent down to pet Deke. The dog sat still for a moment under her hand, but then ran to catch up with Nick. She straightened slowly, her body tingling where it had been pressed close to him. She walked over to close the sliding glass door he had left open for Deke, and lowered the thermostat setting. As Nick had predicted, it took her only minutes to get everything for the barbeque ready to go, including setting the table. He had eight full place settings stored neatly in the cupboard on the side of his kitchen sink. The closer she came to being done, the more she glanced toward the stairs. Even with the air conditioning working full blast, sweat beaded on her face. Her pulse quickened as she considered excuses to visit his bedroom. *Why didn't you just strip for him before he went upstairs?*

Rachel looked at the clock. *Damn, it's only a few minutes to one.* She wet a paper towel and used it to cool her face. After taking two sodas out of the refrigerator, Rachel walked to the stairs, pausing to second guess her course of action once again. A full minute passed, and she nearly returned to the kitchen. With a small grunt of annoyance, she stepped decisively up the stairs, halting only when she was standing outside Nick's open bedroom door. He sat at a small desk across the room with his back to the doorway.

"I brought you a soda," she announced.

"Thanks." He didn't look up from his notebook computer where he typed at a rapid pace. "Just set it down on the night stand."

She did as he asked before unzipping her dress and shrugging out of it noiselessly. Wearing only a red thong and low-heeled black shoes, she approached him with growing apprehension and rising excitement. Nick stopped typing as Rachel's hands clasped his upper arms.

"I don't type well with company watching over my shoulder," he said in a joking manner, attention focused on his fictional assassin's abstract life, with a writer's tunnel vision concentration. "I…"

She felt his body tense as she leaned into him, her bare breasts pressing into his neck.

"On second thought, I think I can work through an interruption." He spoke without turning, his hands reaching behind the chair to stroke her legs.

"I thought perhaps you might need some inspiration in creating a difficult scene like Diego getting laid," she explained in

125

a husky whisper, moving in small, slow, side to side motions. "I figured maybe I could be your...what do writers turn to for inspiration...a...?"

"Muse," Nick finished for her. Leaning back, he stroked her bare skin from upper rear thighs to rear calves, fingers kneading the flesh momentarily at the sensitive area behind her knees. "I have a good feeling about this collaboration, Ms. Muse."

"You'll take your time, though, going over the rough spots, right?"

"Absolutely."

* * *

Rachel lay naked across Nick, their bodies entwined tightly. Her chest heaved against his, trying to draw breath, while at the same time unable for the moment to move her limbs. Bathed in sweat, the two had been immobile for the last couple minutes. Nick stroked her sides, his touch eliciting a moan from Rachel, who propped herself up momentarily, and then rolled onto her back. She reached over his chest to cup his chin with her right hand. She shook his chin, making an admonishing noise in her throat as she took a deep breath.

"Nick...you...dog."

"I was innocently writing about an assassin. I was seduced against...well...okay, not against my will, but at least in spite of my will."

"Just because I innocently flirted with you does not give –"

"Flirted?" He sprung up into a sitting position, growling as he reached for her.

"Don't touch me!" She squealed, trapped under him, her hands captured and held to her sides.

When he leaned into her, his mouth sealed off more exclamations. He released her hands, and her arms wound once again around his neck. She twisted under him, and drew her hands to his chest, pushing him away reluctantly.

"It's nearly three-thirty, Nick. We…we have to get ready."

"Eventually," he whispered, his lips trailing down over her chin, throat, and between her breasts, pausing to glance up into her eyes only when he reached her stomach. "Are you sure?"

"Please let me go." Her hands gripped his shoulders, unable to push him away, as reality battled desire with weak resolve.

Nick spun away and off the bed, turning to give Rachel a hand up onto her feet.

"Thank you." She kissed him, trying to ignore his obvious state of tension.

"Want me to take a shower with you…you know…to save water?"

"No!" She broke away from him, pointing a finger in his direction as she backed away. "You stay right there."

Half an hour later, Nick showered quickly, thinking ahead to how he would question Suzan without getting her guard up. The faint sound of the phone ringing through the open bathroom door roused him from his deliberation.

"Nick!" Rachel cried out as she ran into the bathroom with Deke close behind, the dog sensing her fear. "They have Jean!"

Chapter Ten
Wake Up Call

Nick threw open the shower door and grabbed a towel. In a glance, he saw Rachel's terror. Her fists were clenched, and she hunched slightly forward, trying to control the obvious panic threatening to overcome every other thought. He dried in a rush, putting an arm around Rachel while guiding her toward the bedroom. He pushed her down on his bed.

"Take a deep breath and tell me only the facts," he ordered, hurriedly pulling on his clothes.

Rachel breathed deeply, setting the nightmarish conversation with Suzan firmly in her mind with effort. Tears welled up as she fought down sobs. "Two men…came to her house. She recognized them as friends of the security guy, Brewster, and let them in. They were looking for Brewster. When…when they saw Jean…they…they –"

"Easy, Rach, you're doing fine," Nick soothed, sitting down, and pulling her close. "Keep going."

"One of the bastards took all the kids with him." Her body heaved under his arm in a mixture of rage and terror. "The other one…he's with Suzan. He wants us over there now. Would they trade Jean for me and let her go?"

"They've kidnapped Suzan's kids, too, and her husband's an exec somewhere in the hierarchy they plan on scoring from. These guys aren't trading anything. We have two things going for us: one, they don't know what happened to Brewster, and two, they don't know anything about me. We need to find out how much they know and what they want."

"Tell me what you need me to do." Rachel wiped her eyes.

"Act like a mom with her kid in danger. I'll be supportive, just a friend along to comfort you. I'm hoping the guy at Suzan's house will give us some hint as to what they have planned. I need an Oscar-winning performance from you once you're near him. Collapse crying at his feet, but not too near. I'll lean down to comfort you and then we play psycho. If I miss my chance, or something goes wrong, don't wait for an invitation. This guy will be the key to getting Jean back."

"I'm ready. Let's get going."

"He'll have Suzan let us in so our chance won't come right away," he added, following her out of the room and down the stairs. "Under no circumstances do we let this mook tie us up."

Nick ran around to the passenger side of the Escalade when they reached Suzan's house, supporting a sobbing Rachel to the Benoit's front door. Suzan held open the screen door for them before they reached the entrance. Nick noticed the left side of Suzan's face was swollen. A man wearing a button up, khaki, short sleeve shirt and dark brown slacks stood about ten feet inside the doorway, covering their entrance with a silenced automatic. He was at least a couple inches taller than Nick, and thirty pounds heavier, mostly in his gut. Although probably in his late thirties, the man's thin brown hair was arranged in a comb over.

"Close the door, sweetie, and sit your ass down there on the couch," the man said to Suzan. "Now then, you two strip down to your underwear."

"But..." Rachel started to protest.

"Do it, Rachel," Nick urged, looking fearfully at the man as he quickly stripped out of his shoes, jeans, and t-shirt.

Rachel took off her shorts, and then her blouse. Not having a bra on, she covered herself with folded arms. The tears flowing down her cheeks needed very little acting ability on her part.

"Now then, you can call me Joe. I need some questions answered. If you hesitate in answering, I'll have to get mean. As

129

you can see, I don't need to worry about noise, at least not from my gun."

"Sure...whatever you say," Nick agreed. "Please, we just want Jean back."

"We'll do anything...anything," Rachel added with a heartfelt sob.

"Good." Joe nodded, smiling. "First off, where the hell is Brewster?"

"Brewster came over yesterday and showed us a picture of Jean and Rachel," Nick blurted out. "He said he wanted ten thousand dollars to keep his mouth shut. We agreed to pay him. I gave him the money. He gave us the picture and left, saying maybe we wouldn't see him again."

"Shit!" Joe showed real anger for the first time. "You had ten thousand at your house?"

"I...I have a vault." Nick could tell Joe believed Brewster would have taken off with the money.

"How much more do you have in there?" Joe asked, his voice calming down.

"About thirty grand," Nick said with enthusiasm. "It's all yours. Just let –"

"Well now, I think we might work something out," Joe cut him off. "I need your little lady here to take me wherever she has the safety deposit box everyone's looking for. My partner and I heard there are some very valuable items in it. Jean and the rest of you will have to stay here so Ms. Rachel will be cooperative."

"Please, Joe!" Rachel cried out, falling forward on her knees, pleading. "Let Jean go. I'll go with you and get what you want. Don't –"

Nick crouched next to her, putting comforting hands on her shoulders. He saw Joe take a half step back, enjoying the view. Joe glanced at Suzan, and Nick launched into the man's gun hand, grabbing Joe's right wrist with his right hand. Nick slapped the barrel of the 9mm automatic up as Joe pulled the trigger. Twisting the weapon up against Joe's thumb, Nick ripped the gun from the startled Joe's hand. In the next split second, Nick controlled the silenced automatic and fired point blank into both of Joe's kneecaps. The man screamed in agony, falling backwards to the floor, hugging his injured legs.

"Get dressed, Rachel," Nick ordered, pulling her to her feet. "Suzan, go get some plastic garbage bags, and drag one of your kitchen chairs in here. Hurry!"

"Who...who are you?" Suzan stared at Nick in horror.

"No time, Suzan," Nick replied sternly, locking eyes with her momentarily. "Do as I say and we'll have the kids back safe and sound. Give her a hand, Rachel."

Suzan nodded her understanding. She ran into the kitchen. Rachel followed, buttoning her blouse. They returned moments later with a kitchen chair and the large black plastic trash bags. Joe had stopped screaming. His mouth and eyes were clenched shut as he rocked slightly on the floor in a fetal position. Nick motioned Rachel over next to him.

"Go out to the Escalade," he whispered. "Open the back and bring me the gym bag I put there when we left the house."

Rachel followed his directions without a word. Nick grinned as Joe stopped moaning and began cursing him. Suzan waited next to the chair she'd brought from the kitchen, hugging herself to control the trembling.

"Spread three of those bags out on the floor, Suzan, and then put the kitchen chair on top of them."

Suzan did as she was told. Rachel came in from her task with the gym bag and closed the door behind her. Nick pulled Rachel over to him. He positioned the weapon in her hands, keeping it pointed at Joe, who had begun looking around him, just the way he wanted it.

"If good ole Joe here moves when I don't want him to, you fire another round into his knee," Nick directed. "We need him, so aim carefully."

Seeing the grim look on Rachel's face as she trained the weapon on Joe's exposed left knee, Joe rolled over with a grunt of pain. Nick dressed hurriedly. He shook his head when Rachel looked at him.

"That's okay, just shoot him in the ass if he moves," Nick directed, tying his shoes.

Nick opened the gym bag and took out the roll of duct tape he had placed inside. He tore off eight foot-long strips, hanging them on the kitchen chair. He walked over to Joe, grabbed his belt at the back and dragged the cursing man over in front of the chair.

"You're going to get into the kitchen chair the easy way or the hard way, Joe." He made eye contact with the big man. "But in the chair, you most assuredly are going."

"You son of a bitch! The kids are as good as dead! You hear me?" Joe cried out in rage as Nick propped him up against the kitchen chair and took up a position behind him.

Leaning against the chair back for leverage, he reached over and grabbed Joe under the armpits. With a powerful yank, he pulled Joe up into the seat, eliciting a scream. Nick quickly trapped and duct-taped each of the Joe's struggling wrists to the chair arms. He taped around the chair back and Joe's waist, following with a wrap at shoulder level to the back of the chair. Taping the ankles and adding extra strips completed the task. Nick put one last small strip over Joe's mouth. Then he undid Joe's pants and pulled them down along with his underwear. Nick reached into his gym bag and took out the stun gun he had stored there. He fired off an arc in front of the red-faced Joe, whose eyes widened in abject terror.

"Now then, partner. I know you're just itchin' to tell me everything you know. Ladies, leave or stay, but this won't be pretty. I need to show our friend Joe how important his telling the truth is going to be. That will take a rather painful demonstration just to get him on board."

Nick paused. Rachel stayed where she was, her fingers curling and uncurling nervously.

"I'll be upstairs in my bedroom." Suzan glanced at Joe before nearly running to the stairs.

Nick bent toward Joe, putting a foot on the horizontal brace attached to the two front chair legs. He fired off an arc into the man's exposed testicles. Rachel looked away as the chair jumped and Joe passed out. Nick went into the kitchen. He returned with a towel and glass of water. Placing the towel over Joe's groin area, Nick slowly dripped the cold water over the man's contorted face and head. Joe woke up screaming, a high pitched keening from his throat, muffled by the tape.

"Joe... you see, there are things worse than death. Once you calm down, I'll take the duct tape off your mouth. Then you're going to answer some questions, and we'll start working together to get the children home safe and sound, right?"

Joe's head bobbed up and down violently in agreement.

"That's the spirit." Nick pulled the tape off.

For a moment, Joe mouthed words without sound. Nick held up a hand in a stopping gesture in front of Joe's face. He allowed Rachel to move closer. He could tell thoughts of Jean in the hands of some guy like Joe were eating her up from the inside out.

"Wait for it, Joe, wait for it. I don't want you wasting your breath on what you think I might want to know. Tell me how this plan started."

"Suzan...Suzan recognized...Hunter and her kid. Christ... give me something for the pain!"

"Concentrate, Joe, or you'll be nostalgic for the pain level you're at now."

133

"Her husband...had the photo. She only knew someone was...looking for them. Carl knew the story already." Joe closed his eyes, mouth clamping shut, his head rolling in an attempt to control the pain. Nick slapped Joe's face lightly, bringing him out of it. "When...Suzan told him she saw them at the pool, Carl brought us the photo."

"You knew about the safety deposit box. Do you know where it is?"

"We...we heard Florida."

"Give me the plan you guys hatched, short and sweet."

"Ta...take Hunter down to Florida and get the stuff...sell it to the highest bidder."

"And the rest of us?"

Joe hesitated, but after a glance into Nick's eyes, he went on. "Dead...the moment I... had Hunter on the way to Florida."

"Suzan and her kids too?"

Joe nodded.

"Did you contact anyone else about Rachel or your plan... maybe some investors?"

Joe shook his head in the negative, grimacing as waves of excruciating pain continued to rip through him.

"Good, now what were you to do next with your partner?"

"Tell him when...when I had you two wrapped up...and found out about Carl. He...he was to drive the kids back over in our van...and –"

"Stay here while you and Rachel headed for Florida?"

Joe nodded. "Then he would...drive out in the desert...with the rest of you."

"Your partner must be a real piece of work. Okay, so you call your partner, tell him we're all bound up and ready. Have him

134

drive the van into the garage when he gets here, and come in through the kitchen. Rachel, see if you can find a pen and paper."

Rachel checked the kitchen first. She returned with pen and paper, handing them to Nick.

"Give me the address where your buddy's holding the kids, Joe."

Joe gave him the address.

"I...I can hardly talk...he'll know something's wrong."

"I'm going to find something to help you deal with the pain." Nick grabbed Joe's ears, his face inches away. "If you mess up, Joe, I'll still get those kids back, but when I'm done with your partner, I'll take you out in the desert and keep you alive for four days. When the four days are done, you'll embrace hell with open arms. Are we clear?"

"I...I'll do it... Just give me something to take the edge off," Joe promised fearfully.

"You have chosen wisely. Rachel, go see if Suzan has any heavy duty pain killers."

* * *

Rachel ran to the stairs, hope driving her with energy and purpose. She found Suzan huddled up on the bed, fists pressed against her mouth. When Suzan heard Rachel, she leaped quickly from the bed, her face a mask of misery and concern.

"We need pain killers. Do you have anything that won't knock somebody out, but might take the edge off the pain?"

Suzan looked at Rachel blankly for a moment, and then hurried into the master bathroom. She pulled a bottle of pills off the top shelf and handed them to Rachel.

"They're OxyContin. Two will take the edge off, and then it would be guess work."

"Thanks," Rachel turned to go. Suzan grabbed her arm.

"I...I'm sorry, Rachel. If I'd had any idea what –"

"Forget it. Joe told us you didn't know."

"Is there any chance we can get the kids back?"

"Oh yeah." Rachel patted Suzan's shoulder. "If it can be done, that cold-blooded bastard downstairs will do it. You can come down if you want. Joe's helping."

Suzan followed Rachel downstairs. Nick was binding Joe's wounded knees with towels from Suzan's kitchen, using duct tape to hold them tightly in place, staunching the blood flow. He had already cleaned up the mess from his interrogation of Joe, stuffing the refuse into another black plastic bag. Joe suffered in silence, enduring anything so as not to draw Nick's attention. Rachel handed Nick the bottle.

"OxyContin," Rachel told him. "Suzan says two will take the edge off, but it gets flaky from there."

* * *

Nick emptied two from the bottle. He picked up the water glass he had used to wake Joe up. He stuck the tablets into Joe's mouth, and held the water glass to his lips until Joe sipped enough to get the tablets swallowed.

"Is the garage empty, Suzan?"

"Yes...Joe had me park my car along the street."

"What kind of vehicle did they come in?"

"A van...ah...dark blue," Suzan answered. "It was one of those old beat up Dodge Tradesman vans. They checked to see if it

136

would fit in my garage before Joe's partner took the kids. What can you do about his partner without getting the kids hurt?"

"Let me worry that through, Suzan." Nick looked closely at Joe's face. Some of the pain lines were fading and Joe had relaxed his jaw somewhat. "Talk to me, Joe. Time's running out."

"I can do it!" he cried out, as Nick picked up the stun gun again when Joe was slow answering. "Bring me my cell-phone. It's on the stand near the couch. The number's on speed dial under Craig."

Rachel picked up the cell-phone and handed it to Nick. After finding and entering the number, Nick held the cell-phone for Joe.

"Craig...we're all set. Drive the van into the garage. Come in through the kitchen," Joe said, and then listened for Craig's acknowledgment. "Okay, see ya."

Nick closed the cell phone and pocketed it. He went to his gym bag. Nick motioned for Rachel to follow him over. Nick removed an odd shaped gun from the bag. He held it up for her to see.

"Here's what we do. Suzan, you trigger the garage door open, but leave the connecting door to the kitchen closed. When Craig comes in the kitchen this Taser gun will stop him. Rachel, after Craig's down, I'll give you the gun while I duct tape him. Zap him any time he moves."

"You're like the Inspector Gadget of Assassins," Rachel joked, when Suzan went into the garage through the kitchen to open the door.

Nick smiled. *Damn, good recovery lady. You'll do.* "Just hold the gun in your hand, and hit the trigger if Craig has any life in him after the initial zapping. I need Craig alive though."

Nick turned to Joe, who looked noticeably better. "If you have anything to add in addition to what you've already said, now's the time, Joe. If your partner's story doesn't match yours, it'll go badly for you."

Shock registered for a moment on Joe's face as he frantically tried to think of anything he might have left out. "No, that's it. Honest to God."

"Better hope so." Nick took out two more OxyContin and helped Joe get them down. "Sit quietly. When I hear your buddy, I'm going to tape your mouth temporarily."

"Stay in the living room," Nick said when Suzan returned from the garage. "Keep an eye on Joe, Rachel. Put the tape over his mouth when I tell you to. If he even looks like he's going to make a sound, give him something to make sounds about. I'll leave the stun gun with you. You two stay cool. The hard part will be over shortly."

Nick went into the kitchen after checking that the main entrance was locked, carrying the Taser gun and Joe's silenced automatic. He placed a chair to the right of the connecting door from the garage. With Joe's weapon in his left hand, and the Taser in his right, Nick waited. Ten minutes later, he heard the ragged exhaust sound of the Dodge driving into the garage.

"Put the tape on Joe, Rachel," he called out.

Two minutes later, the kitchen door opened. A huge man with carefully trimmed black beard and hair entered. The Taser needles struck the man's left breast. Craig cried out, his arms flailing wildly as Nick gave him burst after burst until the man fell first to his knees, and then pitched to the floor on his face. Nick kept up the charge until Craig moved only spasmodically. He could smell the unmistakable odor of singed flesh. *Ah...smells like...victory.*

"Come in, Rachel," Nick called out. "Suzan, you keep an eye on Joe."

Rachel hurried in. She took the Taser from Nick. Setting the automatic on the kitchen table, Nick quickly duct taped Craig's crossed wrists behind his back, relieving the man of a 9mm Glock he had in his waistband. He then taped the man's ankles together and, bending them upward, Nick taped the wrists to the ankles. Lastly, Nick put tape over Craig's mouth.

"Put the Taser gun down right where you are, and come search this clown, Rachel. Empty everything out on the floor. I'm going to drag Joe in here before I get the kids."

"Nick," Rachel caught hold of Nick's wrist as he passed by, her lip trembling. "I —"

"It's not over yet, Wonder Woman. Hang on a little longer." Nick jogged into the living room.

"Grit your teeth, Joe. I'm dragging you into the kitchen." Nick applied duct tape to keep the black plastic bags attached to the oak chair. He tipped the chair backwards. With the plastic bags making the quick slide easier into the next room, Nick dragged Joe out of sight in the kitchen.

Nick went into the garage carefully, having picked up Joe's silenced automatic, and some scissors from the kitchen counter before going out. The front seat was empty. Nick breathed easier. He heard the kids squirming in the back seat as he opened the door. Garth, Kelly, and Jean stared back at him, wide-eyed with fear. Nick made a shushing sound, setting the automatic down under the van for the moment. Using the scissors, Nick cut away the plastic ties Craig had bound the kids with.

"Go easy pulling the tape off your mouths, kids," Nick urged.

The kids pulled the duct tape off with some difficulty and muffled cries. Jean was the first to get hers off. She dived into Nick's arms.

"I knew you'd come, Nick," Jean sobbed, tears streaming down from her eyes. "I told Kelly and Garth you wouldn't let them get us."

"You'd better believe it, kid." Nick hugged her back. "C'mon, I want you three to walk out of the garage and go in

139

through the front entrance. Go straight upstairs with your Moms, and stay there until I tell you to come down, okay?"

Kelly and Garth nodded silently at the near stranger. Jean twisted around in Nick's arms.

"I told you the Terminator would save us," Jean claimed happily as Nick put her on the cement. "C'mon, we have to go in the front."

Nick watched Jean help Kelly from the van, and then Garth. When they were around the corner, running to the front, Nick picked up the weapon from under the van. He went inside the house to relieve Rachel. Nick took the Taser from her. She ran into the living room to scoop Jean into her arms, crying in relief. Suzan sat with her arms around Kelly and Garth on the couch, holding them silently, rocking back and forth. When Jean saw Nick standing at the kitchen doorway, she whispered in Rachel's ear. Rachel set her down, nodding in agreement.

"We have to go upstairs for a while," Rachel told Suzan, motioning the woman up from the couch.

After Rachel, Suzan, and the kids were upstairs, Nick checked on Joe and Craig. When he was satisfied neither man could do anything, Nick put Joe's silenced automatic into his gym bag, along with the Taser gun. Nick then went out to trigger the garage door closed. He rooted around until he found bleach and paper towels. Nick placed them on the Dodge's passenger side front floorboard before moving to and opening the rear doors of the van. Craig and Joe had emptied the back, expecting to transport bodies.

In the kitchen, Nick found Craig beginning to roll around in pain, groaning under the duct tape. Nick flipped Craig over and dragged the man out by his legs, down over the three steps, and across the garage floor to the Dodge's rear doors. Nick managed to work Craig's upper body onto the van's cargo floor. After taking a couple deep breaths, Nick flipped the man's legs into the van.

"Damn Craig, you weigh a ton." Nick breathed heavily but smiled when he heard muffled noises. Craig's body rolled side to side.

Nick joined Joe in the kitchen. He helped Joe swallow two more OxyContin. Nick tore off four more strips of duct tape. From behind Joe, Nick cut the shoulder and waist tape.

"I'm going to slice the tape away from your wrists, Joe. Put your hands behind your back immediately. If you don't, I'll push you forward, right on your knees, understand?"

Joe nodded. Nick sliced the tape away from his wrists. Joe leaned forward, crossing his hands behind him. Nick put two of the strips around Joe's wrists. Nick sliced the tape off Joe's ankles and duct taped them together.

"Okay, Joe, time to go in the van. I'm going to ease you forward onto my shoulder and do a fireman's carry out to the van. Don't make this hard, or I'll throw you on the floor and drag you out by your knees."

Nick pulled the man over his shoulders, lifting with his legs to a standing crouch, and slowly trudged out to the Dodge van. He eased Joe inside the cargo area. Nick retrieved his duct tape and wrapped each man two full times around their chests and arms, immobilizing their upper bodies. Craig's eyes verged on insanity. Nick patted his cheek.

"You're lucky I don't have time to play with you, Craig."

Chapter Eleven
Clean Up

Nick closed the van doors. An hour later, Nick had bagged all the men's personal items, and cleaned the living room and kitchen meticulously. His gym bag was repacked. One black garbage bag was tied closed near the front door. He walked to the staircase.

"I'm sure you all are hungry and thirsty, so come on down," Nick called out.

When they were all sitting in Suzan's kitchen, drinking sodas, and eating chips Suzan had served, Nick waited until they were through before speaking.

"Rachel, Jean, and I have to leave. I have a couple more errands to run. Tomorrow's Sunday. Rachel and I would like to have you all over for the barbeque we missed today. Once we leave, this bad stuff will all be in the past. We'll talk tomorrow, Suzan. Talk to no one until then."

"I won't," Suzan promised.

"What if those guys come back?" Kelly asked.

"They won't be coming back," Jean told her with exasperation. "Are you stupid?"

"Jean!" Rachel rebuked her daughter. "You apologize right now!"

"Sorry," Jean sighed. "I didn't mean that, Kel."

"It's…it's okay."

"Can we go tomorrow, Mom?" Garth asked Suzan.

"Yes, I think we should," Suzan answered, exchanging glances with Nick and Rachel.

Nick stood up. "C'mon you two, it's almost dark. I'll go out through the garage and get the van out of Suzan's way. I packed an extra soda, and the Oxy, Suzan. I'll bring back what's left."

"Keep them."

Nick went out to the van with the garbage bag and his gym bag. He heard the loud grunts and groans from Craig as the man now thrashed around the cargo area. Nick opened the rear door. He used the stun gun on Craig until the man vibrated. Nick made a silencing motion with his finger to his lips for Joe, who was staring wide-eyed at him. Joe nodded his head energetically. With the trash and gym bags up front, Nick started the Dodge and backed it out to the street. He then put it in park and walked over to the Escalade driver's window. Rachel had already opened it.

"Follow me. When you see me turn off into the dirt, stay where you are by the street. I'll hike out to you. It won't take me long."

"Okay, Nick."

"Don't get caught speeding, Nick," Jean called out from the back.

"Oh...Jinx! Thanks a lot, Jean."

Nick waved and went to the Dodge. Half an hour later, Nick had driven the van out into the desert on the East side of Las Vegas until the wheels stuck. He took the garbage bag, gym bag, and cleaning supplies out of the van. Nick put on Nitrile gloves from his gym bag, and went to work with the bleach and paper towels, working around Craig and Joe in the back when he finished with the front. Satisfied the van was clean, Nick took out Carl Brewster's weapon, which he had already packed earlier, wiped it off, and set it aside. He repeated the process with both weapons taken from Craig and Joe. With his stun gun and Joe's weapon, Nick went in the back. After leaning the squirming Craig up into a kneeling position against the side of the van, he stunned Craig senseless. Nick crawled around behind Joe, helping him up so he

143

was seated, leaning into Nick. Nick cut Joe's hands free. Joe cried out as Nick forced his numb right hand up and wrapped it around Joe's gun.

"Ready, aim, fire," Nick joked, triggering the silenced auto with Joe's numb finger twice. "Nice shooting, Joe – right between the horns."

Nick propped Joe against the passenger rear seat after taking the weapon back. He used the old tape to bind Joe's hands behind his back once again. Nick went out and brought back Brewster's silenced auto. He cut all the tape off the deceased Craig, balling it up and putting it aside. Nick positioned himself behind Craig's corpse, fitting Brewster's weapon into Craig's hand and aiming it at Joe.

"Say cheese, Joe, c'mon big smile now." Nick fired two shots into Joe's head with Craig's finger. "Man, you two guys can really shoot."

Nick left Brewster's gun in Craig's right hand and added Craig's own Glock into his left hand, allowing them to rest on the dead man's legs. Nick repeated the process with Joe, wadding up all the tape, and makeshift knee bandages, leaving Joe to stare off into eternity with his weapon in hand. He closed and locked the van after a final cargo area wipe down. With his gym bag in one hand and the garbage bag in the other, Nick jogged at a slow pace out to the road, nearly two miles away. When he reached the Escalade, he walked in front where Rachel could see him. He heard the doors unlock. After dropping his bundles off in the rear, Nick hopped into the front passenger seat. He took deep breaths and enjoyed the air conditioned air. Jean was fast asleep on the back seat.

"You look like you could use a beer."

"Absolutely," Nick said, leaning back with a sigh.

* * *

144

"It doesn't get as cool in the desert at night as I thought it would." Rachel handed Nick an ice cold mug. "I'm surprised you're out here in the backyard."

"There's a breeze," he replied, hanging on to her hand for a moment after taking the mug. He kissed her palm. "I like looking at the stars out here. Jean never stirred when I carried her to the bedroom. She was really out."

Rachel sat down in the chair next to him, her own mug in hand. "We're not going out in the desert at dawn tomorrow are we?"

"No, I think we should stay in tomorrow and wait until we talk to Suzan. I'll check out Jim Benoit, then go through those bozos' personal effects for names and addresses. We need to keep watching the news for updates on the roadside intervention I pulled in Bakersfield. We'll stay apprised of any dead bodies being discovered around here too. I should be doing it now, but my batteries need charged."

"You were amazing today. How many times have you done something like that?"

"Counting today, once." He smiled over at Rachel. He could see her watching him, even though it was dark out on the patio. "I trained for hostage situations extensively when I was with Delta, but Delta doesn't conduct hostage negotiations in the manner I did today."

"Maybe they should."

"Oh, you don't go along with the 'we have to be better than them' line of thinking?" He shook his head in a disapproving manner. "By the way, you did exceptionally well today. That was one hard episode for an on-the-job training session."

"It taught me there really isn't anything I wouldn't do if I had to," Rachel admitted. "I'm not sure I'll make as good a psycho as you are, but I might make it as an assistant psycho. Besides, you're a fake psycho."

"A fake psycho?"

"A real psycho would have dumped Jean and me, and laughed while they were driving away. Now I have a real problem. If I ever left you, my daughter and dog would refuse to go with me...damn it."

Nick laughed. Deke sat up from where he lay between him and Rachel. She gave Deke a push on the side of his head before petting him.

"The goofy dog even knows when he's mentioned in a sentence, by name, or not. You really don't think we should make a run for it?"

"We need some time to pass between our first run for it and our next one," Nick explained. "I have to get you up to speed on weapons and defense techniques. Joe confirmed the word is out on where the safety deposit box is. I'm thinking we're going to need a hell of a distraction. I'm working on a simplistic plan where we scout the bank for the usual suspects. We then get very familiar with what they look like and how they operate. They will be expecting helpless Rachel Hunter to saunter into the bank and give them whatever they want. What I want them to get is a Rachel Hunter ready to take out anyone we've deemed a potential bad guy, with me as back up."

"Do you really think I can be that Rachel Hunter?"

"Absolutely," he patted her hand. "If you're not, I'll have a kid and dog to raise."

It was Rachel's turn to laugh.

"Okay, okay, but I don't think a gun battle in broad daylight in Sarasota, Florida would further our agenda," she commented after thinking about what he proposed.

"No gun battles in the streets, Rachel," he assured her. "I want you to hustle into the bank from a running car when we're set, get your business done, and hustle out. They won't have time to grab you going in. Coming out, you will know the bad guys or gals on sight. When they approach, you pepper spray the crap out of them, and stun gun them with no hesitation. Jump in the waiting car and away you go. I'll be on a rooftop with a clear view of the scene. Any heavy action, I'll handle. Any vehicles pulling out after you, same deal. Hopefully, we'll know all the bad guys' vehicles. I'll disable them before you hit the bank. Remember, you're in the right. If they have someone we didn't count on in the bank, stun them and call security. Don't use the spray inside."

"Oh this sounds really simplistic."

"The fun part starts when we get the flash drives and they launch an all-out manhunt for our asses in a spiraling search from ground zero out across the states. They'll be desperate. The kid gloves will be off. That's where our friends Grace and Tim come in. We need to pass off the drives to someone not on the payroll of this syndicate, who can get them high up the ladder. We'll have copies of the drives, because they won't want to deal with some of the folks who'll just need killin'."

"This will be a test of Grace and Tim too... won't it?"

"I'm afraid so. There's so much money loose on this deal, we can't afford to trust anyone. I'd also hate to get those two killed."

"They were the only reason I'm not stark raving mad. Doing a disappearing act is not as much fun as it sounds. I do not want to keep on the run with my daughter for the rest of our lives. I sure envisioned a different kind of day after our...ah —"

"Interlude?" Nick finished for her. "If I told you how many times our interlude flashed into my mind, even while we were all in danger, you'd probably promote me back to full psycho."

"You Satyr!" Rachel leaped up out of the lounge chair, pointing at him. "I'd forgotten all about when Joe made us strip. You were popping right out of your underwear."

147

"What can I say?" He shrugged. "Sometimes my priorities get a bit skewed at inappropriate moments. While you're up, Sister Mary Rachel, get me another."

Rachel giggled. She grabbed Nick's proffered mug on her way inside. When she returned, she wore only a black thong. She handed him the mug over his shoulder. When he glanced back, he nearly ended up wearing the beer.

"I have a kink in my neck. Would you mind working it out for me like you did the other day?" Rachel sipped from her mug while turning the chair she had been sitting in around in front of Nick. She sat down on it with her backside perched out over the edge, leaning with her chin over the chair back."

Nick set the now half-empty mug down near Deke, who lapped up the remainder without hesitation. Leaning forward, Nick splayed out the fingers of each hand near Rachel's temples and his thumbs at the base of her skull. By rotating his thumbs into the jumble of nerves, he had her groaning audibly in under a minute. Slowly, he worked every inch of her spine, his thumbs methodically moving over and against her spinal column, while his fingers probed the shoulder area before trailing down with feathery caresses in tandem with his thumbs. With more freedom than the day before, he massaged the base of her spine with powerful upward pressure while gripping his fingers into her hip area. Rachel cried out, shuddering as she staggered forward, chair in hands, out of Nick's grip. She spun around, breathing heavily, having tossed the chair aside.

"No fair," she whispered, grabbing his hand and pulling at him. "Let's go."

"I need a shower."

"Later!"

* * *

148

"How come you get up so early, Nick?" Jean asked, rubbing her eyes at the entryway into the kitchen, dressed in pajamas, robe, and slippers.

"About five to six hours is about all the sleep I care to have." Nick looked up from his notebook computer, where the character Diego had just killed the hierarchy of a gang in East Los Angeles with a car bomb. "How are you feeling this morning, Danger Girl? You had a rough time yesterday."

"Danger Girl," Jean repeated, giggling as she walked over to pet the ever-present Deke, who rolled over for a belly rub. "I'm okay. That guy didn't beat us up or anything. He told us to stay quiet or he would beat us up. I guess he'll be pretty quiet himself now, huh?"

"That's a very grim way of speaking, DG." Nick saved his file and closed the notebook.

"Oh, right, we're not supposed to speak ill of the dead." Jean grinned up at Nick, who immediately dropped his head into his hands.

"Keep it up, keep it up." Nick covered his face in feigned exasperation. "It won't be funny when you say things like that at the worst possible moment by mistake."

"Okay." Jean sighed, plunking down in the seat next to him. "I'll be more careful. Hey, do you know how to make pancakes?"

"Absolutely." He moved to the counter nearest the stove. He took pancake mix out of the cupboard along with a four cup mixing bowl. After collecting an egg and milk from the refrigerator, he gestured Jean over. "C'mon, I'll show you how to do it, too, Danger. Do you like bacon with your pancakes?"

"Oh, yeah."

* * *

Rachel woke smelling the aroma of bacon drifting up through the house, one of the most tantalizing odors in the world. She sat up groggily, glad Nick had bullied her into her own bedroom after they had showered together. The thought of explaining to Jean a relationship change involving her suddenly sleeping in Nick's bed did not appeal to her. The alarm clock on her nightstand read eight-thirty. She wondered idly how long her two cohorts had been up. After donning her robe, she made a quick trip to the bathroom before going downstairs. She could hear laughter coming from the kitchen. Pausing at the kitchen entryway, she saw Deke doing somersaults to get small pieces of bacon thrown to him. Nick noticed her, and gave her a quick salute.

"You're just in time for breakfast." He walked over to the oven and took the leftover pancakes and bacon out. "I saved you a plate all warmed up. Good thing you came down when you did. Deke is getting demanding."

"Nick taught me how to make pancakes, Mom," Jean told her. "He calls me Danger Girl, and Danger for short. I like it."

"Wonderful." Rachel grimaced as she sat down and took the plate from Nick, along with a napkin containing silverware. "You could have slept in at least until eight, Nick."

"Diego waits for no one," he stated solemnly, while placing a mug in front of her. "How'd you sleep?"

"Great. I don't think I even moved. Did you already check the news?"

"There's nothing on the internet. The local news starts at nine. I've been meaning to bring this up, but you two trouble magnets keep cramming our days full of adventure. I think it would be a good idea to dye your hair darker."

"Mom already bought the dye at the store."

"We should have done it in Monterrey."

"Then they would have known." Nick pushed Deke away from the table. "This way, maybe we get a little extra time."

"These are really good," Rachel pointed at her pancakes. "Did —"

The doorbell rang, and Deke ran to the door. Nick made a calming gesture.

"Easy…easy…not everyone in this town is out to get us."

* * *

Nick walked to the entrance and looked through the security eyelet. Two police officers stood on the front stoop. Nick looked them over carefully, from their shoes to how they wore their belts and badges. As the taller one reached for the doorbell again, Nick opened it, kneeling down to quiet the growling Deke.

"Good morning," Nick greeted them.

"I'm Officer Mendez, and this is my partner, Officer Carrington. Are you Roscoe Weatherby?"

"Yes?" He assumed a questioning look and stood up.

"May we come in? We have some questions for you about a missing person's case."

"Sure," Nick said, opening the screen door, as Rachel and Jean came out of the kitchen. Jean beckoned to Deke and the dog went to her reluctantly. "This is my wife Rachel and daughter Jean."

Some of the tenseness left the police officers' faces at the appearance of Rachel and Jean. Rachel clasped Nick's arm. She leaned into him with a natural grace.

"What's this about, hon?"

151

"Something about a missing person," he answered, gesturing toward the kitchen. "Would either of you like some coffee? We were having breakfast."

"Sure." The dark-skinned Carrington nodded with a smile. "I'll have a cup if it isn't too much trouble."

"Thank you," Mendez added, following Nick, Rachel, Jean, and Deke into the kitchen.

Mendez and Carrington sat down at the kitchen table next to each other, opposite Rachel and Jean, while Nick poured two mugs of coffee. After placing the mugs in front of the officers, he set milk, sugar bowl, spoons, and napkins down too. He sat next to Rachel. Mendez took a picture out of his right breast pocket, setting the picture down in front of Nick. It was a picture of Carl Brewster with a fishing pole in hand, holding out a stringer with two trout.

"Have you seen this man?"

"The day before yesterday," Nick replied, picking up the picture for a closer look and then handing it to Rachel. "His name was Carl something…"

"Brewster," Rachel finished on cue.

"That's it," Nick agreed. "He said he worked security for a neighbor of ours we met over at the Excalibur. Apparently, when our neighbor's husband goes out of town on business, Brewster watches over the mom, and the two kids."

"Do you know the neighbor's name?" Carrington glanced down at a notepad he had in hand.

"Benoit," Nick answered. "We got together with Suzan Benoit and her kids. What're the kids' names, Jean?"

"Kelly and Garth," Jean put in, smiling with enthusiasm, knowing she was playing a part in a very adult game.

"Do you remember what car Mr. Brewster was driving?" Mendez questioned in a more relaxed tone.

152

"I only glanced at it when he left, but I think it was a Toyota of some kind...silver colored. Is Brewster the one you're looking for?"

"The woman he's living with reported him missing when he didn't come home. She said he left early Friday afternoon, saying he needed to check out something. Your address was on his day planner," Mendez explained. "Did he say where he was going after leaving you?"

"He did say something about being late for a meeting with two associates, named Joe and Craig. Suzan didn't say anything about him when we were over at the Benoit house yesterday. They're coming over for a barbeque today. Should I ask her to call you?"

"No, we've been over to see Ms. Benoit already." Carrington put away his notebook, and handed Nick a business card. "She told us she hadn't seen Brewster since Friday. We found his Toyota already, but no sign of Brewster. Thanks for your cooperation, folks. If you remember anything else, please call us."

"Sorry to have bothered you on a Sunday like this," Mendez added, as the two police officers stood up.

"No problem." Nick escorted them to the door.

"Will you be leaving us soon, Mr. Weatherby? Ms. Benoit said you stay in Las Vegas for short periods of time."

"I'll be here for another two weeks. I have business back East after that, but you can reach me —"

"Ms. Benoit gave us the number to reach you from your business card," Carrington finished for him. "We'll call if we think of anything else."

"Goodbye, Mr. Weatherby," Mendez added as the two walked out past Nick.

"Goodbye." Nick watched them walk out to their squad car with the familiar buzz he inadvertently experienced when details

153

flowed together around him to his advantage. *Now if my Roscoe ID holds up, we may last through our two-week cushion.*

"Everything okay, Nick?" Rachel joined Nick at the entrance with Jean and Deke.

"Everything's fine for now. Nice going in there, both of you. The barbeque should be interesting later."

Chapter Twelve
Information Gathering

Rachel and Jean walked into the living room where Nick watched the news. Both had towels around their necks.

"Hey, Nick, how do we look?" Jean asked.

He looked up from the television screen, doing a double take at the obvious change. Rachel and Jean had both dyed their hair a dark brown, with some lighter brown highlights.

"You two look totally different," he stated approvingly. "I think brunette hair coloring would have made a less natural-appearing change. If we can pick up some colored contact lenses for you, Rachel, I think we'll be in good shape. Do you wear contacts, by the way?"

"No, but any one of those eyeglass chains will have colored contacts. I was hoping you wouldn't want us to cut our hair."

"You can put it up," he suggested. "When we go out, some kind of hat in addition to the hair color change wouldn't be a bad idea. Those ball caps I gave you to wear out in the desert would be fine."

"What's up in the news?" Rachel moved behind Nick's seat, while Jean sat on the arm of his chair. "Is that who I think it is?"

Nick returned his attention to the recovering California Highway Patrol officer going over Nick's intervention in Bakersfield from his hospital bed. He had been watching the news cast with growing anxiety. "Yeah, he caught more of a look at the Chevy than I thought. Lucky us, he owns a Chevy Malibu as a personal car. With the half-baked statements from some of the on-lookers who hung around, the cops know the make, model, and color."

"He just wants to thank you," Jean said, listening to the heartfelt appreciation the officer expressed, his face swollen and discolored.

"He does." Nick grinned over at Jean. "You should have heard the poor victim's relatives. They want to sue. They want me drawn and quartered. How dare I take a hand in a private altercation when I knew nothing of the victim's side? My help was a hideous overreaction. The victim nearly beat the cop to death because he's a misunderstood youth and has unresolved issues with police authority. Blah...blah...blah...boo hoo."

Both Rachel and Jean were laughing by the time he reached the end of his soliloquy.

"Since we have the Cad, are we still okay?"

"I don't know. Everyone knows we were headed East. It will point people in our direction. We've already had a taste of how thoroughly people check out rumors lately." Nick laughed suddenly, shaking his head. "On the other hand, no one who knew me would ever consider I'd stop to help a cop at the risk of betraying where I was headed."

"You're a little sick, Nick," Jean rhymed with a giggle for emphasis.

"Yes I am, Danger. I'm also part psychic as well as psycho. I believe there's more to Suzan and her husband than meets the eye. Her recognizing you and your mom was no coincidence. I'm hoping her run-in with death yesterday steered her in our direction. The cops visiting us this morning gave me hope she's come to a decision."

"Her two kids aren't part of this game, Nick. You don't –"

"I'm not going to harm Suzan, Rachel," he stopped her, waving his hand with some degree of impatience and winking at Jean. "Let's not go any further with this for now. Loose ends will either fall in place for us...or not. We'll know soon enough."

"You're too much of a fatalist," Rachel retorted.

156

"Or not enough of one," he argued.

"Are you leaning toward cutting our stay short?"

"Not unless Suzan says something I don't want to hear. There's nothing on the news about Brewster and his buddies yet. No news is good news on that front."

"Would it be okay if Jean and I go shopping?"

"What, bathing suits aren't enough for you two? Oh, all right," he joked. "I put the stun gun and pepper spray back in the Cad glove compartment. Put them in your purse within easy reach wherever you go. Buy a few of those throwaway cell-phones too. I don't want you using your cell-phone for anything."

"About the buying part, we need money."

"There goes the college fund, Danger," Nick complained, as he stood up. "I'll go pick some off the tree. Be right back."

"I guess you'll be writing?" Rachel asked, bumping Jean, who had immediately laughed at Nick's money references.

"Yes," Nick answered, on his way upstairs. "I think I'll finally give Diego a steady love interest, who turns his life upside down, and bleeds him dry."

* * *

"Mom sent me up," Jean announced from Nick's open bedroom doorway, fighting off Deke. "She says it's almost five, so Suzan, Kelly and Garth will be here soon. You've been writing all day. Is it really that much fun?"

Nick saved his file, and closed up the notebook computer. He pushed away from his desk and stretched before joining Jean and Deke at the doorway.

"Writing is an escape to a different world where I make things happen the way I want them to."

157

"Cool." Jean led him toward the stairs. "You're like king of the world."

"Exactly. If something bothers me in real life that I can't do anything about, I use my fantasy world to make everything work out the way I want it to."

"Maybe I can be a writer. How did you get started? Did you write stuff when you were my age?" Jean looked back at him questioningly as they went down the stairs, with Deke leaping the last few steps.

"No, not for quite a while, but I read a lot. Reading gave me an idea of what kind of fiction I liked to read. I loved action/adventure type fiction, so when I started writing, I wrote what I liked reading."

"Mom says you write novels about an assassin." Jean turned at the bottom of the stairs to face him with a smile forming. "I thought you said you write fiction."

"You're beginning to annoy me, Danger."

Jean giggled. She ran off to the kitchen with Nick following her.

Now I'm getting tagged by eight year olds.

"We're all set, Nick," Rachel told him as he walked in the kitchen. "Corn is on the boil. The baked potatoes are in the microwave, and I've coated the steaks with barbeque sauce. Did you want to wait to start the coals?"

"No, I'll do it now," he said, making pantomime gestures at Jean of him choking her.

"Why are you threatening by daughter, you brute?"

"She started it."

"Did not."

"Did too."

158

"Nick, go start the coals. You should be ashamed of yourself."

"Yeah Nick," Jean added, joining Rachel near the stove with folded arms.

"I..." Nick began. Deke streaked out just as the doorbell interrupted Nick's intended rejoinder. He shook a finger comically at Rachel on his way out of the kitchen. "This isn't over."

At the door, Nick checked through the security eyelet. He opened the door, gesturing Suzan and her kids inside with a smile while keeping an arm around the excited Deke.

"Hi, Ross," Suzan said.

"C'mon in. I'm starting the coals now. This is Deke. He likes everybody."

"Hey, my mom bought me some new card games," Jean chimed in as she hurried over to greet Kelly and Garth. "We can play cards until dinner, and then watch movies if you want."

"Sure." Garth crouched down to pet Deke. "We don't play many card games."

"Can we play in your room?" Kelly looked up at Nick apprehensively.

"Absolutely," Jean replied, parroting Nick, and giving him a little wave. "We'll be upstairs, Dad."

"I'll call you when we're ready to eat," Nick agreed.

"Okay," Jean acknowledged. She led Kelly and Garth toward the stairs.

"Why don't you go on in the kitchen, Suzan? Rachel's already there. I'll start the coals and join you both in a couple minutes," Nick suggested, patting his leg to get Deke to follow him.

"Thank you."

* * *

Suzan entered the kitchen, waving at Rachel. "I like your outfit. I see you and Jean did a dual hair coloring. The eye color change is a nice touch too."

"We were overdue for the color change." Rachel gestured at her black short shorts, and pink sleeveless top. "Jean and I went shopping for clothes this morning. How are you holding up?"

"I was hoping you and Ross could tell me that," Suzan answered, sitting down at the table. "How are we all doing?"

"I better let Ross handle that question. How about a drink? I bought some Berringer White Zin."

"Are you having some?"

"Sure, I've only been waiting for you." Rachel went to the refrigerator for the already-opened wine, which she poured some into two wine glasses on the counter. Rachel set a glass in front of Suzan and sat down opposite her.

Nick walked into the kitchen, having left Deke out back. He sat down next to Rachel with his own beverage. Suzan took a gulp of wine nervously.

"Who are you really, Ross? I know you're no US Marshall."

"I was asked to take in Rachel and Jean for a short time by the US Marshalls in charge of her case. We need to stay here for a couple weeks before moving on."

"What...what you did yesterday...I know you can't be a cop. You're a stone-cold-killer," Suzan blurted out, taking another hit of her wine.

"I'm here to protect Rachel and Jean. Let's leave it at that."

"You recognized us at the Excalibur, didn't you, Suzan?"

Suzan nodded. "I tried to keep the kids from hanging around with Jean, but Brewster saw you. He wasn't there to watch out for me and the kids. He was there to keep an eye on us for my husband's employers. My husband wants out, but he's in too deep, and knows too much. Jim's invaluable to them right now. When they don't need him anymore, we're afraid he'll end up like your husband, Rick. Some Tanus employees told Jim what happened to Rick. They gave him a family picture of you, Rick, and your daughter. Everyone in the organization was to be on the lookout for you and Jean."

"Brewster showed it to us." Rachel saw Nick nod his head for her to go on. "You and Jim weren't contemplating blackmailing anyone, were you?"

"Hell no! We didn't know why they killed your husband. Jim figured they gave him the picture as a warning not to try and leave the organization. Look...I have to ask this...is...is Brewster...you know...coming back? I heard you tell Joe you paid Brewster off."

"We didn't pay him off. He's in much the same condition as Joe and Craig. Do you know if Brewster had to check in with anyone periodically?"

"He probably did. You're worried they'll send someone else, aren't you?"

"Would they call you up when they didn't hear from him?"

"It's never happened before. Carl's been watching us for the last six months."

"I think you should call your husband and tell him to get in touch with Carl's real employers," Nick suggested. "Jim should be the one to tell them you haven't seen Carl for a few days, which you thought was unusual."

"That's a good idea." Suzan considered Nick's suggestion. "Is there any way you can help Jim and I get free of Tanus Import/Export? Yesterday convinced me they don't need a reason to kill us. It's only a matter of time. They keep ramping up their

161

demands on Jim. He thinks they'll use him as a fall guy if the feds bust Tanus."

"Rick was blackmailing Tanus because of me," Rachel admitted. "They tortured and killed him to find out where he had taken the flash drives he'd made of their operations."

"Oh shit…" Suzan whispered. "What happened to put you on the run? Weren't you in Witness Protection?"

"There's a leak in the program and they found out where we were."

"If Rachel and I recover the flash drives, do you think Jim could decipher the information for us?"

"Are you nuts? They'll kill us for sure then. You just said the Witness Protection Program has been compromised."

"We believe those flash drives will bring down Tanus Import/Export," Nick explained, hoping they hadn't already lost any chance to recruit her. "They would be your family's ticket out, because the government will need someone to testify as to the validity of what's on the drives. The organization has already recovered from Hayden Tanus's death. US Marshalls are working to close the leak right now."

"I'll have to talk with my husband." Suzan finished her wine. Rachel refilled Suzan's glass, and then her own. "I know better than to call him with something like that. He'll be home in another three days."

"You should call about Brewster though," Nick reminded her. "I don't want any suspicion on you. I went over his buddies' stuff. I didn't find anything tying them in with Tanus Import/Export, so I believe they were going to do just what Joe told me: sell the drives to the highest bidder. If you do get assigned a new guy, would you let me know?"

"I owe you our lives. I'll tell you if they send a new guy. Do you think it would be possible they'd trust me because I told them Carl was missing?"

"As you already perceived, they're using you and the kids to keep Jim in line."

"I probably should lay off the wine."

"I'll put the steaks on." Nick walked over to the counter for the steaks.

"I'll try to convince Jim to help you."

"Thank you. I think it's your only way out."

* * *

"Remember what we talked about," Nick instructed, crouching next to Rachel. "Only the first pad of your finger touches the trigger. If you wrap the finger, you'll jerk the shot. Hold the weapon firm, but don't clutch it like a life buoy in the Arctic Ocean. Last call, Danger, what do you have for readings?"

"No wind, no heat wave, seventy-eight degrees," Jean called out, spotting for her mom's shot. "You have a go, Mom."

Nick watched Rachel's finger squeeze the trigger. He shifted his attention to the cast iron targets he had placed at two hundred meters. The weapon fired and a moment later the plate clanged.

"Yes!" Jean pumped her fist. "Nice shot, Mom."

"It's not even in the same ballpark as the shots Nick makes."

Nick nodded approvingly as Rachel sat up, excited and tingling all over from having hit the target her first time.

"Over two football fields," Nick corrected her. "I'd say you did very well. Let's not get into comparisons. I've shot thousands of rounds. You shot once. How was the recoil?"

"Not bad with this recoil pad you gave me." Rachel touched the shooter's vest Nick had helped her put on.

163

"Can I try it, Nick?" Jean asked.

"I don't think so, Danger. I brought along a twenty-two caliber rifle with a hunter's load. Without wind, I'm betting you can hit the same target with it. It will actually take more skill, because although the telescopic sight I put on it is accurate to five hundred meters, the .22 hunting slug doesn't always act predictably beyond a hundred and fifty yards. Spot the rest of this clip for your mom, and then we'll work on your skills - if it's okay with her."

Rachel shrugged. "I'm going to hell anyway."

"Debatably, the greatest sharpshooter of all time was Annie Oakley," Nick told Jean. "Annie Oakley was only about five feet tall. She was an expert with rifle, pistol, or shotgun. Annie learned to shoot at age eight with her Dad's old .40 caliber cap and ball rifle. My .50 caliber sniper rifle is a baby's toy next to that old Kentucky rifle."

Jean's eyes and mouth were getting wider as she reacted to Annie Oakley's legend the way Nick figured she would.

"Annie outshot every sharpshooter in Europe when she toured with the Buffalo Bill Troupe. More importantly, she brought home food for the table and to trade when she was just a girl. So, Danger, I doubt your Mom will be going to hell because you shot a rifle at age eight. It's been done before."

"I'm only seven," Jean immediately qualified her age. "I'll be starting before Annie Oakley did."

"Well, your mom's a natural, so it probably runs in the family. Maybe you two will get so good, we'll go on tour as the Terminators."

"You really are sick, Nick," Rachel noted as Jean laughed. "Spot me for three in a row Jean and mix up the order. Let's get this Wild West Show on the road."

When Rachel turned to the sniper rifle, Deke stuck his nose up the back of her blouse, launching Rachel straight up in the air, much to Nick and Jean's amusement. Rachel started looking around on the ground and amongst the packs.

"What are you looking for?" Nick asked finally.

"A ball or something this damn dog will chase out in the sand. I think it's time for some live practice."

"Don't listen to your wicked stepmother, Deke." Nick covered the dog's ears.

"Quit foolin' around, Mom. Get shooting. I don't want to miss my turn."

"I'm warning you, Deke." Rachel pointed at the dog, who 'gruffed' and pulled on her pant leg. "Some folks think dog meat is a delicacy."

* * *

An hour later, Nick and Jean were packing the gear. Rachel had taken Deke with her for a walk to get away from the noise an un-silenced twenty-two makes. When they were putting their packs on, Rachel led Deke over the small bluff toward them.

"How'd she do?"

"She hit nearly every time."

"I'm going to be a sniper when I grow up," Jean announced. She giggled at Rachel's stunned expression. "I knew that would push your button."

"I blame you for this, Mr. Oakley." Rachel turned on Nick, who had been laughing, but now was retreating with hands up in surrender fashion.

Nick changed the subject. "It's getting hot. Let's go see if I can rent our Excalibur Cabana." He started hiking toward where they had left the Escalade. "We'll see if Suzan and her kids want to meet us there. If you wear your ball cap, and look inconspicuous enough, maybe I'll let you toss in a few quarters at the slot machines, Wonder."

"I'm not liking these nicknames," Rachel muttered, falling in behind Nick, with Jean and Deke bringing up the rear.

"You could be Nikita," Nick suggested, stopping to glance back at Rachel.

"Who?" Rachel thought he looked unusually surprised as she and Jean reacted without recognition to the name.

"Oh, come on, you never saw the 'La Femme Nikita' television show?"

Rachel blushed, remembering, while Jean continued to look mystified. Deke began jumping around as if he recognized the name.

"La Femme Nikita was a TV program about a secret organization, where Nikita killed people for some pseudo government organization," Rachel explained.

"That is so cool!" Jean exclaimed. "I like it way better than Wonder Woman. Nick and Nikita, assassins for hire. I like it."

Nick and Rachel exchanged glances. Nick started walking again, throwing his hands in the air. "Okay, I'm going to hell. I'm doomed."

Rachel mouthed 'you are the one', and high-fived Jean behind Nick's back. Nick looked around, sensing something. Rachel and Jean were looking at the ground as they followed him. Rachel peeked up in time to see him shake his head and continue on.

"I think I've been served," he called out over his shoulder.

Chapter Thirteen
Error In Judgment

"Thanks for inviting us." Suzan toasted Nick and Rachel with her iced tea glass. "I didn't think you two would want to socialize with me."

The three were relaxing inside the cabana Nick had rented again at the Excalibur while watching the kids swim. Nick made sure Jean, Kelly, and Garth had pool floats, dive batons, and dive masks to keep them entertained.

"We needed to talk, and the kids like the pool. Did you contact your husband about Brewster?"

"Yes, last night. Jim said he'd inform his bosses. He told me he's still planning on being home Thursday. I'll explain your idea then. Have you talked to your Marshall contacts?"

"Not yet," Nick admitted. "I need to sell them on what I have in mind when I call. I don't quite have the sales pitch down. It has nothing to do with what we talked about. They will be enthusiastic about the flash drives and a corroborating witness. I need them to turn their heads as to how we acquire the drives. Have you noticed anyone hanging around you don't recognize, or a car on your street you haven't seen before?"

"No, and I've been watching."

"Is this freaking you out?" Rachel asked.

"Of course, but nothing could be worse than watching my kids dragged away. How long have you been in hiding, Rachel?"

"Over a year."

"Jesus! And now you're on the run."

"I had it coming. Jean didn't though. I'll do anything to make things normal for her again."

Nick saw three young guys and two girls, all in their late teens, pointing at the kids. The group had left the Excalibur a moment before, wearing swim gear and carrying towels. The tall dark-haired young man in the lead said something to the others and they all laughed. He headed directly for the kids. Nick stood up. *Great, another bunch of yuppie larvae figuring they can do anything they want.*

"What's wrong?" Rachel peered around Nick. "They're just kids."

"That's what I'm hoping." Nick looked around for some Excalibur employees. It being Monday, there was a minimum of staff on duty and none near the pool.

"No!" Jean shouted, as the dark haired teen grabbed the end of Jean's pool float.

"Get away from the little girl, Dexter," Nick warned him, walking to the pool edge cattycorner from the group. "Don't make me tell you twice."

"Oh crap," Rachel murmured under her breath, as the group started gesturing and mouthing off at Nick. Rachel picked up her purse.

"Swim over here kids," Nick told Jean, Kelly, and Garth, ignoring the insults and threats.

Nick watched one of the teenage girls doing her best to talk the others into walking to the other pool, but the dark haired pack leader had other ideas. *Walk away, kid.*

"Don't, Glenn. Let's go to the other pool!" The teen peacemaker tried reasoning with the leader to no avail. He walked purposely around the pool toward Nick with the others following. Glenn's companions looked at Nick uneasily as they drew closer. They were looking for fear, and not seeing it.

"We want the pool floats, Pop. Your kids have been hogging them long enough."

"They don't belong to the Excalibur, Dexter. They belong to me." Nick put up a warning hand when he saw that Glenn was planning on walking up to get in his face. "That's close enough, Dex."

Glenn stopped, the smirk on his face made Nick forget why he didn't want to end up in a Las Vegas jail.

"What makes you think we won't stomp your sorry old ass into the cement?" Glenn laughed.

Nick smiled when he heard a familiar crackling arc. The teens jumped back in surprise as Rachel joined Nick with the stun gun from her purse.

"Run along kids and I won't have to zap anyone," Rachel urged.

"Good thing you have the old lady along for protection." Glenn spat on the cement between them as he backed away with his friends.

"Nikita handles all my light work, punk."

"That was tight, Mom," Jean said as the teenagers walked away toward the other pool after a few parting words.

"I hope you didn't mind my ad lib, Nick," Rachel whispered, as Suzan motioned her kids out of the pool.

"Not at all." Nick shook his head. "It was one of those escalating tragic sequences. You pulled the plug on it. Nice."

"I think we've had enough excitement for today." Suzan held up one of the throw away cell-phones Nick had Rachel buy. "I'll call you if anything comes up. Thanks for the phone."

"No problem." Nick gave Kelly and Garth a little wave. "If Jean dreams up any adventures we think you two will be interested in, we'll give you a call."

"I think I'm getting my psycho on," Rachel remarked as Suzan and her kids walked away. "I wanted to toast that Glenn kid."

"Oh lady, when you stop being afraid, and start contemplating violence, it's very habit forming." Nick put his arm around Rachel's shoulders. "Shall we go home and call the US Marshalls? I wonder what our canine interior decorator has been up to while we've been gone?"

"I left Deke a soup bone so big he'll still be working on it when he's too old to chew."

* * *

"You don't call. You don't write..." Grace droned on. "Have we offended you in some way, my little stud muffin?"

"Am I on the FBI's most wanted list next to the Al-Qaeda hierarchy?"

"Not yet, but there are people working on that very scenario. How are Rachel and Jean?"

"Real good so far, and we have a plan. It involves an item unknown to you before: a safety deposit box with flash drives Rachel talked her husband into making from Tanus Import/Export. The real story is Rick was caught and tortured by Tanus because Rachel had a little get rich quick scheme. The extra heat is because of those drives."

"Oh...my...God..." Grace uttered in a hushed voice. "A ton of money's being dropped on this problem, isn't it?"

"It sure is. Have you and Tim decided on whether to move on with your lives, or step up?"

"I should have shot you that night at the restaurant, you smartass weasel."

"Time is running short," Nick said, watching the indicator on his phone, smiling to himself as he pictured Grace fuming at the other end of the line. "Any more additions I'll have to save for my memoirs if you're not interested."

"Make it good, because you're very close to starring on America's Most Wanted."

"We lucked into a corroborating witness who wants out of the Tanus operation. The wife believes her husband can decipher what's on the flash drives. They want protection. I'm supposed to find out whether the US Marshalls can provide any."

"Holy Guacamole, cowboy! You stepped in it this time, didn't you?"

"It's all yours, Grace, if you want it. Is the DOJ sealed yet?"

"They caught a deputy director and one of the bureau chiefs, all thanks to the tail you picked up on the way to Monterrey. The weird ass breaks in procedure, allowing a sniper suspect to have an accident in custody, cemented the deal. Tim and I were on the hot seat for a short period of time. We've been put in charge now."

"Sweet," Nick commented. "Here's the plan then. Rachel and I will get the drives. We'll get our witness to make sure of what's on them. Then we'll hand the drives and the witness over to the US Marshalls."

"Instead, we meet up with you and Rachel, retrieve the drives, and take you all into federal custody," Grace countered.

"No offense, Frumpy, but you heard the plan, and you ain't in it until I say you're in it. Time's up. I'll call in one hour."

"Was she disappointed in me?" Rachel asked anxiously as they sat together out on the patio with Deke, having already put Jean to bed.

Nick laughed. "I think you have more pressing problems than whether Grace has a lower opinion of you or not. Hey, did you inhale that beer?"

"I was nervous."

Nick watched Rachel shift in her lounge chair, crossing her legs. He reached over to run his hand along her thigh. "You don't look nervous. You look edible."

* * *

Rachel slapped Nick's hand with a gasp of false indignation. A shiver streaked from the balls of her feet to the nape of her neck. Thoughts of US Marshalls and flash drives were fading faster than ice cream over a campfire. She had showered, joining him on the patio in only her blouse and shorts. Nick took her right hand in his left, turning it palm up. He used only the whisper of contact with his fingertips down Rachel's bare arm and over her palm to the very tips of her fingers. He rotated the feather soft touch around and up her arm again. She leaned her head back with a moan, gripping the opposite arm of her chair with the other hand.

Her arm was on fire. The skin without Nick's attention felt cold and bleak, awaiting the returning warmth of his fingertips. Nick undid her blouse, and she shrugged it off impatiently. Rachel lifted up from the lounger as Nick gripped the waistband of her shorts. He pulled them from her smoothly. Moving off his lounger, he settled onto the edge of hers, and began his fingertip message with both hands. Down from her cheeks, over shoulders, breasts, ribcage - ever so slowly - hips, thighs, ankles, feet, toes, and up again. Rachel tried to relax. She tried to absorb his soothing touch, but her breathing quickened, her blood raced, and her body tensed. Nick returned his attention finally to her palms and wrists, tracing gentle circles. She crumpled into the lounger, his fingertips on her palms calming the tingling firestorm.

"You drive me nuts," she whispered.

"Why's that? You mean the massage? I figured I'd relax you. Didn't you like it?" He continued the circular stroking of her palms.

172

"It's incredible, but why not just –"

"I haven't been with a woman I liked in a long time… maybe ever."

She sat up into his arms, their faces inches apart.

"You mean that?"

"Absolutely."

Rachel's lips touched Nick's as lightly as his fingertips had explored her body. Neither moved to end the exquisite caress or probe more deeply. Her breasts brushed against his bare chest, causing his fingers to encircle and tighten on her wrists. She felt him tense everywhere except at the sensuous contact with her mouth. It was at this very moment Deke decided to make his presence known in the form of a cold wet nose on Rachel's back. She lurched against Nick with a squeal of protest, arching against him as Deke poked and sniffed.

"Do somethingggggggggg!" Rachel writhed more deeply into Nick.

* * *

Nick reached around her with his left hand, grabbing Deke's nose, and shaking it playfully as Rachel settled down.

"Deke, your timing could be better, pal." Nick peered around Rachel, eyeballing the dog reproachfully as Deke sat and gave him a paw.

"Tell me you are not shaking that beast's paw," Rachel said through clenched teeth, clinging to Nick with her head against his right shoulder. He realized she could feel the movement of his arm at her side.

"You told me I can't hurt him."

She huffed. "I changed my mind."

173

"Perhaps we should go up to my room and start over."

"No, I'm not in the mood."

"Okay," Nick sighed, pushing up and away from Rachel. "I was going to do your back next."

She sprung up from the lounge chair and into his arms. "What'll we do with the hellhound?"

"Give him a beer," Nick whispered, trailing kisses along her neck, evoking a protesting shudder and moan. "Deke can drink it in Jean's room."

"You have to call Grace back," Rachel reminded him reluctantly, at the same time moving side to side gently.

"Shit!" He thumped his forehead on her shoulder.

"I'll go get Deke settled in Jean's room. You call Grace. I'll meet you in your room."

"You better not be asleep when I get there."

"Yeah, right." She laughed. "C'mon Deke, let's get you locked up for the night."

Nick picked up his satellite phone and called Grace. She answered on the first ring, and he noticed the light was green.

"Hey, no trace - you are so helpful."

"The shit hit the fan, Nick, just as I suppose you imagined it would. I was to contact the Attorney General only if you called. I did and he brought in the Homeland Security Chief. Apparently, our two wayward justice department members corroborated the existence of Rachel's magic flash drives. They want them so badly they may overlook your transgressions."

"How much about my transgressions do you know?" Nick asked warily, repressing memories of missions over the last decade as they flitted through his mind.

"Let me put it this way, Nick." Grace's lilting tone immediately irritated him. "I know writing best sellers is a hell of a

174

cover gig. It seems CIA and NSA pooled their resources after the Khobar Towers bombing in 1996 into funding this neat clandestine group. Only the word leaked. It was shut down before it actually went into operation. At least that's what congressional oversight thought. How am I doing so far, Obi-Wan?"

"Oh, those transgressions."

"Want to fill in the blanks for your friends at the US Marshall's office, Nicky?"

"Never going to happen," he retorted, his mind racing. "We'll deal with me later. Not that I'm complaining, but how did a couple of lowly US Marshalls end up on top in this mess?"

"It seems because we were the only ones working to keep Rachel and Jean alive, the Attorney General decided that, with all the suspicious happenings and leaks, Tim and I would be the logical oversight for the people who almost got us killed."

"Please tell me you don't have a task force."

"Nope," Grace chuckled. "Tim and I know better than to speak about this crap to anyone. We have access way beyond our pay grades and can call in help from anywhere we need it. We answer only to the Attorney General."

"Here's the deal then. There may be a dust-up where the safety deposit box is."

"Meaning the bad guys know where the box is. You and Rachel know where the box is. The authorities, in the form of Tim and I, know nothing."

"You have a talent for summarization, Grace."

"I can round up enough people I trust to escort you and Rachel into the bank to get the drives, Nick," Grace replied, anger creeping into her voice.

"But then you'll have our hole card. Think about it logically, Grace. What happens when we hand over the drives without leverage? I can make copies. You won't be allowed to. If you get leaned on too hard, those drives can keep you and Tim in business. I'll be like the Oracle. When you have questions about the way our justice system is progressing on the case, I can fill in details for you about what they may be covering up."

"And if we don't take the deal?"

"I'll find a way to get those flash drives. Then it will be a hot time in the old town tonight, baby."

"We're in," Grace agreed. "It's getting late. You've worn me out. When can you get those drives?"

"You'll know when I have them in my hands or close to it."

"I'll bet you're writing this all into a Diego best seller, aren't you, you prick?"

"I may be able to dish this heroic episode of reality into a treasure chest's worth of fiction."

"I'm thinking Tim and I need to go down to Pacific Grove. I'll talk to some of your friends down there. We might need a hole card against you, big shot."

"Listen closely, Grace." Nick's voice became nearly unrecognizable in its sheer menace. "It would be very dangerous for you or Tim to approach anyone I know. Are we clear?"

"Sure Nick, sorry."

"You will be, if you ever forget what I just said." He ended the call. Only the thought of Rachel in his bedroom enabled him to set the satellite phone down without smashing it into the cement.

"How'd it go?" Rachel asked, as the bedroom door swung open, and she propped herself up on the bedcover.

"It's a work in progress." His mind went blank at the sight of her in a sheer black-silk teddy.

She turned onto her stomach, looking up at him over her shoulder. "I bought this while Jean and I were out shopping. Still want to do my back?"

176

* * *

"Come on, Mom," Nick whispered, guiding a very groggy Rachel toward her own bedroom. "You know you'd blame it on me if Jean wakes up and checks your room."

"Damn, Nick, can I sleep in tomorrow?" She turned in his arms, hugging him to a stop midway down the hall.

"You sleep in every morning." Nick held her, kissing the top of her head. "What would be different about tomorrow?"

"Brat! Everyone sleeps in compared to you. What time is it anyway?"

"Nearly one-thirty."

"That was a wonderful few hours." Rachel pressed tightly into him, moving her lips to his bare neck. He knew she could feel the desired affect her movements had on him. She twisted away toward her bedroom. "Goodnight, Nick."

"I am so going to wake you at five, you little tart."

Rachel gave him the wave off, continued into her bedroom, and closed the door. Nick walked by and quietly opened Jean's bedroom door. Deke streaked by him toward the stairs. Nick followed quickly, finding Deke panting at the locked glass patio door. He barely had time to slide the door back far enough before Deke jammed through the opening and over to the nearest desert plant.

"Sorry about that, Deke. I should have let you out earlier. That'll teach you to stick your cold nose into my business." Nick waited, but Deke ignored him and walked over to his gnawed soup bone. Ignoring Nick's urging to bring the bone inside, Deke laid down with the bone between his front paws and went to work on it. "Okay, but you'll be out for the night. I have to lock up buddy."

He closed the door, waiting a few more moments, hoping Deke would change his mind. When the dog stayed where he was, Nick locked the door and reset his security system. He returned to the bedroom and his bed. He found it difficult to sleep with Rachel's scent everywhere, but started to drift off after fifteen minutes. No sooner did the first stage of sleep overcome him than the phone rang on the night stand next to his head. He grabbed it up before it could complete the ring, hoping the sound had not disturbed Rachel and Jean.

"Hello."

"Ross? You have to come over here," Suzan's voice sobbed into his ear.

"Calm down, Suzan," he urged, moving from the bed, and pulling on his jeans with one hand. "Tell me what's happening, one step at a time."

"We had a bunch of hang up calls, and then a van parked across the street at around midnight. No one is getting out of it. I… I waited for them to go away, but they're still here. Should I –"

"No, you were right to call. I'll come by and check the van out. Does it look like a delivery van or one of those minivan types."

"It's a big one. I mean…it's not one of those little ones."

"What color?"

"Dark Blue."

"Okay, stay in the house with the kids and don't come out. I'll jog over so it'll take me a couple minutes. I'll come to the door if everything is okay."

"Thanks Ross."

Nick hung up and hurriedly put on his socks and tennis shoes. He took a black t-shirt from his drawer and put it on before taking the silenced Heckler & Koch .45 caliber handgun from his vault. Nick grabbed the light jacket he had fitted to carry the H&K,

178

and jogged down the stairs. Five minutes later he slowed, checking out the cars near the Benoit residence on the street. No van was in sight when he went up to the Benoit house and tapped on the door, his hand on the H&K grip. Suzan answered the door. She began crying the moment she saw him. *What the hell?*

"I'm sorry...I'm sorry..." Suzan sobbed, retreating from the door. "I'm supposed to tell you everything's okay. I...I can't. They were going to kill us."

"How many?" He went through the door and grabbed Suzan. "Think. How many guys came in the house?"

"Three...but I think there was a fourth, because someone started the van when the three men left."

"Is the van they drove a dark-blue full-size like you said, and when did they leave?"

"Yes, the minute you told me you'd be over."

"They're hitting my house. Shit! Keep the throwaway cell on you. Pack up your kids. Go stay at a motel until I contact you." Nick left the house at a run, cutting down the street in back of his house. He saw the security lights and heard Deke barking at the back of his place. He knew the neighbor at the rear of his property did not have a dog so he leaped their fence at a run and moved to the next fence bordering their properties. He pulled himself up to look into his backyard. Deke heard him. The dog left the patio door to investigate the fence. Nick went over quietly, slipping down next to Deke. Staying along the border of his fence, he rounded his backyard. He crossed to the patio inside the security light's glare, with the dog shadowing his moves.

Inside the living room, he saw two men waiting, their eyes on the front entrance, with silenced handguns. Knowing he had locked the sliding glass door, and the men inside would not have opened it with Deke in the backyard, Nick moved to the sturdy lounger Rachel had lain in earlier. He took off his belt, and looped one end around Deke's neck, and the other he cinched around a table leg.

Gripping the middle sides of the lounger, Nick used it as a battering ram and plowed through the patio door glass. Once through, he tossed the lounger left, while he dove to the right, drawing his H&K. The two men fired wildly at the lounger. One went down immediately with a .45 caliber slug through his head. Nick shot the shoulder of the second man, the .45 slug potent enough to knock the man down flat. Nick covered the distance between himself and the wounded man in seconds. The man was feebly trying to roll toward him. Before he could turn, Nick slammed the butt of his weapon against the man's temple, stunning him. He quickly disarmed him, and dragged the man into the kitchen to the cupboard where he kept his duct tape.

Keeping his eyes on the downed man in the living room, He duct-taped the wounded man's wrists and feet behind him, and together. Then he made sure of his kill. He quickly frisked the dead man for ID and weapons. With those items, he returned to the kitchen and repeated the process, evoking a groan from the trussed man. Deke started barking again, so he hurriedly dragged the wounded man onto a kitchen chair, and duct-taped him to it securely. With the confiscated weapons on the kitchen counter, he carried Deke over the broken glass and into the garage.

"Stay here for a moment. This may get a little messy," Nick told the dog while pulling a stun gun out of the Escalade's glove compartment. Leaving Deke out in the garage, he returned to the kitchen.

After checking to see how much blood was flowing from his captive's shoulder wound, he stuffed some towels inside the man's shirt, and duct taped them in place. He unfastened the man's pants, and yanked them down with his underwear. Filling a glass of water next, he flung it in the man's face. The man regained consciousness, groaning for help, only to be slapped in the face with hard, flat hand swipes.

"Can you hear me now?" Nick shook the man's chin.

"Oh shit!" The man's eyes widened when he recognized who had his jaw in a vice-like grip.

180

"I see Suzan must have told you what happened to the other guys who tried this crap on me." Nick fired off an arc. "I'd advise you to start talking, beginning with what route your partners took the woman and girl."

"Route 93 out of the city, then hit Interstate 40 all the way to Georgia, then..."

"I get the picture. They left you and the dead man to kill me. What then?"

"Follow in your vehicle with the body. Please, man...that's the honest to God's truth. Don't –"

"Shut up. Who connected you to us?"

"Craig and Joe. They...they were supposed to kill everyone but the woman."

"Including Brewster?" Nick interrupted, pissed off Joe held out on him.

"Yes."

"Then you guys are independents?"

"We had a buyer for the drives."

"Who?"

"Tanus's rivals, ah, Fletcher Exports."

"Then what?"

"When Joe and Craig didn't show, we came looking for them. Please, that's all of it...I don't know anything else."

"That's what they all say."

181

Chapter Fourteen
Rescue The Hard Way

With Deke in the back of his Escalade, Nick raced after the dark blue van. Attaining speeds in excess of a hundred and ten miles per hour, he crossed the Arizona border in minutes. After the slight slowdown crossing over, Nick again drove all-out on the long stretch of US 93 toward Interstate 40. A three-quarter moon cast some light over the nearly deserted highway. Whenever Nick saw taillights ahead, he turned off the Escalade's headlights.

Fifteen miles before the Interstate, he spotted taillights mounted far enough off the road to be a van. He shut off his headlights, and floored it. Once he confirmed that the license matched what the man at his house had told him, he paced the vehicle three car lengths back, and switched to cruise control. With the window down, Nick kept the steering wheel controlled in his right hand. He leaned out the driver's side window, aiming the H&K .45 at the van's left rear tire. He hit it on the third shot, immediately braking while waiting for the van to pull over.

When the van drove onto the roadside, kicking up dust and dirt, Nick turned off the road with it, keeping a fifty-yard distance between the vehicles. Having already pulled the fuse on his interior lights, he opened the door, exiting quickly with his weapon in hand. He kept to the blind side of the van, working his way quickly and quietly toward it. Two men, swearing and slamming the doors as they emerged, approached the damaged tire from both sides. They stood assessing the damage at the left rear tire with a flashlight in the driver's hand. Nick shot four times with deadly accuracy, two .45 caliber slugs through the head of each man, running up on them to fire once more from point blank range. Continuing around to the driver's side, he opened the door and got in, ready to fire. The cargo area was sealed off from the van's front seating.

Nick quickly dragged the bodies around to the van's passenger side, confiscating the keys and paraphernalia the two men carried. He opened up the rear compartment, his heart pounding. Rachel and Jean lay bound and gagged on their sides. The mind numbing tension of his race across the desert slowly seeped from Nick, leaving him drained, momentarily, of all thought and energy. He took his knife out and carefully cut Jean free first, gently helping her take the gag off. Jean's lip trembled and her eyes misted as she worked Rachel's gag off while Nick cut away the bonds.

"Oh Nick, thank God!" Rachel cried out, hugging Jean tightly.

"The Cad's back about fifty yards. We have to get out of here. Our luck's run out. I'll follow you back to the house."

"Is...is Deke okay?" Jean asked.

"He's in the Cad. There's broken glass, so I didn't want to leave him. Take him upstairs when we get home. Start packing. I have to do some clean up. Then we need to go."

Nick helped Rachel from the van with Jean still in her arms. He walked with them to the Cad. With a cry of pure joy, Jean dived into the backseat with a wild Deke. Rachel let Nick guide her into the driver's seat and shut the door.

"Drive the speed limit. Don't pick up any hitchhikers."

Rachel barked out a quick laugh, which turned into a sob as she covered her face. Nick reached in and took her hands.

"Training or no training we'll get ahead of this thing, Rach. No more chances - no more playing house. I really screwed the pooch last night. You go on now. I'll follow shortly in their van after I change the tire."

Rachel nodded, taking the handkerchief he offered through the open window. She started the Cadillac and watched him jog back to the van in the Escalade's headlights.

* * *

"Mom, where's the Terminator going?" Jean peered anxiously over Rachel's shoulder with Deke's head next to hers.

"With us, Baby, with us," Rachel answered, driving away from the roadside.

When Rachel reached Nick's house, she parked outside. She waited until he arrived before getting out with Jean and Deke. Nick remote-opened the garage door and drove the van inside. He exited the van, walked out of the garage, and closed the door. He walked over to Rachel and Jean, fending off Deke on the way.

* * *

"You look like shit, Nick."

He flashed a tired grin. "Hey, thanks. You and Danger don't look like a bowl of Rice Krispies either. We've only begun. Let Deke do his business, then take him inside. Bypass the mess. Everyone go upstairs to pack like we talked about. If you could sweep up the broken glass, Rach, I'd appreciate it. I'll clean everything else. Let's go. We have a lot to do. After we leave their van near the border, I want to make it a ways down Interstate 40 before we stop for the day."

"I'm scared, Nick," Jean said suddenly.

Nick knelt down in front of Jean. "Look, Danger, I know getting kidnapped every other day is the pits. I promise you this, the next time you or your mom gets taken, it'll be because I'm dead. We Terminators are awful hard to kill."

Jean hugged him. "I'm glad you came. I...I didn't feel much like a Terminator."

"Me neither, kid." He hugged her back tightly. He then held her at arm's length. "What say we blow this town?"

184

Jean nodded enthusiastically. Rachel took her hand, touching Nick's shoulder as she went past. Inside the house, Rachel took Jean and Deke upstairs and began packing. Nick went out to the garage. He loaded the other two bodies, dragged from the house earlier, that were stacked behind his Malibu into the van with the others, and covered them with a tarp. He loaded magnesium flares on the van's front seat and opened the garage door. After backing out to the street and parking the van, he drove the Cadillac in and shut the garage door again. He spent the next half hour loading equipment into the false floor in the cargo area. When he went back inside, Rachel was already cleaning up the broken glass.

"We're all packed Nick," she paused to tell him, gesturing at the three suitcases. "Jean is taking a shower. I'll go in after her. Then it's all yours."

"Good deal." He took the first two suitcases out and loaded them. Rachel met him at the door with the third one, giving him a quick kiss before returning to her sweeping.

It was nearly ten o'clock in the morning by the time Nick had put a tarp over the broken patio door and finished his house cleaning. By ten thirty, he had his bags packed and in the Escalade with the rest. Rachel, Jean, and Deke sat together on the couch watching a movie when he came down the stairs after showering. He carried the clothes he had worn through the early morning hours with him.

"We're all set, crew. I think it would be better for you to follow me. It's still daylight, so I'll have to drive this damned van out a ways off the road before doing some final touches to it. When you see me turn off into nowhere, pull alongside the road right where I leave it and I'll join you as soon as I get the van taken care of."

"Okay, Nick, we'll be out front." Rachel switched off the TV. She walked outside with Jean and Deke into the Las Vegas heat.

185

Nick backed out of the garage, sealed up the house, and handed the keys to Rachel. By the time he gave everything the once over, Rachel had the Cadillac ready to go with Jean and Deke in the backseat. He gave her a wave, and carried the small shoulder bag he had packed to the van.

After passing a town called Cloride, Nick looked for the first available spot to turn off. Five miles down the road, he turned into the desert, keeping the van speed up to avoid getting stuck. He made it in nearly two miles before the rear of the van sunk to the axle. Taking papers, match booklets, and charcoal lighter fluid out of his bag, he doused the clothes he had worn earlier and the front seat area with lighter fluid. He opened the van's cargo doors, pulled aside the tarp, and threw two of the unlit magnesium flares from the front seat onto the bodies. Nick coated everything in the cargo area with lighter fluid. He lit a booklet of matches, and threw it into the back, closing the doors. After igniting the front in the same manner, he left at a dead run with his bag.

He made it to the Escalade soaked in sweat, having run the two miles in brutal desert heat, pouring water from a quart container over his head every hundred yards. Rachel drove off the second he closed the passenger side door. They were nearly a quarter mile down the road when the van exploded. Nick had been watching for it. With the magnesium flares, he figured it would burn white hot until nothing of any consequence was left.

"Can you give me about an hour, and then I'll take over for you?" Nick reclined his seat.

"Oh sure, I do all the hard work and you sleep it off," Rachel deadpanned.

"I'll make it up to you later, Nikita," he promised, his eyes already closed.

Nearly an hour later he woke up, looking around tensely. He relaxed when Rachel smiled over at him.

"What the hell! You have a built in timer or something?"

"Inner clock - perfected over the years." Nick stretched. He looked back at Jean and Deke. Jean sat with her head against the seat, sleeping soundly, while Deke lay across her lap. "Want to make a pit stop and get something to eat?"

"I was hoping you'd say that. A sign we passed just before you woke up claimed there's gas, food and lodging up ahead about five miles. How far did you want to go today?"

"Flagstaff, if we can. The guy I questioned convinced me they were selling the drives to a rival outfit called Fletcher Exports. If those guys were independents then we've bought some time. We'll make Sarasota ahead of schedule. We needed more work in the desert before pulling off what we have ahead, but it can't be helped now."

"Do you think there are any more free lancers out there?"

"I'm sure of it. As long as we keep on the move, I think we'll be okay. Hooking up with Suzan was a blessing and curse. She nearly killed us all, but if we can get together with her husband once we retrieve the flash drives, our bargaining position will be greatly improved. I better call her, and then Grace."

Nick pulled his satellite phone from the bag at his feet. He called Suzan on the throwaway cell-phone he'd given her. She answered a moment later. "It's over, Suzan. You can take the kids home. Our deal's still on, but we won't be seeing you until the drives are in our hands. It probably won't matter, but did anyone see those guys visiting your place yesterday?"

"I can't say for sure. They came after dark. They're really...gone for good?"

"No more surprise visits," Nick told her. "Will your husband be coming home on time?"

"Yes, he called earlier."

"I'll give you a call this weekend sometime after you get a chance to talk with him."

"Okay, thank you."

"You bet." Nick hung up. He called Grace next. She answered the phone without setting off a red light. "We're on the move, Grace. The timetable may have been moved up a bit. Are we still dealing?"

"It's a go, Nick. They're not all happy but, surprisingly, the Attorney General is. He's suspected there was a lot more to all this. He's very happy with our progress - considering how little of it you've worked with us to achieve. Can I talk to Rachel?"

"Sure, but make it quick. She's driving, and cell phone usage by the driver is against the law."

"Hand her the phone, wise guy."

"She wants to talk to you." He handed Rachel the phone.

* * *

"Hello, Grace," Rachel greeted the Marshall, as she turned the Escalade onto an off ramp leading to the gas, food and lodging she had seen advertised on a sign earlier.

"Listen closely, Rachel. Don't reply," Grace urged. "Nick's a killer. He's some kind of psychopathic hit-man according to all the rumors flying around. We're not sure if he does it under some pseudo government network authorization, but we know he's not some innocent novelist. You and Jean need to get free of him, Rachel. When you do, call me, and I'll help you deal with the flash drives."

"I'm sorry for putting you and Tim through all this. What you just outlined will never happen. Nick's already saved our lives a few times on this damned excursion." Rachel glanced over at Nick, who was looking straight ahead.

"Damn it, Rachel! Use your head! How the hell do you know he won't waste you all the moment he has those flash drives?"

188

"I just do."

"You're in love with him, aren't you, dummy?" The tenor of Grace's voice betrayed her anger. "Think of Jean."

"I am thinking of Jean. Nick's our best shot at being free again."

"With harps and clouds maybe."

"Are we done?"

"Think it over care –"

Rachel handed the phone to Nick. "Hang it up for me, Nick."

Nick disconnected. "She trying to sell you the sell out?"

"Yep. Grace thinks you have it in mind to get the flash drives and bury the rest of us in the desert."

"The only thing the flash drives mean to me is a chance at having you, Jean, and Deke in my life on a permanent basis. I have money. What the hell does Grace think I'm going to do with the flash drives?"

"She thinks you're a cold blooded psychopath without a conscience and you'd do it just for the power trip."

"Oh, well sure, there's that, but I'm a nice guy when you ignore those small flaws."

* * *

"I feel better." Nick sat down at the table with Rachel and Jean.

"You smell a little fresher." Rachel sniffed toward Nick, earning a quick head slap.

"You try running full speed for a couple miles in the desert and then –"

189

"Sleep your time away to a restaurant," Rachel quickly filled in for him while Jean giggled at her two adult companions. "I think the clean t-shirt helps the most."

"After washing up, I went out to give Deke some water and dropped the foul smelling thing off in the back. Did they take the order already?"

Rachel nodded. "I didn't order the food yet, but I did order our drinks. She'll be bringing us coffee and –"

"A milkshake," Jean piped in proudly.

Nick laughed. "She conned you again, huh?"

"Miss smarty-pants pointed out we could wind up dead anytime, so it's kind of stupid to worry about her diet right now."

Nick quit laughing abruptly, looking over at Jean. "Not funny."

"I got a milkshake out of it."

The dark-haired waitress in her middle thirties served their beverages, smiling at Nick appraisingly while setting the drinks down. "Have I seen you around here before, Sir?"

"I get that a lot." Nick smiled back. *She doesn't look the type to be a fan of Diego, but Grace didn't either*. "This is our first time visiting Ash Fork though."

"You look familiar, but it's been a long day. I'm probably a little batty. Are you folks ready to order?"

"We'll have your special." Rachel wagged a warning finger at Jean.

"Make it three." Nick handed the menus to the waitress.

The waitress paused after taking the menus. "I can't think who you remind me of, but - I know this sounds goofy - are you someone famous?"

"Roscoe Weatherby," Nick said, holding out his hand to the waitress with a friendly smile. "I'm only famous, or infamous, as the case may be, to my wife and daughter here."

The waitress chuckled, shaking his hand. "Terry Jenkins. You look a lot like Brad Pitt."

Rachel and Jean were still laughing as Terry walked away.

"It wasn't that funny." Nick pretended annoyance at his companions' amused disbelief that the waitress would think he might be Brad Pitt. "I do look a lot like Brad."

His statement brought renewed laughter. His satellite phone beeped in the bag next to him, where he'd stored his H&K .45. Nick took the phone out of the bag. "I'll be right back." He walked outside with the phone, unwilling to take any chances some noise or conversation might give away their location to the caller. It was still nearly ninety degrees outside in the Arizona town, and he felt the sweat start forming again after being in the air conditioned restaurant. Staying in the shade, he walked away from the restaurant entrance, but kept alongside the building wall providing cover from the five o'clock sunlight.

"I'm here," he answered.

"Ready to come in from the cold, Nick? Eliminate the family problem and we'll have you on a book tour in France, all expenses paid, plus a nice million for your retirement fund. We can heal this unfortunate rift between us easily. What do you say?"

Nick remained silent, inwardly masking the disappointment of hearing Frank's voice.

"Thought your US Marshall friends nailed me, huh? This won't go away, Nick. The DOJ is only one small thread. We have inroads everywhere. National security is all one big happy family. If one of our family units gets too hot for a while, we cut off contact until it cools down."

"You're on my bucket-list, Frank," Nick stated calmly. "Kiss your wife, girlfriend, or significant other. Play video games

191

or baseball with your spawn. You won't know when or where, but I'm going to do my part for national security in a small way, by erasing your back stabbing ass."

Frank laughed. "Turn that record over will you, Nick? You'll never get close."

"I don't need to."

"There's a reason we don't party together or exchange Christmas cards, Meat. We understand how some facets of our operation might one day go off the deep end, so anonymity is highly guarded."

"I'm glad you don't believe I can find you, Frank. I promise not to be vengeful, and kill everything you ever loved right down to your kids' pet gerbil."

This time, it was silent on Frank's end of the conversation.

"Okay, let's deal," Frank said finally. "We know the safety deposit box is in Florida. We also know you're heading there."

"If you know everything, why don't you get a court order and take the box? Oh, that's right, whoever you're in bed with would be on the DOJ's radar, along with our little covert group. You could have played this straight up with me, Frank."

"What? Keep financing your pretend world, give you a ready-made family, and throw all our other assets under the bus? You're insane, pal. It doesn't work like that. I follow orders, just like you used to do. I can see you don't want the easy way back in. Why don't I give you an alternate way out of this mess?"

"I'm listening."

"We open the way into the bank for you and your sweetheart. You give us the flash drives. Then you and your family run along and live happily ever after."

"I don't think so," Nick retorted. *Shit, there'll be pros shadowing our way into the damn box.* "What is this all about anyway? We get the drives. I nail the bad guys and everybody's

192

happy. I might not even come looking for you under the right conditions."

"Unlike you, they know where I live. We could out you to the whole world, Mr. Bestseller. We've already put the bug about your past in your US Marshall friends' ears."

"Then there wouldn't be any reason for me not to release everything I have stored concerning the last ten years. How many people know where you live, Frank?"

"Wait a minute, wise guy, are you...hey, not bad," Frank muttered. Nick waited patiently for Frank to sort out his complex conniving thought processes. "Would this square us, Nick?"

"Depends. If you feed me legitimate targets and manage to seal up any other possible leaks to this travesty, I could be persuaded to let bygones be bygones."

"Say I give you a name or names and everything in the information department gets nice and tight. What happens to the drives?"

"Are you on them?"

"No, but a whole bunch of unintended consequences could arise if an unedited version of those drives hit the streets. It's a deal breaker if I don't get to pare them down for uninformed eyes."

"One condition - I keep an unedited version of the drives. Also, my US Marshall friends get on your edited version list too. If I see anything out of sync you're not taking care of, I'll be able to remind you."

"You'd be a damn target forever...oh –"

"Now you're getting it," Nick interrupted. "If my adopted family or I have any trouble at all, the unedited version would be out in the open, along with ten years of covert assassinations."

"This extortion racket of yours is guaranteed to wear thin."

"You'll be in a position to make some really nice jumps in pay grade, Frank. I need you to post your proposition to me, including all the little details about why these names are the ones to take care of. I want a vid with you doing the presentation. We're past the Texas Hold Em' phase of this relationship. Put your cards on the table."

"Agreed. How do I know you won't kill me later anyway?"

"You don't, but since I know you live in a fancy estate in Reisterstown, if I wanted you dead, you'd already be dead."

"Christ!"

Nick pictured Frank's hand trembling as he gripped the phone, looking wildly around in a panic. He could practically hear the thought streaming into Frank's mind: *'The son of a bitch could be right outside my house!'*

"Don't blaspheme. See, now we have the cards face up."

"All right, I'm impressed." Frank uttered what Nick wanted to hear in a wavering, hushed voice. "I'll put together the presentation. It will be sent to your usual drop. Give me some time though...at least a day. Don't do anything hasty, Nick."

Nick leaned his head against the restaurant wall, imagining Frank at his desk in the study located in the east-wing of his estate. Having targeted Frank with his spotting scope in the past, he knew where Frank spent most of his time. "Quit glancing around your study like a caged animal. Everything's going to be all right."

Nick grinned when he heard a desk chair moving and the phone being juggled. "Will you relax? There's no need to duck away from the window. I told you we have a deal. Just make sure you sell me on the proposition you present."

Knowing the layout of Frank's study intimately, Nick calculated Frank was probably hiding behind his bookcase. He confidently pondered what Frank was thinking at the moment as he leaned comfortably with his eyes closed, guessing Frank's thoughts: *'My God... is he really out there? Where the hell are my men?'*

"You look like a little kid, peeking around the book case like that." Nick gambled and won, hearing Frank's breathing pick up.

"Nick, don't do anything stupid. Like you said, we have a deal. I'll have everything you need posted by tomorrow."

"Sounds good, buddy." Nick chuckled. "You know, a man like you should have some nice blinds instead of those sheer frilly curtains."

"Jesus…"

Nick ended the call. *Oh yeah.* He went to the Cadillac and checked on Deke. With the sun visors up, vehicle windows cracked open, and the SUV recently air conditioned, the temperature inside was comfortable for the dog. Deke would be okay through the meal. Opening the passenger side rear door, Nick petted Deke for a couple minutes. The rear seat area was considerably cooler than outside, so he gave the dog a final stroke and returned to the restaurant. Rachel looked up questioningly. He could tell she expected the worst. He smiled to make her relax a little.

"Your food's getting cold." she informed him.

"After being out in the oven, I'd rather it was cold. Well, ladies, it looks like we stay in Ash Fork tonight. After dinner, we'll go find a good air conditioned motel with a swimming pool."

"All right!" Jean added her support enthusiastically. "It's early. We can rent movies and everything."

"What happens tomorrow, Nick?"

"Detour," he answered, patting Rachel's hand.

Chapter Fifteen
Double-Cross Again

Rachel sat near Nick's sniper rifle, far back from the window, with the spotter scope in her hand. The suite Nick had picked out in downtown Denver was their third habitat in the two weeks since they'd arrived. She felt the usual guilt well up in her as she glanced over at Jean, sleeping in her bed with Deke lying at the foot of it. Nick insisted she be with them now, no matter what they had to do.

All of what seemed some scatterbrained nightmare he had thought up for a novel unfolded. First, they had watched Nick's handler, a guy named Frank, give a detailed briefing as to how this man in Denver was behind the attempted hit on Rachel, Jean and Nick. Then Nick had run the transmission again, showing all the flaws in Frank's presentation: his tone, body language, and even slight facial expression changes.

Rachel smiled, remembering how Nick had explained it.

"The prick doesn't know I've spent months observing him. He's a gambler. I'll give him that much."

"Maybe he's just scared. He looked convincing."

"We're going to Denver. We'll take our time. We'll keep in touch with Frank. I'll give him a time frame for when the job will be done. It would be easier for me to show you, rather than just string together words with no reference. I'll make it educational, too, involving lots of geometry."

"I hate math," Rachel kidded.

Nick had been right. Rachel sighed, leaning back in her chair after glancing at the watch Nick had given her before leaving the room. They were staying at a nice Ramada Inn with an indoor pool for an entire week, checked in separately. Nick, Jean and Deke stayed in one room, and Rachel in the other. Nick explained that, when Frank did sweeps of new motel check-ins, they hopefully would not show up on the radar until moving to the next location. Three days later, Nick finished with his recon, identifying the optimal place to assassinate Senator Anthony 'Tony' Ambrose, the man Frank had fingered. The killing would be blamed on a tragic overreaction to the Senator's continuing sponsorship of anti-gun legislation. Nick moved them out of the Ramada Inn, much to Jean's dismay, and into an even plusher hotel near central Denver. From his new outpost, Nick was able to anticipate the most likely place a second team would be stationed to take Nick out after the Senator was dead.

Rachel shook her head, still somewhat disbelieving this could be happening as if they were using Nick's template. But there was no denying the facts. Two days after Nick's prediction, a sniper team had arrived in the very room where Nick's sniper rifle was aimed. He had explained the angles, wind shear, and all the reasons for their appearance, as if he had called them to the very spot he anticipated. He'd spent two days finding every inroad to the sniper team's room without being seen. Rachel looked again at her watch, breathing deeply as Nick had suggested. Her job was back-up: relay positioning and movements in the room when Nick went in. She was only to shoot if he went down.

Five minutes later, Rachel scoped the sniper team's room, waiting for Nick's signal with her headset in place. She had all the lights off in her hotel room. Only a faint glow illuminated the sniper team's room. They had one man on watch twenty-four hours a day, which is another reason Nick had waited this long.

"All the reasoning, inside information, and final positioning in the world won't get it done," he explained to her after observing the team for a day. *"Waiting, covering all the angles, and patience is the only way to get the shot and protect your ass. They'll be hot to trot at first, but as hours and days pass, they'll get sloppy. I can tell they haven't worked together long. They're already getting antsy. No way to get the drop on them if the spotter's doing his job, but as you'll see, I will get the drop on them."*

"Confidant, are we?" Rachel had kidded him.
"I better be," had been Nick's grim answer.

197

Rachel heard Nick's single click in her headset, which meant she needed to be in position. It was a hundred meter shot Nick had told her he hoped to God she wouldn't have to take.

"It's not that I don't think you would," he'd said. "It's because my hoped-for setup will be history if you have to take the shot. Remember, first pad of the finger, slow movements only, and squeeze the trigger. I should have at least one of them down, even if I'm dead. Put another round through him, too, anyway. Repeat the procedure striking both men. Pack up. Get in the Escalade with Jean and Deke. Head for parts unknown. I'd suggest Idaho, North Dakota, or Utah. Find a very small community. There's a hundred grand in the false bottom of the Escalade I showed you. It'll get you through until you find work."

Rachel grabbed his hand before he left, moving her body into him. "What made you decide to adopt me and Jean?"

"When you invited yourself to sit down with me at the restaurant," he answered with a grin. "I like a woman who shows an interest."

Nick repeated the single click, meaning he was at the door.

"Hold." Rachel sighted in on the shielded sniper nest covered with bedclothes. "One man at the gun. Other out of sight...he's approaching the gun...back turned to you..."

Rachel jerked in spite of knowing what would happen next, glad she had remembered to keep the pad of her finger off the trigger until ready to shoot. Two crackling charges felled both sniper team members. Nick stayed low to the floor, jolting the men until they were unconscious.

He closed the door and hurried to the fallen men. He disarmed each of them, while keeping the silenced muzzle of his own weapon covering them.

"Everything's okay, Rach. Neither of these boot camps is armed. This is an insult. How dare Frank send 'Beavis and Butthead' after me?"

Rachel laughed.

"I'm going to be a few minutes longer than I'd hoped. Without any silencers, I'll have to rig this up the old-fashioned way. Pack up. I'm going to hit the good Senator tonight."

"What?" Rachel yelped incredulously, cringing as Nick put a knife into the fist of one downed man and forced it into the chest of the other. "We're...we're not in position for the shot."

"The most righteous Senator Ambrose is in bed with his mistress," he explained, while positioning the stabbed man over his comrade and using his hands to crush the man's skull under him with a stone flower vase. "That'll teach you to stab me, you varmint."

Rachel laughed again, unable to look away from the horrendous killing of two unconscious men, ending in a cartoon dialogue joke. She glanced again at her daughter guiltily. *Go straight to hell. Do not pass go. Do not collect two hundred dollars. You're as big a monster as he is.*

* * *

Nick waited for twenty seconds more, making sure the two men were dead. He took a black plastic bag out of his pocket, and loaded in his two Taser guns, H&K .45, jacket, and gloves. Taking out a fresh pair of Nitrile gloves and donning them, he left the room, making sure the door locked. With the ball cap down low over his face, he made his way out of the building by his planned route.

"I'm going to the Cad. I'll drop off this stuff and pick up my next outfit for the visit to Senator Ambrose."

"Why do you have to kill the Senator?"

"Because Frank was right about one thing: Ambrose is trying to kill us."

The tone of his answer prompted Rachel to dispense with the questioning.

"We'll be packed and ready to leave when you get back."

Nick parked the Escalade around the block from the apartment building where Senator Ambrose's suite was located. Putting on a dark blue windbreaker and ball cap, Nick carried a small shoulder bag with him to the alleyway entrance. He used the access code stolen during his first days in Denver, and made his way up the stairwell through the predawn silence. Outside Senator Ambrose's door, he listened intently for a few moments, before using his access card to get in. After shutting the door silently, Nick took off his shoes. Seconds later, he stood at the entrance to the Senator's bedroom, where the outlines of two bodies breathed in varying degrees of sleep.

Nick crept over to the woman's bedside. He placed the chloroformed white pad next to her nose. When her breathing changed, he removed the pad and moved to the Senator's side. He gently pulled the cover back from the Senator, who was lying on his back, snoring slightly. Nick position himself above the Senator and jammed his knee into Ambrose's Solar Plexus, driving the breath from him. Ambrose's eyes popped open as he gasped and flailed. Nick put a gloved hand over his mouth, easing the knee back until Ambrose could breathe.

"Hi, Senator. Stay quiet. Keep your arms at your sides and legs still, or I'll crush your chest. Nod if you understand."

Ambrose nodded. Nick removed his hand.

"I'm Nick. I have some questions for –"

"Nick…McCarty?" Ambrose managed to interrupt with a wheeze.

"One and the same," Nick confirmed. "How many other people besides you and Frank know about me?"

"You…you murdered the only others who knew about you."

"If you're the lone boss man, why does Frank always make it sound like there's a board of directors?"

"No one has all the pieces. I formed the group after –"

"Khobar Towers. I know. Do you deal all this shit out on a whim, or do you actually run it by a committee?"

"We've split off from everyone…but everyone reports to me in some way through Frank. How did you find…Frank…? Frank gave me up?"

"Yep. I believe old Frank is tired of taking orders from you and shit from me. He rigged it up so I'd kill you and another team would kill me. It didn't work out. Was Tanus a real national security threat?"

"We have to take some bad with the good. Come on McCarty, you…you can't be that naïve," Ambrose blustered, starting to move around. "To get intel, we need bad men to get it for us, and bad men like you to end the lives of ones who cross the line. Now get the hell off me."

"I like that," Nick smiled, sealing the Senator's mouth once more, as his knee dug in again. "Bad men to end the lives of the ones who cross the line. Works for me, Tony. Adios."

* * *

"Sorry we had to leave so quickly, Danger," Nick told Jean, sliding in behind the steering wheel and looking back at the little girl with her ever present lap dog.

"It's okay, Nick." Jean shrugged. "I'm getting to like this traveling. We get to stay in different cool places. Too bad it's so hard to find places that'll take Deke."

"It usually just takes a little extra money." He started the Escalade.

"Are we going to Washington D.C.?"

201

"Why would we go there?"

"To meet up with your friend, Frank."

Nick feigned surprise. "I'm shocked at you, Rachel. I think you're getting a little bloodthirsty, my dear. We can't just flit around the country, hunting poor dupes of the government/media complex down on a whim. You are a monster. Shame on you."

Halfway through his performance, Jean was giggling, and Rachel's mouth had dropped open in actual shock. Her eyes narrowed suddenly. She punched Nick's arm.

"Okay, good one." She leaned back, arms folded across her chest. "My daughter seems to know when you're making fun of me faster than I do. How sad is that? Now, where the hell are we going, and do you think I'll ever get the job at your friend's café in Pacific Grove?"

"That's our goal." Nick steered the Cadillac out onto the road. "We're heading for Sarasota. I'm hoping to be in Missouri before we call it quits today. We'll take Danger to the best hotel we can find. You and Deke should be entertained enough with the portable Playstation and DVD player, right Danger?"

"Sure Nick, but we are going to stop to eat, aren't we?"

"Yep. But I'd like to be out of Colorado when we do. We'll stop the moment we get into Kansas. As for my old buddy, Frank, we're going to play a little game with him and buy some time. I'm going to wait for his call and –"

"Pretend you're coming after him," Rachel interrupted, grabbing Nick's arm. "You are such a monster. He'll be going nuts wondering when and where."

"Is this my plan or yours, Miss I'm Going To D.C.?" Nick glanced at her with an award winning look of annoyance. *She's good.* "Yes, I'm betting Frank has to pretend he doesn't know anything about anything. It will be impossible for the weasel to simply take off, especially when they find the surprises we've left behind. He knows I would arrive in a roundabout fashion, so who knows how big a dragnet he'll put out for me between Colorado and D.C.? If I convince him I'm coming, he knows I'll recon every possible item in his life. He will indeed be preoccupied with my arrival - enough so he will pull his resources out of Sarasota."

"Leaving us to deal only with the thugs we expected before."

"That's the plan. I figure we can take our time once we split off for the South."

"You'll have to be subtle and not openly threaten him. If... what?" Rachel laughed, seeing the quick glances she was getting from Nick as she lectured him on the obvious. "Sorry. I didn't mean to insinuate you don't already have every detail of your conversation with Frank planned out, Master."

"Very well, you're forgiven, young Jedi." Nick glanced back at Jean, who had her Playstation already out and headphones on. "I figure the room-temperature Senator will be discovered very soon. It'll be interesting to hear how the cops play it out with what I left them. Frank will know instantly, which will lead him to try and make immediate contact with 'Beavis and Butthead,' who are also at room-temperature. I'll bet he doesn't have any assets in the area to clean up the mess either. Although I took all their personal stuff, you can bet their DNA and fingerprints are on file somewhere. They'll be looking into that scene very closely. I believe he'll be calling right around the time we stop to eat."

"Those guys... the sniper team...do –"

"Don't go there, Rachel," Nick cautioned. "They were paid to take us out. We're driving toward Kansas because we were better."

"You were better."

"When you told me to hold up at the door, I was going in. Chances are, without my spotter, I'd be dead. You can bet 'Beavis and Butthead' had skills. Don't short change yourself. If all goes as planned, you and I may develop into one of the best teams around."

"As long as we don't raise Jean up in the family business, I'll go where you go."

"Hey, don't limit your daughter's potential, Mom."

"Not funny!"

"Calm down." Nick laughed. "Hell, you figured to be dead by now."

"We'll never really be safe after this, will we, Nick?" Rachel reached over to put a hand on his thigh.

"No one is really safe. Many times, having value means greater safety. If we make it through this, we'll be quite valuable. Unfortunately, it may mean I won't be able to put a bullet in that prick Frank's head for a while."

Later, Nick exited for gas and a pit stop off Route 70, in a town called Brewster, past the Colorado/Kansas border. As he drove toward the indicated gas station and restaurant his satellite phone vibrated next to him. He grinned over at Rachel, who was shaking her head.

"Now that's timing." Nick saw Frank's ID on the digital readout as he picked up the phone. "Assassins R Us, Nick speaking, how may I direct your call?"

"I know what you're thinking, Nick," Frank said.

"No, you don't."

"You're wasting your time. You'll never get to me."

"Why...whatever do you mean, Frank?" Nick asked in a lilting voice. "Has something happened to make you think you're in danger?"

"I...I have to hand it to you. They think Ambrose had some kind of attack. They're hushing it up because of the mistress waking next to him with no idea what happened."

"Gee, that works out really well for you, Frank. Maybe you were a little shortsighted in your cleanup idea."

"Small damn doubt about that. Jesus! You can't really be coming to D.C., Nick. You're not that stupid."

"Now see, I don't really think of a nice trip to the nation's capital as stupid. I consider it kind of a vacation - or even an adventure." He pulled off the road for a moment to finish the call, with Rachel watching him closely.

Frank's voice came across as slightly panicked. "What can I do to make this right, Nick? I'm really in a position to help you."

"How sweet, you're going to help me now."

"Don't be an ass. We can work this out."

"Let me think about it for a couple weeks, Frank. Maybe you'll be around when I make the decision - or maybe not."

Nick ended the call and steered onto the roadway again.

"How we doing?"she asked.

"Five by five, Rach, five by five."

* * *

Rachel checked the speedometer once more, glad for the cruise control. It had taken them over ten hours, with stops for gas and food, to get across Kansas. Every time she had taken the Escalade off cruise control and operated the gas pedal manually, Nick had been forced to nudge her back down to seventy miles per hour. He kept reminding her that the last thing in the world they needed was to be stopped for speeding. After an hour of driving, seventy seemed like twenty on the highway. *I've had about as much of the amber waves of grain as I can take without going stark raving mad.*

"Did you say something?"

"I'm sorry." She met Nick's gaze. "Did I curse Kansas out loud?"

"It feels like you age a couple years driving through here, doesn't it?"

"I kept glancing back at Jean the last half hour expecting her to be a teenager."

He laughed. "She and Deke are good travelers." Rachel saw him glance back at Jean, who was again dozing off. "They sleep when they can and play when they can. I'm glad Jean thought to get a Frisbee when we stopped. Did you know Deke was a champion Frisbee player?"

"It was a surprise to me. I guess we should have tried him out with balls and Frisbees before this. Work, eat, sleep, and life slips by without a stir. I noticed the goofy dog sleeps with his head on the damned thing now."

"Deke's grown quite attached to it."

Hearing his name, Deke looked up with the black Frisbee in his mouth, gave it a few chomps and put his head down again.

"The border's only five minutes away...thank God! Where do you want to stop?"

"I've been to Concordia before when Kansas has worn me out. It's not far from the border. We should be there by seven. We'll stay at the Day's Inn, off of Route 70. They allow pets and Danger will like the indoor pool and hot tub. I know I will."

"Sounds wonderful. I've noticed it doesn't take much to make you happy."

"These days, we have to take the good times where we can get them. Didn't you like our stay in Denver?"

"Too much tension," Rachel admitted. "All I could think of was what you were going to do and whether we'd ever make it out of there alive."

"Okay, then this drive through Kansas was pretty nice, right, relatively speaking?"

"Gee, where was that count your blessings crapolla three hundred miles ago when I could have used a pick me up?"

"It looked like you were having the time of your life. We'll check in separately again. I'm glad I had time to get a Colorado driver's license for you. It makes checking into hotels a lot easier. This day and age, they need your life history even when you're paying cash for the room."

"I was surprised how fast you managed to get my false ID. How did you get the license, Nick, or is that need-to-know?"

"An old friend. We hadn't seen each other in years. I have quite a few contacts across the country, but none I trust more than Jake. He does it professionally, so you can bet you're listed in Colorado's DMV as Jane Austin."

"I liked the name you picked out."

"I was surprised you'd read *Pride and Prejudice*. I figured you more for one of those Thomas Hardy fans."

"Not likely." She shook her head slightly with obvious distaste. "I read *Jude the Obscure* in college. I nearly committed suicide afterwards."

"My thoughts exactly." Nick chortled in agreement.

"You must trust the false ID guy implicitly."

"I saved his life in the first Gulf War when we were just kids. Jake doesn't ask and he doesn't tell. It's the first time I've asked him for anything. You should have seen his face light up. We'll go see him under better circumstances. He hasn't been to Pacific Grove in over seven years. Jake has a wife and three kids. That's why I didn't want to have a big meet up. No one knows we've kept in touch. I have to keep it that way."

"Does he know what you do?"

"Jake thinks I'm one of the good guys."

"So, you lied to him."

"Exactly."

Chapter Sixteen
Down Time

When they reached the Concordia Days Inn, Nick took Deke off to the hotel side. He played Frisbee with the dog for a half hour until Rachel and Jean were checked in. After noting what room they were given, he went in and asked for the room adjoining theirs. Although the clerk did a double take when asked for a room next to the one he had just rented out, he completed the transaction quickly under Nick's Roscoe Weatherby card.

"I'm friends with the lady and little girl who were just in to register," Nick explained, when the clerk gave him the room electronic keys.

"Oh." The clerk smiled. "I was wondering. Anyway, we have a very nice Continental breakfast served in our dining area every morning. Enjoy your stay, Mr. Weatherby."

"Thank you."

Nick rejoined Rachel and Jean, who were allowing Deke to lap up a bowl of water after his Frisbee exercise in the dusky light. It was still nearly ninety degrees outside. Nick sent them ahead to the rooms while he parked the Escalade closer. Jean decided the pool and hot tub were preferable to dinner, so Nick put on his swim trunks and shorts hurriedly. He went out to play more with Deke while Rachel and Jean were getting ready. He put Deke inside with food and water. He then ordered soda and beer inside the hotel restaurant.

With the beverages in separate ice buckets, Nick entered the pool area where Rachel and Jean were already swimming. He watched Rachel in her black bikini glide smoothly from one end of the pool to the other, as did the other half dozen men in the pool area with their families. Nick placed the towels and ice buckets on an empty table, along with his bag containing the satellite phone, keys, and stun gun. The pool area was crowded and noisy, but the people thinned out quickly, having been at the pool longer.

Rachel followed Nick into the hot tub nearly forty-five minutes later. Jean played in the swimming pool with three siblings near her age: two girls and a boy. Rachel pointed at the satellite phone Nick had in hand.

"You're going to call Grace, aren't you?"

"You know me so well."

"It couldn't wait until morning?" She settled in next to him.

"We haven't called her since we were on the road to Denver. I have to see if anything's changed before we move on," he explained. "I waited until I had a beautiful woman, a beer, and a hot tub before calling her."

"You think I'm beautiful, big boy?" Rachel batted her eyes at him comically, nearly making him lose the last gulp of liquid through his nose.

"Don't..." Nick choked while avoiding Rachel. "Let me get this over with."

"Oh fine. One measly compliment and then it's back to business." She moved away from Nick haughtily.

He hit the key to speed dial Grace, shaking his head at Rachel.

"Nick, is that you? Speak up, boy. You're the only caller who can get through to me without an ID."

"It is I, Nick the novelist, checking in with my favorite Marshall. How's Timmy and Lassie?"

"Oh, you're a real crackup. All hell is breaking loose around the country. I want to know where you are and what you had to do with it?"

"Huh?" He waited for Grace's reaction.

209

"We have a dead senator in a Denver love pad with his mistress, and a sniper team nearby who apparently came to blows and killed each other in a fit of angst over God knows what. The real kicker is the senator and this sniper team were connected by the same closed down clandestine operation your name popped up in. Care to comment?"

"In what way? What…you think I caused some senator to screw himself to death, and talked two sniper guys into a duel, all while I'm hiding out with Rachel, Jean, and Deke the dog? Wow, you really do have a high opinion of my abilities, Grace."

Rachel was in a full blown, hands-over-mouth, convulsions of laughter, with Nick making quieting gestures at her with his hand. She moved further away from him.

"Okay, that does sound stupid when you put it like that," Grace admitted. "We hadn't heard from you for weeks and…well, we were worried you were connected with Denver."

"We're laying low, Grace, sorting things out. Are we still on for the drives?"

"Yes. They're willing to meet your demands and let you extract the drives any way you can. We're to cover for you unless the op gets turned into a wild-west show, in which case we disown your ass."

"I wouldn't have it any other way, Frumpy. Talk to you soon." Nick ended the call as Rachel moved in close again.

"Denver caused some waves, huh?"

"Yep, but we surfed right over them like Banzai Jack. I love it when a plan comes together."

* * *

Rachel knocked on the door, and Nick let her in. He was dressed in khaki shorts and a strapped t-shirt. Rachel moved into

210

his arms, the thin pink cotton pullover nightgown doing nothing to insulate the feel of her body against his. She held him tightly, her cheek resting against his shoulder.

"Good Lord, woman, you smell good," he whispered.

"It's called Scent of Arousal. Like it?"

"More than I can say." He forced her toward the bed. "It smells just as wondrous as it did last night."

"Last night?... Oh, don't Nick, Jean's up. I told her I was waking you for breakfast. I thought you'd be comatose after, well, you know?"

"Our extended interlude?"

"Yes." She laughed, feeling Nick's attention right through her clothes. "You look like you've been up for hours. I'm glad Jean went to bed early yesterday."

"Me too." He guided Rachel over to his notebook computer set up on the desk with his satellite uplink attached. "Fletcher Exports definitely ranks up there with Tanus. I can understand why they want to get their hands on the flash drives. I did some hacking around and found some interesting new hires on their payroll sheets. We may not be flying blind when we get to Sarasota."

She looked over the pictures Nick had on the screen and gasped. She pointed to a husky, clean shaven man with dark hair. "That's the guy I saw with Tanus, when they finished torturing Rick. He's working for Fletcher now?"

"Yep. He's among the hired-muscle I think would be waiting for us in Florida," Nick answered, nuzzling her neck. "I guess it explains how Fletcher Exports all of a sudden knows the drives are in Florida. I'm surprised Tanus didn't whack this Javier Martine before he had a chance to switch sides."

Rachel moaned, her hands dropping to her sides, as she jutted back against him. Suddenly she spun around, grabbing his hands. "Nick, I want that Javier guy."

211

"To play with or just do yourself?" he asked curiously.

"I...I don't think I could torture him."

"Good. One step at a time, Nikita. I believe you've earned it. Let's see what part our Javier plays in Sarasota before you carry out the death sentence." He pulled her right hand up to his lips, while he ran his fingertips up and down her arm until she shuddered.

"Huuuuummmmm...don't do that. You know it drives me nuts," Rachel complained, but moved into him instead of pulling away.

Nick lifted her up and into him, his hands supporting her bottom. Her legs wrapped around his hips and their open mouths met in tense anticipation. She groaned, feeling him poke into her through the flimsy nightgown. She reached down and tore it upwards toward her waist. She unfastened Nick's shorts, never parting from his lips. A knock on the door startled them both as Nick had been on the verge of impaling Rachel.

"Hey, in there...Deke and me want to play Frisbee before breakfast," Jean's voice called out, followed by a short gruff bark from her sidekick.

"Oh my God!" Rachel whispered, panting for breath as she slid down away from Nick, her face flushed.

"We'll be out in a minute, Danger," Nick yelled back. "You and Scruffy the Wonder Dog go back to your room and we'll be right there, okay?"

"Okay, Nick."

"So, this is what married with children is all about." Nick gave Rachel a quick kiss before turning away to get dressed.

Rachel seethed. "She has your timing."

* * *

212

"I like staying here, Nick," Jean commented as they walked toward the restaurant at the Days Inn. "How long can we stay?"

"Maybe one more day," he answered, exchanging glances with Rachel. "Deke really likes this place too. We still have a ways to go on this leg of our journey, kid. Tell you what, when we finish in Florida, we'll head back to California this way. We'll make a real sightseeing trip out of it with no more than a few hundred miles a day driving."

"I'm flying back if we don't stop at least three times in Kansas," Rachel added.

"Three times it is, then," he agreed. "I –"

He looked out at the parking lot, where three young men were walking along, checking out cars. Jean had wanted to stay late at the pool, because her three friends were there, so they were eating late. The parking lot security lights had come on as the sensors detected the approaching night. Rachel followed Nick's line of sight toward the lighted parking lot.

"What's wrong?"

"Those three gentlemen wandering around out in the parking lot are looking to boost a car," Nick answered, stopping to watch them. "I'll go put in a word at the office. I'm sure they have some security guys here. I don't know what level of expertise they have, but I damn well don't want the Escalade taken right under my nose."

"This is Missouri, not New York, Nick. Are you sure they're not simply checking out the different models?"

"I'm pretty sure." He grinned over at Rachel.

"Why don't you go get them, Nick?" Jean looked around Rachel at the parking lot. "Where'd they go?"

"Around the corner, looking for an easy one. I'm not Batman. I don't want to draw any attention, so I think I'll leave this up to the proper authorities. You two go on in the restaurant and order me up anything that looks good."

213

"Don't do anything that'll put us on the road again tomorrow, Batman," Rachel warned. "I need another day and night break after Kansas."

"We won't have anything to be on the road with if they get the Escalade, Nikita," Nick pointed out with some exasperation. "It is one of the most stolen vehicles around."

"You should have Lojack." Rachel giggled at his reaction.

"That would fit right in with my secret identity. Get moving."

He waited until Rachel and Jean entered the restaurant before jogging toward the office. The same desk clerk who had checked them in the night before was on duty. He smiled at Nick.

"Hello, Sir, may I help you?"

"I believe you have three young guys looking to steal a car in your parking lot. Right now, they're looking for a quick one with the keys in the ignition. Do you have a security man on staff?"

"Yes, we do," the clerk answered, picking up his phone. A few seconds later he engaged someone on the phone, and then hung up. "Our assistant manager handles security matters after six. She'll be right out."

"Okay, should I wait?" Nick wondered if the trio had reached the parking lot where his Cadillac was parked yet.

"Yes, Ms. Tobler will, ah, here she is, Sir."

Nick turned around. He watched a brown-haired woman in her late thirties, dressed in a black skirt and light blue blouse approach. She had on black shoes, flat at the heel and was only a couple inches shorter than Nick. Her brown hair, cropped in short straight fashion, lent a lean hard look to the woman's face. She stuck her hand out as she approached.

"Leslie Tobler, Mr…"

"Weatherby, Ms. Tobler, Roscoe Weatherby." He shook her hand, appreciative of the solid grip. "I saw three young men out cruising your parking lot on foot. Two were about my height, light complexion, wearing jeans, white t-shirts, and ball caps. The third was a couple inches taller than me, dark complexioned, wearing jeans and a black parka. He had on a ball cap too."

"Wearing a parka, in this heat... maybe you're on to something, Mr. Weatherby. Would you walk with me and identify these three men?"

"Ah, do you have a weapon, Ms. Tobler? The guy with the parka's probably packing something lethal, and the other –"

"Why don't we have a look first, Sir?" Tobler smiled reassuringly at him. "I have my cell-phone with the Concordia police on speed dial. If the three look suspicious, I'll call it in while we keep an eye on them."

"Sounds good. They were on their way around the building to our left."

"Fine," Tobler acknowledged, setting a brisk pace toward the entryway. "Where do you hail from, Mr. Weatherby?"

"Nevada, Ma'am."

"Leslie, please," Tobler urged with a slight English accent, veering to the left as they cleared the entryway. "Anywhere near the Las Vegas area?"

"Yes, we have a house there," Nick answered, not liking where the questions were going.

"Have you heard about the bodies they've discovered in the desert? It was on all the newscasts."

"No, we've been taking in the sights on the way, trying to keep clear of the news."

"I know what you mean." Tobler glanced over at Nick's bearded countenance. "I guess they still lose a few bodies out in the Las Vegas desert even now."

"They sure do." *Too bad the damned discovery wasn't a couple months away though. This may play hell with my stay another day plan.*

"There's one of them." Nick pointed to a t-shirted man looking into car windows in a line of parked cars. "His two friends are down the way, working back towards him."

"I see them." Tobler sighed, taking out her phone. She pushed a button and waited. "This is Leslie Tobler, assistant manager at the Day's Inn on Third Street. We have three men casing our parking lot and... Yes, that's right. Okay then. Fifteen minutes."

"Fifteen minutes?" Nick repeated with some concern, seeing the taller one of the three glance their way. *Maybe they'll abort the heist.*

Instead the man walked toward them, exaggerating his already affected glide. Nick watched parka man's hands as he approached, with his two buddies falling in behind him.

"What you lookin' at?" Parka man asked Nick.

"I'm Leslie Tobler, head of security at Day's Inn," Tobler broke in with confident tone. "Do you have a room here, Sir?"

"It's a free country, cuz," parka man retorted. "We just checkin' out the rides, Mrs. No need to go Dick Tracy on us."

"The police will be here shortly," Tobler continued. "I would advise –"

"What?" Parka man backed off a step, reaching into the pocket of his jacket. "I'll show you shortly –"

Nick dropped and leg-whipped parka man off his feet, spinning to trap his adversary's hand in the jacket pocket. Tobler had calmly stepped back and sprayed parka man's companions from a keychain pepper spray can she had in hand. They stumbled back in agony, but Tobler pressed the attack, spraying until the two dropped to the ground gagging and yelling. Nick flipped the gasping parka man to his stomach, crossing the man's arms behind

216

his back, rendering him immobile. He held him there while patting the parka pocket.

"Are you all right, Mr. Weatherby?" Tobler kept her eyes on the two she had sprayed.

"I'm fine. This one's armed. Feels like a 9mm."

"I'm very sorry about that," Tobler apologized. "I assumed incorrectly they would run away and avoid a showdown with the police. I –"

Tobler paused, leaning toward the two on the ground, who were beginning to crawl away. "Stay right where you are or I give you another dose right in your eyes!"

The two immediately stopped crawling. They wiped at their mucous covered faces with the t-shirts they had on, while grunting out strained pleas not to spray. Tobler reached toward parka man's pocket, but paused when she saw Nick shake his head.

"I'd advise allowing the police to find the gun on him, Leslie. I'll hold him still until they get here."

"Quite right, Mr. Weatherby." Tobler took her position again in front of the other two. "I greatly appreciate your help. Perhaps I could comp your room."

"No, that won't be necessary. I'm glad it's worked out so far. Would –"

"You...you dead!" Parka man regained his voice. "You and your bitch! I'll –"

Tobler leaned around Nick, and shot off a small dose right into parka man's eyes. It was all the grinning Nick could do to keep from being bucked off by the writhing man under him. Parka man began vomiting. Nick pulled him slightly back away from it as the man continued to gag.

"I very much dislike being called that name," Tobler explained, as people were gathering. Approaching sirens wailed in the distance.

217

* * *

A tense Rachel, holding Jean's hand, approached Nick, looking stricken. Nick shook his head in the negative slightly. Rachel pulled Jean away into the forming crowd. Jean was smiling.

"Batman strikes again, Mom," Jean whispered.

"It looks like he had a little help from the Huntress," Rachel whispered back. "Oh boy, I bet this means we're on the road again tomorrow."

* * *

"Hey, I heard you come in." Nick walked from the bathroom, drying his hair. "What's Danger up to? Did she go to bed already?"

Rachel looked away from the screen of Nick's notebook computer. "I rented her the latest Harry Potter movie. She and Deke are propped up in bed watching it. I see you've really collected a lot of information on Tanus and Fletcher employees."

"It will make our Sarasota adventure less exciting if we can spot some of the players near the bank. My software program didn't register a break in Tanus's firewall until just before my shower. The names and faces you have on the screen are the latest." He threw the towel aside.

Rachel put her arm around Nick's waist as he stood alongside her chair. He had put on black boxer shorts before coming out of the bathroom. She kissed his side, leaning into him for a moment. "Leslie was pretty good with the cops. They hardly asked you anything."

"She put them right on the defensive, then steered her way into the middle of their investigation. I made a simple statement,

218

backing up her version, and she made them leave me alone. Leslie had all the right questions for them, too, about whether the police had priors on the young men, or if they fit car theft profiles in the area. She called hotel managers she knew and confirmed those clowns had been spotted before, after robberies at other hotels.

"I have your meal on warm in the microwave."

"Bless you." He pulled her up from the chair. "I'll eat, check on Danger, walk the wooly mammoth, and then see if I can entertain you for a few hours."

"Wow, aren't you ambitious? Sit down, and I'll bring the food and drink. You must feel a lot better after your shower."

She brought out the carton with Nick's order from the restaurant and set it down in front of him on the table near his notebook computer. She retrieved napkins and their drinks before sitting down with him. Lips parted slightly, she watched him eat the food in his black boxer shorts. Nick noticed her appraisal.

"I'm underdressed for dinner, huh?"

"Overdressed." Rachel ran her hand along his thigh. "How's your meal?"

"Other than having it with plastic utensils, it's great."

"Are we leaving tomorrow?"

"I'd like to stay," he answered between mouthfuls of his hot turkey sandwich. "They found the van in Las Vegas. Leslie asked me about whether I'd heard the news when I told her we had a house in the Las Vegas area."

"They'll never pull your name out of that hat, Nick," she kidded him.

"The quickest way to get into trouble is to start assuming facts not in evidence. I'm thinking we need to stay another day because we don't want the cops around here getting suspicious of us fleeing the area after my run in with the locals tonight. They have our information on the register, including the Escalade's license plate."

"So, we stay."

"We'll play it by ear tomorrow and see how it goes."

"Hey Nick, I've wanted to ask you something about your writing. How did you ever get your assassin stuff published?"

He leaned back with Rachel's hand in his. "What makes you ask?"

"I've always heard it's hard as hell to get published."

"It took me three years for an agent to get beyond the first paragraph. A writer has to send out a query first with what they call a hook. If an agent or publisher likes your hook, they ask to see more. I had some requests for partials, but nothing panned out until near the end of my third year trying."

"What did you do besides kill people while you waited?" she needled him.

"I wrote more books. By the time my first manuscript was picked up, by a publisher instead of an agent, I had four more books in the series done. Editing took up most of the two years after I hit the best seller list for my first book."

"You must have had a lot of rejections in three years."

"Quite a few," he admitted.

"Did you ever want to shoot them?"

"Very funny." He stood up. "Want another one?"

"Sure." Rachel handed Nick her empty can. "Did you ever get discouraged, or think about giving up on the idea of writing?"

"Nope. Writing gave me an outlet. It was pure enjoyment. I had a woman editor during the second year say she liked the idea, but the writing needed work. Usually you only get a form letter rejection. She sent an attachment with what she claimed were suggestions. I opened up the attachment in her e-mail, thinking it would be a critique pertaining to my manuscript. Instead, it was a list of basic things not to do while writing a novel."

"So, you hunted her down, right?"

"You are so out of line." He returned with their drinks, chuckling at Rachel's banter. "No, I didn't hunt her down. It was cute. At least it wasn't another form letter."

"The editor insulted you," she argued, feigning rage. "How dare she insinuate the only thing good in your manuscript was the idea. Let's go get her now."

"Right, Nikita, we don't have enough people to kill as it is. We need to start hunting down agents and editors from my past that sent me rejection notes. I don't think so. I have a better idea. Let's go watch the end of Harry Potter, play some Frisbee, put Danger and her sidekick to bed, then come back here. You can lecture me some more on how to handle rejection."

"I'm thinking you probably won't be getting anymore rejections." Rachel shifted over into Nick's lap.

Chapter Seventeen
Sarasota

"Uh oh, here comes the Huntress." Rachel avoided looking directly at Leslie Tobler as she approached their table.

Nick nodded, winking at Jean, who smiled back. They had decided on an early breakfast in case there were any developing complications.

"Good morning, Mr. Weatherby." Tobler smiled at Rachel and Jean. "You're not leaving us soon, are you?"

"Good morning, Leslie, this is –"

"Jane Austen and her daughter Jean," Tobler finished for Nick, holding out a hand to Rachel. "*The* Jane Austen?"

"Uh, no." Rachel laughed, shaking Tobler's hand. "Would you like to join us?"

"I'll have a cup of coffee, thank you," Tobler replied as their waitress appeared with Tobler's order as if by prearranged agreement. "I only noticed one vehicle registered for both of your rooms. Are you all traveling in one vehicle?"

"Yes, we met in Las Vegas and decided to travel together," Nick answered. "We have business in the East and decided to take the trip in my Escalade."

"Where at in the East?"

"You ask a lot of questions, lady," Jean piped in. "Mom says it's rude to question people."

Nice one, Danger, Nick gave Rachel a small head shake as he could tell she intended to rebuke Jean.

"Quite right, Jean, I suppose it is," Tobler admitted. "I apologize if my questions are out of line. Our skirmish with the three young gentlemen last night caused quite a stir. It seems they

222

are indeed responsible for many of the vehicle thefts in the area. The police wondered how I noticed their out of the ordinary behavior."

"I see," Nick acknowledged. "Did they have more questions for me?"

"No, I told them what you informed me of last night about the three as if I had noticed the odd behavior and not you. I explained you simply lent a hand when the young men became violent. I wondered if my taking credit for your exemplary perception was out of line?" Tobler watched Nick appraisingly.

"Not at all. The three of us are trying to travel with as little fanfare as possible. I'd rather we didn't attract any unnecessary attention. Did it help raise your intrinsic value with the police?"

"It did." Tobler stood up with her coffee. She shook hands with Nick. "I hope you'll stay with us again in the future."

"We will. Thanks for the help."

"It was nice meeting you, Ms. Austen, and your daughter." Tobler gave Rachel and Jean a small hand wave before turning to walk away.

"I owe you one, Danger," Nick said. "You sure ended Leslie's fishing expedition in abrupt fashion."

"Does this mean we get to stay another day? My friends said they wouldn't be leaving until tomorrow. They're visiting family here for another day."

"We'll stay another day if I can keep off the police blotter, Danger."

"Nick, we have some time this morning, can...can we go buy some stuff to play softball with?" Jean continued on a roll. "Mom was going to sign me up for the Mini's Softball League this year."

"I did promise to teach her the basics," Rachel added. "I don't suppose softball is one of your many talents, is it?"

"I've played most sports," Nick answered. "I'm sure between the two of us, we could give Danger some practice. Deke will, of course, want to play, which could be a hindrance or help, depending on if he retrieves balls, or plays keep away. I do have to spend at least a few hours on research today sometime between baseball and pool parties. I have a couple solid Tanus hits on guys I'm certain they will be using in Florida. They fit the profile with large paychecks and no expertise in anything resembling the import/export business."

"I can monitor the pool party while you –" Rachel began.

"I think not," Nick interrupted. "I don't want either of you on your own without me. Now, if you two are done eating, let's go find a sports store around here and get some equipment. We'll be on the road again tomorrow, so another activity to pursue while traveling is a good thing. I know Deke will approve."

"Yuck! He'll make the softballs all slimy," Jean complained.

"I'm telling him you said that," Nick warned.

* * *

"Let's get clear on our agenda for the next few weeks," Nick said, as they entered the Sarasota, Florida city limits. "I contacted my friends who own condos down here shortly after hearing where the bank was located. We're still in the off season. They were certain they would have one ready for us. I called them at the last rest stop after talking to Grace and –"

"How'd that go?" Rachel broke in.

"Don't ask," Nick cautioned with a shrug. "It's a process. Anyhow, my friend has a condo we will all be happy to stay in. It's part of a complex, where each building has a set number of condos and structures bordering different small lakes, with all the Florida wildlife inherent to the area, including alligators."

224

"Wow, alligators?" Jean cried out excitedly.

"Yep. They can't train them. They can't make boots out of them. The damned dinosaurs traipse around anywhere they want." Nick smiled back at Jean in the rear view mirror.

"Good. I like alligators," Jean stated.

"Sure, they're all cute and cuddly until someone's pet or child ends up as dinner for one." Nick supplied the counterpoint with some exasperation.

"Huh?"

"Nick, I don't think –"

"I'm just giving Danger the Wild Kingdom rundown of Florida. Alligators are on top of the food chain. Everything else is on the menu for them. I could gun down five people in the street and everyone would be looking into my motives, childhood, and religious background. They would waive the death penalty and put me in a cushy cell with cable TV. If I put a bullet in an alligator, I'd be lucky to survive the week."

Rachel was already laughing, but Jean watched Nick with uncertainty.

"What...what do we do about Deke?" Jean asked, hugging the dog.

"Teach him how to say 'please don't eat me'," Nick quipped, earning an immediate punch to the shoulder from Rachel, who could not stop laughing. "We won't let any alligators get Deke. Now, if we can move from the animal kingdom for a moment, I'd like to return to our actions while living at the condo. We can go swimming in the condo pool, play softball, and even fish in the lake. What we will not be doing is wandering around Sarasota. I have another friend who will quite happily look after Jean while you and I recon our target site, Rachel."

"These friends of yours know something about you then?"

225

"I've used their condo as a retreat before when I've had business in the Gulf or down in the Bahamas. Gus Nason, the guy I'm having watch out for Danger, is an old associate. I have my own contacts. I've never revealed them to anyone."

"Whatever made you establish a retreat in Sarasota? I mean, why not down further in the Miami area?"

"Weather plays less of a factor, and if something goes wrong I wanted to be further away from the trouble point," he answered truthfully. "Your bank down here - SunTrust Bank - I've been looking at street level surroundings on Google. Everything about the place is perfect for our snatch and grab. It's on Main Street and there's a wooded parking lot across the street. We can set up very early in the morning and begin the tedious process of finding out who's watching the bank at any moment. If a couple of the gentlemen I have pictures for turn up, we will definitely have some fun."

"You scare me when 'fun' is mentioned anywhere in a dialogue we're having. Although you did mention fun when we bought the softball equipment."

"What was fun about that?" Jean questioned, looking around the seat at Rachel. "You beaned me on the second pitch, Mom."

"I said I was sorry a hundred times!" Rachel lifted her clenched hands up in front of her. "Please...please...please forgive me."

"Good thing Nick bought me a batting helmet," Jean added, trying not to laugh as Rachel whipped around in the seat.

"Oh waaaahhhh! Get over it. That's baseball." Rachel gave Jean the wave off and looked at Nick's solemn expression. "You got something to say, Hemingway?"

"Threw at her own kid in a Mother/Daughter softball game." Nick shook his head mournfully. "Oh the shame! Oh the trauma!"

226

"Oh, barf," Rachel retorted, hearing Jean laugh.

Ten minutes later, Nick turned into a gated community, complete with guard. Nick stopped and told the guard why they were there. He waved them inside. Nick drove to a picture-book residential street, stopping in front of a house with beautifully manicured landscaped palms and flowers.

"I'll get the keys and we'll be on our way."

"Don't you want them to meet us?" Rachel asked.

"Deniability, my dear." Nick got out of the Escalade. "If they don't see a woman, child, and dog, I'm a single occupant vacationer."

"It's okay to admit you're ashamed to be seen with us."

"Why you..." Nick reached in through the open window on the driver's side toward Rachel, evoking squeals of protest from both Rachel and Jean, while growing a Deke head with jaws around his wrist. "Why you...traitorous mongrel...see if you ever get a beer again. I'm going to cut your Frisbee up into tiny pieces."

Nick backed out amidst jeers from his companions. Five minutes later, Nick exited the house and slipped into the Escalade driver's seat.

"Our condo is right across the lake we passed," Nick told them.

"Can we go swimming?" Jean asked.

"Of course, but let's get settled in first before using the pool."

"This place is gorgeous," Rachel exclaimed in open-mouthed awe, looking around the condominium after they split up the bags and took them into the separate bedrooms. "A full kitchen, laundry, and balcony overlooking the lake. I could be happy here for a few weeks. I only saw a couple people coming up here. Is that because it's the off-season?"

"When the winter hits full bore up North, this is the retreat from the cold. Let's take Deke down and play some Frisbee. He'll need exercise after our final road jaunt here. The refrigerator is stocked. My friends always have cold cuts, bread, cereal, and milk too."

"You haven't mentioned your friends' names," Rachel pointed out.

"No, I haven't. Let's bring along Deke's water dish and the cooler. We'll wear his butt out while sipping our drinks in the shade on lawn chairs."

"What about alligators?" Jean looked out at the lake from their balcony.

"Good point, Danger." Nick dropped down on his knees in front of Deke. "Repeat after me, Deke. Please…don't –"

"Nick!" Rachel grabbed Nick by the ear, yanking upwards on it. "Stand up here. We'll stay away from the lake while playing Frisbee, Jean."

While Jean tossed the Frisbee to Deke, Nick and Rachel sat together in the shade. Nick handed Rachel two photos of men. They looked like mug shots."

"These are the guys we'll really be looking for first. Keep them and memorize their faces," he told her.

"What do we do when we see them?"

"It will be more fun to show you." Nick grinned over at her.

* * *

At eight o'clock, Nick sat at the dining room table writing on his laptop while Rachel, Jean, and Deke watched *Madagascar*. Nick had been banished from the living room when he was unable to stop laughing at what was supposed to be a poignant moment in

228

the movie. Knowing how infrequently he had been able to write lately, Nick decided against launching a protest. The doorbell rang right on time and Nick checked the security eye in the door before opening it. Rachel stopped the movie, looking back at the door anxiously.

A clean shaven black man, inches taller than Nick, walked in the doorway and shook hands with Nick. To Rachel's surprise, they then hugged each other. Deke had crept nearer the entranceway in order to stay apprised of who came in. The dog sat attentively behind Nick, watching the reunion with interest. The man looked overly lean to Rachel, but with huge shoulders. He wore jeans and a black t-shirt. His hair was cut very close to his scalp. Rachel left the couch with Jean in tow, curious to meet the man Nick had only mentioned.

"Gus Nason, this is Rachel, Jean, and Deke." Nick gestured to his companions, while Gus smiled and shook hands with each of them in turn, including Deke. "Gus will be helping us out with logistics and support."

"Did he save your life too?" Rachel smiled up at Gus.

"Ah, no," Nick answered for his friend. "Gus handles anything and everything I need when I work anywhere in the Gulf. He lives in St. Petersburg and owns a very nice boat he takes fishermen out with when he needs money."

"Or I transport the Kingfisher here to and from his work as he calls it, for quite a bit more money than my fishing enterprise pays," Gus added.

"Is that a Boston accent?" Rachel asked. "I like it."

"Born and raised there, but hated the weather. Usually, people are so shocked I don't speak cornpone, they never notice the accent."

"Sit down, Gus, and I'll get you a beer." Nick gestured for his friend to sit down at the dining room table. "You want to take a break from the movie, Danger, and sit with us?"

"Sure," Jean answered happily, slipping into a seat opposite Gus and next to Rachel. "Do I get a beer too?"

"I don't think so, young lady," Rachel commented, giving Jean's hair a tug.

"Did Nick just call you Danger?" Gus asked Jean.

"Yeah, like the girl in the comics. I'm Danger Girl. I can shoot and everything. Nick says I'm part of the Terminator team."

"The Terminator?" Gus laughed long and hard, with everyone but Nick and Deke joining in. "Oh, very good…did you come up with that, Danger?"

"Yep," Jean acknowledged proudly.

"These two know more about you than anyone, ever."

"I'm in the process of changing my lifestyle," Nick explained in deadpan fashion, which evoked more laughter from Gus. He turned to Rachel. "Unlike my friend in Denver, Gus here knows I'm not one of the good guys."

"It's true," Gus agreed. "Some problems can't be solved by good guys. Well, what's my part in this enterprise, Terminator?"

"Rachel and I will be on recon during banking hours, starting tomorrow. I need you to look after Danger and Deke while we're gone. When we've arrived at the moment for making a withdrawal, you'll drop Rachel off at the SunTrust bank entrance and ride around until she calls for a pick up. There will be some excitement on her way from the bank to your car. We'll handle that. You just drive the car."

"Oh. 'Drivin' Ms. Daisy', huh? Only in a hail of bullets?" Gus asked.

"There won't be any hail of bullets, Gus. There might be a few guys dropping to the sidewalk on Rachel's walk to your car. I also need you to rent a new car each day to come over here with. Rachel and I will drive it over to the bank."

"I like that part." Gus leaned forward. "What kind?"

"You pick. Don't make it too flashy. We'll need to have the windows all very dark."

"Do you know how to play softball, Gus?" Jean asked.

"Sure thing, Danger. You a player?"

"Yep. I can hit pretty good. My mom beaned me, though, last time she pitched."

"Oh, for God's sake," Rachel exclaimed, dropping her head to the table while the others laughed.

"I like your new crew, Terminator," Gus announced.

"Danger's been handled a couple times on our drive from the West Coast. I don't want her touched again."

"Count on that, brother. Swimming, softball, and I'll teach Danger how to fish. Can we go to the beach? They have a spot here in Sarasota where dogs are allowed."

"Can we, Nick?" Jean implored.

"Sure, if Gus is comfortable with the beach, I'm okay with it. Rach?"

"I...I guess it'll be all right."

"I see you're worried, Rachel. Don't be. I can imagine what happened to the guys who bothered Danger on the trip. With me, I'm more of a preemptive strike kind of guy, so we'll be here waiting every day when you two get done at the bank."

"Thank you." Rachel grabbed Jean's chin. "If she mentions the beaning one more time, she'll need a bodyguard to keep me from pounding on her myself."

Deke popped up to grip Rachel's wrist with a short 'grrfff,' while Jean giggled appreciatively, wrapping her arm around Deke's neck.

Gus chuckled. "Looks like she already has one."

* * *

"I really liked Gus," Rachel mentioned as Nick slowly drove down Main Street at nearly ten o'clock in the morning. She watched Nick's notebook computer screen, while the video transmitter Nick had mounted above the front door frame on the passenger side sent images being filmed. Rachel could direct it slightly, or zoom in.

"I really like this Buick Lacerne. You're getting the license numbers clearly, right?"

"Yes, Obi-Wan, all is as it should be, Master. You guys talked for three hours and never said a damn thing about how you met or what stuff you two did together."

"I think I like the sound of Master." Nick ignored Rachel's quick glare as he sidestepped the rest of her comment. "It may be vaguely entertaining to know every detail about everything, Rachel, but it does nothing for our safety, or the people we deal with. We're in the thick of it now."

"You mean we do it by the book," Rachel said sarcastically.

"There is no book. We do it by the same rules I've stayed alive with for over a decade."

"You admitted breaking all the rules getting here."

"This is why I work alone." Nick turned into a parking lot down the street and headed the opposite direction on Main Street. "Would you like to risk the lives of everyone Gus cares about so you can gather a few more interesting facts?"

"No, but –"

"But nothing," Nick cut her off. "You and Jean were taken away from me with the most obvious of ploys. I make mistakes when I'm flying by the seat of my pants. If those guys would have needed to question you, instead of needing something only you

232

could get for them, guess what? You'd have told them your entire life's story."

"What about you?" Rachel argued, changing the transmitter position slightly with the joystick Nick had given her to use. "If you were –"

"I'll never be taken," Nick interrupted again. "We can park now. Maybe I can find a spot under one of those trees in the parking lot across the street."

"We don't have to shut off the car and the AC while we broil, do we?"

"I'm a psycho, not stupid. I don't underestimate my enemies and I don't project abnormal intelligence into common thugs doing a boring job. There's a spot."

Nick drove in a semicircle, parking with the front of their rented Buick pointed at an angle toward the front of SunTrust Bank's main branch. He took out his spotting scope and checked the scene around the bank's front entrance. Rachel used the mounted transmitter with digital zoom to scan the area on Nick's notebook computer.

"I'm good. How about you?"

"We have only limited vision on the cars on our side," Rachel answered.

"These guys won't be sitting in a hot car all day," Nick explained. "For one thing, the cops would be called in by bank security. One of the reasons you see a bank's security guard walk around in front of the bank has nothing to do with getting a breath of fresh air. They look for cars parked too long in front of the bank with idling motors - or double parked cars."

"That's the reason you had me film so far down the street in both directions."

"There are plenty of little shops on Main Street. They'll be watching the bank with at least one of each team within grabbing distance. The other one will hover close to the car in case the

233

grabber misses. We have a number of objectives. We need to ID our two teams and their vehicles. It will be important if we can determine whether they're aware of each other. I'm betting Tanus doesn't know where Javier went, so they'll be flying blind. They'll suspect Javier went rogue on them, but they won't know with whom. Fletcher's people will know Tanus has a team here. By the way, this is an inexact science."

"Why is this starting to sound very familiar to me?" Rachel looked up at Nick from the notebook computer questioningly.

"Ever see any of Clint Eastwood's 'Spaghetti' Westerns?"

"I knew it!" Rachel laughed, pointing her finger at Nick. "This is the plot from *A Fistful of Dollars*. The man with no name comes to town and plays off the evil Rojo brothers against the equally evil Baxter clan. You're not playing by some assassin's rulebook, you're following the script from a 1960's Italian Western."

"I don't plan on being caught and tortured by the two sides. Damn," Nick complained. "I never figured you saw those movies."

"I was a tomboy and I loved Clint Eastwood." Rachel reached over to grasp Nick's hand. "Maybe that's why I love you."

"I'm Brad Pitt, remember?" A chill ran through Nick from where she grasped his hand.

"You're a cold-blooded killer with no conscience. The man with no name saved a Mother and her child in *A Fistful of Dollars*, too, on a whim."

"Maybe I love you because I can't think of anyone else who would have made the connection." Nick brought Rachel's hand up to his lips. Flashes of her in his arms the night before, muffling her screams of pleasure with both hands, romped through his head.

"So, how do we play Tanus off against Fletcher?"

"We find out first if those two guys from the mug shots I showed you are down here for Fletcher Exports."

"And...and we turn them over to the cops," Rachel added excitedly.

"After the cops drag those two away we'll only have the Tanus team to deal with for a few days. I'll give Fletcher's people a call and tell them Javier tipped off the cops. That will cause some excitement. We'll hit the bank the moment we only have Tanus waiting for you. I'll take them beforehand."

"Gus drives up. You get out, dressed like a model, with red hair and all your accessories. Gus will back your play if you need help. As we discussed, you can bet Tanus owns a couple people inside the bank. The moment you access the safety deposit box, their team outside will know it. Since I found out Javier switched sides, I've decided against having you bludgeon your way through. Hopefully, with Fletcher and Tanus at each other's throat, we can get far away from Sarasota before they know we're gone. I'll get the flash drives copied and then we'll begin negotiating."

"What if they have more people than you think and they follow Gus away?"

"Let me worry about pursuit. We want –"

"There, Nick." Rachel paused the video taken while cruising earlier, pointing to a blue Ford Five Hundred parked across the street from the bank. It had Louisiana plates.

"I'll take a stroll first and see if I have any luck. There are little shops along this side of the street for me to saunter past." Nick took two photos from the folder, along with their rap sheets. "Vertinski here was busted in Baton Rouge for drugs and assault."

Nick turned the computer toward him for a moment. He hacked into the Louisiana Department of Motor Vehicles, querying their database for a stolen Ford Five Hundred with license plate matching the one across the street from the bank. Nick started laughing.

"Dum...da dum dum," Nick intoned the popular opening to the TV series 'Dragnet'. "He's a genius, Rach. The dummy didn't even have sense enough to switch plates. Oh man, if he's around the car, this could be our lucky day."

Chapter Eighteen
Stakeout

"Nick, be careful. Don't let a little positive stuff screw up your bad karma."

"Ha ha, very funny." Nick gave Rachel's hair a tug before exiting the Buick with ball cap and sunglasses on. He had dressed in khaki shorts, gray t-shirt and tennis shoes with no socks before leaving the condo with Rachel. The heat after being inside the air conditioned Buick nearly dropped him to his knees. He pointed at the throwaway cell-phone near Rachel. "I'll have mine at my ear like all the other cell-junkies do so we can stay in constant contact."

Taking a few deep breaths and feeling droplets of sweat forming everywhere, he closed the Buick door. He walked briskly toward Main Street while phoning Rachel's cell-phone.

"Rachel on the run, Rachel speaking."

"Oh, you are just too cute for words." Nick rounded the parking lot in front of a Spanish-style building. He stepped up on the sidewalk, glancing at the cars parked diagonally near a line of shops with awnings. "I see it and the genius."

Vertinski stood, arms folded across chest, in front of the second shop, leaning against the building. He wore mirror type sunglasses, a sleeveless white t-shirt, loafers and tan shorts. Nick stopped in front of him, smiling up at the heavily built man.

"Excuse me, Sir, do you know what time it is?" Nick asked politely, pointing at Vertinski's Rolex watch.

"I don't know," Vertinski growled, not making any move to turn his wrist. "Go ask inside, meatball."

"Sure, sure." Nick scurried back as if frightened, and then walked away up the street. He lifted his phone up again. "It's Vertinski."

"I heard you playing with him, dummy."

"I'm going across the street to the bank to start up a savings account. When I get done taking pictures in there with my really good digital camera, I'll leave and take a picture of the gorilla posing right in front of his stolen car. We'll post the picture to the Sarasota police department and kick back to watch the fireworks."

"Showoff."

Nick took his hand-held digital camera out as he walked into the air conditioned bank with an audible sigh of relief, clicking away with his camera, while talking to Rachel. While he waited in a seat near the desks for his turn to talk with a consultant, he snapped pictures without being obvious. His mouth tightened when he saw one of the security guards come out of the rear.

"We have a tiny problem."

"What, you can't walk from the bank to the car because of the heat?"

Nick smiled. "No, Vertinski's partner works as a bank guard."

"Oh joy."

"We're going to really cause a stir when I get out of here. I shouldn't even start up an account now, considering their hiring practices."

Thirty minutes later, Nick had a savings account with five hundred dollars in it under his Roscoe Weatherby name. He also had pictures of Vertinski's partner. As Nick walked from the bank, he fiddled with his papers, zooming in on the immobile Vertinski and the stolen Ford. Nick crossed the street down from Vertinski, almost directly in front of the rented Buick. Vertinski did not glance his way, so Nick moved quickly to the Buick. He entered with a sigh as the cool air hit him.

"C'mon, Geeks R Us, get busy with the pictures," Rachel ordered, turning the notebook computer toward him.

Nick popped the memory chip out and plugged it into his computer. The pictures were automatically downloaded into a file. Nick looked at each one of them with satisfaction.

"Not bad for off the hip shots. Look at the one for Vega, the security guard. Oh boy are the cops going to love this stuff. They have one wanted felon out casing the bank and an inside-man felon as a security guard. Nice setup."

He looked up the Web address for the Sarasota police department and uploaded the pictures with date stamp and explanatory note. He included Vertinski's and Vega's mug shots with partial rap sheets. Next, he had Rachel call in on her throw away cell-phone, explaining to the police how she had spotted the two. Until she talked them into checking their computer for the pictures, they were less than enthused. When they suddenly wanted to know everything about her, she ended the call. Twenty minutes later, police squad cars ringed Vertinski and his Ford. A second team carefully entered the bank. They emerged with Vega five minutes after they went in.

"Dum...da dum dum...daaaaaa..." Nick crooned.

* * *

"Tell Gus why we couldn't have hit the bank right after the police took Vertinski and Vega away," Rachel directed. She brought refreshments over and set them down on the condo's dining room table.

"I don't need to tell him," Nick replied, exchanging grins with Gus as the two sat across from each other. "He trusts my judgment. Come to think of it, Danger and Deke trust my judgment too. Why, oh why, can't you?"

"We had the advantage, Nick." Rachel ignored the laughter at Nick's rhyme.

"Rachel, you didn't know all the players," Gus told her gently. "If Tanus has someone working the safety deposit boxes, or notes which ones get accessed, they could have tipped off a Tanus team not right outside the bank. Fletcher Exports screwed up with their two picks, leading to a nice first day. Predicting actions by Tanus on the heels of the police action may have led to disaster."

"I wasn't making fun of you, Rachel. I'm tired. We had a busy, hot day. Sit back and relax. While you were catching up with Danger's day, I sent a note into Tanus headquarters, letting them know Javier Martine ended up at Fletcher Exports. I then put a note into Fletcher Exports, warning them not to send anyone else to Florida if they know what's good for them, as if it came from Tanus. Now, we need to find out who the hell is down here from Tanus."

"Other than scripting your plan like an old western, what's the purpose of all this?" Rachel asked, not at all mollified by his explanation.

"To make your walk in the bank like a day at the beach," Gus answered for Nick. "Nick shows up at the bank every day, doing something different inside, including getting a safety deposit box. How am I doing, brother?"

"Too damn good," Nick muttered. "Either you've known me too long, or I've known you too long."

"They won't have a clue, Nick," Gus reassured him.

"Jesus...that is good." Rachel smiled for the first time since she sat down. "I go get the flash drives and pass them to you inside the bank. You take the drives and put them in your own safety deposit box. Then, even if something goes wrong outside, they don't get the flash drives."

"First, we have to stir the pot between Tanus and Fletcher. I want them watching each other with the same enthusiasm they're watching for you. In the meantime, I'll spend the next three days

240

adding a checking account, money market account, and a safety deposit box. I want everyone around to believe I'm just some new local businessman."

"Did you have any luck spotting what vehicles might be owned by Tanus?" Gus asked.

"We didn't find any out of state license plates, but I still have to check for rentals," Nick answered. "Vega was a surprise. I need to examine the SunTrust employee records more closely. I checked, and he used an alias to get the job. Fletcher found out about the drives recently. Tanus has had time to establish people at the bank we may not be able to spot."

"This is getting complicated again," Rachel pointed out.

"We're not getting the flash drives at any cost. Our side will not take casualties. Today was only our first day, Rach, and we had a good one. Let's not piss on our good fortune by hurrying fate. Moving on, how was your day with Danger, Gus?"

"Between Miss Outgoing, Deke, and the damn Frisbee, I nearly had the whole beach crowd checking us out."

"Jean told me she had a great time with you," Rachel said.

"We have to go to the beach again tomorrow to meet up with her new friends vacationing from Pennsylvania. I told her as long as she cleans up the dog dung, I'm fine."

"She was out like a light at eight o'clock."

"Her birthday's coming up in a few days, isn't it?" Nick asked.

"Yes, and you've already spoiled her rotten on this trip, so I don't have a clue what to get her."

"I have to go. Thanks to Danger, the chick magnet, I have a date tonight," Gus announced, standing up.

"You Philistine, using Danger and Deke to troll for women. How could you?" Nick asked, already shaking his head in fake disappointment.

241

"They were an attraction today," Gus acknowledged. "How was the Buick?"

"Perfect. Anything you can get similar to it would be a help. I'd be able to mount the transmitter easily again. The windows were just right too. It should be nice on your date."

"No use wasting a beautiful new car rental." Gus shrugged, waving on the way out. "See you two tomorrow."

"Bye, Gus." When the door closed behind him, Rachel turned to Nick, who was at the refrigerator for more refreshments. "How do you do it, Nick? I figured we'd storm the bank without a second thought when the cops left today."

"Patience and a healthy survival instinct, Rach. There are too many variables right now to do anything hasty. I thought you liked the idea of switching safety deposit boxes."

"I do. I'll be less pessimistic tomorrow morning."

"Do you think Deke needs a walk?"

"He's out cold next to Jean. I went out with him for a while before Jean went to bed. Want to try out your patient approach in some other endeavor?"

"I thought you'd never ask."

* * *

"Damn, no rentals around, and no suspicious out of state license plates."

They were parked in the same spot as the day before in a Pontiac 6, this time with Rachel behind the wheel. Nick worked the computer, while Rachel watched the bank and surrounding area with Nick's digital spotting scope.

"I guess it was too much to hope for, that they'd be as obvious as those two yesterday." Rachel held up two sheets of pictures. "Like you said last night, they've been down here waiting for a long time. I haven't seen anyone resembling the men or women on these photo sheets you made up."

"I didn't spot any Tanus people inside either. I guess it's time for me to make another appearance in the bank. I'll set up a safety deposit box today. I'm hoping the bank has someone in particular who handles the area where the boxes are."

"You'll be a lot less comfortable, but I like your outfit better." Rachel gestured at Nick's gray slacks and light blue short sleeved pullover shirt. "You'll look a lot more presentable today."

Nick pulled his notebook computer case from the backseat. "This will be what I'll have with me every day. You'll go in with a large black purse with blank flash drives already in it when we decide it's time. After taking the real drives out and putting them into a small zip lock bag, you'll lock your box back up and come out. I'll be holding the case in such a way you will be able to brush by me in the bank and drop the drives in. Then, you take a seat and mess around filling out something while I copy the drives. I'll put the originals into my own safety deposit box. I want you to then look around nervously while I complete the transfer and leave the bank ahead of you. With any luck, the bad guys will have gathered by then, waiting for their moment."

"If I didn't trust you –"

"Yeah, this plan would be awkward. I could ditch you right then and there, leaving you to take the heat. Instead of that traitorous scenario, I'll get my bag somewhere safe and cue Gus. I should have a good idea who the grabbers will be. I'll take them out and give you the word to hurry the hell out of the bank and into the car with Gus. I don't want you exposed for even ten seconds, so once the Tanus guys hit the deck, you run for the car. I'll meet up with you at the condo. We'll have all the poker chips then: original flash drives still in a safety deposit box, us with copies, you and Jean out of danger."

"Wow, it sounds so simple when you put it like that."

"Off I go." Nick opened the door to a furnace blast of humid hot air. "Good Lord in heaven! I'll keep you on the cell while I'm playing businessman inside. Watch for guys paying attention to me."

"Okay. Just shut the damn door."

Nick closed the door and adjusted his sunglasses. He hurried diagonally across the street so as to end up at the SunTrust bank entrance. He called Rachel while walking across the threshold.

"Nick, bring me back a Diet Pepsi."

"Sure thing, Princess." He walked to one of the people at a desk, asking about opening a safety deposit box. Fifteen minutes later, the man who had helped him fill out the paperwork guided Nick to the safety deposit box area, cautioning him on what would happen if the keys were lost. He buzzed the rear section. A pleasant faced blonde in her mid-thirties came to the window. Nick recognized her immediately.

"Rene will help you from here, Mr. Weatherby." The man shook Nick's hand.

"I see you have your signature card all filled out. Sign and date the sign-in sheet and I'll take you back to the boxes."

Nick signed in and Rene let him into the back. She found his new safety deposit box number and inserted her key, gesturing for Nick to insert his. Once he had the box in hand, Rene led him to a line of small rooms.

"Let me know when you're ready to return the box to the room, Sir."

"I will, Rene, thank you."

"Rachel," Nick spoke into the cell-phone after closing the door. "We have contact. Rene's working in safety deposit box land. You have her on your sheet."

"Rene Santora?"

"Yep. What do you think about following her home tonight, trussing her up before work in the morning, and blowing all these complicated plans to hell? We could walk right in and back out if there's no tipster in here."

Rachel started laughing and took minutes to calm down before being able to speak.

"What…what happened to patience?"

"Patience took a hike the moment I saw a familiar face in here." Nick leaned back in his seat visualizing what he would need to do. "We do it exactly as I outlined, only I won't have to drop any guys on the way to the car. We get away clean."

"You won't kill her, will you?"

"It would be easier if I did."

"You cold-hearted bastard," Rachel murmured. "She's just an employee. You're screwing with me, right?"

No. "Of course I am. I'll be out in a couple minutes."

* * *

"You haven't said a word since we drove away from the bank." Rachel pointed out as Nick drove their rented Pontiac. "Are you plotting?"

"I called Gus. He'll be meeting us at the condo. I'll get changed into a suit and tie. He and I will go over to Rene's house for recon. If our research reveals no dogs, children, or husbands, I'll put her out of commission before dawn tomorrow."

"Why use Gus instead of me?"

"Gus can immediately drive back to St. Pete and return the Pontiac," Nick answered. *She's suspicious already.* "The moment the bank opens tomorrow, we'll make our flash drive withdrawal in the new rental Gus brings us. We'll only be gone a couple of

245

hours. I'll have the condo locked down tight with a motion detector while we're gone, which will alert me the moment it goes off."

"You're going to kill Rene, aren't you?"

"What? You're on a first name basis now with the woman who would have painted a target on you the moment your safety deposit box was accessed?"

"She wouldn't have known why. Maybe they told her it was a police investigation."

"Look, Rachel, I just need to disable her until around noontime. Once we have the flash drives copied, we'll lay low at the condo until I'm certain there's no heat on my Weatherby identity. I did have to give them the condo address to start my accounts. I'll go fool around with my new accounts and visit my safety deposit box while you and Jean stay with Gus at the condo. It will give me a chance to see if our withdrawal stirs up anything. If we're lucky, Santora won't tell anyone so as to stay out of trouble with Tanus. The two teams may then be back in place watching each other while we hit the road."

"When do we bring Grace and Tim back into the mix?" Rachel asked, her voice sounding slightly relieved at Nick's explanation.

"After I arrange a get together with Suzan and her husband at a neutral spot and we decipher the information, I'll bring the Marshalls into it. I'll give Suzan's husband unedited copies. Then I'll tell them to set up a meet with Grace and Tim. We'll lay low. I'll plot targets until the shit hits the fan. Even with the drives and a corroborating witness, we'll need to be in lockdown mode until I see Grace do the right thing."

"What about Frank?"

"Frank stuck it to me with the setup in Denver. We'll wait to find out if Frank survives the flash drive revelations. There's no use in negotiating with Frank if he's indicted. Our work for getting you and Jean back to a normal life depends on how many untouchables are on the flash drives."

"Untouchables?"

"People who escape the taking down of Tanus and who might still pose a threat."

"Can't you make them do something about these untouchables?"

"We'll see, but there might be a name or two only a .50 caliber solution will remedy. Frank would be an extremely valuable guy to have on our side if that happens."

Nick parked near his Cadillac in front of the condominium complex. Inside the condo, they said their hellos, and he went in his bedroom to get dressed. When he came out, he looked like a bank executive in the slate gray suit he had changed into. While Gus waited at the Pontiac, Nick made sure his alarms were in place and activated on the condo. They drove to Rene Santora's home on Gillespie Avenue.

Nick pulled on white Nitrile gloves and exited the Pontiac as Gus drove away. He walked up to the house and rang the doorbell, noting no alarm pad was in place. He smiled when he pulled up a corner of Santora's welcome mat and found her hideaway key, saving him the lost time picking the lock. Twenty-five minutes later, Gus picked him up in front. Nick opened his laptop and inserted the memory chip from his camera into the slot on the side. Moments later, he was scanning the inside pictures of Santora's home on the computer screen.

"How's it look?"

"Piece of cake," Nick answered. "No squeaky spots, guns, dogs, or roommates. Her bed is only thirty feet away from the rear entrance. I copied the hard drive on her computer too. The woman is helpless."

"It's perfect if you kill her."

"You barbarian."

* * *

"I like this. Very few houses and no traffic." Gus scanned the area near Santora's house at three in the morning. "I'll be around."

Nick nodded. He left the Pontiac, dressed all in black with a small bag. Seconds later, he stood outside the rear entrance to the house with his night vision goggles in place. He had earlier rigged the door so it could not be locked. Slipping inside, he gently closed the door and stood listening intently, leaning against the wall. Minutes passed with no sound, other than Santora's refrigerator kicking on and the air conditioning going through a cooling cycle. He moved into Rene's bedroom while the air conditioning covered the faint sounds he made. He wet a thick gauze-like pad and covered the woman's face.

Nick heard her snore slightly. She quieted as he watched her glide quietly toward death. He cursed suddenly as a motion picture replay of Rachel, Jean, and Deke bombarded him. *Son of a bitch*! He pulled the chloroformed pad away and carried Santora into the attached garage. He maneuvered her unconscious body behind the steering wheel. Nick retrieved his bag, a small pillow from the bedroom, and a kitchen towel. After making sure movement on the steering wheel hub did not activate the horn, Nick put the woman's head on the pillow and positioned her face sideways into the now padded steering wheel hub.

He duct-taped her wrists together, and then taped them draped around the steering column and wheel, adding numerous wraps around her upper body. He taped her ankles together and to the brake pedal. Slipping the seat belt around her waist, Nick fastened and tightened it until there could be no movement. He then carefully duct taped the kitchen towel in place around her mouth and head, ending with a final revolution of tape to keep her head immobile. Nick shut the car door. He left the garage open to the air conditioned air from inside the house.

Gus received his call and returned to Santora's house where he picked Nick up.

"What did you do, take a nap in there?"

"Very funny."

"You didn't kill her!" Gus exclaimed in overly dramatic fashion, laughing in short snorts of derision. "Oh, you poor neutered puppy, someone's cut your man bearings off."

"Shut up and drive."

* * *

"I should have known you'd be up," Rachel commented, walking into the dining room area where Nick was typing, already dressed in his suit, minus the coat. "I missed not slipping into your room last night."

"Did you?" Nick looked up at the same time Deke did as the dog lay behind his chair. "I'd like you to be ready in an hour. I don't want to be waiting at the bank entrance when it opens. I want you to go in about half an hour after they open the doors."

Sensing a change in Nick's demeanor, Rachel walked over, grabbed and shook Deke's nose playfully for a moment, and sat next to Nick. He felt her reach around and run her right hand up and down his back. He clenched his teeth together, unable to halt the familiar passion sweeping through him at her touch. She leaned in against him, her head on his shoulder. He could feel the heat where her breast pressed into his arm through the flimsy silk nightgown, and her scent seared his senses.

"You don't like me much this morning, do you?" Rachel asked, her left hand moving down Nick's stomach and over his belt. "Well, okay, maybe you do like me."

Nick's hands knotted into fists on either side of his notebook computer.

249

"Did you kill her?"

"No, but I should have. Our excursion this morning is in jeopardy because I left her alive. I'm lucky Gus didn't walk away from this last night. It puts his life in danger along with all of ours."

"Knowing you, the risk will be small," she whispered.

"I'm not in the risk business, Rachel. I'm in the dead bang cinch business. Better go get ready so we can make the risk as small as possible."

"I love you."

"What if I'd killed Santora?"

"You didn't."

"I would've in a heartbeat," he replied, turning and locking eyes with Rachel.

The dark, cold, and lifeless nature of his piercing stare made her shudder and look away.

"I believe you." She gave him a final tense hug before standing up. "I'll go get ready."

Chapter Nineteen
Old Friends

Gus arrived at eight o'clock sharp, laughing when he saw Nick with Jean out on the patch of lawn bordering the condo complex in suit pants, white shirt and tie, taking turns throwing Deke the Frisbee. Gus parked the black Lincoln Town Car under the awning-covered parking section near the building's front. He exited the Lincoln, also dressed formally, and walked over toward Nick.

"I see you're passing the time before our morning enterprise gainfully." Gus grinned down at Jean, who came over and gave him a hug, while Deke dropped the Frisbee in front of him. "I'm beginning to see where you're going with all this, Nick."

"Good. Maybe you can fill me in. Danger's going with you and Rachel. I'll take the Escalade with Deke in the back. I'm not leaving anyone this morning."

"It's your show," Gus agreed, his tone somewhat surprised.

"I'll get Rachel."

Nick entered the condo. Rachel met him at the door with his suit coat, and he looked her over approvingly. She wore a sleeveless burgundy dress with black high heels and tan nylons. The neckline plunged modestly. Her hair fell in waves past her shoulders. She turned after handing Nick his coat.

"Zip me, big boy."

He did as ordered. "I see you have your bag. Do you have the ID's you'll need to access your box?"

"Yes, and I have the Ziploc bag for the drives. I'm not sure it's such a good idea to take the pepper-spray and stun-gun though. I shouldn't –"

251

"Leave them in your bag," he directed, locking up after she cleared the doorway. "They won't search you. The stun-gun and pepper-spray give you added insurance in case I missed something or Santora has been found. I checked the local news earlier. It was all quiet. I expect they haven't seen you around at the bank in quite a while. They're sure to give you a bad time at check-in. Stay frosty and don't take any shit. Have them call over the branch manager if they give you the run around."

"I will," she acknowledged with some condescension, having heard the directions many times. "It won't be so hard since you didn't have me dye my hair red."

"Did you just give me attitude?"

"Maybe...ouch!" She jumped as Nick smacked her butt with a resounding slap. "You...you spanked me!"

He smiled as he took Rachel's arm and pushed her forward. When they reached the Lincoln, Nick opened the rear door for her, giving Jean a small wave.

"A couple hours from now we'll be lying out by the pool," Nick told them, closing the door. He turned, and took Deke's leash from Gus. "I'll call you the moment I go in. We'll stay in constant contact once we're in the bank. Anybody in front looking suspicious, let us know."

Gus nodded. He walked around to the driver's side of the Lincoln while Nick walked Deke two spots over, opening the Cadillac's rear door and motioning for Deke to jump up. Nick left first as they had previously arranged. He drove to the bank, parking in the spot they had used for surveillance. Looking around with his spotting scope, he saw only a few cars parked near the shops along Main Street. The traffic was sparse. In the few minutes before Gus arrived, Nick only spotted one person going into the bank. He watched the Lincoln pull up in front of the bank, and then drive away, leaving Rachel walking confidently into the bank.

Nick waited fifteen minutes. Leaving the Escalade with notebook computer bag in hand, he walked quickly over to the

SunTrust bank and went inside, phoning Gus as he did. A woman was signing Rachel into the safety deposit box area when Nick came through the entrance.

"Rachel's in," he relayed to Gus. "Open up a three way for us with her."

"You're on," Gus replied simply.

"Everything okay, Rach?"

"They're all here. I'll be out in ten minutes."

"Hang up, put your cell on vibrate. Once you've left the drives with me, sit down in the waiting area. I'll call you when we're clear."

He walked over to a teller's window in the nearly empty bank and deposited two hundred dollars before moving to the forms desk, where patrons could get deposit and withdrawal slips. They also had forms for obtaining ATM cards. Nick took one of those and began filling it out carefully. Rachel walked out of the safety deposit box area a few minutes later, spotted him, and walked over to the form table. She put the Ziploc bag with flash drives on the table, picked up some deposit slips, and went to sit on one of the chairs in the waiting area.

Nick put the filled out form in his bag with the flash drives. He signed into the safety deposit box area and retrieved his box with the help of Rene Santora's replacement. Inside the private viewing room, he opened up his notebook computer and started the tedious process of copying the flash drives over to his hard disk, and to a new set of flash drives. When he completed the process, he put the original flash drives in his safety deposit box. After storing away the new copies and notebook computer in his bag, he waited for the attendant. When she came over to help him, Nick returned his safety deposit box to its slot and left.

"Gus, I'm on the way out of the safety deposit box area. Are you across the street?"

253

"Yes, and there's a woman pacing out here: brunette, mid-thirties, designer blue and green jogging outfit. She's moving around as if waiting for a running partner. I don't like it."

"I'll take a look. Get Rachel back on with us now."

Nick walked to the entranceway and stopped near the security guard. He knelt down as if to rearrange or check the contents of his notebook computer bag, all the while watching the woman doing small stretches out front. She finally glanced at the bank entrance, giving Nick a facial view. Nick took his partially filled in form out and walked to the forms desk once more.

"I know her. She's not Tanus or Fletcher. Rachel, I want you to go get the security guard at the front to walk you out to where Gus is going to be. Don't engage the woman at all. Don't look at her. Don't pause. Have your stun gun ready even with the security guard next to you. If she so much as asks for the time, zap her. We have to flush her partner out. Gus, is that warehouse place we used a couple years ago on the dock between here and St. Pete still abandoned?"

"Yeah, the rebuilding money fell through during the mortgage dump."

"Take a drive around Sarasota for the next thirty minutes, and then take them there. You know the drill. Don't drive anywhere you're not in the middle of traffic. Use the approach near the water, where the buildings are on your left. Stop fifty yards from where the access winds around to the left."

"Got it."

"Leave now, Rach."

"What if the security guard won't walk me?"

"Make a fuss if he bulks, but don't go out to Gus without him."

Rachel stood up with bag in hand. She walked quickly to the security guard, engaging him in conversation for a moment. The man nodded agreeably, and held the door open for Rachel.

"She's on her way, Gus."

Nick went to the front entrance and watched her progress. When the woman saw the security guard, she took out her cellphone and made a call. She did not approach Rachel. The Lincoln was waiting when Rachel reached the street. She thanked the security guard and slipped into the passenger seat next to Gus. A white Lexus drove by in front next, stopping long enough for the apparent jogger to jump in before it followed the Lincoln. Nick left the bank and jogged toward the Cadillac. He opened up the cargo area and stripped off his coat and shirt, throwing them in the back. Deke sat up on the passenger side front seat when Nick opened the driver's door.

"You're going on a field trip with me, Deke," he told the dog, slamming his door and gesturing Deke into the back seat.

* * *

"I hope you ladies enjoyed our scenic tour of Sarasota," Gus spoke up, as he drove toward St. Petersburg.

"What are we doing, Gus? Is the woman from the bank still following us?"

"She's back there. Every once in a while I catch a glimpse of her white Lexus."

"Where're we headed now?" Jean asked.

"A warehouse spot near the ocean almost to my house," Gus answered. "We'll only be stopping there for a moment before we go back to the condo."

Because the traffic thinned out considerably, both Rachel and Jean saw more of the Lexus as they traveled. When Gus turned into a dock area, lined with graffiti covered warehouse buildings, Rachel looked around worriedly. Gus slowed to a crawl as they drove along the litter filled access road. The Lexus had plainly followed them.

"What the hell are you doing, Gus?"

255

"Calm down, Rachel," Gus urged as he approached a winding curve.

Gus stopped the Town Car. Rachel and Jean watched the Lexus get larger in the tinted rear window. It stopped only twenty yards behind the Lincoln. A few seconds after the Lexus halted, its windshield shattered. Rachel and Jean both jumped. The passenger side door of the Lexus started to open; but the woman they could see plainly through the now open windshield area suddenly pitched backward, her left shoulder a bloody pulp. Gus turned the Lincoln around.

"Close your eyes ladies," Gus advised.

He drove by the idling Lexus. Neither Rachel nor Jean looked away. The Lexus driver no longer had a head. His woman companion moved only slightly. As the Lincoln accelerated, Rachel saw Nick's Escalade round the curve and stop next to the Lexus. Rachel turned toward the front. She knew the end of this particular story.

"That's the Terminator," Jean said quietly, still watching out the back window.

"Yes it is, honey," Gus agreed.

* * *

"Hello, Kate." Nick peered into the Lexus, his H&K at the ready. "Does Frank have anyone else down here right now?"

"An...an army," the woman moaned, clutching her wound where the .50 caliber slug had ripped the top of her left shoulder off. "Christ...Nick...you did this on purpose."

"You know me and loose ends, Kate. This is going to hurt a little."

* * *

256

Kate's high pitched scream dropped into an agonized wail as Nick backed off from prodding her wounded shoulder. Nick had revived the woman twice in the last forty-five minutes, noting that blood loss would quite shortly put an end to the interrogation. Kate's story had not changed in any significant detail as Nick had taken her through it three times.

"Now, Kate," Nick urged. "Is –"

"Pleaaaaaasssssseee…Nick," Kate sobbed grotesquely, head writhing from side to side, her blue and green top soaked in blood. "No…no more –"

"Just a little more, baby," Nick implored in a soft but urgent voice. He added a new question. "Where were you to take the flash drives?"

Kate hesitated. In doing so, she knew instinctively it would mean more pain. She began crying piteously. "You…you cared for me once."

"About as much as you cared for me, Kate. You knew who Frank sent you down here against."

"I never thought…you'd protect the Hunter woman. I told Frank I thought you'd send her down here to get the drives…and…and if she didn't get them you'd –"

"Write her off?"

Kate's mouth moved for a moment, but no words issued forth. She looked away from Nick, life and pain fading from her anguished features. "Jason…Bidwell…"

Nick heard the rattling exhale of life, as the final loss of all worries in this world erased the lines from the woman's face. It took nearly thirty minutes for him to position the Lexus. Five minutes later, he watched the vehicle sink beneath the ocean's surface.

* * *

Deke ran into the condo, charging across the room to Jean, his whole body wagging. Jean immediately began wrestling with him on the floor near the dining room table where Gus and Rachel sat drinking coffee. Nick, carrying the clothes he had discarded before setting up his trap, walked in only seconds after Deke and closed the door. Jean gave him a hesitant wave from where the dog had her pinned on the carpet. Nick waved back and threw the clothing over a chair back before sitting down.

"How we doing, partner?" Gus asked.

"Pretty fair," Nick answered as Rachel reached over to cover his hand with hers. "It seems my little feint toward Washington didn't draw everyone away from the area. The good news is those two in the Lexus were the only ones. Frank had his own insider at the bank; but it's no one we have to worry about, because Rachel won't be going in there again. I made the call to the cops about Santora. They won't be finding the Lexus and its occupants anytime soon."

"Did you know the woman outside the bank personally, Nick?" Rachel asked.

"I knew both of them," he answered without any change of expression. "The woman gave me a name: Jason Bidwell. He's the one they were to take the drives to. I believe we can count Frank out of helping us return things to normal."

"As in Jason Bidwell, former senator, financier, and big time trader in carbon offsets?" Gus rattled the facts off with a low whistle and small shake of his head. "We're going to need a bigger boat."

"We?" Nick exchanged smiles with Gus. "You signing on for the duration or something, Gus? I figured to transfer some funds and you'd be on your way like always."

258

"I think I have a chance to finally get even with you, brother."

"If you mean Jamaica, we've been square a long time." Nick's smile diminished into a tight-lipped grimace. "What the hell makes you think I have you on the pad for Jamaica? Those two runs off the keys, when no one else in the world would have anything to do with me, evened us up just fine."

"Those were cake-walks." Gus waved Nick off with some annoyance. "My brother's a doctor now up in Boston because of Jamaica. You need me on this, just like I needed you back then. Burning Jason Bidwell will bring all kinds of hell down on you, Nick. I like your new family here, if you haven't scared them off with that stunt today."

"Stunt? Well, maybe it was a little creative, but –" Nick started.

Gus cut him off. "Without me, your ass would've been hanging out in the breeze."

"Which is why I brought you into the Florida part of this," Nick reasoned. "I didn't turn your offer down. For the first time, I don't know where this shit ends. Bidwell's just the newest addition to a growing list of guys we can't run from. If word gets out you're in this with me, no one you ever knew will be safe, Gus."

"We'll just have to be careful then, won't we, Boss?" Gus stuck out his hand. "Don't worry, it's going to cost you a nice tidy sum I ain't decided on yet."

"If we pull this off, my friend, you'll be able to retire in style." Nick shook Gus's hand. "Best think it over tonight before throwing in with us."

"Hey, what are friends for, right Rachel?"

"That's right, Gus," Rachel nodded her head happily. "I'm glad you're staying."

Nick shook his head. "Would this be a good time to tell you those two folks in the Lexus were friends of mine too?"

259

* * *

Deke ran full out to the fence after the bouncing softball. Gus ran toward second base to help Jean who waited halfway to the fence for Deke to bring the ball back. Rachel streaked around second base, while Nick moved from first base to cover home plate. Deke dodged Jean and faked Gus off his feet to one knee. When Deke reached Nick, he dropped the ball with Rachel still ten feet from home plate. Rachel squealed and barreled into Nick, who had grabbed up the ball and moved to block her. They went down in a heap as Gus and Jean ran up to umpire the action. Deke poked his nose into the squirming, two-player pile. Suddenly, Nick's right arm shot up from under Rachel with the softball in his hand.

"Yoooooooouuuuuuuuuurrrrrrrrrr out!" Gus and Jean yelled in chorus to Rachel.

Rachel sat up on Nick with an outraged look, red faced and panting.

"No fair!!! I scored before he tagged me."

"Oh waaahhhhh. Get off me you big baby... you are so out." Nick used the softball to bop Rachel in the forehead, which set Gus and Jean off on a laughing jag.

Rachel went for Nick's throat, forgetting about the ever vigilant Deke. Rachel's left forearm ended up in Deke's mouth, while the dog stared her down with a growl.

"Damn it, Deke! I had my first homerun, you ungrateful cur!" Rachel complained, disengaging herself from Nick and the dog. "Now I have slobber all over my arm and forehead, and I'm out. Thanks a lot."

Deke barked. He plopped down on his paws next to Nick.

"Nick, your dog never hits the cutoff man." Gus knelt next to Deke and stroked his head.

"Deke is the star. He doesn't need no stinking cutoff man, right Deke?" Nick received a short grunt of acknowledgment from the dog.

"He slimes the ball anyway," Jean added.

"Put a fork in me, I'm done," Nick stated, lying back over home plate.

"I'm taking off too." Gus stood up. "Will you require a new vehicle to check out the bank tomorrow, Ace?"

"Only for a short time," Nick answered, sitting up. "I want to see if Santora goes to work tomorrow. I'll go alone. I don't want anyone to even get a glimpse of Rachel."

"What about the flash drives?" Rachel kicked Nick's leg, while keeping an eye out for Deke.

"I've already compressed all the content," Nick answered, slapping Rachel's foot away and standing up. "They're all ready to send over to Suzan's husband. Then we'll hang around and wait for his input. If it matches or enhances what I gleaned from the drives, we'll call Grace and put her in touch with Suzan. They'll have plenty of bargaining power. Suzan and Jim will have to handle their own deal with the government."

"Can we go swimming again, Nick?" Jean asked.

"Absolutely."

"I'll leave you to it then." Gus handed the glove he had been using to Rachel. "See you all tomorrow."

"Bye Gus," the three chorused in varying tones as he walked away.

"I need a beer," Nick announced as he picked up their equipment bag and began stuffing it with balls.

"What happened to your iced tea craze?" Rachel took charge of the bat.

"It turned into a beer craze the moment I had to endure ninety degree heat and humidity."

261

"Can I have a beer too, Nick?" Jean asked as they walked with Deke toward the parking lot. "Deke always gets one."

"Sure, Danger."

"Nick!" Rachel pushed him off balance.

Nick shrugged at Jean with his 'I'm not in charge' look.

"Well, how about a shot of Jack Daniels?"

"Jean!" Rachel ran after her giggling daughter with Deke nipping Rachel's heels.

Nick watched his team of terminators for a moment before shaking his head and walking after them. *Oh boy.*

Nick and Rachel watched Jean practice swimming laps from the lounge chairs they had set in the shade of the building that housed the bathrooms for the condo pool area. Nick had packed a cooler for their sojourn to the pool. Deke lay next to his water dish, sleeping in the shade between the lounge chairs.

"It looks like Danger finally wore out Deke today."

"Maybe, but I don't trust that dog." Rachel noted Deke's head didn't pop up at his name. "We have the whole pool to ourselves this afternoon."

Nick glanced at his watch. "It's nearly six. Everyone else is probably eating by now."

"I heard you talking to Suzan."

"I gave her the domain address on the internet where she could access the information off the drives I uploaded. She said her husband Jim would go over the information right away. I'll call her tonight after we get something to eat and see what he thinks."

"It may be dangerous for you to go over to the bank tomorrow. What if Frank sent more people? They'll be looking for you this time instead of me."

"I figure I have a day before Frank figures something's happened to Kate and Jessops."

262

"I'm sorry you had to –" Rachel began, having heard Nick call the woman he'd killed by name for the first time.

"Don't." Nick cut her off with a quick wave of his hand. "Kate made an error in judgment. It cost her. They would have killed you, Jean, and Deke without blinking an eye. If the name she gave me pans out with Jim Benoit, there will be lots of pond scum floating to the surface. Bidwell would have a few layers between him and this mess. The sooner we put the Benoits together with Grace and Tim the better. Some of the heat on us will most definitely cool once the rats start scurrying for cover."

"And then what?"

"We go rat hunting."

Chapter Twenty

Slight Correction

Nick spotted Javier Martine the moment he walked through the bank door. He was talking to Rene Santora in front of the safety deposit box section. Nick walked over to where customers stood in line to access a safety deposit box. Santora immediately closed off her talk with Martine. He glanced at Nick and walked away. Santora smilingly waved Nick to the window.

"Hello, Mr. Weatherby." Santora checked the ID Nick slid into the tray under the window.

"Hi, Rene." Nick appeared to look at her nametag. He then did a double take, pretending surprise. "What happened to your face?"

Rene smiled crookedly at Nick, patting her splotchy face, the result of hours in contact with duct tape. She pushed the sign-in sheet clip board around so Nick could sign it. "I'm okay, just a little rash."

"Oh. Good." Nick signed the clipboard sheet and handed it back.

Rene let Nick in the back. After helping him get his safety deposit box, she settled him into one of the rooms and left him alone. He took his satellite phone out of the case holding his computer and called Rachel's throw away cell-phone.

"Hello?"

"Hey, Rach, guess who I spotted in the bank this morning."

"I'd rather not. I thought you weren't going to call. My heart stopped when the phone rang. Even Gus looked at me weird. Are you all right?"

"I'm fine," he answered, surprised how tightly wound his companions were. "Our Javier was inside talking to Rene."

"Holy shit! Tanus is after him too. Why would, oh…Rene must be feeding Fletcher instead of Tanus."

"Which would explain how Frank had two people on site. He must be in charge of acquiring the drives for Tanus, the prick. Since I'm here, and I see Javier's hanging around, too, why don't I follow him and see what happens?"

"Aren't you afraid whoever Frank has in place will ID you?"

"They didn't make me yesterday. Frank's probably still trying to reach Kate and Jessops. Your girlfriend Rene looks okay."

"My girlfriend? Bite me! I'm feeling better about you risking your neck already. Have fun."

"Still want to have a meet with Javier?"

"From a couple hundred yards?" she asked.

"Not this time, Nikita. Sarasota and sniper killings do not mix. It will have to be up close and personal. Whether you want a piece or not, Mr. Martine will have to be sent in search of an afterlife very soon."

"Can I get back to you on that once you see if it's feasible?"

"Absolutely."

* * *

Rachel hung up the phone. Gus waited patiently for her to enlighten him. Jean was in her room with Deke, playing video games, while Rachel and Gus had coffee at the dining table.

"Nick says Javier Martine, the guy who helped kill and torture my husband Rick, is at the bank. He was talking to Santora, so she was spotting for Fletcher, not Tanus. Nick is going to follow Javier."

"I take it from your side of the conversation, he offered to set Javier up for you."

"I asked him about doing it when we found out Javier had transferred to Fletcher," Rachel admitted.

"Be careful what you wish for. Are you going to take him up on it?"

"It seemed like a good idea when it was an unknown in the future."

"Reality's a bitch."

"Gus, what happened in Jamaica?"

"That's classified," he joked guardedly.

"We could trade Nick adventures," Rachel coaxed. "C'mon, Gus, it'll be fun."

"You don't know Nick if you think it would be fun to tell stories about his adventures, Rachel." He raised his hands palm outward toward her in a stopping gesture. "That guy's one of the most dangerous men on earth. When he suddenly showed up with you, Jean, and Deke under his wing, I checked to see if the earth had flipped on its axis. The fact he and I hooked up in the past professionally doesn't mean I don't get a tingle of dread when I see him. Watching him playing softball with you, Danger, and that damn dog was the most disconcerting thing I've ever seen."

Rachel laughed. "Then you definitely don't want to know about our traveling road show. I have no illusions as to what Nick is, or what he's capable of."

Gus leaned back in his chair, arms folded across his chest, as if coming to a decision. When he leaned forward again, he began talking while looking down at his cup.

"My younger brother Phil graduated from college seven years ago and received an internship at Boston General. He decided a trip to Jamaica with his friends, Damian and Julie Butler, who are sister and brother, seemed like a great way to celebrate. Phil did so well in school, and because he's the only family I had left, a vacation to Jamaica seemed like a good graduation present. Phil claims he and his friends were at a party on the beach. He ended up bound and gagged along with his friends by the Jamaican Posse. They wanted a million dollars ransom. The Butler kid's parents and I were able to round up the money, but as happens many times, we were sold out by the official in charge of helping us exchange the money for hostages. They ended up with the money and held on to the kids. No one cared a crap about it in either the Jamaican government or ours."

"On an island like Jamaica, why would it be so hard for their police to find out who in this Posse was responsible?" Rachel asked, captivated and on the edge of her seat, hearing the tale.

"The cops are corrupt and the gangs own the ghettos. The Butlers and I went to Jamaica, hoping to petition the government for help. The US embassy claimed their hands were tied. The Jamaican government told us we should have come to them first. I had provided gear and support for Nick in the Dominican, Haiti, and Cuba in past years. Like he said yesterday, there were a couple jobs no one would touch, operating without backup. After watching Nick work, I never turned down a job with him. Anyway, I sent a message to his Internet drop. Three days later he was on my doorstep with his infamous equipment bag. He listened to the story and asked if I could land him at a particular place off the Jamaican coast, near Kingston. He slept on the way. I took him where he had requested. He told me to stay moving until he called me. Two days later, he told me to anchor at the place I'd dropped him off at. Nick showed up with a guy tied up and gagged in the raft."

"Interrogation," Rachel stated.

"You have some experience with a Nick question and answer session?" Gus asked, somewhat surprised.

"Oh yeah. Enough to know Nick found someone he was sure knew where your brother was. Then he found out the information in short order."

"Then you do know. Nick went back in with a MAC10 and a bag full of hand grenades. I only have my brother's version as to what happened. Phil told me he and the Butlers were chained in some dank hole under a bar in Kingston. They heard explosions, screams, and gunfire. The trap door to the hole was opened. One of their terrified captors tumbled down inside with them, followed by a guy dressed all in black with his face and arms blackened. Phil said the captor let them loose and Nick shot him in the head. Nick led them up into what was left of the bar, where Phil claimed the floor was covered in blood and bodies. He told me Nick guided them out, shot anything that moved and tossed grenades at random until they reached the Jeep he'd acquired.

"Nick called me with coordinates to hook up at in the Port of Kingston. When I backed in next to the pier, Nick hustled the three kids on board and we were out of there. The kids looked like hell. They'd been beaten and tortured. Nick helped the kids get cleaned up and their wounds bandaged while I hightailed it home. When we were all safe at my dock in St. Pete, Nick tossed me a bag full of money. I tried to make him keep it. He smiled, patted the other bag he had, and said he'd already acquired his fee."

Gus laughed. "You should have seen Phil and the Butlers during the trip to St. Pete. After they were cleaned up and doctored, the three of them avoided Nick like he was the devil himself - not even a damn thank you. Nick told me to sneak everyone back where they belonged without saying anything to anybody. He gave the three kids a quick lecture, telling them to forget they ever saw him and how they ended up in St. Pete. They didn't need convincing. Apparently, the official who had sold us out was one of the first casualties. A lot of the Kingston Posse hierarchy went to hell, too, so the Jamaican government wasn't all that upset. Phil completed his internship and marred Julie Butler. They have a three-year-old daughter.

"Nick never mentioned anything to you about it at all?"

"Sure he did." Gus answered. "He said 'Piece of cake.'"

* * *

Javier Martine exited his Ford Mustang in front of the Solano Vista apartment complex, wondering if he should call his contact at Fletcher Exports to report he had talked with Rene Santora. Although Rene had told him she had taken ill suddenly, Javier believed something else was going on. She had dodged his questions about whether the log had been checked pertaining to the Hunter safety deposit box and why she hadn't called him. *If those idiots, Vertinski and Vega hadn't been arrested, I'd be by the pool with a beer. If that dork with the beard hadn't come over when he did and interrupted us, I wouldn't have to meet Santora later.* As Martine closed his apartment door, someone knocked. He checked out the security eye in the door and saw a familiar man.

"What do you want?" Javier recognized the man who'd interrupted him and Rene at the bank.

"Rene sent me over with a letter." The man held up an envelope.

I will kill that bitch for sending this asshole to my place. Martine flung open the door angrily. The crackling arc from a stun gun was the last thing he heard before the pain and blackness engulfed him.

Javier groaned. His eyelids fluttered open and he quickly realized movement was impossible. Plastic ties fastened his ankles to something solid, pulled tight enough to nearly shut off circulation. He could feel his arms fastened painfully in the same way behind his back. A towel had been duct taped around his mouth and head. From what little he could see and feel, Javier

269

knew he was duct taped to his kitchen chair and his pants were down. Directly in front of him, the bearded guy from the bank watched him with a detached look. Javier grunted in an attempt to get his captor's attention and show he wanted to speak.

He heard a slight knock. The bearded man went to answer the door as if he expected someone. Javier groaned unintentionally when he saw a woman follow the man into the kitchen. Martine recognized her right away, despite the hair coloring: Rachel Hunter. He saw from her eyes that she recognized him too. The bearded man handed her the stun gun. Rachel leaned down with the weapon, bracing herself with a hand on Javier's left shoulder, but the man pulled her hand away. He adjusted her slightly so no part of her was in contact with Javier.

"Remember my husband Rick?" she asked him, just before the crackling sound heralded a pain so intense Javier's shoulder popped out of its socket when he jerked. He again passed out.

When he came to, every nerve ending on fire. The bearded guy grabbed his nose with plastic gloved fingers until Javier's eyes bulged open, and then released him.

"I'm going to uncover your mouth for a moment. Give me the name of your boss at Fletcher, or Rachel here will tickle your balls with the blue arc again."

"Max…Max Stoddard!" Javier cried out the moment the man from the bank peeled down the gag. "Please –" he began before the bearded man pulled the gag back into place.

"Just like I did a moment ago, Rach," the bearded man directed, stepping aside.

Rachel Hunter leaned toward Javier's widening eyes once again. She gripped his nose shut with her own plastic covered fingers, and glanced at the bearded guy while Javier's vision turned grainy.

"Like this?" he heard her ask as if from far away.

"Perfect."

* * *

Nick looked over his handiwork carefully. Javier Martine sat on his couch in front of the big screen television mounted on the wall. The ESPN sports channel was selected on the screen at normal volume. Javier clutched the channel changer in his right hand. In his left, a two-thirds full beer can was propped up on his left thigh. The missing third of the beer had been carefully poured down Javier's throat. Javier's eyes were closed as if he had fallen asleep watching sports. Nick had cleaned the apartment thoroughly.

"I'll get the rental first and swing by to pick you up," he told Rachel. "Slip out of here and lock up as you leave. Don't exit if anyone is in view of the door. Keep your hat pulled down over your face and don't look up, just like when you came in."

"Oh, was I supposed to do that on the way in?"

He growled as Rachel smiled at him innocently. "One of these days, Alice, one of these days," Nick wheezed through clenched teeth while looking up at the apartment ceiling with cocked fist. "Right to the moon, baby, right to the moon." He completed his Ralph Kramden *Honeymooners* imitation with a few final shakes of his fist in her direction.

She laughed. "Not bad. Bullwinkle the moose, right? Can you do Rocky the Flying Squirrel too?"

"Let's get going before I'm forced to give you an attitude adjustment," he replied, slipping out into the night. *She'll be okay.*

Rachel walked out to Nick's rental and slid into the passenger side seat. He drove around the block to where he'd had her park the Escalade and stopped behind it.

"Do you think they'll suspect murder?" she asked before leaving the car.

271

"No forced entry, no telltale marks… at least none they'll spot without getting real close. My guess is they'll accept the scene the way I left it. Javier's apartment is locked from the inside. I saw his rap sheet. I doubt the cops will give him a second thought. Rene is the one I'm interested in."

Rachel sighed. "You were probably right the first time about my girlfriend. She's feeding Tanus and Fletcher. So, who tipped off Frank's people yesterday?"

"I don't know, but we're not going anywhere near that bank now. Rene will be in trouble with some hard people. I'm betting Frank's insider will be checking the logs of who accessed what after Kate and Jessops are missed. Word will get to Tanus that the drives are gone, and Rene will be answering questions about how it happened. I copied the drive from Javier's rinky-dink computer. I'll see if he has anything on there I can use. Get going. I'll see you at the condo."

She grabbed Nick hard around the neck, her face inches away from his.

"Thank you."

"I'll expect to collect my fee later," he whispered, his lips caressing hers, making her pull away with a moan of regret. She quickly left the rental and hurried to the driver's side of the Escalade.

* * *

Gus threw Deke's well-chewed Frisbee over the patch of lawn where he had seen Nick doing it. It was near dusk and the parking lot lights had already flickered to life. Both Deke and Jean chased after the Frisbee, with Jean trying to block the dog's path back to Gus after Deke beat her to the toy. Nick saw Gus look up as the Escalade drove into the parking lot, followed closely by the rented Pontiac.

"Hey, Gus." Nick waved, getting out with his equipment bag in hand. "Have you tired either of them out yet?"

"Not hardly. How's the banking business?"

"Oh, you know, same old stuff - one less problem, one new one." Nick waved at Jean as Rachel walked over to join them. "Did you eat yet?"

"No, I figured we'd all go out to a little place I know in Sarasota. I'll guide you to it, and then go home from there. You're buying dinner though, Daddy Warbucks."

"Of course," Nick agreed.

"I'm starving!" Jean called out, running over with Deke in hot pursuit.

"The deciding vote's in," Rachel added. "Let's go wash up and get Deke settled in. I hope the place has Long Island Iced Tea."

"I guarantee it," Gus grinned, putting a comforting arm around Rachel's shoulders.

"I'll go out on the porch with my uplink and see what Jim Benoit deciphered from the drives."

Forty-five minutes later, they arrived at the restaurant. Even Jean laughed with her mom as they looked at the sign that read 'Hemingway's Retreat', although Nick noticed Jean could not figure what her mom was enjoying so much. Gus jumped out of the Pontiac, pointing at Nick with a jabbing index finger, thoroughly enjoying Rachel and Jean's reaction. Nick stared up at the restaurant sign, shaking his head.

"This is a very nice place, Hemingway, so watch your manners," Gus advised, and then turned to Rachel. "I stayed at his place in Pacific Grove and met his friends a couple years back. We ate at his buddy Joe's place. It was fun watching the Terminator here get insulted through an entire meal by the guy waiting on us."

"I'm starving!" Jean repeated.

273

Gus led the way inside. Although the restaurant was crowded, they were seated immediately. Rachel wasted no time ordering a Long Island Iced Tea for herself, and a soda for Jean. Nick and Gus opted for beers. When the waitress arrived with their drinks, Rachel downed nearly a third of her very potent drink, which sent a warning signal to Nick. After ordering their meals, Nick spoke up quickly to capture Rachel's attention.

"Jim Benoit confirmed Jason Bidwell is the driving force behind Tanus. He also explained the connection I asked about, which seems to link Tanus with the late Senator Ambrose. Jason Bidwell and Fletcher's Max Stoddard teamed up a few times in the past to take out a half-dozen government officials in South America and Mexico. Jim gave me the key to deciphering the encryption they used, so I can begin making a list of possible suspects interested in our demise."

"Since Ambrose was on the drives, do you think you're implicated on them, too, from something you did for Tanus?" Nick's revelation had the desired effect of drawing Rachel's interest, as her drink seemed forgotten.

"I'll know tonight when I go over the information with Jim's key. It doesn't matter. I'm bringing Grace and Tim into this tonight anyway."

"If Grace wants to round up the Benoits right now, your place in Las Vegas and –"

Nick gestured for Rachel to keep it down. "There were a goodly number of suspicious things in Las Vegas which might draw the Marshalls' curiosity. It can't be helped. I'm hoping for a little discretion on Suzan's part, but it will be out of my hands once the Benoits hook up with the US Marshall Service."

"How long will we be here, Nick?" Jean interjected.

"You don't want to be on the road for your birthday, huh Danger?"

"It is only two days away. A couple moved into the condo complex today. They have a daughter only a year older than me.

274

We talked when she came over to watch us toss the Frisbee around with Deke. Her name's Ginny. Even Gus liked her."

"What do you mean even I liked her?" Gus glanced sideways at Jean, who giggled at his overplayed stern demeanor.

"You scare off more kids than Nick does."

"Gus has to look foreboding when he's looking after you, Danger."

"He's wrecking my social life," Jean continued, trying to imitate the frown Gus was leering at her with.

An hour and a half later, Nick guided Rachel into the passenger seat of his Escalade while Jean jumped into the back.

"She all right, Nick?" Gus asked, looking the rather pale Rachel over from behind Nick's shoulder. "I guess we shouldn't have let her have that third LT."

"I...I'm okay," Rachel assured Gus, looking up at him with a crooked smile. "I just...needed some fresh air."

"We'll see you tomorrow, Gus." Nick gave Rachel a slight push on the side of her head. "Bring your fishing pole. I have a feeling we'll be doing some planning and watching the news after I dump this on the US Marshalls tonight."

"I'll bring my fishing gear, but do we have to bring Danger with us? She's bad luck."

"Am not!" Jean called out, poking her indignant face up from the back.

"See you all tomorrow." Gus pointed at Jean, and then spun around toward the rental.

Nick shut Rachel's door. Fifteen minutes later Nick parked the Escalade in front of the condo complex. Nick handed Jean her mom's purse.

"You take this Danger, and I'll help your mom inside." Nick shook Rachel's shoulder. "Wakey, wakey."

"Okay, Nick," Jean agreed, opening her door with Rachel's purse in hand.

Nick saw movement near the pillars at the end of the walkway.

"Danger!" Nick hissed, stopping Jean's movement out the door. "Get back inside."

"What's wrong, Nick?" Jean hurriedly closed the door again and locked it.

Rachel stirred when Nick shook her. The urgency in his voice woke her completely, heart racing, and breathing coming in short gasps.

"Rachel!" Nick took her chin in his hand. "Are you with me?"

She nodded. Nick reached into the glove compartment for his H&K with silencer, cocking it.

"Tuck this next to your waist, so the grip pokes toward your right. That's it. Now clamp it against you with your left hand on the barrel. I'll come around and help you out of the Cad. Keep your right arm over mine as I guide you toward the condo. Stay slightly crouched over. I'll walk you with my right hand on the grip. They don't want you dead, so if someone's there, they'll want to talk. The moment we see who it is, drop like you're too drunk to stand and reach for the sidewalk."

"I...I don't feel too well, Nick."

"Good. Then you won't have to act. Danger, don't move out of here or show yourself."

"Okay, Nick. Take care of my mom."

"I will." Nick hurried around to Rachel's door. He opened it, and leaned in to assist her out.

Nick kicked the door shut, and slipped his right hand onto the butt of the H&K .45 caliber. He kept up a running dialogue telling Rachel they were almost to the condo. As they reached the

276

sidewalk surrounding the complex, three figures stepped out of the darkness in front of them. Nick recognized Rene Santora, but didn't recognize the two men with her. They were both several inches taller than him.

"Mr. Weatherby." Rene chuckled. "Having some trouble?"

Nick peered at her, while holding a groaning Rachel tightly to him. "Rene? From the bank?"

"It's me, and I'll bet this is Rachel. How long did you think it would take me to check the logs?"

Rachel dropped forward drunkenly to her knees, hands reaching to ease the fall. All eyes followed her down. Nick fired before the men had a chance to look away from Rachel. Forty-five caliber slugs ripped into their brains, throwing them backwards off their feet, where they landed splayed out on the walkway, twitching as if in shock at their sudden demise. Rene's mouth opened to scream. The butt of Nick's H&K struck her in the forehead, landing Santora next to the quieting men. He scooped Rachel up to her feet with his next movement, then propped Rene up in a sitting position, and handed the stunned Rachel his weapon.

"Watch her, Rachel, while I put these two in the Escalade."

"Okay, I got it."

Nick looked around the deserted area. Seeing no one in view, he quickly pulled the men's shirts and undergarments up over their heads to absorb the blood from their wounds. He then grabbed the first man under the armpits and dragged him to the Escalade, returning moments later to take the second one. By the time he had secured the two bodies into the cargo compartment and retrieved the duct tape he had stored there, Rene Santora had begun to moan. He taped Santora's mouth for the second time. After securing her wrists behind her and ankles together, Nick pulled Rene up and over his shoulder. Rachel walked along with him, holding Santora's purse. He deposited Santora next to her companions. He added more tape to bind her ankles to her wrists. Rachel handed him the purse. Nick rooted around in it until he found car keys. He closed up the back and went around to open the door for Jean.

"C'mon, Danger, we're going up to make sure Deke's okay. I go in first, though. I'll level with you. I'm not sure Rene and her two goons didn't hit the condo first. I'm hoping Deke made enough noise they didn't want to attract attention. Are you okay, Rach?" Nick took the weapon from her carefully.

"I'm okay." Rachel hugged Jean to her.

In the condo, Deke was waiting for them in full wild dog mode. He streaked out past them and down the steps to the grass below.

"Apparently Deke is okay." Nick patted Jean's shoulder. "You two go on in, and I'll bring Deke when he finishes his business. I'm going to call and disturb Gus too. He won't be happy."

Chapter Twenty-One
Last Thread

Nick used the time waiting for Gus to clean up what he could with bleach and cold water. He played Frisbee with Deke, covering for his outdoor cleanup activities in case someone came by. Gus arrived, armed and ready.

"Look after Jean. I'll go find out if we need to worry about other unexpected visitors. What do you have?" Nick asked, noticing Gus was clutching something under his loose parka.

"Uzi."

"That'll work." Nick used the remote on Santora's keys to find out which car was hers. "Send Rachel down, Gus. Deke, go with him."

Deke followed Nick's gesture and padded up the steps after Gus, Frisbee in mouth. A couple minutes later, Rachel hurried down the steps to where Nick waited next to the Escalade.

"Are you sober enough to drive?"

"I am now," she answered. "And I brought my license with me."

"Follow me in the Escalade with Rene's Volvo. It's the black one over there." He pointed and handed her the keys. "When we get to the warehouse area, turn out your lights. Stay close behind the Cad, but not so close you'll run into me when I stop. I'll be going slow."

"Sorry about all this, Nick."

"Nothing to be sorry about. Let's go see if we have anything else to worry about. If not, we'll correct our error. I wish you didn't have to go along, but I need Gus to look after Jean, just in case."

"I know. I'll be right behind you."

Forty minutes later, Nick had finished positioning the two dead men in the front seat of the Volvo. He walked around the Volvo to where Rene Santora lay against the driver's side rear tire. Nick propped her up, taking the stun-gun from his back pocket. Her eyes widened as she moaned and shook her head vehemently back and forth.

"Here's a little sample of what happens if I don't get answers to the questions I have for you, Rene." He gave her a short jolt. It was enough to make the woman convulse, smashing her head back into the Volvo's rear quarter panel.

He revived her with gentle slaps to the face with his gloved right hand. When she groaned, Nick grabbed her chin, shaking it gently.

"You awake, Rene? Nod your head in my hand if you are."

She nodded.

"Who thought of the idea to come over and try for the flash drives, Rene?"

Nick peeled the tape off her mouth.

"Mine...honest to God," she blubbered, her sobs bordering on hysteria. "My boss...he'd kill me if he found out I let your bitch get in and take the drives."

"Who do you work for?" he asked as a test.

"I...I get paid by two different firms, Tanus Import/Export...and Fletcher Exports."

"Give me the name from each firm you would call boss."

"You'll kill me anyway...you sadistic bastard! I'm –"

Nick gave her a prolonged jolt. Rene ended her convulsions nearly under the Volvo rear wheel, and he sat her up once more. After a few moments, he shook her chin again, focusing the woman's attention.

"It's only around one in the morning, Rene. That gives me quite a bit of time to help you remember."

"Jason...Jason Bidwell runs Tanus now...and...Max Stoddard at Fletcher!" she gasped out as Nick released her in preparation for another jolt.

"Very good. Now, who are the two guys you brought along with you?"

"They...they worked for Tanus. Their names are Overman...and Sweeney."

"Why didn't you just dummy up after my first warning?"

"That was you? I couldn't...Christ...he told me I had someone watching me at work too. They'd have checked the logs. I talked those two into helping me get the drives. Then we could have dealt with —"

"You should have run, Rene," Nick interrupted. He put the tape back in place, and pinched off her nose.

Rachel had been dozing in the passenger seat. She jumped in a panic as the driver's side door opened.

"Easy, Rach," Nick said soothingly. "It would appear we can stay in Sarasota until I get the Marshalls hooked up with the Benoits. I'll call Grace in the morning. This all had an upside."

"What?" she asked skeptically.

"It took your mind off Javier."

"Javier who?"

* * *

"Gus!" Jean called out, running over to hold up a stringer with an eighteen inch bass on it. "Look at the fish I caught!"

Gus walked toward Nick, Rachel, and Jean, with Deke running around his legs in circles as he approached the condo lake front. He took the stringer from Jean with the proper amount of respect.

"Now this is a fish, not one of those guppies Nick's been pulling out and throwing back."

"Nice to see you too." Nick looked over at Gus from where he reeled in his latest cast.

"Hi, Gus," Rachel greeted him with a wave from where she sat on a lounger in the shade.

"Hey, Danger, where'd you get the new groupie?" Gus pointed at a large blue heron going over to check out Nick's line whenever he reeled it in.

"That's Charlie," Jean answered, returning the stringer to the ice chest. "He showed up when Nick pulled a guppy out."

"Hey!" Nick argued, gesturing at Jean. "That was a nice fish. Charlie here liked him, right Charlie?"

The heron remained silent, but moved closer as Nick cast again.

"Anyway, Charlie's been hanging with us ever since I fed him Nick's guppy," Jean explained. "He doesn't even care when Deke's running around."

"I can't believe you've enticed 'Mr. Freeze' out of the air conditioning for the third straight evening fishing expedition. What's your secret? He complained so much last night, I almost shot him."

"Here's the secret." Rachel held up a clear mug. "It doesn't let the beer get warm. You put it in the freezer until it's time to pour your drink. Some liquid freezes inside of it and doesn't thaw. Jean and I bought them at the store today."

"It…it's a miracle." Nick pretended to be deeply moved, as he held up his frosty mug.

"We bought you one too." Jean took another frosty mug out of the cooler. She handed it to Gus along with one of the beers.

"Man, that looks good." Gus sat down next to Rachel. He poured his beer slowly into the mug and took a sip. "Oh yeah."

Nick jerked on his pole. It bowed under the strain. Jean ran over immediately, with Deke on her heels. Charlie the heron moved out of Deke's way as Nick handed the pole to Jean, letting her get a grip first. She played the small bass expertly, bringing it in without tangling the line or picking up a snag. The heron, seeing Jean was bringing in a live one, moved to watch right over her shoulder. Gus laughed at the sight of the little girl with a dog on one side and a blue heron hovering on the other. Nick picked up the line as the fish thrashed around in the shallow water. He unhooked the fish and threw it over in front of Charlie. The happy heron scooped it up and moved down the way to savor his treat.

"I'm going to throw the Frisbee for Deke, Nick." Jean handed him the pole.

"Okay, Danger, we'll kick back for a little longer. Stay in sight."

Nick sat down on the other side of Rachel.

"The bank looked business as usual when I did my rounds," Gus said. "I didn't spot any new people except for one of the managers filling in for Rene. I drove by the warehouse area. There's still no interest there. Did you two get any calls?"

"Nope," Nick answered. "Not since I closed the loop between the Benoits and the Marshalls. I'm hoping for some news soon though."

"Grace and Tim are probably in shock you sent them copies of the drives too. I bet Grace hasn't slept since you delivered the info."

"Be grateful for small blessings," Gus cautioned. "At least there isn't a manhunt for all the missing people around here."

"I'll drink to that," Rachel said. "Wouldn't it be nice if they nailed the big fish, and we could relax without any more worry?"

"Yeah, that'll happen," Nick scoffed. "I'd like to see –"

Nick's satellite phone rang. Nick picked it up with a smile, knowing only one man had his number. "His ears must be itching."

"Flash drives incorporated," Nick answered.

"We had a deal!"

"I'm going to hang up if you plan on speaking to me from that alternate reality of yours, Frank." Nick noticed his device read green. "I take it the US Marshalls are helping the DOJ probe your little love nest, huh?"

"There's a firestorm up here. You'll be incinerated along with the rest of us, you moron!"

"I didn't see your name or my name on the drives, buddy, and I was looking for yours real close. Is Bidwell setting you up for the fall, Frankie?"

There was silence on the other end of the line until Nick started humming the 'Beat The Clock' theme song, as both Rachel and Gus waited anxiously.

"I can give you Bidwell, Nick."

"I'm not too crazy about your gifts, Frank." Nick watched Rachel shaking her head and mouthing the word 'no' silently. He gave her his annoyed look while waving her off. "I imagine things are moving rather quickly."

"Let me send you the info. You see what you think and get back to me…quickly."

"I'll take a look."

"Nick, have you seen Kate Fuller and Sam Jessops?"

"Who?"

"You bastard!"

284

* * *

"Hey, you," Nick whispered, putting a warm hand on Rachel's hip as she lay next to him, "It's almost five-thirty. You'd better creep into your own bed."

"Uummmmmmm…" Rachel moaned sleepily, shivering at the feel of Nick's lips tracing paths along her neck. "You're getting up, aren't you?"

"Diego's calling to me. I only have a couple more scenes. Then I can start assembling it to send out."

"Assembling?" Rachel questioned, turning over on her back, with Nick shifting alongside her. "What's there to assemble?"

"I have editing notes for scene breaks and chapters. When I finish the novel, I separate the chapters. Then I begin outlining my timeline, character list, and synopsis according to chapters." Nick moved his left hand over Rachel's stomach, followed by his lips with whisper soft kisses. "When I…finish with those items…it's time for the first…editing pass."

"I thought all you…oh…Nick…"

At seven-thirty, Nick typed at a furious pace, the excitement of his novel's finish obliterating all other thought. Rachel held her place instead of rounding the hallway corner. She watched Nick type, intrigued by the smile spreading on his face as he typed. It was at that particular moment an even more curious Deke silently goosed Rachel, his cold nose contacting bare skin under Rachel's robe.

"Eeeeeeeeeeeeeee!" Rachel squealed, flattening against the hallway wall.

"Deke!" Nick called out. "Get away from her, you perv."

The dog shook himself. He padded over to head butt Nick's thigh.

"Okay, okay." Nick stood up with exaggerated effort. "It's time to walk Rachel and Jean's dog again. I wonder what Rachel and Jean did before they had a dog walker."

"We had more time for mundane things like dog walking before we took over the first two places on everybody's hit parade. Sit still. I'll take him out."

"Dressed liked this?" Nick separated Rachel's robe, his hands running up her sides. "I don't think so."

Rachel shivered, pulling up Nick's t-shirt as he drew her close. Nick held Rachel off, allowing only the nipples of her breasts to contact his bare skin as he leaned forward to kiss her. Rachel swayed side to side against him, their lips meeting, parting, and joining again.

"I'm hungry," Jean stated emphatically, giggling as Nick and Rachel collided, burst apart, and turned to the little girl guiltily with Rachel snatching her robe together.

"You are this close, Danger," Nick growled, holding the index finger and thumb of his right hand a fraction of an inch apart, "to having all video game privileges revoked until you're eighteen. I'm walking Deke."

Nick made as if to throttle Jean, while circling around Rachel with Deke on his heels.

* * *

"Can I help make pancakes, Mom?" Jean asked the red-faced Rachel.

"Ah...sure," Rachel answered, moving around Jean and into the kitchen. "You do realize, you little sneak, between you and Deke, I'll have a heart attack before I'm forty, don't you?"

286

"You really like Nick, don't you Mom?"

"There's an understatement."

Nick brought Deke back from their morning jaunt in time for breakfast. He unfastened Deke's leash and sat down at the dining table with Jean, who had just begun eating her pancakes.

"Want some pancakes, Nick?"

"Sure."

Rachel came in a moment later with her own plate and one for Nick. She returned to the kitchen for coffee, as Nick slid his cup from next to the notebook computer to where he was sitting. Rachel filled his cup and hers before sitting down.

"Is Gus coming over tonight again?"

"He wants to do a drive by at our favorite dock. Then he'll stop by to see what I've decided about Frank's offer."

"Oh come on, Nick, you can't be seriously considering doing his dirty work again," Rachel argued, giving him a disgusted look.

"Actually, our dirty work too," he corrected her. "I checked the Internet news. The Feds hit Tanus this morning. If they can't nail Bidwell, we'll be looking over our shoulders forever. I don't play that game. Frank's intelligence was very good on the Denver deal. Granted, he threw in a takeout team, too, but –"

"I'm afraid your luck's going to run out," Rachel interrupted, seeing Jean watching them with wide eyes. "We're so close, Nick. Can't we give Grace and Tim a chance to do this legally?"

"Frank sent me the info. I looked it over last night. There's only a one week window. It would take Gus and I a couple days to get into position. The moment word got out the drives were in the Fed's hands, Bidwell took off for Nassau, where he owns a piece of Coral Reef Boat Rentals. We know the area real well."

"But…but what about us, Nick?" Jean asked.

287

"I think it may be time to ask Grace and Tim for a bit of protection. I'll come up with a story about how we should split up for now until they get the bad guys and –"

"No!" Rachel slammed her hand onto the table in anger. "We're not leaving you, and you're not leaving us!"

"Mom's right. You said we're a team," Jean added, her quivering lip betraying emotion she tried desperately to hold back. "I don't want you to go."

Deke, hearing and smelling something different in the air, shot up between Rachel and Jean, his paws on the table, tail wagging.

"Look, you two, have I done something to earn this kind of disrespect from my team? With Frank's recent track record, I don't want either of you anywhere around me on this. He has zero interest in you two since the drives were made public. Because of the high stakes on this, there's high risk too. Besides, this'll be out at sea, where we'd have nowhere to run. Secondly, who the hell will be looking after my dog if you two come with me?"

Rachel knew Nick was right. Anger at the sudden decision clouded all other thought. She bit her lip in order to remain silent. She patted Deke down to the floor and took her plate out to the kitchen without another word. Jean looked from Nick to Rachel in disbelief. Something had changed, but what, the little girl could not understand. She reached across the table, covering Nick's hand with her own as Rachel listened from the kitchen.

"You…you'll come back for us…won't you, Nick?"

"Absolutely."

* * *

Gus knocked on the door, holding the briefcase Nick had requested with charts of an area off the coast of Nassau. Rachel answered the door, giving Gus a slight smile before waving him in. Gus followed her inside and down the short hallway. Jean and Deke were sitting on the couch together watching a movie. Nick looked up from his computer and gestured at a chair next to him at the dining room table.

"Hey, Gus, have a seat. Any bad news from our favorite dock?"

"Nope, not a sign." Gus nodded with a smile at Rachel, who held up an iced mug from the kitchen. "I brought the charts you asked for. Did you decide to play for your little friend in Washington again?"

"It's not a forgive and forget, but he sure has some interesting intel."

Rachel set the mug down in front of Gus, and then joined Jean and Deke on the couch.

"Wow, what the hell did you do, brother, kick Deke?"

"My decision is unpopular. In three days' time Bidwell will be fishing off the Nassau coast in a Coral Reef Rental luxury boat called the Tequila. Remember the drug cartel guy four years ago?"

"Yeah. I believe we had a two week recon on that job."

"This is a strictly volunteer excursion. Frank may have something unexpected for us after I send Bidwell to his reward."

"Has he screwed you before?" Gus asked with some hesitation, knowing Nick did not like questions on past ops from people with no prior knowledge.

"Did you happen to hear about some mysterious deaths in the Denver area?"

"No shit!" Gus exclaimed, real surprise highlighting his features. "Damn, Nick, a sitting US Senator? He didn't die in his sleep, huh?"

"Sort of. There were two special op guys who supposedly killed each other nearby on the same night. They were there for

289

me, courtesy of Frank, after offering up his boss for me to guide into the happy hunting ground."

"So that's what all this talk about deals was about. I can outfit us against something in our weight class, but I doubt we could run from a destroyer or a helicopter gunship. I'm in though. You have plans for your family they're unhappy with?"

"I called my US Marshall friends. They're flying down here tomorrow morning. They'll be picking up my three upset companions. Rachel's very excited about it, aren't you Rach?"

Rachel held up her right arm, right hand and middle finger. Gus laughed and spread out the first chart on the table.

"Show me what you have in mind, 'Family Guy'.

* * *

Gus arrived with Rachel, Jean, and Deke at the park where they had played softball together. Nick had picked the spot out for handing his charges over to the US Marshalls. Rachel left the passenger side of the rental Buick after Gus popped the trunk lid. She took out their bags and set them over by the sidewalk. Gus turned and handed Jean an envelope while Rachel unloaded the car.

"Nick said to give you this. Happy birthday, Danger."

Jean opened the card and read the words as tears filled her eyes: 'I love you, Danger. Take care of your mom and Deke. We'll have a real party when I see you next time. I'll be thinking of you, Deke, and your mom every moment. Happy birthday, kid. Love, Nick.' Jean hugged Gus over the seat back and left the car with Deke. Gus drove away.

Ten minutes later, a dark blue Ford van pulled up next to the curb. Grace stepped down from the passenger side of the van, smiling happily at her three former clients. Rachel made a stopping gesture as Grace began hurrying over to them.

"Tell Tim to get out of the van and open all the doors, Grace," Rachel directed.

"What?" Grace looked at Rachel as if she had gone around the bend.

"Please, just humor me."

Grace stood still for a moment and then returned to the van. She opened the passenger side door and the sliding door on the side.

"Tim, get out and leave your door open. Open the rear doors too."

"This some kind of joke?" Tim asked in confusion.

"Just do it. I guess Rachel's still a little gun-shy."

"Okay," Tim agreed, getting out and walking to the rear of the van to open the cargo doors. "I guess I can't really blame her."

"Me either," Grace agreed. She walked around to the front, holding up her hands. "Okay?"

Rachel nodded, relief plain on her face.

Grace approached. She hugged Jean while Tim walked over to pick up two of their bags. Deke followed him around, tail wagging.

"You afraid we might be bad guys?" Grace asked. She embraced Rachel.

"No, I was afraid you didn't do exactly what Nick told you to do and not come after us alone," Rachel answered. "We wouldn't be hugging right now. You, Tim, and everyone extra in the van would be dead."

"Jesus…" Grace looked around the immediate area, her hand inadvertently reaching into the bag at her side.

Rachel caught Grace's wrist with both hands, a pleading look on her face. "Please Grace, for God's sake, don't do anything stupid. Let's just go, okay?"

"Sure," Grace agreed, moving her hand away from the bag.

"Oh! Hey, Grace." Jean remembered the envelope Nick had handed her to hold onto until she saw Grace. Jean reached into her carry-bag and extracted the envelope from a pocket in the bag. "Nick said to give this to you."

Grace took the envelope from Jean and opened it. She unfolded the type written sheet of paper inside. It read: 'If anything happens to Rachel, Jean, or Deke, you and Tim had better be dead.' It was unsigned but Grace had no doubt who typed it. Grace shivered although it was another hot, muggy, Florida day. She put her arm around Jean's shoulders.

"We better get moving."

Five minutes later, the van drove away. Three hundred yards away, Nick quickly packed up his sniper rifle.

Chapter Twenty-Two
Nassau Operation

"Oh my goodness," Nick announced in a nearly reverent tone, looking out over the dead calm surface with his digital range-finding binoculars. "Gus, we've hit the jackpot, my friend."

Gus sat ten feet behind where Nick stood, listening to the chatter on the radio. He took off his earpiece and joined Nick at the wheel house observation window. Two miles away, Bidwell's boat Tequila lay at anchor nearly five miles off the Nassau coast. Nick handed the binoculars to Gus. It took Gus a minute to sight in the vessel, where a party had been going on for the last three hours. A speed boat had brought four bikini-clad women, along with two men Nick did not recognize, out to the Tequila. Until this time, Nick had only spotted Jason Bidwell and two crewmembers.

"What am I looking at besides a wild night on the high seas?"

"See the guy with the blonde comb over and pot belly?"

"Yeah, he's doing some kind of dance with one of the women. That's just...disturbing."

"He's Max Stoddard. It appears Tanus and Fletcher may not have been rivals. Either that or their CEOs decided the better part of valor is party time in Nassau."

"Oh my, that does work out well for you, doesn't it? Do you think Frank knew about Stoddard?"

"He knew." Nick took the binoculars back from Gus. "You can bet he tracked us by satellite the moment we entered Bahaman waters. Bidwell's the one putting pressure on him back in Washington. I believed Frank about Bidwell making him the scapegoat. At least we don't have to worry about my buddy trying to take us out before I get Bidwell."

"I'm not happy about sacrificing my baby to this mission."

Nick laughed. "Your baby? Gus, this tugboat looks like that scow they used to go after 'Jaws'. I'll buy you a brand new boat. If you think Frank will be acting honorably towards us after I off Bidwell, then stay with The Loose Lady."

"My boat's name is The Lucky Lady, you cretin," Gus corrected him.

"Not after tonight." Nick grinned, focusing on the ship again with his binoculars. "These clowns ought to be passed out soon. The ladies will be on their way back to shore in a few hours, hopefully with those guys they came on board with and a couple of the crew."

"You were never this picky about collateral damage before."

"I've been domesticated. What'd you think of the boat I picked up on Andros Island for us to get home in?"

"It's a damn glorified rowboat, you cheapskate. My skiff is bigger," Gus needled him.

"Beggars can't be choosers, buddy. Your master mariner rep is on the line," Nick said, taking a break from watching the Tequila. "You went over the boat from stem to stern and gave me the thumbs up on throwing away twenty grand on it. Can we sail the glorified rowboat home or not?"

"Don't get all huffy, Captain Ahab. Weather willing, I'll get us back to St. Pete."

"Ahab? This is the tropics, brother. I'm like James Bond in Dr. No." Nick sat down next to Gus.

"James Bond, huh?" Gus chuckled. "Who would I be?"

"You'd be like James Bond's sidekick in Dr. No: Quarrel."

Gus brightened, leaning forward. "He was the go to guy for anything Bond needed. A tough guy who…hey, wait a minute! Quarrel gets killed."

294

"Oh, sorry, Quarrel... My bad."

* * *

Nick zipped up his wetsuit. The Lucky Lady floated in darkness, while the Tequila anchored with running lights, as is common practice to keep from being struck by another ship. Gus helped Nick with the one piece buoyancy compensator and tank vest, which also incorporated a weight belt. Nick checked his gauges. He took a couple practice breaths with his regulator, setting it for minimum air flow.

"I still don't understand why you didn't blow their heads off with your long range cannon," Gus said irritably. "You're taking this James Bond stuff too far."

"Like I've never approached a boat with scuba gear before," Nick retorted, fitting his mask into place.

"Sure you did," Gus agreed. "But you attached enough C-4 to vaporize the boat. Why assault the damn guys in the boat?"

"Finesse, my dear Quarrel, finesse," Nick said in his best James Bond voice. He put on his fins and positioned himself aft. "I have chloroform, plastic ties, stun gun, and my trusty H&K .45 in the waterproof pack. Stoddard being on board with Bidwell makes me think there may be more to this get together than sex, drugs, and rock & roll. When you look through the sight of my sniper rifle, you'll see real fast why taking potshots from a rocking boat ain't an exact science. Remember, don't fire that damn thing unless I'm dead. Chances are you'll kill me."

"Ha, ha, very funny. That's a long swim, genius. Why don't we –"

"Bloody hell, Quarrel, mind your business." Nick put the regulator in his mouth, clasped his hand over the mask and went into the ocean off the fantail.

Gus shook his head. He waited for Nick's thumbs up to hand down the grappling hook and line, followed by Nick's equipment bag.

Nick took a final reading with his compass, built into the gauge pack. Allowing enough air out of the buoyancy compensator to take his dive down to fifteen feet, he then headed toward the Tequila. Breathing in and exhaling with measured discipline, he kicked forward at a steady pace in the absolute darkness. He popped up every few minutes, ensuring his course still intersected with the lighted boat.

Nick looked up in relief when he reached the Tequila. They had left the aft ladder in place. After discarding the grappling hook, he aired up his buoyancy compensator and slipped out of it. He fastened a compensator strap around the ladder base, leaving it floating in the water. He pulled his mask down around his neck, undid his fins while clinging to the ladder, and climbed up slowly. Peeking over the fantail, Nick waited a full five minutes before boarding the Tequila. After setting aside his mask, fins, and bag, he took off his gloves. He extracted the H&K .45 caliber automatic, silencer in place, and set it down within reach. Nick eased out of his wetsuit, using a towel from the bag to dry off.

He found the crew members first, asleep in the wheelhouse on cots. He retreated to his bag, and then returned silently to the wheelhouse with H&K .45, chloroform, and a large gauze pad soaked in chloroform. He kept his weapon trained on the crewmember to the left, while holding the chloroformed pad lightly over the other's nose until his breathing changed. Nick pressed the pad tighter, until the man breathed no more. He repeated the process with the man on his left. Padding down the ladder carefully in his bare feet, he cleared his head with deep breaths.

Bidwell and Stoddard slept the sleep of the wasted downstairs. Nick took his bag with him down into the cabin area and gave each of them a light chloroforming before flipping each one over and plastic-tying their wrists behind their backs. He plastic-tied the ankles next, adding one tie between ankles and wrists. Nick went up to get some air, and returned to the cabin. He found an ice bucket holding empty bottles of Champagne. He took the bottles out and poured a little ice water over each man until they groaned their way into consciousness. Nick placed a chair near the bunks and kept up his ice water treatment.

"Wha...what the hell?" Bidwell spluttered, looking around wildly. He saw Stoddard bound as he was across the narrow space between bunks. "Stoddard!"

Stoddard blinked stupidly and threw up. Nick doused him with ice water, and pulled him off the bunk to the floor. Nick sat down and picked up his stun gun. He fired off a crackling arc which had both men trying to scramble away. Stoddard twisted on the floor, looking up at Nick without recognition.

"Who? Who are you?"

"I'll be asking the questions, Max, and we all know what happens if I don't get answers. Why are you two supposed rivals in the gunrunning, drug, and human trafficking business here together?"

"We had to call a truce...especially with what's surfaced lately," Bidwell gasped out fearfully. "There were these drives –"

"I know all about the recent disclosures. You guys know a man named Frank from Washington D.C.? He used to be an underling of Senator Ambrose. Now, I hear he takes orders from you, Bidwell."

"Oh Christ...you're that psycho, McCarty! Frank said he had you killed. That son of a bitch sent you after us, didn't he?"

"How about you, Max?" Nick ignored Bidwell's question.

"Frank Richert?" Stoddard asked, his eyes now wide open.

"Yep."

"How…how did he know we were setting him up to take the fall?" Bidwell's voice faded in tenor along with all hope of seeing another sunrise.

"Don't know," Nick admitted. "He's a sneaky one, our Frank."

"He'll have you killed too." Stoddard's voice sounded stronger. "We can protect you."

"No thanks, Max."

"This is all because of that Hunter bitch! The stupid slut and her dimwit husband brought all this shit down on us!" Bidwell raged, rocking back and forth on the bunk.

"This is one of your boats, Bidwell," Nick interrupted Bidwell's rant. "Where do you keep your cruising around money?"

"Fuck you, McCarty!"

"I was hoping you'd say that." Nick stunned Bidwell until he flopped around in boneless fashion.

"Honest to God, I don't know where any money is, Mr. McCarty," Stoddard whimpered, trying to scoot even further into the bunk's base.

"Is there anyone else besides you and Jason here looking for the Hunter woman, Max?"

"We stopped looking for her when the drives were released. We met down here to…to reorganize. We needed to let our people pour enough money into the right pockets so we could recover."

"I believe you, Max." Nick picked up his chloroform pad. He soaked it once again and bent down toward the cringing Stoddard. "Breathe deeply Max, and go to sleep. If you fight it, I might change my mind and have two drowning victims instead of one."

Stoddard breathed and died. Nick threw some more water on Bidwell, who cried out as Nick began slapping him awake.

"Now, you were saying about the money, Jas?"

"It's in a safe, behind the galley cupboard!" Bidwell cried out as Nick fired off another arc near him. He quickly rattled off the combination.

Nick found nearly fifty thousand dollars and some drugs in the safe. He came back from the galley a few minutes later, his bag stuffed with money. Nick had left a couple thousand dollars and the drugs behind before closing up the safe. "That's more like it."

Nick cut the ties off Stoddard's body and worked the corpse up into the empty bunk. He then cut Bidwell's plastic ties on his ankles. Nick guided Bidwell up the steps and over to the fantail.

"I need a drowning victim. Any volunteers?"

"Oh God no!" Bidwell screamed. "Please —"

Nick threw Bidwell over the fantail and then dived into the water after him. Nick grabbed Bidwell by the hair and surfaced. He held him under the water while clinging to the boat ladder for five minutes. Nick ducked down and put Bidwell over his shoulder. He worked his way up the ladder, tossing the dead man into the boat. Nick retrieved his cutters and cut the plastic tie on Bidwell's wrists. After shouldering the dead man once again, Nick made his way down to the berthing area and dumped Bidwell on his bunk.

Over the next fifteen minutes, Nick packed up. When he was ready to leave, he turned on just one of the galley burners without flame, and left the oven door open and flame on. He went up to the fantail and into the water, donning his fins and compensator quickly at the base of the ladder. He made it nearly halfway to The Lucky Lady when he felt the concussion from the blast. He continued surfacing every few minutes to check for the small light Gus had turned on. Gus took his bag and gear, hauling up the compensator and tank so Nick could climb aboard without the weight.

"I hope you have the skiff ready, Quarrel. I'll change when we get to the other boat."

"All set, James," Gus played along.

"Well done, Quarrel. Do you have Lucky here rigged to run toward Florida?"

"Of course, James."

"I'll be in the skiff, Quarrel. Please hurry, won't you?"

Gus gave Nick a push and went to set The Lucky Lady on the autopilot he had rigged up. By the time he hurried down to join Nick, the boat was picking up speed with running lights on. Nick released the mooring when Gus jumped down into the skiff.

"I hope you're wrong about my boat, James." Gus watched The Lucky Lady churn away.

"Keep that happy thought, Quarrel."

Before they reached their backup boat, the two men heard muffled explosions off in the direction The Lucky Lady had been headed, lighting up the horizon.

"At least you survived, Quarrel. Good show, old man!"

* * *

Gus quickly slipped the mooring ropes into place, holding the boat he had dubbed Second Best in his St. Petersburg berthing. Nick jumped across to the pier, comically kneeling down and kissing the wood planks.

Gus laughed. "Fuck you, Nick."

Nick turned his head without straightening, to peer up at Gus. "Man, that trip reminded me of the old movie *Wake of the Red Witch*. Did you miss any swells on the way here, or did you accomplish your mission of hitting every single one?"

"Sailing into St. Pete from Nassau in a thirty-footer is not for the faint of heart," Gus admitted. "Especially when you have to hug the coastline of every rock poking out into the ocean so as not to become a new satellite target. Get your lazy ass back aboard and

300

help me with the gear. We're going to go clean up and wash the salt out of our throats at the local pub."

"Sounds good," Nick agreed, re-boarding the boat. "Do we have to shower down here on the pier or do you actually have a bathroom at your place."

"You used to be a lot less whiny before you were domesticated." Gus put an arm around Nick's shoulders. "What about all those sweet little ports of call we stopped at as we rock-hopped home over the last couple weeks? You look salty, brother, a real Hemingway-esque character."

"After the first week of touring those sweet little hell-holes, I considered giving myself up. I spent six months in the Afghan mountains once with more amenities."

"You're getting soft. This trip toughened you up."

"Why, thank you, Gus. That is so sweet." Nick pushed Gus away. "Let's get the hell off this boat. I need to start planning Frank's demise."

"Can I come?"

"Yes indeed, Quarrel." Nick shifted to his James Bond persona. "You know of course, old man, your survival would again be in doubt with this upcoming sticky situation."

"Show me the money, James, show me the money."

Chapter Twenty-Three
Homecoming

Grace and Tim sat in Frank Richert's outer office, his secretary having seated them with the promise Mr. Richert would see them very soon. Rachel stood outside the office with Jean, waiting for Grace to summon them. Grace claimed this would be the last step in securing their release from US Marshall protection. Richert had requested the meeting after the deaths of Jason Bidwell and Max Stoddard were made public.

The burned hulk of Bidwell's cruiser Tequila had been found by Nassau authorities. It was deemed accidental death, a burner left on causing the fire. The four corpses found aboard showed no sign of foul play. The case was closed. Another vessel in the area on the same night had made the news also. The official story had been drug runners caught in a crossfire. Nothing but unrecognizable debris had been found. Grace knew Rachel suspected the worst. Nick and Gus were dead. Now they would be at the mercy of the man she believed responsible.

"Mr. Richert will see you now," the secretary announced, standing and opening the door for Grace and Tim.

Inside the lavishly adorned office of dark oak, leather, and pile carpeting, a middle-aged man sat behind an oaken desk with a beautiful view from the picture window behind him. He looked up with a smile and took off his reading glasses. Grace looked Richert over carefully as the man stood up. His slate gray suit was tailored impeccably to fit Richert's paunchy five foot eight form. Grace figured the brown hair to be a rug, but a credible one.

"Marshalls Stanwick and Reinhold, thank you for coming," the man greeted them, holding out his hand to Grace first. "I'm Frank Richert. We've talked a few times on the phone during this unfortunate investigation into Tanus Import/Export and their cohorts at Fletcher Exports."

"It would have been helpful if your agency had been more forthcoming, Mr. Richert," Grace said, shaking the man's hand.

"Actually, I knew so little about the case, my assistants had difficulty finding anything in relation to the two firms," Richert replied, shaking Tim's hand before gesturing them into the seats fronting his desk. "In light of the news coming from Nassau, I thought this would be a good time to meet and clear the air."

"In light of the news, the only reason my partner and I came in today with our clients is to assure their safety. Your agency has had many dubious dealings with both the firms under investigation."

"My agency's investigations into terror networks worldwide put us into contact with quite a number of suspicious entities," Richert stated with straightforward confidence. "As an important information gathering branch of the NSA, we do have what would appear to be strange dealings in our investigations. These specious rumors of our being an assassination-for-hire mob need to be put to rest with the criminals who started them. I wished to meet with Ms. Hunter and her daughter only to congratulate them on helping take down this potential threat to national security. I want to pledge my support in integrating them back into their normal lives."

"I'm glad to hear that, Mr. Richert. If anything does happen to my clients, I have been ordered by the Attorney General to personally take your agency apart piece by piece. Are we clear on that?"

Richert's mask dropped for a split second, allowing a glimpse of what lay beneath his office façade. "Of course, Marshall Stanwick. I'm sure Ms. Hunter's troubles are in the past."

"I'll go get Rachel," Tim said and walked out of the office.

* * *

Rachel jumped a little when the office door opened. Tim stepped through, smiling widely at them.

"It's all good. Richert's so full of bullshit, his carpet's brown, but I think your running days are over. C'mon in for the weasel's little ceremony and we'll get the hell out of here."

"Thanks Tim." Rachel grasped Jean's hand.

"I wish the Terminator was here," Jean whispered.

"That makes two of us, honey," Rachel whispered in reply, brushing away a tear, cursing the way her eyes filled upon hearing Jean's familiar title for Nick.

* * *

"I'm done for the day, Lisa," Frank said, waving to his secretary on the way out. "I'm going to take the rest of the afternoon off."

"Very well, Sir, you're certainly cheerful today, Mr. Richert," Lisa observed.

"Things are finally starting to swing our way again. See you tomorrow." Frank went out the office door, whistling tonelessly on his way to the elevator.

On the parking garage level, Frank looked around as he left the elevator angrily. The lighting on the left side of the underground lot near where he had parked his Mercedes was out. He flicked his remote and opened, started, and turned the lights on in his vehicle. Not wishing to ruin his nearly perfect day, Frank took a deep breath and walked carefully over to his car. Sliding into the driver's seat, Richert used his remote to turn on a classical music CD. He leaned back happily, reveling in the rich sound of a piano concerto. He felt a slight sting on his neck, swatting at it with his right hand. Seconds later, darkness swept into him on a wave of despair. Light, sound, and consciousness fled, leaving only a fleeting moment of abject terror.

Frank awoke with a painful throbbing behind his eyes. A pitiful mewling cry belched out of his mouth as realization lanced through him in a heartbeat. He was naked and strapped into a chair. One dull forty watt bulb illuminated the dank cement room only slightly.

"Ni...Nick?" Frank heard chairs scraping as if pushed away from a table and two dark figures walked around him on either side.

"Hello, Frankie, long time, no see," Nick greeted him with a pleasant lilt to his tone. "I want you to meet my old friend Gus Nason."

"Glad to meet you, Mr. Richert," Gus said formally. "You sure have caused a lot of trouble, Sir."

"We...we can make this right, honest to God, Nick," Frank rattled off in high-pitched stumbling fashion. "I'm in charge of everything. Anything you want...anything...I can get it."

"I'm afraid that ship has sailed, Frankie," Nick put a consoling hand on Richert's shoulder. "It sailed the moment you called in a strike on Mr. Nason's boat, The Loose Lady."

"The Lucky Lady, damn it," Gus corrected.

"Not for Frankie, Gus." Nick grinned over at his partner.

Richert began to sob, his shoulders shaking as a real emotion overcame him: fear.

"Awwww... don't get so upset, Frankie. I'll make this real easy on you, for old time's sake," Nick promised, bending down to give Richert a hug. "I have my notebook computer all set up. You're going to help me transfer all the ill-gotten gains I know you have in offshore accounts into my offshore account."

"You'll kill me anyway!" Frank cried out. "I'll give you everything - just let me go."

"Ah...no." Nick shook his head. "You know how this works, Frankie. You can give me what I want and go out painlessly, or you can scream for death over the next ten hours, and then give me what I want. I'm only making the offer once though. If you start playing me, you'll get ten hours of wishing you were dead, no matter what information you give me. What'll it be, ol' buddy?"

"O...okay," Frank sobbed in gasping breaths, tears streaming down his cheeks.

"You see, Gus." Nick looked up at his friend. "I told you Frankie would be cooperative."

* * *

Grace stopped the rental van in front of Nick's Pacific Grove house.

"Wow, this is gorgeous. I guess Nick really liked you two."

"He gave me the keys and paperwork," Rachel replied tiredly. "I don't have a clue about the legal ramifications."

"Nick's coming back!" Jean piped in angrily from the backseat, where she and Deke huddled together.

"Easy Jean," Grace soothed, exchanging a knowing glance with Rachel. "I didn't mean to imply anything. Is Deke okay? I know they gave him something for the flight."

"He's better since riding from the airport with his nose out the window," Jean answered, hugging the dog's neck.

"We really didn't have to fly straight here from D.C. after our meeting with Richert, although it will sure be nice to drive over and see my place. Too bad we couldn't get a flight leaving Washington until nearly midnight. Getting stuck in that damn Dallas/Fort Worth hellhole until nearly dawn really frosted me. I'm lucky Tim volunteered to stay in D.C. and cover my tracks."

306

"I didn't want to stay around there any longer. That Richert guy gave me the creeps."

"This from a woman traveling around with Nick," Grace retorted, opening her door. "C'mon, let's get your stuff inside. I'd like to see the inside of Diego's home."

Twenty minutes later, the two women sat in the kitchen drinking coffee, while Jean and the still-groggy Deke watched television.

"I'm as spacey as the goofy dog," Grace complained. "At least with everything the Benoits have given us, you won't have to testify anywhere. Are you really going to live out here now? This is your first chance in a long time to get back in touch with friends and family."

"It's great knowing I can do that, but I'd rather come out of hiding slowly. After being with Nick, I don't see the world in quite the same way anymore."

"Look..." Grace leaned over the table, lowering her voice. "We both know Nick won't be back. Tell me about him. Was –"

Grace's cell-phone rang. She checked the caller ID with some irritation and then answered it with a sigh. "Yes, Timmy, we're here safe and sound in lovely California. It's so thoughtful of...what?"

Rachel watched Grace's bored expression turn into bewildered, open-mouthed shock. Grace glanced furtively at Rachel while listening intently to her partner's voice. Minutes ticked by as Grace simply acknowledged what she heard with short grunts of acceptance.

"Okay...call me if anything else comes up, Tim. I'll check your place, too, after I sleep all day. Yeah, right...you can clean your own damn place, pal. See ya'." Grace ended the call and hesitated to speak for a moment.

"Grace! What the hell's going on?" Rachel asked impatiently, dread washing over her in a cold, clammy wave.

"Richert's dead. They found him slumped over the steering wheel of his car, halfway home, along the roadside. They think he had some kind of stroke. Tim says it's lucky he didn't crash into –"

Rachel erupted in laughter.

"What?" Grace looked at Rachel as if she were nuts, and then leaned back in her chair, comprehension flooding in along with stunned disbelief.

"Oh come on, Rachel. You don't think? No way…"

Jean ran in from the next room at the sound of her mom's laughter with Deke trying to keep up. Rachel hugged Jean, teary eyed, and barely able to keep her fading laughter from turning into sobs of relief.

"What's wrong Mom?" Jean asked worriedly, holding onto Rachel tightly.

"The Terminator's back," Rachel whispered.

Jean pushed away in jubilation, pointing excitedly at Rachel. "I told you."

* * *

Gus sat on his beach chair, looking out over the surging surf, smashing against the rocks at Otter's Point. He pulled up the collar of his down jacket for the third time since arriving for what he had lately come to consider Nick's weekend dawn patrol. No painting could do the little beach justice, Nick had told him countless times. After less than two month's living in Pacific Grove, Gus now accepted the fact that he was hooked. With a sigh of satisfaction, he reached for the Sunday paper he had carried down to the beach with him. Deke ended his leap from the granite wall a few feet above the sand to a spot not more than six inches from the startled man's feet.

308

"Eeeeyaaaaaahhhh!" Gus fell sideways, grabbing his paper while fending off Deke's lavish attention. "Holy mother of God, Deke! You shaved five years off my life!"

Gus ceased fighting the dog off and simply sat up in the sand with Deke across his lap. It was only then he heard raucous laughter over the wind and beach noise. Gus glanced to his right as Nick and Jean descended the stone steps to the sand, having a merry time at his expense. Jean had her strainer and bucket in order to pursue the hunt for treasure in Otter's Point's myriad tide pools. Nick carried beach chairs and a backpack Gus knew contained a stainless steel coffee thermos with mugs. Jean waved hello as she passed by. Deke pawed sand over Gus in his haste to follow her, leaving Gus using his newspaper as a shield. Nick was still laughing when he reached down a hand to the less-than-entertained Gus.

"Oh... that was so funny," Gus growled, allowing Nick to pull him up to his feet.

Nick brushed sand off his friend with overdone zeal and righted the beach chair.

"Good morning, Gus." Nick set up the three beach chairs he had carried down with him. "Would you believe I'd never have let Deke off the leash if I'd known he would launch himself from the walkway?"

"Not even for a nano-second, you prick."

"Good, I'd be disappointed if you thought these entertaining inspirational gems I think up for you were an accident. Coffee?"

"Ha, ha, I beat you to the beach for the first time since being talked into moving here to the Arctic." Gus held out his hand for the mug Nick filled from the thermos.

"The Arctic? Oh...turn that record over, will you?"

"I might as well be living in Boston," Gus proclaimed, blending the perfect amount of nostalgia for a place with weather he detested, along with enough insinuated guilt to set Nick's teeth on edge. Gus chuckled as his familiar barb lanced home for a fleeting moment.

Nick stood up with manufactured outrage. He grabbed up his beach chair, waving at Jean, and calling out to her. "Come, Danger, we must move on. I've been insulted once too often by this uncultured rube."

Jean met Nick's indignant demeanor with a smile, waved back, and continued her sifting endeavor with the forever curious Deke hunched over the rocks, waiting patiently for new discoveries to sniff at. Gus pulled on Nick's coat with his free hand.

"Sit down, fool, before you stir up the sand. Where's Mrs. McCarty?"

Nick barked out a short laugh and sat down again. "I got Rachel so good this morning. You know how she hates it when I'm always up before she stirs. This morning, I inched out silently from beside her and spent ten minutes carefully making her into the bed. The only thing showing from the covers was her face. Then I snuck out of the room and closed the door. It took some doing, but I managed to keep both Deke and Danger from ruining my little charade before we left for the beach."

Gus shook his head, smiling at what entertained the cold-blooded killer sitting beside him. "I figured when we came back from Vegas after the wedding, you two would settle into humdrum married life. Here it is nearly six weeks later and you're still trying to annoy her like always. How do you do it?"

"I'm thinking of getting Deke a kitten."

Gus nearly snorted coffee through his nose, as he had just begun sipping the brew.

"Damn, Nick!" Gus laughed. "You need to get back to work. This family life has released your inner demons. It's not pretty."

"I sent Diego's newest adventure in last week. My agent called me Friday and claimed it's my best work yet," Nick said defensively.

"We both know what work I'm talking about, partner. What'd you title your book anyway?"

"Caribbean Contract," Nick answered with enthusiasm. "Diego took on a partner in this latest literary masterpiece of mine."

"He wouldn't happen to be black and a master mariner, would he?"

"Why yes, Gus, how perceptive of you. Did –"

"You're toast, Hotshot!" Rachel's voice warned, her voice carrying over surf, wind, and conversation.

"Uh oh." Gus smirked, as Nick studiously kept from turning toward Rachel's voice. "Your evil ways have caught up with you, Hemingway. It looks like a triple team. Rachel recruited Dan and Carol on the way. The Dynamic Duo has joined with Wonder Woman to put the Joker in his place."

"When I get the galley for editing from my agent, I'm writing out the smartass partner," Nick replied, evoking laughter from Gus.

By this time Rachel had forged ahead of Dan and Carol to stand with arms folded over her chest.

"Hi, Rach," Gus greeted her, while Nick turned away.

"He made me into the bed! That's six mornings in a row!"

"Ah… you neglected to mention this wasn't your first caper, Joker," Gus pointed out. "Hi Dan…Carol."

"I wouldn't sit too close to Nick this morning, Gus," Dan advised, smiling knowingly.

"You should be ashamed, Nick," Carol added, trying not to laugh.

"And you, young lady!" Rachel pointed at Jean, who was dancing around with Deke, in a victory dance. "Your mentor here won't be around every minute. I will have my revenge!"

Gus stood up while Nick continued sitting, looking off to the left as if completely absorbed by the horizon. "Now look, I know tucking the covers around you and sneaking off may be a little –"

"Tucking the covers?" Rachel snapped incredulously. "Is that what he told you? He duct-tapes me into the bed, damn it!"

Gus started howling in laughter, walking away while trying to stop. His reaction set off Dan and Carol, who also stepped back a few paces. Gus noted Nick then peeked over his shoulder at Rachel. Seeing her lip quivering as she resisted laughter, Gus watched with amusement as Nick jumped up and put an arm around her shoulders.

"Good morning, my love." Nick kissed Rachel's cheek.

"Don't you good morning me. It took ten minutes to get out of bed this time, you brat." Rachel turned her head away, but allowed Nick to draw her closer.

Gus approached the group again with some trepidation, but did so more confidently once he saw Rachel's arm slip around Nick's waist. "I told Nick he needs to get back to work."

"He needs a vacation, Gus," Carol interjected. "Nick just finished a book."

"I'm afraid I agree." Rachel leaned her head against Nick's chest. "A long vacation."

"Besides, I have a job," Nick stated. "Deke and I walk Danger to school in the morning while Rachel…ah…sleeps in."

"Nick told me he was going to stop," Jean joined in, seeing she was missing her favorite part of Nick's morning ritual lately: the aftermath. She beckoned the group to follow her. "C'mon over and look at the shells I found this morning."

"Actually," Nick whispered to Gus as they brought up the rear, "I told Danger I ran out of duct tape."

"Idle hands are the Devil's workshop," Gus admonished.

"Maybe you're right," Nick allowed.

The End

Made in the USA
Lexington, KY
29 May 2017